CITY of the SUN

by
Don Yates

PublishAmerica
Baltimore

© 2003 by Don Yates.
All rights reserved. No part of this book may be reproduced in any form without written permission from the publishers, except by a reviewer who may quote brief passages in a review to be printed in a newspaper or magazine.

First printing

ISBN: 1-59286-253-5
PUBLISHED BY PUBLISHAMERICA BOOK PUBLISHERS
www.publishamerica.com
Baltimore

Printed in the United States of America

ACKNOWLEDGEMENTS

To my wife Betty who demonstrated great patience while I disappeared into my jungle world.

For our children who always enjoyed a good story.

Thanks to Sandra Rush for her tireless efforts in helping me with editing and proofing.

CONTENTS

Chapter 1	Memories	7
Chapter 2	The Beginning	14
Chapter 3	The Journal	22
Chapter 4	Preparing for South America	38
Chapter 5	Arriving in Lima	55
Chapter 6	North to Trujillo	78
Chapter 7	Iquitos — Gateway to the Amazon	98
Chapter 8	Into the Interior	131
Chapter 9	Where Danger Lurks	162
Chapter 10	City of the Sun	199
Chapter 11	The Golden Garden	215
Chapter 12	The Serpent is Found	230
Chapter 13	Protector of the City	247
Chapter 14	Unwelcome Guests	264
	Epilogue	282

1
Memories

My wife and I have retired to a small farm in the Shenandoah Valley of Virginia. Our children and their families are invited to spend time at the farm to relax and get away from the pressures of life in the city. They are invited to stay as long as they care to; it provides us the opportunity to spend time with our children and grandchildren. These visits are special, because we can relax together and enjoy each other's company without the burdens of the working world intruding into these moments of family gatherings.

Last year one of my single sons came for a visit and questioned me on a subject that sparked the interest for me to prepare what you are reading. I have a well-stocked 5-acre spring fed pond with several tall shade trees, which provide a perfect atmosphere for relaxing and letting the world slip by. While preparing our lines in anticipation of catching one of the largemouth bass that live in the pond, my son asked, "Dad, I have a magazine I would like you to look at." He opened his tackle box and removed a magazine and handed it to me saying, "Please open where I have the yellow tab located." As I reached for the magazine I was aware he was scrutinizing my face for evidence of a reaction to what I was about to see.

It was a recent issue of a popular magazine featuring archeological sites and artifacts. Opening to the indicated page I saw a picture of an object I had not seen for more than twenty years.

"I see you trying to hide your reaction to the picture, but your eyes give you away," said my son. Putting his fishing rod on the ground, he turned and said, "That article says that the artifact in that picture is on display in a museum in a city in northern Peru. It also states that the museum will not disclose how they acquired the artifact. I've seen a picture in your den of you, Uncle Serge and Uncle Jason holding a golden statue of a serpent coiled around a branch much like the one pictured in that magazine. You know the picture I'm referring to, the one where you are holding that statue in front of a stone structure in the jungle. Where did you find the artifact you were holding?" My son had caught me completely off-guard with the magazine and his questions. Suddenly, memories of a danger filled adventure in the jungles of the Amazon flashed through my mind. Memories I had filed in the far recesses of my mind, never suspecting anyone would be interested in reliving the events of my past life.

My children were aware of some of the events of my life, my love of archeology and the lure of searching for artifacts from ancient cultures. They were also aware I had traveled extensively as a young man, and that I had a few very close friends I had known for many years. Beyond this knowledge, they knew very little except that their father had been a practicing engineer, who worked in the Washington, D.C. metropolitan area until his retirement.

I slowly laid the magazine down on my lap and said, "I never thought you kids would be interested in what I had accomplished as a young man. If you're really interested, I could tell you about a trip your uncles and I made to South America in 1978, and how I had my picture taken holding that statue. Come to think of it, I've never told your mother much about that trip. It was dangerous, but we found some amazing things in the jungles of Peru. You better get a beer out of the cooler for me; this story will take some time to tell." As my son handed me a beer, I leaned back against a tree and made myself comfortable. Within moments I found the memories of the Amazon and our search for a lost city beginning to return to me as if it was yesterday.

That evening while relaxing on the front porch, my thoughts returned to that afternoon at the pond and the story I related to my son. My wife joined me for some quiet time and I told her of the events of that afternoon. She paused for a few moments and said, "I married you realizing that you were a man who had traveled to many areas of the world. But, to this day you've never really given me many details of your travels. I know you have a passion for archeology and you have traveled extensively, but when Serge or Jason visit, it's as if another person is revealed. As for the story you told today by the pond, I've always wondered about the details of that trip. If I were you, I would make a record of your travels, if for no other reason than as a keepsake for your children. Remember, by the time you're old enough to care what others have done, they may have passed away before you have the opportunity to ask them about their early lives."

After a short period of time my wife stated she was ready to retire for the evening, and asked if I was ready for bed. I told her to go ahead, I would follow shortly. With only my thoughts to keep me company, I began to dwell on my wife's words. Her suggestion of preparing a record of my travels kept returning to me, I had always wondered what my father had accomplished in his early adult years. He died before I had the opportunity to do what my son had done today by the pond.

During the next week my son found several opportunities to ask for further details concerning the story I had related to him. As I added more details he became completely absorbed in the story and hung on my every word. After I had finished telling the story he had numerous questions and I could see his interest was genuine.

A few weeks after my son's visit, I found myself on the front porch reliving memories of times past. Memories that would be lost with my death, unless I recorded them. That night I resolved to begin a record of my life's travels, if for no other reason than for my children to know whom their father was before he became their dad. Yes, they knew me as "Dad or Father," but I felt they needed to have the ability to know who I was as a young man. What were my hopes and dreams. What adventures had I participated in during my lifetime.

We live in a world of unexpected events that can affect our perspective of the world, as we know it. This story tells of such an event. A series of occurrences that led to my being a passenger aboard a plane destined for Peru, South America, attempting to find a lost city in the jungles of the Amazon River Basin.

My story begins during the time I was in the military stationed in Europe, specifically Nancy, France. I took advantage of many weekends to travel into the French countryside discovering a world very different from the world I had known while living in Washington, DC. I discovered that history in Europe was much different than in America. Within a few hours drive from the military post where I was stationed I could visit cities with city walls built hundreds of years ago. I soon discovered that ancient history was within my grasp in many of the European countries I visited, but I discovered a lifelong passion in the city of Pompeii, Italy. A passion that would forever more cause my blood to race at the very thought of discovering an object that had remained hidden for eons of time. This occupation was the study of ancient cultures and their ways of life, which included searching for artifacts from these early cultures.

After my visit to Italy I returned to France and my military duty station. My duties were varied and I was kept busy, but after the days work my time was my own. I found the study of ancient cultures and their artifacts a lure that would always attract me to search for the unknown. The library on the base was small with a limited amount of materials dedicated to archeology and the study of early civilizations. Within a few weeks I had exhausted everything that was available on the subject, and realized I would have to look beyond the base library for more materials. I decided to visit the University of Verdun on weekends in hopes of gathering further information.

During the middle of 1963 I struck up a friendship with a young student at the university by the name of Serge Gaston. His studies included archeology and anthropology, and he seemed enthusiastic about participating in some private field research. I mentioned my interest in perfecting my abilities in field research and suggested we investigate any local sites he might be aware of. He informed me that he lived near the village of Toul and that he knew of several sites he had always wanted to search. He suggested that we should be able to get some fellow students who would be willing to help with the excavations.

Until my separation from the military in the fall of 1967, Serge and I spent many pleasant hours delving through old manuscripts in local libraries searching for interesting sites to explore. We spent our vacations in caves and ruins throughout France and Germany, refining our skills at excavating and recording our finds. Our collection of old bones and projectile points grew month by month and our knowledge of field research grew with each new adventure.

In the summer of 1966, our continuing research led us to a 19th century estate that was referenced in an old book on local country estates. The property was located northeast of Nancy, France in lightly wooded rolling hills. We were able to obtain permission from the property owner to perform some limited excavations, with the understanding that we would leave the grounds as we found them. During the early spring we made several weekend trips to prepare the site for our extended stay in the summer. After the spring rains had come to an end we decided to take several weeks vacation to investigate the area where our research indicated the estate might have existed.

Our field investigations involved camping in the area of our excavations, so planning ahead was of great importance. After planning for several previous research sites, we had developed a good system of anticipating the supplies we would need for the area we were to work in. You always have the awareness that the unexpected can happen, so preparing for this was always a task I enjoyed. We had to be self sufficient, because we usually were many miles from where supplies could be obtained. Also, having spent enough time in the military, I felt it necessary to always carry some form of self-defense. This was to be a habit that stayed with me throughout my years of field studies, and many times I've overcome problems due to this precaution.

As the day dawned on our newest adventure, Serge and I found that we were prepared to leave at dawn. Serge had scheduled several weeks earlier for some students to gather at his home and travel to the site with us. These were students that had worked with us before, and knew how we liked to run an archeological research site. We had a clear summer morning to take to the road, so with our vehicles packed, we left for the countryside. The following weeks made such an impact on my life that I knew my life's ambitions would always include archeology. During this time I realized I would always be searching for the unknown, always looking for something that is waiting to be found. The mystery of uncovering an object in the soil and realizing that it had rested in that spot for centuries, undisturbed, will always cause me to drop what I'm doing and investigate a possible new find. When you expose an object in the soil, realizing it has remained in that position for centuries, it presents a mystery that needs to be solved. The questions that come to you at that moment are many and varied; such as who dropped it, what was the person like that owned it. The day I found the coins was the high light of our time during this excavation.

Within a few days we had uncovered some of the foundation of the main house as shown on the old plot plans. We proceeded to dig several test pits inside the foundation walls in hopes of discovering if a cellar had been built under the house. We had dug three 4-foot by 4-foot pits, several feet deep and had found remains of glass, pottery, nails and various debris. While digging the fourth test pit, at about 16" below grade, I noticed the stones of the foundation wall were joined in a peculiar pattern. A pattern that indicated that they had been removed and replaced at some time after the construction was completed. As I was uncovering the soil inside the wall I came upon the remains of a leather pouch with draw strings. I slowly uncovered the leather fragments, realizing at the time that my heart was racing at the prospect of what I might uncover hidden just below the thin layers of soil. The leather fragments were flaking away as I slowly scraped the soil from around the bag, and then the glint of gold was uncovered as I brushed the soil from the bag. I sat in silence, just looking at the coins, not believing my eyes.

I realized this was something that only Serge and myself should know about. I quickly covered the bag and coins and proceeded to move to a new location. That evening I suggested to Serge that we needed to talk privately. The work we were doing at the site was very strenuous, and by sundown everyone was ready to bed down for the night. As everyone began moving towards their tents, I suggested to Serge that we needed to update our journal concerning the work that had been completed that day. Sitting by the fire that evening, I related what I had found inside the foundation of the main house. I stated that a find like this should be kept between us, because the potential for problems when money is involved is always present.

We were only days away from completing our excavations and recording the items we had found. Serge announced at the next evening meal, that we would close the camp and all work would cease Friday morning. He indicated we were very pleased with the results from the work everyone had contributed, and we felt the excavations were a success. Friday dawned clear and bright, and the camp was bustling as tents were lowered and the last items of research were packed for storage. After paying everyone and saying our farewells, by mid morning Serge and myself were the only ones left at the site. I could see the anticipation on Serge's face as he watched the last of the students driving away from the site.

We quickly grabbed tools and ran to the spot I had located next to the foundation wall. Within moments I had uncovered the fragments of the bag and the coins within it. I carefully revealed 53 gold coins and 2 rings, each with a gemstone. As I removed the coins from the soil I said, "Look at the condition of these coins. They look like they're in mint condition."

Serge began spreading the coins out and picked one up saying, "Have you taken a good look at these coins? These are 19th century American coins."

As I picked one up I realized it was one of the famed $20.00 United States double eagles, it was dated 1860. After cleaning the coins we found them to carry the dates of 1859 and 1860, with the mintmarks of "O." How did these coins find their way to a secret hideaway under this house in eastern France? As we sat in the dirt, we realized that this find might possibly give us the ability to fulfill some of the dreams that we had discussed so often. We had spent many evenings discussing the possibility of continuing our education in archeology, but neither of us had the funds. Now the possibility to attain our goals was before us. I told Serge the coins could possibly bring more than $100,000.00; this could be our answer to financing our educations.

My time in the army would soon be over and I had informed Serge that I would be returning to the United States to continue my education. Serge decided he would remain in Europe and continue his education in Paris. He reassured me that he would always keep his eyes open for opportunities for further research, and I should be prepared to travel on a moment's notice. We had spent many years together and a friendship had developed that I hoped would last for many years to come. It was agreed that we would stay in contact with each other, and keep records of any interesting sites that we might find for future research.

As winter was coming to France, my time for rotation back to the United States had arrived. Preparing to leave was difficult; I had developed many close friends both in the military and in the local towns. I knew returning to my parents' home would be difficult, my family had continued with their lives without my presence. Lives had changed while I was away and would I be able to fit in? Would I be able to pick my life up where I had left it, and if so, would I want to continue my life as it was. Many questions went through my mind during the last few weeks before my flight. Questions concerning home, family, friends and most of all, my future.

Serge and I spent many quiet evenings at a local family inn discussing plans for searching for lost civilizations and discoveries that were waiting to be found. We were determined that we had to prepare ourselves in every way possible for the opportunity that might present itself.

My last day in France was spent saying my goodbyes and then boarding a train to Paris for my flight to the United States. Serge met me in Paris, with the parting encouragement to continue my education and keep my eyes on the future. He felt that in a few years we would be ready to seriously try our hand at setting up an expedition. We only needed to determine where and when that expedition would take place.

2
The Beginning

When you leave family and friends at the age of 20, you consider life is an adventure, one you are totally prepared to enjoy. You don't ask to many questions about your future, because you are focused totally on the present, the future will take care of itself.

I enlisted in the U.S. Army almost on impulse. I had not given much thought to career or even the branch of the service I would enter. I had already determined that I did not want to serve onboard a ship, so the Navy was not even considered. My father had served in the Army during the Second World War, so if it was good enough for him, it was good enough for me.

The recruiting officer made it very easy to voluntarily sign my life away, especially when you wanted to enlist. Within ten minutes of walking into the recruiting office, I had signed on the dotted line. I was given directions to meet other recruits within 30 days in Baltimore, Maryland and by the way, congratulations on joining the U.S. Army for the next three years. I remember returning home and announcing that I had just enlisted in the army, the family was stunned. When asked why I had taken this action, I indicated I wanted to have the opportunity to travel. The next 30 days passed quickly, and on a cold November morning I said goodbye to my parents and got on a bus destined for Baltimore, MD.

Those were the thoughts that ran through my head as I sat in a cab returning to my parent's home in Washington, D.C. Six years had passed since I had left home, six years of personal growth and independence, years of making decisions on my own.

I enjoyed seeing my family, but soon realized that I was a visitor. The family had continued without my presence and though I was welcome, I knew I was intruding in their lives. My parents tried to make room for me in their lives, but after a six-year absence it was difficult to have me back in their home.

During my years in the Army I had been trained in mechanical engineering, so my first task was to find employment. Within a week I had found employment with an engineering firm in Maryland and located an apartment near the University of Maryland.

After settling in to my new home I wrote to Serge of my situation and that I would begin my studies in the spring of 1968. I enrolled in the university's engineering schools and also began several courses on archeology. The university offered some very interesting courses on ancient civilizations, with the possibilities of field research during the summer months.

By 1973 I had received my degree from the university and in the process I had struck up a friendship with a fellow student studying architecture and ancient cultures. During the summer of 1972 while participating on a colonial excavation with the university in southern Maryland, I met Jason Williams. Jason was an intriguing individual who spoke several languages and loved the outdoors. He was an adventurous individual who imagined he was destined to find lost cities in the jungles of South America. Though Jason excelled in architecture, he was intrigued with archeology, especially the ability of ancient craftsmen to build structures with limited tools and technologies. It soon became evident that Jason was an individual that Serge and I could use in future archeological research projects.

After graduation, Jason and I continued with graduate studies in archeology and continued participating in summer excavations every summer with the university. These excavations required my being absent from the office for extended periods of time, which always required extensive explanations to my managers. Realizing that few employers would tolerate their employees taking 3 or 4 months off every year, I decided that providing my services as a private consultant would best suit my lifestyle. This gave me the ability to provide engineering services on a schedule I could set. As a private consultant I was able to provide a sufficient income for my needs, but if unexpected expenses arose I had funds from the sale of the coins to fall upon.

As the years passed my involvement in ancient cultures began to occupy more of my time. I was constantly in touch with Serge, who was studying in Paris and gaining experience in field excavations in Europe. Early in 1977 I received a letter post marked from Paris, as I opened it a sense of excitement came upon me. As I read, I soon realized that Serge had come upon something that was cause for great excitement. He stated that he had come upon some early 18th century documents concerning the Peruvian Amazon River Basin, in South America. He suggested that Jason and I start concentrating our studies on the early cultures of South America, specifically the Inca. He also indicated that we should try to obtain maps of the eastern area of Peru where it borders with Brazil. His letter ended with his intention to travel to the states sometime in 1978 for further discussions on this matter.

As I related to Jason the possibility of going to South America and looking for Inca ruins, our excitement had no bounds. This could be the field research we had always dreamed of. We gathered from Serge's letter that we had approximately one year to get all we could on the civilization of the Inca and the country of Peru. This would also take us into the rain forest of the Amazon River basin. I had never been in this type of terrain, so preparing for a trip of this magnitude presented quite a challenge.

I had acquired some basic information concerning the Inca through my years of study, but I realized I would need more detailed information for an expedition into the interior of eastern Peru. As I began researching the Inca Empire, I became more fascinated in the study of these amazing people.

The empire of the Incas had always intrigued me, how people that had built an empire that stretched twenty-five hundred miles down the coast of South America and held over 12 million subjects under its control could be toppled so quickly by less than 200 Europeans.

Before expansion of the Inca Empire began in the early 1400s, the Incas lived in or near their capital city of Cuzco. At its height in 1532, the empire consisted of most of Peru, much of Chile, and parts of Ecuador, Bolivia, and Argentina. It included coastal and desert regions, rain forest, and parts of the Andes Mountains. This was all accomplished without having horses, the wheel, or a written language. The Incas expanded their empire through war and diplomacy, but they also knew how to keep what became theirs. They were good organizers, ruling one of the best-run empires in history.

In one hundred years, they conquered millions of people who had languages and customs quite different from their own and made them all a part of the Inca Empire. As these people were conquered treasures were taken and shipped to storehouses in Cuzco. The Incas and other Andean people considered gold to be the sweat of the sun, and silver to be the tears of the moon.

The Incas were skilled stone-masons as evidenced by their use of bronze chisels and stone hammers, with which they fitted together enormous blocks of stone of different shapes and sizes that were held together without mortar or cement. One aspect of the Inca that had intrigued Jason and myself was their engineering abilities. They built a network of roads that covered hundreds of miles and their architecture was known for its great size and skillful construction. Archeological research has provided many articles that have demonstrated Inca craftsmen had made quality artifacts from gold and silver.

With this basic information in hand, we began gathering information on the empire of the Inca and the country of Peru. In a short period of time we realized how little we knew about the Peruvian people and their spectacular country.

During my studies I had become familiar with the fortress cities of Machu Picchu, situated high in the Andes, and Sacsayhuaman near Cuzco. We also realized our knowledge of the three mainland regions were very limited, especially the selva, a region of forests and jungle along the eastern foothills of the Andes. The jungle was of great importance to us, because it seemed that we were destined to travel into that area in the not too distant future.

I found my life had taken on more direction now that Serge had set a destination for an expedition. As the months passed Jason and I spent most of our free time gathering copious amounts of data on the Incas of Peru.

Our studies revealed that in many Indian societies authoritarianism prevailed, but no society had a more totalitarian state than the Incas of Peru. From the Cuzco Basin of the southern highlands a Quechua-speaking group of Indians began gradually to dominate the people around them. Their ruler was called the Inca, and the people are known today as Incas from the title of their kings. By 1525 the Inca Empire had consolidated approximately 7 million people in an area of some two thousand miles from north to south, and from the Pacific Coast to the edge of the jungle foothills east of the Andes.

The Inca conquests were most successful where established states and regimented societies, with strong central authority and class structures, had already existed. There, the conquered people accepted the new rulers more readily. But in less developed regions of farmers and herdsmen it would require a large Inca garrison to keep the people under their authority. These peoples were not worth the effort, and they were never fully brought into the empire. The Inca conquests were great examples of generalship and statesmanship. Persuasion was mixed with military threat and action and with the use of diplomacy, intrigue, and alliances with people already conquered, dictatorial methods were employed. The adoption of the Inca language, Quechua, of the Inca cult of the sun, and of Inca customs which were forced on the entire empire, and all classes were strictly regimented.

The Inca emperor held title to all land and allotted it among the religious institutions, the state, and the commoners. The government owned and controlled the entire means of production and distribution. The individual could own neither private property nor productive capital. The emperor was aided by a council of nobles who served as governors of the provinces of the empire. The Inca emperor, his royal family, and their descendants were at the summit of political and religious life. The emperor, possessing absolute power, was worshiped as the direct descendant of the sun and was so exalted that only his full sister could marry him. The noble class, including the military leaders, priests, and civil administrators who ran the empire for the Inca, lived in pomp and splendor. When they died, they were buried with their wives and retainers, who were given a stupefying potion and then strangled. Important persons were buried above ground in stone chambers. Inca builders were known for their magnificent palaces, temples, forts, and other public works, the stonework was so finely done that the stones were fitted together without cement.

Religion played an important role in the public and private lives of the Inca. The people believed that nature was created by their most important god Viracocha, the supreme deity, believed to be a bearded white-skinned man who had created other gods, as well as men and animals, and who had given the people their possessions and knowledge. The ruling family prayed chiefly to the sun god, Inti, who was the direct ancestor of the emperors, which was the second most important deity. Others were the thunder and moon-gods and the goddesses of the earth and sea. In addition, animals, mountains, and caves were worshiped as containing supernatural power and hundreds of objects and places were regarded as *huacas*, or sacred shrines. The principal temples were used for ceremonies to the imperial gods, although temples generally were not employed for public worship but were the residences of priests and noble virgins, as well as homes for images of the deities.

Sacrifices and offerings accompanied by prayers were a main part of the Inca religious ceremonies. Crops and animals, mainly llamas, were sacrificed to keep the good will of the gods. Human sacrifices were made on special occasions. Most people considered it an honor to be chosen for sacrifice. Our research found that the Inca considered funerals sacred. They believed that people lived in either heaven or hell after death.

As our studies progressed and our depth of understanding of the Inca Empire grew, we began to appreciate the complexity of these people. Though these people never developed a system of money and the wheel remained unknown to them, the government was prosperous. They constructed many roads and bridges, but humans and llamas were the ones to carry the burdens from place to place.

The Inca studied the stars and planets and used their observations to predict the seasons of the year. They knew how to perform certain mathematical calculations, which they used in designing buildings, roads, and terraced fields. Special officials who used the Quipu, which was a cord with knotted strings of various lengths and colors, did record keeping. Each color or knot represented a different item, and knots of varying sizes at certain intervals designated numbers.

The totalitarian nature of the Inca Empire, with all power at its head, was an important factor to its sudden end. In 1532, Francisco Pizarro landed on the coast with a small army of Spaniards, whom many of the Indians regarded at first as supernatural beings. After marching inland, the army seized the emperor Atahualpa and held him for ransom. The emperor paid the ransom, which was a room filled with gold and another one filled twice with silver, and then he was murdered. With the head of the entire political and religious system suddenly gone, the Indian Empire was helpless before the newcomers. There was no clear rule concerning the emperor's successor, and three years passed before an effective opposition was organized. By that time it was too late and the Spaniards put down the revolt. At that time a large part of the population retreated too less accessible regions in the interior. These people moved to the eastern flank of the Andes, an area of humid tropical forests.

I received a letter in the fall of 1977 from Serge that introduced a new element of danger in the forthcoming expedition. The letter was short and brief, Serge would arrive in the spring of 1978, but he cautioned me with a reminder of our last major excavation in France.

That evening I contacted Jason and told him of the letter and that we needed to get together. Over a quick meal I explained Serge's reference to our excavations in France during the summer of 1966. I retold the incident of finding something and why we decided to keep it to ourselves. As we sat in my small kitchen, I told Jason that Serge must have some reasons to suspect that his research had attracted someone's attention. If this was true, and he was cautioning us, then he must feel that we should also take precautions with our research.

We decided to be more observant of our whereabouts and more security conscience with our research materials. I usually left books and papers lying on my desk or stacked in my car. Serge's warning served as a reminder that someone else could be interested in what we were researching. The question that was foremost on our minds concerned what Serge had come upon. How could it generate enough interest to cause others to want to shadow us? Our curiosity over this situation, was a cause for many sleepless nights to come.

The letter ended with a request to find information on the eastern flanks of the Andes down to the Amazon River. Also, to gather what information we could on a frontier city called Iquitos.

As we finished a bottle of Cousino-Macul from Chile, we realized that our research had taken on a sense of danger. We sat up into the early morning hours making plans for accelerating our research and how to protect the information we gathered. I knew Serge well enough to feel that his statement of caution was given after considerable reflection on the consequences his words would have on me. He knew I would remember that evening by the fire, and that I would begin to take steps to safeguard our research.

Jason left by 2:00 in the morning and as I attempted to settle my mind to gather a few hours sleep, I wondered what Serge had come upon. Could it be something like the rumor of *El Hombre Dorado*, "The Golden Man," which drew Spaniards to the realm of the Chibchas who had a custom of covering a chieftain with gold dust at the time of his accession? Also the legend of *El Dorado,* a land whose riches would surpass anything the Spaniards had found. With these thoughts going through my head I fell into a troubled sleep.

The next few months involved gathering information on the tropical forest tribes of eastern Peru. The Indians of the rain forest belong to about 40 different tribes. They live in scattered tribal villages and speak a variety of tribal languages. Most Peruvians speak Spanish, but many also speak Quechua or other Indian tongues. It was becoming evident that Serge and Jason's ability to speak Spanish would be very helpful as we traveled in Peru.

The culture of the tropical forest tribes was characterized generally by simple village societies of small kinship and community groups that lived mainly along rivers and coasts, cultivated tropical roots and plants, fished and hunted, and in many cases were warlike and cannibalistic. Arawakan tribes were also in eastern Peru and southwestern Brazil. In the rain forest could also be found the Jivaroans and Panoans with a patchwork of different language groups occupying the upper tributaries of the northwest and southwest portions of the Amazon Basin.

I realized that entering the Amazon Basin could be a very dangerous adventure, not only was their danger from the wildlife, but also from the people living in the rainforest. On the eastern side of the Andes, the Jivaros were known to shrink the entire head of a victim; and in the lower Amazon Basin, the Araras flayed and preserved the complete skin of their enemies. I wondered if these customs were still practiced at this time.

The land east of the Andes Mountains has two sub regions – the highlands and the lowlands. The highlands consist of the eastern foothills of the Andes. Unlike the dry western foothills, they are covered with green forests. The lowlands consist of low, flat plains east of the highlands. Thick rain forests and jungles cover most of the lowlands. The Eastern Highlands and the rain forest have a wet and dry season. It seemed only practical to travel in the dry season, which is from May through October.

Our studies revealed that a trip into the jungle would involve a need for someone who had knowledge of the area. I was determined to question Serge as soon as he arrived as to what his plans were to obtain the services of such a person. We would require the help of an experienced individual to accompany us into the jungle.

3
The Journal

The winter of 1977 - 1978 seemed to take forever to end, as I anticipated the arrival of Serge in the spring. I resolved to devote as much time as possible to gathering information on Peru and the area east of the Andes mountains.

I had several engineering projects in the Washington, DC metropolitan area, which occupied much of my time, but I was able to divert some of my attention to research on Peruvian antiquity. Having a goal and the challenge of preparing for it can become all engrossing. Knowing this, I knew that the engineering would help balance my workload in trying to prepare for a trip to South America.

As the first weeks of 1978 passed without word from Serge my anticipation only became worse. I was constantly on the alert for some form of communication from Europe. Then in February I received a letter postmarked Paris, France. Serge stated that he would arrive at Washington National Airport, March 16th on flight 198 from Paris. He requested I meet him, and asked if there would be room for him to stay at my place.

I leaned back in my chair, pausing to reflect on the last time that we had seen each other. We had been communicating for more than ten years, but we had not seen each other for all that time. The possible realization of this expedition was the culmination of years of study and research, years of preparing for this moment. As my thoughts wandered over the past years and the many unknowns that still confronted us, I felt overwhelmed with the prospect of traveling to Peru.

We had been so preoccupied with studying about Peru and the Inca that the prospects of traveling there had always seemed to lack a touch of reality. Now the reality of flying to Peru was upon me, with the realization that all the studying and training was finally to be applied. Since early in 1968 I had prepared for this, now I was to see if I was up to the challenge.

Peru is the third largest country in South America, with an estimated population of 25,000,000 people. Most of the people speak Spanish and since 1975 the Peruvian government has made Quechua, the language of the Inca, an official language along with Spanish. Serge and Jason both speak Spanish, but Jason also speaks Quechua. During Jason's early teen years he had lived in Lima with his parents and had the opportunity to acquire the ability to speak the language of the Inca. He also had the opportunity to visit the coastal pre-Inca temple ruins at Pachacamac; this early introduction to Indian Civilizations of the Central Andes laid the foundation for his interests in early civilizations. I felt somewhat reassured in that two of our party could speak the language of the country we would be traveling in for a few months. Neither Serge nor myself had traveled to South America, but with Jason's previous time spent in Peru, travel should not be too difficult.

A knock at the door brought me out of my day dreaming and upon opening the door, Jason steps in asking, "What's new?" I handed the letter to him and stated that time was short and we had better finalize our preparations for the anticipated trip to Peru. Also, we better start getting our personal affairs in order for an unexpected departure, which also included applying for passports, and vaccinations for yellow fever and malaria.

Though my work and research kept me fully occupied, I tried to keep in contact with my family. They were aware of my lifestyle, which included absences of months at a time. Not wanting them to be overly concerned for my safety, I informed my parents that I would be out of the country for a few months and would contact them on my return. With the potential problems of security, I felt it best not to involve my family in the details of the forthcoming trip.

I had confirmed that flight 198 was scheduled for arrival at 10:00 a.m. As the date quickly approached, my anticipation of seeing my friend and the information he carried kept me in a constant state of readiness. As the days crept by with preparations as complete as was possible, without knowing our destination, Jason and I spent hours pouring over maps and reference materials. Questions such as, what part of the Amazon Basin were we entering? There were two cities of some size such as Iquitos in the north and Pucallpa in the south. Both cities had airports and located near rivers. Until Serge arrived our questions would have to go unanswered, though our curiosity would be unbearable.

As the 16th of March dawned, I was dressing and preparing to enter the early morning traffic on the Capital Beltway, which surrounds Washington, DC. I was determined to arrive at least by 9:00, which would require leaving at least two hours before the scheduled arrival time.

Airports can provide an interesting display of humanity, especially at a time when they have the least amount of control over their scheduling. People rushing to and fro, those who are waiting for loved ones and those preparing to bid farewell. As I sat waiting for the flight, I relaxed with a cup of coffee and tried to let the frenzied atmosphere of the terminal recede into the background. As the sights and sounds of the terminal faded, I found myself reliving my years in France, my military life, and my desire of searching for ancient artifacts waiting to be discovered. The last ten years seemed to blend together as I sat waiting for a flight from Paris and the return of a friend who might hold the key to fulfill my many dreams. I'm suddenly brought back to reality by the public address system, announcing the arrival of flight 198 from Paris at gate 21.

I rise and begin weaving my way through passengers and friends to gate 21; I feel the tightening of my stomach and the nervousness of seeing a friend after so many years.

I soon found myself in the waiting area for gate 21, and begin hearing conversations in English and French throughout the room. The excitement and anticipation around me was contagious and I found myself standing on my toes to catch a glimpse of Serge, as he would be entering the waiting area. As the passengers are emerging from the access way, everyone seems to gravitate towards the area roped off for the convenience of the disembarking passengers. The shouts of greetings surround me just as I see a familiar face. A face I haven't seen for more than ten years, older, more confident, slowly scanning the crowd. I wave and call out Serge's name and his look of recognition brings a smile to his face that reminds me of Europe so long ago.

We grasp each other's hand and I could see that we were both at a loss for words. With evident emotion in my voice I said, "My dear friend. It's so good to see you again. How was the trip?"

Serge also seemed to have trouble finding his voice as he looked down at me and said, "As you have been known to say, you're a sight for sore eyes." With a chocked laugh from deep in his chest he proceeded to give me a bear hug and said, "The trip was smooth and uneventful, but the anticipation of seeing you again has kept me on the edge of my seat."

After being released from his hug of greeting I stepped back having forgotten the strength of my French friend. Serge stands a fraction over six feet tall and weighs about 190 pounds, the strength of his greeting was a good indication that he was staying in shape. I could see that he had not let the last ten years keep him from his favorite sports of rock climbing and scuba diving.

As we both took a moment to gather our emotions I said, "Let's get your bags and get out of here. We've got lots of catching up to do."

As we neared the baggage claim area I motioned to the leather satchel Serge was carrying and said, "Is that attached to your wrist?"

Serge grinned and said, "No, but what's inside needs to be protected. Wait until we leave here and I'll tell you what I have in the satchel."

After retrieving his baggage from customs and finishing the legalities of entering the United States, I indicate for Serge to follow me to the parking area. While traveling north on interstate 270 towards Frederick, Maryland, I gave Serge an abbreviated description of what Jason and I have been doing since his letter in the fall of 1977.

While driving I'm aware of Serge leaning forward and lifting his leather satchel onto his lap. As if he's collecting his thoughts, he slowly begins to explain that his grandfather had passed away early in 1977. He explains that as his grandfather became aware of Serge's interest in archeology, the old gentlemen began requesting him to visit more often. He lived in the suburbs of Paris in a small, quiet village and enjoyed discussing the various excavations that Serge participated in. In 1976 he requested Serge to spend a weekend at his home, he indicated he had some important matters to discuss. Suddenly I sense a change has come over Serge, I quickly glance at him and said, "Are you all right?"

I hear him sigh and as he shakes his head no, he says, "The memories are still difficult to deal with. I had grown to love the old man and his death was difficult for me to handle."

After a few moments, he begins slowly, as if he were reliving the memories he's about to reveal. He describes arriving on a Friday afternoon to find his grandfather relaxing by the fire in a warm wood paneled room filled with books. Many of the books bring back memories of quiet times with his grandfather in that very room. Later that evening while sharing a glass of cognac, his grandfather asks Serge to relax by the fire until he returns.

As Serge is speaking I'm able to detect some excitement entering his voice at this point in his story. I control the urge to ask questions or to hurry him. He would tell the story at his own pace and I would not interfere; though I certainly wanted him to hurry with what was next.

His grandfather returns after a short interval carrying a tablet-sized, worn leather case and a wooden box. Even at a distance the age of the case and box was obvious, these must be something the old gentlemen treasures. He seats himself slowly holding the items on his lap. He begins to explain to Serge that some things need to be handed down to the next generation with great care. Because some items will never be appreciated for what they are or what they could mean if not given to the appropriate person. At this point he leans forward and in a confidential manner explains, that no one in the family is aware of these items, as he pats the leather case. He had acquired it from his father's grandfather and only after observing Serge's interest in archeology had he decided to entrust these items to him.

As his grandfather leans back and tastes his cognac, he states that he had read the journal and wanted to solve the mystery revealed in its pages. Then the First World War brought a halt to a young man's dreams. His dreams of exploring were brought to an end on a French battlefield by German mustard gas. He lived, but his strength was never the same. He places his hands on the leather case and says that he had hoped before his death that someone in the family would have the training to put the information in the journal to practical us. He lifts the case and hands it to Serge and tells him to read what is written in the journal of his great-great-grandfather Phillip and they would discuss it the next morning. After Serge accepts the case, his grandfather takes the box and hands it to Serge saying, "Your great-great-grandfather Phillip carried this in Peru." At that point he rises, says goodnight and leaves for his bed. I had kept quiet as long as I could, but without thinking, I said, "Well what did you do?"

Serge looks at me and smiles and says, "I refilled my glass and with the journal and box under my arm, I went to my room to read." I had been so preoccupied with the story Serge was relating that only at that moment did I realize we were only moments from my home. I informed Serge that my home was very near, and he suggested I contact Jason and that the three of us get together for a meal and a story.

I have a small home west of Frederick city on ten wooded acres. It's quiet, peaceful and provides just the type of privacy I desire. Having been raised in Washington, DC, I have great appreciation for the quiet style of country living that can be found in these green, rolling hills. As I approach the house Serge was appreciatively nodding his head. I could tell he felt comfortable already, even before he stated that the place looked peaceful.

We carried the luggage in and I took him to his room, with a suggestion that if he would care to rest awhile I would contact Jason. I suggested dinner at seven that evening, and then we could relax and let Serge present his findings. He agreed, so I left him to unpack and get some rest, and I went to call Jason. I waited until after 1:00 and called Jason at the office, he quickly accepted the invitation for seven that evening.

Serge was up and about by 6:00 and decided to get some air while I prepared the meal. Within 30 minutes I heard a car and soon after Jason and Serge came into the kitchen, I could see introductions would not be needed. Everyone seemed to enjoy the meal, but you could feel the anticipation throughout the meal. Both Jason and myself were impatient to hear of Serge's discoveries, so when I suggested clearing the table for Serge to set out his materials, everyone quickly responded.

Serge gathered his dishes and turning towards the kitchen he said, "I'll put these in the sink and get the journal from my room. Get comfortable I'll be right back."

Jason and I were sitting at the kitchen table as Serge returned with the satchel under his arm. As he seated himself, he said, "This journal could possibly be the adventure of a lifetime." I suggested that Serge quickly explain to Jason how he had acquired the journal, since I had been briefed on our trip from National Airport. While Serge was speaking, I got a bottle of Courvoisier and three glasses. As Jason was brought up to date, we each tasted our cognac and Serge with a sigh begins.

Serge opens the satchel and withdraws a worn leather-bound portfolio with leather straps tying it closed. Jason and I watch as he carefully releases the straps and opens the journal. The pages are yellowed and the edges are cracked and broken from age. As he opens the journal I can see the entries have been made with a quill pen.

Serge explains that his great-great-grandfather Phillip Gaston, who was an adventurous young man wanted to see more of the world than France, this was his journal. At this point, Serge turns the first page and we move closer to see what is written.

"It's written in French," exclaims Jason.

"Hey, relax," I said. I looked at Serge and said, "Do me a favor and read the journal to us. Jason doesn't read French and I would like to hear the journal read before reading it for myself." Though I can speak and read French, I also wanted to hear the journal read for the first time. I would quietly read it alone at a later time. As Jason and I sit back in our chairs, Serge takes another taste of cognac and begins reading.

The first entry is dated 1853 and describes a trip on a merchant ship from Toulon, France through the Straits of Gibraltar to Mogadore in Morocco. After a layover of several days they set sail for Cape Town located in the Cape Colony of southern Africa.

Serge stops reading and looking up from the journal says, "If you remember the history of that area Phillip was unable to use the Suez Canal because the French canal builder Ferdinand de Lesseps had not received permission to build a canal through the Isthmus of Suez in Egypt at that time."

The journal continues with a description of sailing around the Cape of Good Hope and making their next port of call at Zanzibar in the country of Zanguebar. He describes the port and the many strange sights of this far off country. From Zanzibar they sail into the Indian Ocean and stop at the island of Ceylon for two weeks. Next they sail north across the Bay of Bengal to the city of Calcutta, located on the Ganges River. During the next two months, Phillip makes notations of traveling up the Ganges River to the cities of Agra and Delhi. His descriptions of temples, ruins and the riches of the country are very detailed. Numerous sketches are made of buildings and locations as if he planned to return at a future time.

The next entry is dated 1856, indicating that he was preparing to sail from Bombay and return to France. Very few notations are made concerning his return trip to Europe. In a short entry dated 1857, Phillip states he is purchasing a small country estate north of Paris at St. Denis. He is also pursuing studies at a university in Paris on ancient cultures.

Serge pauses for a moment, sips his cognac and states that Phillip seems to have returned from India, a man of some means. He wonders if his great-great-grandfather had returned from India with something of more value than the knowledge of the country?

During the next few years, there are entries describing excavations in Nantes, Narbonne and in the Pyrenees Mountains. By the year 1866 there seems to be a growing interest in the South American Indians of Peru and the Spanish conquests by Francisco Pizarro.

Serge comments that the next entry is underlined, it reads April 1869. While researching the travels of Pizarro and the Spanish conquests in Peru he comes upon a notation that a soldier of fortune named Diego de Aranda had deserted from the garrison in Pisco in 1548. Phillip writes, I must travel to Aranda to investigate this individual, he may have left a record of his travels.

Phillip writes that he is aware of a small city by the name of Aranda situated on the river Douro in north central Spain. He travels to Aranda and while searching through the library of the local university he discovers an old journal wedged between reference books in a basement storage room. Upon opening the journal his wildest hopes have been rewarded. The first item written in the journal states, this is a record of the travels of a gentleman from Aranda, written by Diego de Aranda. Phillip realizes he would not be allowed to remove the journal from the library, so he spends several days copying the pertinent information concerning Diego's travels to Peru.

As Phillip reads the journal he quickly realizes that Diego traveled to Peru for only one reason, to find his fortune. He writes that he sailed from Cadiz for Peru in 1542. The ship makes a stop at the Canary Islands before sailing for South America. His next entry states that they sailed across the Atlantic Ocean without incident and made landfall in Rio Janeiro, Brazil. Diego makes a notation in his journal that if only he could have been with Francisco Pizzaro when he returned to South America in 1532. He states his parents insisted he continue his education, which prevented him from signing on ten years earlier with Pizzaro. With a new Viceroy being sent to the new colony to impose order it was not difficult to sign on for the voyage as an officer with the army.

Diego continues with a description of sailing around Cape Horn and the storms that threatened to capsize the ship on a daily basis. The next port they put into is Valparaiso and within a few days they are sailing north to Lima. Very little is written until a notation dated 1545 that he has been transferred to a garrison south of Lima in the city of Pisco.

Phillip makes a notation that the entries dated 1545 thru 1547 deal with everyday life in a garrison on the frontier of civilization. Diego seems to dwell on locating treasure, and is cultivating a friendship with a local Indian named Mazco. He states that Mazco tells of a city far to the north, hidden in the jungles of the Amazon.

Diego's next entry describes the arrival of Pedro de la Gasco in 1548 who was sent to rule the colony. With the colony in turmoil between the Spanish and the Indians, Diego feels that eventually the Spanish may have a difficult time holding the new colony under their control. He makes a quick notation that he has heard that the city Mazco has mentioned could be located on the Napo River. He hopes to convince several others in the garrison to accompany him on a trip into the interior with the help of Mazco as a guide. He writes that the city is described as an ancient city of a people who disappeared before the Inca came into power. His last entry states that they will leave quietly in the early hours of the morning, Diego has ten men who will accompany him to find the city.

The entries for the next few months are few, Diego describes crossing the Andes at the city of Pasco and then using canoes to travel upon the rivers heading north. By the time they get to the Napo River, he records that four of their number has been killed by Indians or from deadly animals. Their food is low and they are eating mostly fish from the rivers, but they must use great care, because of the small fish with sharp teeth. He writes they will strip the flesh from a man in minutes. Diego also notes that Mazco seems more withdrawn and sullen as the days go by. The men treat him almost as a slave and Diego worries that one morning he may wake to find that Mazco has abandoned the party.

The journal continues with comments concerning the trip north on the Napo River and when the river splits, Mazco indicates they should enter the left branch. Diego notes the river is very rough and in many places they must carry the canoes up river to less troubled waters. He notes the river twists and turns as a serpent, causing them to proceed at a cautious pace. After carrying the canoes around a second waterfall, the decision is agreed upon that the canoes would be hidden on the left side of the river and the party would continue on foot. They discover once away from the river, the jungle thins and travel is easier. After passing two tributaries entering the river from the left, Mazco states they are to go up the second tributary.

Diego indicates the men are losing heart in finding the city and three are sick and barely keeping up with the rest. He states Mazco reassures him that they are only three days from the ruins. That morning they have a meeting to discuss if the party should turn back or continue. Diego suggests that the sick remain in the camp with one of those not ill, and Diego with the remaining two would follow Mazco up the river for three more days. If nothing is found, they would return to the camp and then return to the coast.

Diego's next entry describes finding a valley with two step pyramids built of stone, similar to Inca temples, but these seem to be of a finer construction. He also comments that a cylindrical tower of unknown origin is in the city. He makes a few sketches that depict a city surrounded my mountains, but his goal is treasure not archeology. His next entry is 15 days from the previous entry and his only notation is that the city is beyond his greatest expectations. This is the last entry until 1550. A short entry states he is sailing from Lima for Spain. He mentions no treasure, only that after eight years in South America he longs to return to his home in Aranda, Spain.

Phillip states that after reading Diego's journal, he traveled to the area of Aranda searching for evidence of Diego's return. Although three hundred years had passed, he finds that the family was able to acquire some prominence in the city after 1550. During the next ten years Diego purchases a large estate and lives out his life as a wealthy landowner. Phillip makes a notation that he feels Diego truly found a city in the jungles of the Amazon and returned with some form of treasure.

The next entry in Phillip's journal is dated 1871, where he states that he is sailing from Marseilles for South America. He is hoping to use his notes from Diego's travels to find the city in the jungles of the Amazon. During his trip to Peru, Phillip makes very few entries in his journal.

The notations in the journal after Phillip's arrival in Lima indicate that he visits various ancient cities in the Andes. He mentions visiting the ancient capital of the Inca Empire Cuzco. A city built in the shape of a puma, with sophisticated water systems, paved streets and no mention of poverty. He describes the huge walls of the city buildings with their intricately laid stones.

His next entry must have made a great impression on him. He states, I have seen Cuzco's magnificent Cathedral, which was built on what once was the Palace of Inca Wiracocha, and made in part from stones hauled from the fortress of Sacsayhuaman outside the city. The altar is of solid silver. Next to the altar is the painting of the crucified Christ known as *Nuestro Senor de los Temblores*. He also notes having seen the cathedral's bell in the north tower, known as *Maria Angola*. It was made of a ton of gold, silver and bronze, and suggested to be more than 200 years old.

He continues with a description of the remains of Coricancha, the temple of the sun, the most magnificent complex in Cuzco. The walls had been covered with 700 sheets of gold studded with emeralds and turquoise, and windows were constructed so the sun would enter and cast a reflection off the precious metals inside. The mummified bodies of deceased Inca leaders, dressed in fine clothing and adornments, were kept on thrones of gold. In the same room, a huge gold disk beautifully wrought and set with many precious stones covered one full wall while a sister disk of silver, to reflect the moonlight was on another wall. Below the temple was a garden filled with life-sized gold and silver status of llamas, trees, fruits, flowers and even delicately handcrafted butterflies. Within the garden the earth was represented as lumps of fine gold, with stalks, leaves and ears of corn that were of gold. There were also more than 20 sheep of gold with their lambs and the shepherds who guarded them, all of fine gold.

Phillip makes a side note that the wealth that the Spanish came upon in Peru must have been overwhelming. And to think, such beauty was melted down into bars for transport to Spain. He writes that he is beginning to have an appreciation for the power and beauty of the Inca Empire. Their architecture, weaving and metallurgy deserve serious study; I must visit other sites for a more complete understanding of these people before traveling north to the Amazon.

He notes that after traveling through Cuzco that he wants to travel to the fortress of Sacsayhuama on the hill overlooking the city. The massive stones used in the construction indicate great skills in handling extremely large stones. The complex has a double wall in a zigzag shape. The fort also once had at least three huge towers and a labyrinth of rooms large enough for a garrison of 5000 Inca soldiers. Phillip seems to be impressed with the construction abilities of the Inca and estimates that tens of thousands of workers must have labored on the massive structure for up to seven decades, hauling the immense stone blocks that make up the double outside walls, and erecting the buildings that transformed the complex into one of the most impressive in all the empire.

Serge pauses, looks at me and says, "Do you realize that Phillip seems overawed by what he sees? Here's a man who has traveled, seen magnificent sights in many parts of the world and he speaks of the Inca Empire in awe. I hope you can appreciate my excitement after reading this and in asking you and Jason to study the early peoples of Peru. As you will see, I believe Phillip found Diego's lost city."

As Serge continues to read, he has no trouble keeping our attention. The anticipation of what remains to be read has my full attention, and as I glance at Jason I can see he also has barely moved since Serge began reading.

Phillip's next entry states he is traveling north along the coast to the city of Truxillo. It was founded in 1535 and named after Francisco Pizzarro's birthplace in Spain, Trujillo was used by the Spaniards as a resting spot on the route between Lima and Quito. This was the city in 1820, which became the first Peruvian city to proclaim its independence from Spain, and the liberator Simon de Bolivar, moving down the coast from Ecuador, set the seat of his government there. He writes he will spend a short time in Truxillo and after securing a guide he plans on using the city as a jumping-off point to cross the mountains and travel down the Huallaga river east into the jungles of the Amazon. He states he has been cautioned about several tribes in his area of proposed travel, specifically the Jivaros and the Guayape. The Jivaros have been known to shrink heads of those they capture. Several weeks later he writes that he has secured a guide named Tejo, who says he knows the jungle and will guide him to the Napo River.

His notations concerning the preparations for the trip seem confident and he seems to place a lot of trust in Tejo. The following pages have short entries concerning the crossing of the Andes Mountains, which he estimates, are over 4000 feet in height in the area he is traveling. He mentions having to cross several streams and then having to cross the Tunguragua River. The next entry states he had arrived at the Huallaga River and had acquired a canoe for traveling to the village of Lagima, where the river meets the Tunguragua. Phillip writes that Tejo has cautioned him about being watched from the jungle and to always keep the canoe in midstream.

There are very few notations in the journal, and what entries there are have not been dated, but he indicates the river continues to flow through thick jungle. As the days pass, the river seems to be widening, which Phillip notes will soon deposit them into the great Amazon River.

His next entry describes waking in the canoe where they had decided to spend the night, due to the danger from Indians they had seen on shore. As he awakens he puts his hand over the side of the canoe to gather water to wash his face, but instead of water his hand hits a hard surface. He peers over the side of the canoe and floating along side the canoe is a Caiman as long as the canoe. As they drift with the current of the river, they slowly part company, to the relief of Phillip and Tejo.

Phillip, as if apologizing, states he has lost all track of time, as they seem to constantly see the same vegetation along the river day after day. Tejo prepares several types of fish to eat and goes ashore to gather fruits and tubers for their meals. Tejo is constantly cautioning for silence, because of the threat of warlike tribes along the river.

Serge pauses in his reading, stands and stretches saying, "I need to take a small break." Lifting his glass from the table he says, "I would appreciate a refill, reading is a dry business." I reached for the bottle of cognac and said, "The story is so engrossing that I have forgotten my manners as a host. Would you care to have anything to eat?"

Extending his glass for me to fill, Serge says, "No, the cognac is sufficient. I also remember the first time I read the journal, it was impossible to put down until I had finished reading it."

Our attention had been totally absorbed in the reading of the journal, as it describes the journey of a man in the 19th century, daring all the odds to venture into a world completely alien to his own. Jason comments that the odds seem completely against Phillip surviving to see the Napo River, much less finding the lost city. I quietly agree with Jason that what I've heard so far paints a very bleak picture for success.

Reaching for the journal, Serge prepares to continue reading. As I anticipate what is to come, my mind dwells on Phillip and what great odds were against his attaining success. He was an experienced adventurer, but it was possible this trek into the unknown would be more than he could accomplish.

The journal continues with the canoe drifting on a lazy current, until one day the current begins to move with more purpose and they soon find themselves swept into a much larger river. Tejo announces that they have arrived at the Amazon River, and they will soon see the Napo River.

The next entry describes a tribe that Tejo insists will be friendly. He suggests that Phillip offer something as a gift that the headman would prize, if he does, they would be able to restock some of their provisions and be given some time to rest in safety. They approach the shoreline slowly, with many of the tribe watching their canoe from the shore. Tejo stands and calls out a greeting and is immediately answered with much shouting and waving. Phillip is told to remain in the canoe until Tejo calls him. After a short period of time, Tejo returns with a short, dark skinned man, who Tejo introduces as the headman. Tejo motions Phillip from the canoe and tells him to give a gift to the headman, whose name is Moura. Phillip reaches into his vest pocket and hands Moura a pair of spectacles, which he proceeds to demonstrate how they are to be used. As he puts them on, he knows he has made the right choice as an offering to Moura.

They are escorted into the village, which consists of pole and thatch houses with platforms for beds. Moura guides them to his house and motions them to be seated, after which he quickly gives instructions to several women. Moura then turns to Tejo and begins speaking in one of the Indian dialects, which provides Phillip the opportunity to observe the village and its people. He realizes he is observing a typical hunter-gatherer society. He notes several dugout canoes near the riverbank and fish drying on nearby racks.

The women return with bowls of food, and Moura motions Phillip to eat as he and Tejo begin to eat. Phillip indicates the meal consisted of a corn meal, squash, and yucca.

As Phillip begins to eat, Moura says something to Tejo and hands him a small bowl of red sauce, and motions to Phillip. Tejo tells him to dip his food into the sauce, as a way of showing respect to Moura, but he warns Phillip the sauce will be like eating fire. Phillip realizing that he must use the sauce or insult Moura, dips his yucca and places it in his mouth. As the liquid fire spreads from his mouth and down his throat, Phillip begins looking for something to drink, hoping it will put out the fire. During Phillip's attempts to find something to quench the fire, he observes Moura and Tejo rolling in laughter at his reaction to the spicy sauce he had just eaten. Tejo, still laughing hands a cup of Masato to Phillip, which he immediately drinks. As Phillip regains his ability to breathe, he asks Tejo what was in the cup that he had just swallowed. It helped with the fire, but it planted another fire in his stomach. Tejo states it is Masato, a drink made from fermented yucca. After the meal Phillip states he needed assistance to the house they have been given for their stay due to the masato.

An entry three days later, states Moura has directed his visitors are to be given yams, squash, and yucca for their trip. They are also given woven armbands that Tejo indicates will give them safe passage to the Napo River. As they enter their canoe and paddle into the river, Phillip asks Tejo if he had questioned Moura concerning his knowledge of any ancient Inca cities in the area. Tejo states Moura had heard rumors of a city of ruins in the jungle where the Napo splits and the river twists like a snake. He also warns that the headman gave a warning that the snake spirits, which guard the city for the ancients, will not allow strangers into the city. When questioned if Moura had ever visited the city, with fear in his eyes Moura quickly stated, never.

Within several days, Phillip writes that a river of considerable size is seen on their left flowing into the Amazon. Tejo begins paddling towards the shore, while announcing that the new river is the Napo River. He explains they must carry the canoe up river a short distance, because of the strength of the current of the Napo River as it flows south.

The next entry states that they have been able to resume traveling up the river by canoe. Tejo states that it will be several days before they come to the fork in the river, the branch to the left is the one that Moura has spoken of that twists like a snake. Phillip makes a short note that both branches are flowing with a strong current, but they are able to enter the left branch without great difficulty.

Within a few days travel on the river, they notice the current has gained in strength and the river twists as Moura had predicted. He also writes that the terrain seems less flat, though the jungle grows thickly along the riverbank, he writes that the terrain has become hilly. Phillip notes that they came to a twenty-foot high waterfall, which they had to carry the canoe around and enter the river upstream from the falls. Another entry indicates that Tejo had pointed out a young Puma watching them from the jungle while they were carrying the canoe. As they carry the canoe Phillip is reminded of Diego's journal, which he also commented upon two waterfalls while traveling up this river.

Within a day they come upon the second waterfall, which is thirty feet high or more, Phillip notes that the terrain has gradually become rougher as they have progressed north. He writes that having asked Tejo if they could continue up river in the canoe, he indicates that it will not be safe if the water continues to get rougher.

A quick entry states, they have hidden their canoe on the left bank of the river and have proceeded on foot. They have passed the first tributary entering from the left and looking for the second as described in Diego's journal.

Serge sets the journal down and stretches, drinks a little cognac and says, "The next entry was put in by Phillip to guard the location of the city." He picks the journal up and resumes reading.

I'm writing this before the sunsets, so I will be brief. I realize that I have kept a record of my travels, and that if I ever return and it gets into the wrong hands, I could lose everything. If I find the city I will leave a coded message in these pages, for any of my future generations to follow, if they have enough adventure in their souls to do so.

We have found the second tributary and have turned west walking deeper into the jungle. The jungle shows no signs of man, it's as if no human being had ever set foot in this part of the world. I have noticed several outcroppings of limestone that show signs of having been quarried in the past. The ground in many places is strewn with rocks of considerable sizes, and we seem to be gradually climbing as we continue west.

A quick entry states, I have found the valley where the city is located, it is more than I had ever imagined. In many ways it resembles Inca architecture, but it shows influence from another culture, possibly from the north. There are two temples, one to the sun god and one to mother earth, and a larger temple of a strange cylindrical design. A number of other structures are located here, much work is needed to be done, but I'm almost out of time. I have contracted a jungle sickness that Tejo is familiar with and he is helping me, but I must return to Lima as soon as possible and return with more help. The city is well hidden, look for the Serpent coiled around a branch, and you will be at the entrance to the city. If possible we will begin our journey home in two days, I will make no further entries in this journal unless they are of great importance.

An entry dated 1873, indicates Phillip has arrived in Lima, thanks to Tejo and the jungle medicine given to him at Moura's village. He will sail for France on the next available ship.

Serge closes the journal with a sigh and leans back in his chair. As I look at Jason I realize its taking us a few moments to adjust to Serge not speaking. We were so caught up in the reading of Phillip's travels that it was difficult to return to the reality of our present century.

I found my head swirling with questions concerning the city, treasure and Phillip, it was almost more than I could absorb in one evening. Looking at Serge I said, "Is there any evidence that Phillip brought anything back from the city?"

Serge nodded and said, "There was nothing definite, but around 1874 he purchased a large tract of land next to his present estate in St. Denis. Then in 1876 he had a new home built for himself and his new bride. I have every reason to believe that my great-great-grandfather found the city that Diego de Aranda had written about in 1548. He also had a hand sketch of the rivers and villages marked in the journal."

I could see that Serge was exhausted, so I suggested we conclude our discussions for the night and resume the following day. Speaking for myself I had numerous questions as I suspected Jason did also. With weary steps we all retired to our beds with thoughts of a city hidden within the jungles of the Amazon.

4
Preparing for South America

The smell of hot biscuits, bacon, and eggs with fresh coffee is a sure way to bring men to the breakfast table. I had been up since dawn and decided everyone could use a good breakfast, I knew there was much Serge still needed to bring us up to date on. I called out that the food was ready and they better get a move on. I could see from their response a second call would not be needed.

When breakfast was finished and the dishes put away, I suggested we take our coffee out to the porch to relax. The weather was unseasonably warm and the day promised to offer some early spring temperatures. As we sat enjoying the mid-morning peace and quiet, I knew that if Jason did not speak up that I most certainly would.

Unexpectedly, Serge broke the silence with a chuckle and smiled asking, "Now that our stomachs are full would you care to hear more of the story?" Our response was immediate as we both encouraged Serge to continue with the story.

Serge begins by reminding us of his grandfather giving him the journal and his excitement after reading it. Serge states that he was attending classes at a university in Paris that was well known for its school of archeology. He had taken several courses instructed by Professor Marcel Segault, a noted teacher of ancient cultures. He had acquired great respect for the professor, who was considered a very learned man.

Professor Segault was a well-respected teacher and researcher on the campus, and he fostered a close relationship with his students. It was known that the professor would disappear every summer and it was assumed he participated in excavations in exotic parts of the world.

With the teacher-student atmosphere fostered by Professor Segault, Serge soon felt comfortable in disclosing the existence of the journal to him. Requesting his opinion of the possibility of such a city existing in the Amazon jungles of Peru.

As Jason and I groaned, Serge quickly responded, "I know, it was a thoughtless thing to do, but I was young and lacked the experience of not trusting everyone."

As Serge continued, he stated that the professor dismissed the possibility of a city in the Amazon, but stated he would be willing to give the journal a brief reading. Serge felt uncomfortable giving the journal to the professor, so he stated he would copy the pertinent pages. He was careful to copy only parts of pages to give a brief introduction to what Phillip had uncovered. As the weeks passed Serge noted a change in the professor's attitude towards him. He soon found that he was invited to the professor's home for social events, but the visits would eventually turn to questions concerning the journal.

During the spring semester Serge was invited to an archeological excavation east of Paris and spent a week with several researchers and the professor unearthing 14th century artifacts. Serge noticed that he was the only student invited to participate from the university.

Serge became aware that Professor Segault was fostering a relationship with him, but for what reason. The professor usually had very little to do with his students outside the classroom. At this point he started suspecting the journal was the reason for the sudden attention the professor was giving him. He realized he had better start distancing himself from the professor as quickly as possible.

The semester was due to end in a few weeks and with the time needed for preparing for finals, Serge was able to decline the professor's social invitations without seeming to be rude. He knew that after the semester it would be best to return home. Professor Segault's curiosity concerning the journal was causing Serge to be concerned for the safety of the journal. Several times he had met Jacque and Michel at the professor's home, and had wondered what these men had in common with the professor. They reminded Serge of very large street thugs uncomfortably dressed in suits. They always seemed to display proper manners, but there was an undercurrent of danger just below the surface of their mannerisms. He recalled noticing that Jacque carried an automatic in a shoulder holster. Serge never felt comfortable enough to ask the professor about the men, but he felt uncomfortable whenever they were around.

During the last week of the semester, Serge recalled a disturbing incident that brought him to a realization that the journal could be attracting unwanted attention. The professor had insisted that Serge come to his home for an evening meal to celebrate the completion of his studies. Serge realized that if he declined the request, he could make the professor suspicious of his continued avoidance of him. To his surprise there were several guests and among them some students that he recognized, which provided the opportunity to spend time with the students. As the evening came to an end Professor Segault requested Serge to remain for a farewell drink. Hoping the evening could end on a pleasant note, he accepted the invitation. The professor seemed very relaxed as he light-heartedly commented on the classes and excavations they had been able to work together on. Serge watched as he poured a generous amount of cognac into the glasses and handed one to Serge. As the professor sat in a large leather chair, he stated that he hoped that some day they would be able to share further adventures in archeology.

The professor continued ideally speaking of various studies and students, while Serge's mind became aware that the professor had nothing of any substance to discuss. Was there a reason for the professor in delaying his departure? While only giving slight attention to what the professor was saying, he realized he had not seen Jacque or Michel since the guests had left. Suddenly, a surge of panic ran through him, could the professor have sent Jacque and Michel to his home to find the journal? Without disclosing the panic he felt he excused himself and thanked the professor for a wonderful evening, but it was late and he really must leave. When he left the house he realized the professor had kept him over an hour beyond the other guests. If anyone had wanted to search his home, they certainly had the time to perform a thorough search.

While pursuing his graduate studies in Paris, Serge had rented a small cottage in the countryside outside of Paris. He enjoyed his privacy and the peace of a rural setting; these were not amenities easily attainable in the city. The stone cottage had been built at the turn of the century and was extremely sturdy. There was a large barn and several smaller buildings all in acceptable condition. One day, while cleaning the barn, Serge stumbled upon a trap door in the floor of the tack room. Upon investigating he found a ladder leading down to a tunnel, which he discovered led to a wood storage shed located at the back of the cottage. He had spent time disguising the trap door in the wood shed, he just hoped it would fool any intruders.

He arrived to find the cottage dark with no outward signs of intruders. After carefully approaching the house and noticing no signs of forced entry, he approached the front door. With his adrenalin pumping, he unlocked the door and immediately turned on the lights. The house appeared in order, with no signs that uninvited guests had been in his home. As he carefully walked through the rooms of the cottage, he became aware of things not quite the way they should be.

He couldn't put his finger on any one thing; he had an eerie feeling that someone had been in his home. The urge to confirm the safety of the journal was overwhelming, but someone could still have him under surveillance, so with great restraint he forced himself to retire for the night. Sleep didn't come easy, but he finally fell into a troubled sleep.

He awoke with a start, with the feeling that someone was watching him. Calming his nerves he forced himself to dress without appearing to hurry, all the time being conscious of any sounds in the house that seemed out of place. During the time spent dressing his mind was constantly thinking of the journal and its safety. He left the house and started to walk to the barn, all the time trying to be cognizant of anything out of the ordinary. Everything seemed normal, but he felt he was still being watched. Once in the barn, he walked about as if he were looking for something. After confirming the barn was empty, he walked quickly to the tack room. Nothing seemed out of place or disturbed. In one corner was an old desk with a metal folding chair. A worn wool carpet, which had seen better days, was placed under the desk. After entering the tack room he closed the door and locked it.

When Serge had found the tunnel and trap door, he had decided to place a lock on the tack room door that could be secured from inside the room. After securing the door he lifted the carpet revealing the trap door. With a sense of urgency he could barely contain, he lifted the trap door revealing a ladder leading down into darkness. Without hesitating Serge began to descend into the darkness below. After descending several steps on the ladder, he reaches through the ladder rungs to the back wall and grasps a lantern hung from the wall. Removing a lighter from his pocket he lights the lantern and continues down the ladder into the tunnel.

Serge describes standing at the bottom of the ladder for a moment and trying to listen for any sounds that may reveal anything out of the ordinary. During this time he also notices that there is dust on the lantern indicating that no one had used it recently. With only silence greeting him, he proceeds into the tunnel for approximately 30 feet. The original designer of the tunnel had excavated a small room on his left, which had been used for some form of storage. At the present time it contained several wooden barrels and crates, everything looked as if they had not been moved in years. With great care, Serge lifted a crate that had been placed upon a barrel and set it upon another crate. He reached into the barrel, moving some old burlap bags to reveal a black metal box. Lifting the box out he produced a key and opened the box, where upon he could see the journal was safe.

With a sigh of relief, he re-locked the box and placed it back in the barrel, covering it with the burlap bags. He then replaced the crate upon the barrel and stepped back to confirm that everything was as it was before he entered the room. As he retraced his steps back to the ladder, he realized that he must contact his partner in the United States and proceed quickly to Peru before others could use the information found in the journal. Until he was ready to leave for the Unites States the journal would stay hidden in the tunnel.

Serge leans over and sets his coffee cup on a side table, and looking at us he says, "I've told you this short story to emphasis why I cautioned you to be aware of securing your research data. I have every reason to suspect Professor Segault and his two companions have tried and will continue trying to steal the journal. After the episode at my cottage I decided to do a little investigating on my own." Serge indicated that he was curious about the summer absences of Professor Segault. Many of the professors at the university taught summer classes, but the professor would always disappear during the summer months. It was also well known that the professor lived very well for someone earning the wages of a university professor.

Hopefully without attracting too much attention, Serge discovered that the professor would have private sales of artifacts. Everyone questioned assumed they were items the professor had discovered during his summer absences. Serge also felt that if the professor suspected he was aware of their interest in the journal, that they might become more aggressive in their attempts to acquire it.

I asked Serge if he felt the professor could be aware of his leaving Europe. He indicated that his absence would go unnoticed for only a short time. He felt that they were aware of my address, since he had never made any attempts to hide any correspondence that he sent me. He stated that he felt we had a small amount of time to prepare for our trip to South America, before someone came looking for us.

Jason spoke up at this time and asked if I still owned the hunting cabin in West Virginia. I had been so preoccupied the last few months, that the cabin had been forgotten as a possible refuge.

Snapping my fingers I said, "That's a great idea. I had forgotten about that little place. It's nothing fancy but it would provide us with a place to make our final preparations before leaving for South America. Several years ago I had wanted to have a secluded place to retreat to, somewhere away from people and the demands of society. I had located fifty wooded acres west of Martinsburg, where my closest neighbors would be deer and turkey. Once or twice a year I like to spend a long weekend fishing and relaxing."

Serge slowly nodded his head and said, "I don't want to produce undue concern, but the professor is not to be underestimated. I would suspect that he has this address and when he discovers that I have left France he will conclude that I have come to see you."

I spoke up and said, "The cabin would be a good place to lose ourselves until preparations were finished for our trip. I must warn you that living at the cabin will require a different style of living than everyone was used to. The cabin has no electricity and running water, but it's loaded with privacy."

Setting his coffee cup down Serge said, "Should we take some camping equipment with us? It sounds like we will be roughing it."

Smiling I said, "I have some camping gear and we can purchase anything else that we will need." As each of us paused to dwell on the situation, silence seemed to settle over the porch like a blanket.

Rising from my chair I said, "There's a little coffee left in the pot, can I refill anyone's cup?" While walking from the kitchen with the coffeepot, I said, "Serge you've given us a lot to think about, but do you have any encouraging information on the forthcoming trip to South America?"

With a smile, Serge said, "Funny you should ask. Let me tell you about Julio."

He stated that during the years of 1973 thru 1975, while taking graduate classes at a university in Paris he had met a young man from Peru. He was attending selected courses on South American cultures, particularly the Inca. His name was Julio Garcia and Serge was very impressed with his knowledge of the Inca Empire and its associated artifacts. As the months passed a friendship developed based on respect for each other's talents and their desires for challenging the unknown. Serge had invited Julio on a couple local archeological excavations and had been impressed with his professional approach to field research.

One evening before Julio was to return to Peru, Serge had invited him for a farewell dinner. Serge had decided that he would reveal some of the material in the journal to Julio and see what his reaction would be to the possibility of the existence of a city in the jungle. Serge knew he would need someone familiar with Peru if we were to have any success in finding the city, and he felt comfortable with asking Julio if he would care to join our expedition. Serge stated that he felt Julio should be aware of Jason and myself. This revelation did not seem to trouble Julio, but seemed to give him more assurances of the possibilities of success. The atmosphere during the meal was light and comfortable, but a little depressing with the knowledge that they might not see each other for many years. As the meal ended, Serge invited Julio to relax and listen to a short story. He proceeded to tell of having seen a journal written during the 16th century describing a city in the jungles of the Peruvian Amazon. He stated that he was only able to see parts of the journal, but what he had seen, convinced him that an expedition to Peru would be something he would be attempting in the near future. Serge proceeded to describe some of the details from the journal, without revealing any key geographical locations. Julio seemed completely captivated by the tale, and suggested that if Serge were serious about this research he would like to be included in the expedition.

After a moment's hesitation, Julio reveals that the reason he had come to the university was to research the possibility of records left by early European travelers. The director of the Museo de Arqueologia has employed him for several years in Trujillo; he had come upon several documents hinting at the existence of a city in the jungles of the Amazon. He states that he feels he can trust Serge and reveals that the director has every reason to believe that it could be the fabled City of the Sun. If it is, the director had already indicated that the museum was willing to offer a $100,000.00 reward for the recovery of a very prized relic.

Early Inca tales tell of a golden serpent coiled around a branch, with eyes fashioned of emeralds. The nobles of the city wore a small replica of the serpent as a status of their positions.

The people of the city worshipped the sun and mother earth, but there was a strong sect of serpent worshippers within the city. They believed that the serpent was the earthly guardian that the sun god had sent to guard their city. Julio indicates the director of the museum should be very interested in what Serge has found and would probably want to meet with Serge to discuss the possibility of searching for the city.

As the evening grew late, Julio suggested that he had to get some rest before his flight in the morning. Again he mentioned his interest in pursuing the possibilities of an expedition into the Amazon to search for the city.

Realizing that Julio would be a great asset to the group, Serge suggests that when he returns to Peru he contact the director of the museum, with the proposal that he join with Serge to find the city. This would provide the director with a personal representative to accompany the expedition, and to provide assurance that anything that was found would be given to the museum.

Julio seemed genuinely excited about the prospect of participating in the expedition, and stated he would relate everything to the director. He reassured Serge that he would contact him as soon as he had an answer from the director.

Serge leans back and smiling says, "I have here a letter from Julio that I received two weeks ago, requesting that we come to Peru. He says we have permission from the director of the museum to go in search of the city, and Julio will be allowed to accompany us." Looking at Jason and I he indicates that we have little time to get things in order and leave the country.

Still smiling Serge reaches into his pocket and produces a piece of paper and said, "Gentlemen, here is a draft in the amount of $10,000.00 to be used to help finance our trip. In the letter Julio sent he states that he had suggested that the director offer a 10% advance, since the museum stood to gain much if the city was found."

As the day was advancing, I suggested that we had better start making decisions concerning what was still needed to be done, and start preparations for our move to West Virginia. Serge asked Jason if he could take him to a large bank in town to cash the draft, and to pick up a few personal items. I mentioned I would start making a shopping list of what would be needed for our stay at the cabin, while they were in town. With our initial goals set for the day, we all proceeded to leave the porch and get ready to begin our projects.

As we were rising, it must have dawned on each of us, that this was the beginning of what we had all been waiting all our lives for. I stopped and looked from Serge to Jason and with great enthusiasm I shouted, "Yes." We laughed and slapped each others backs with the excitement that we all felt, I could see from their faces that they also felt like shouting.

While Jason and Serge prepared to leave for town, I went to the kitchen to clean up after breakfast. As I was washing the dishes my mind started reviewing what I had stored in the basement. I usually kept a small surplus of canned goods, bottled water and general items, in case of a power outage. As the last of the dishes were finished, Jason called out that they were leaving, and asked if I needed anything. I responded, "No, I will make a list and pick it up later." After putting the final touches to the kitchen, I took pad and pen to the basement to make a list of what I had stored and what still needed to be purchased.

The basement is partially finished, with a bedroom and laundry room, which also doubles as a storage area. I had hung shelves in the large laundry room and periodically stored extra items I purchased whenever I went shopping. I also had items that were set aside for my semi-yearly trips to the cabin. These items were first on my list to confirm their condition for immediate use. I had a Coleman 2-burner propane cook stove, with a case of propane bottles. These items went on the top of the list. I also had several Coleman gas lanterns, which would be needed, since I had no electricity at the cabin. Several cases of canned fruits and vegetables were stacked against the wall, with a case of beef stew. I felt that with the canned goods I had at the cabin and these supplies no one would go hungry.

I used the bedroom as an office and general storage room. Entering the room my eyes fell on the walnut gun case against the far wall. As the years had passed I had learned never to under estimate your opponent, if Professor Segault and friends were serious about getting the journal then I might need some form of protection at the cabin. My years in the military had given me an interest in weapons, and I enjoyed using various weapons at the range I had fashioned at the cabin. I withdrew my keys from my pocket and opened the cabinet and the top drawer, which held several handguns. I had fashioned the inside of the drawer to hold several hand guns within molded forms, to keep the weapons from sliding when the drawer was opened. The first pistol my eyes fell upon was a .44 caliber 1880 Remington revolver with a 7.5" barrel, a well made cartridge pistol, but not very successful because of the weapons made by Colt. Then I reached in the drawer and with care removed a mint condition Smith and Wesson .455 caliber hand ejector revolver. This weapon had been chambered for the .455in (11.5mm) cartridge, a special version that Smith and Wesson had made for the British Army.

After replacing the Smith and Wesson, I picked up a 7.65mm German Walther PPK a compact 20oz. pistol that was very convenient to have if problems suddenly come about. One of the things I like about the PPK it has an external hammer activated by a double-action lock, which means, it can be carried safely with the hammer down on a round, and fired simply by releasing the safety and pressing the trigger. This option could make the difference in a tight spot where quick action could make the difference in who gets off the first shot.

Finally my eyes fell on the last weapon in the drawer, a .45 caliber Colt Remington model 1911A1 with a 5" barrel. This pistol held seven man-stopping rounds, and I knew it would be one of the weapons I would be taking with me. I also picked up the Walther PPK; these two weapons would be sufficient if we had trouble while at the cabin. I opened the lower drawer and removed a box of cartridges for each weapon. Setting everything on the desk, I recalled asking Serge if he knew what type weapon his great-great-grandfather Phillip had carried with him to Peru in 1871.

He said that the weekend his grandfather had given him the journal he had also given him the revolver Phillip had carried with him to South America. It was a .41 caliber revolver manufactured by F. P. Devisme, a Parisian gun maker. Serge stated it is an excellent weapon with barrel and cylinder blued and the remainder casehardened. I remember commenting that I would enjoy seeing this weapon some day.

Realizing I was wasting time, I turned back to the gun case to retrieve several other items that I felt would be needed. I keep several items locked in the gun case for safety, these are items I use when I go camping or hunting. Opening the drawer I realize without a doubt that these items will be going to Peru with me. A quality pair of German made 10x42 binoculars with rubber armoring and with slip-proof grips, a compass mounted on transparent base plate with sight mirror, 6" Buck knife, heavy duty military flashlight and a pair of good quality 2-way radios. Turning to the closet and opening the door I pick up a pair of boots I've been breaking in over the last few weeks. I had purchased a pair of waterproof hiking boots for the trip, anticipating some wet, rugged terrain would be encountered. As I started to gather some of the items to carry upstairs, I knew we had better coordinate what we would be taking to South America. I made a mental note to ask Serge if he had coordinated with Julio to have some items stored for our arrival in Peru. In particular, good quality hand weapons, I knew I could not carry any of my own weapons with me on the plane.

I spent the next few hours cleaning the house and putting things in order, I suspected it would be several months before my return. With the prospect of a lengthy absence I paid my bills for the next three months and cancelled the paper. I would have my mail held and telephone turned off, hopefully this covered everything that needed to be done. Whenever you leave for an extended period of time you always feel you've left something undone.

Later that afternoon Jason and Serge returned, and I brought them up to date with what I had accomplished. Serge indicated he had Jason drive him to the airport and he had purchased our tickets with cash, so no trail would be left by using a credit card. Holding the tickets, Serge states that we will be leaving in three weeks on United Airlines from National Airport with a stop in Miami.

I indicate our passports are in order and both of us have had our vaccinations for yellow fever and malaria. I suggested that we spend the next few days pulling loose ends together and then quietly leave for the cabin.

Jason says he will return to his house and will return in two days, which should give him enough time to bring his affairs together. Opening the freezer and taking out three steaks, I asked if I could tempt Jason to stay for supper.

Without hesitating, he grins from ear-to-ear and said, "Do you have any cold beer?"

Chuckling I said, "The beer's cold, but you'll have to start the grill."

Laughing, he grabbed a beer and a bag of charcoal and went looking for the grill.

Everyone seemed to enjoy the meal and the conversation, as you would expect, centered on our forthcoming trip. I asked Serge if he had coordinated with Julio to get some supplies for our trip into the jungle. He stated he had provided a list of items in a letter, which he had sent the day after receiving Julio's letter confirming our trip to Peru. He had requested clothing appropriate for traveling in the jungle, such as long-sleeved shirts and close-woven trousers. He hoped the clothing would protect us from most biting insects. He also stated he wanted the clothing comfortable, durable and preferably made of natural fibers.

Recalling my concern earlier in the day while gathering my equipment in the basement, I asked if he had mentioned weapons to Julio. Serge indicated that he had asked Julio to try and get three 9mm Spanish pistols, hoping that they might be readily available.

Finishing his steak, Serge looked at Jason and I and said, "Do you guys have good hiking boots?"

Jason and I both indicated that we had prepared ourselves with good quality waterproof boots. "It sounds like you two have been busy these last few months," Serge stated as he leaned back with a sigh after finishing the steak.

I stated that after hearing from Serge that we could be leaving in the near future, we had accelerated our preparations for his anticipated arrival. I felt there were very few loose ends that still needed attending to. As the hour grew late, Jason stated he had better get going, he had much to accomplish in the next two days. I reminded him that when he returned we would be leaving for the cabin, so anticipate not returning for the next few months. Serge spoke up and said that the tourist card we will be issued upon our arrival in Peru is valid for 90 days, so we have a three-month window of time to find the city.

The next two days seemed to pass in a blur of activity, as we packed for the move to the cabin. As the boxes began to form a formidable pile, I was reminded that we only had two vehicles to transport people and supplies.

As the third day dawned Serge and I were up early finalizing our packing. While I prepared breakfast, Jason pulled up to the house in his car. I could see several things stacked in the rear seat. During breakfast we began comparing notes on what was required and not required for the trip to South America and the couple weeks at the cabin. After eating and cleaning the kitchen everyone gathered in the dining room to make final decisions on what was necessary to be packed for the trip. We spent the rest of the day packing and loading boxes into the two cars.

I think everyone realized the time had finally come that we had all waited for, without saying a word one after the other yawned and said goodnight. I turned out the lights and as I walked to my room, I couldn't help thinking about the months of preparations that had been part of our lives. The time had finally arrived to test our abilities in the field, and this time the site would be dangerous, far different from research in Europe and the United States. As I lay in my bed with the moonlight streaming through the window, I wondered if I would return to this bed and this room ever again. Life can take many twists and turns as we walk its paths to our destiny, would the path I was about to follow lead to success? I rolled over enjoying the feel of fresh sheets on my face, as sleep quickly came over me.

I awoke to the sounds of the others moving about in their rooms. This morning would not require calling anyone from his bed. The anticipation of leaving was motivation enough to have everyone rising early and preparing for an early start. Within an hour the cars were packed, and the house was locked and secured. Standing on the front lawn, Serge cautioned that he hoped we had left no trails that others could follow.

Serge and I took the lead with Jason following in his car; rush hour traffic was over by this time so I entered Interstate 70 west towards Hagerstown. As I drove in silence I realized both of us were so preoccupied with our thoughts, that very little conversation took place. Within thirty minutes Interstate 81 was approaching and I prepared to take the ramp for the south exit. I commented to Serge that we would be traveling south to Martinsburg and then turning west. He slides down in his seat and asks to be awakened when we arrive. I had forgotten his ability to catch a quick nap at anytime and anyplace. Within a few minutes he was lightly snoring and I drove on with the silence of my thoughts to keep me company.

I tried to keep the car from bucking and rocking as much as I could, but to no avail, Serge came awake asking if we were in trouble. He quickly straightened himself and looked out the windows to get his bearings.

Glancing to my right I said, "No, just going up my driveway."

His next question was to confirm that if I was sure this was my driveway. I stated that it was my driveway and I deliberately left it in this condition to discourage unwanted visitors. He laughed and agreed that very few people would want to visit someone where their vehicle would be damaged from just driving up the driveway.

As the cabin came into sight, I could see that initially nothing looked out of place. I drove to the right of the cabin, and parked near the shed. I motioned Jason to pull next to me, as he approached the cabin. Early spring temperatures were still a few weeks off, and as I stepped from the car I could feel a slight chill in the air. Everyone seemed to stop for the moment to experience the isolation you can feel when you stand in the middle of the forest. Except for the cabin and the two outbuildings no other manmade structures could be seen.

Turning to Serge I said, "Now you can appreciate why I enjoy getting away to this place."

He nodded as he slowly walked to the front of the cabin, turning his head to observe the surrounding woods. Jason asked if I had any neighbors in the area. I mentioned that there were a couple homes, but you can't see them. When the leaves come out on the trees you really have the feeling of being isolated, but at this time of year you can see further into the woods. Jason commented that he enjoyed peace and quiet, but it was a bit too isolated for him.

As I opened the trunk of my car, I suggested we start unloading the vehicles. I picked up a box and carried it to the cabin and opened the door. Serge noticed that I did not unlock the door and asked if I left it unlocked. As I set the box on the floor, I told him that I never left anything of great value in the cabin, and if someone wanted to get in I'd rather they walked in instead of breaking in. I shrugged my shoulders and said, "I've never seen any evidence that someone has entered the cabin."

As Jason came through the door carrying a suitcase, I suggested that I show everyone where we could place our supplies. The cabin consisted of a large main room with a fireplace on the right wall with a stone mantel and hearth. There were two bedrooms with a storage room between them. Each bedroom had a double bed and dresser. I indicated my bedroom was on the right, and Jason spoke up stating he would take the sleeper sofa located along the left wall of the main room. I asked if he was sure and he indicated it was fine, that Serge could have the other bedroom.

Smiling, and shrugging my shoulders I said, "Well... if it's all right with you. I'll continue with my tour." I opened the door to the storage room, indicating that sheets and blankets were located on the shelves. As I walked through the room I opened a door at the end of the room onto a small deck, stating, "The privy is located behind the shed." I reminded them that this would not be like staying at the local motel in town.

As the evening approached, I indicated that I would put something together to eat, while Jason and Serge finished unpacking and storing our supplies. I also asked Jason to get the lanterns lit and to get some water from the post hydrant located at the well. I had explained earlier that I had a well installed, but without a submersible pump. I did not want electricity run to my property at the time, so I installed a post hydrant to draw water from the well. It's a very convenient way to get water without requiring electricity.

After our meal, we decided to relax on the front porch, and watch the sun drop behind the mountains. It was pleasant sitting on the porch, listening to the evening sounds from the forest.

After several minutes, Serge broke the silence saying, "I'd like to get our maps tomorrow and compare them to the sketch Phillip had made in his journal."

Jason quickly turned and looked at Serge and said, "You never mentioned that Phillip had drawn a map in the journal."

Serge indicated that he deliberately had withheld that information in case someone ever intercepted any of his correspondence with us. I announced that we had acquired some good maps and hopefully they would confirm some of Phillip's directions. While the sun was setting a light evening breeze began blowing, carrying a slight chill, which quickly drove us into the cabin. I indicated that Serge could take an oil lantern to his room as I would and Jason could keep one in the main room for his use.

After lighting my lamp I turned and said, "Oh, by the way. If you need to use the privy during the night, you should take a flashlight. Also, watch out for the bears."

Jason looked at me with alarm in his eyes, and I quickly said, "Only joking." I could see these next two weeks might not be too boring.

I awoke to the sounds of birds singing and realized I had enjoyed a very restful night's sleep. I quickly dressed and entered the main room where I could see Jason had already risen. The smell of bacon cooking drew my attention to the front door, which was open. I found Serge on the porch working over a cook stove making breakfast with a fresh pot of coffee on a side burner.

I had a large wooden table in the main room near the fireplace, which we used to eat our meals. After breakfast Serge asked if we could get our maps and try to locate some of the landmarks Phillip had mentioned on the map in his journal. While Serge went to his room to get the journal, Jason and I cleared the table and laid out our maps. I also indicated that I had a geography book dated 1878, which might come in handy for place names Phillip might refer to. Serge seemed very interested in the geography book and readily accepted its use.

As Serge begins to read from the journal he indicated that Phillip was staying in Trujillo and was planning to cross the Andes Mountains and travel overland to the Huallaga River. Looking at a current map I indicate that he probably traveled through the city of Otusco, but that city did not appear in the geography book of 1878. At the present we had no idea if Otusco existed during Phillip's travels. Serge mentions that Phillip records crossing the Tunguragua River. I found the river in the geography book, but our modern maps indicate no such river. I suggest that the Maranon River could be the modern name for the Tunguragua River of Phillip's time. Jason states that he would have had to cross the Maranon River to get to the Huallaga River, which Phillip agrees was his goal.

The next entry state Phillip is sailing down the Huallaga River to the village of Lagima, where it meets the Tunguragua River. I indicate that I have found the village of Lagima in the geography book, but not on our maps. The closest town I could locate is called Tarapoto, which is near the Mayo River. It's possible that this could be the same place Phillip visited but using different names. I indicate the maps show the river continuing into the jungle, this part of the river is called the Huallaga, Maranon River. I state that I feel comfortable that Phillip traveled down this river to the present city of Nauta, where the Ucayali River joins the Huallaga, Maranon River becoming the Amazon River.

Pointing to my map I said, "Present day maps indicate the city of Iquitos is located on the Amazon River, it would seem that Phillip must have sailed through this area to get to the Napo River."

Serge speaks up and indicates that once we are in Peru we will be flying to Iquitos, which would be the last sizable city we would see before entering the jungle. Serge then returns to reading from the journal at the point where Phillip describes entering the Napo River.

Jason points to my map and said, "It looks like we will be sailing past the present city of Mazan before seeing the Napo. I hope the people are friendly."

At this point I put the geography book away stating that it shows nothing along the Napo River, at that time it must have been uninhabited jungle. Our modern maps seem to confirm the next landmark that Phillip refers to as a major fork in the river. As we trace the Napo River northwest we come to the city of Sta. Clotilde, where the river does split. It is possible this is where Phillip and Tejo turned left and traveled up the river that twists like a snake. As Jason keeps moving his pencil along the river we note that the river splits again, and the branch to the left is shown as a twisting river. Our maps indicate this river is known as the Curaray River, which very possibly could be the same twisting river, the headman Moura had spoken of.

As Serge continues reading he mentions the waterfalls and the two tributaries entering the river from the left. I indicate that the waterfalls do not appear on the maps, but the two tributaries are shown. I state the second tributary seems to flow from Ecuador, do you think we will be crossing the border into that country?

Looking at the map Serge shakes his head negatively stating, "Phillip states they traveled west from the river, and Diego had indicated three days travel. I think the city is located in Peru, but only time will tell. If the city is within the borders of Ecuador, we could have some serious problems. I would suspect that our presence would not be welcome."

This was the first time the three of us had the opportunity to compare the journal with modern maps. I was greatly encouraged by comparing the sketch from the journal and the descriptions Phillip had made of his travels, to modern day maps. In many ways they agreed with only minor differences that could be resolved upon our arrival in Peru. As I looked around the table, I could sense that everyone felt confident about our trip to South America.

As Serge was closing the journal, Jason asked, "Serge do you have any idea what the coded message Phillip mentioned in the journal could be?"

Serge opens the journal to the sketch that Phillip had made of his travels to the city, and turns the page to reveal a rough sketch of a stepped temple. Written under the sketch of the temple is the words "Temple of the Sun, look to the door for the way." Under the sketch Phillip had drawn a picture of a large serpent coiled around a branch. Serge looks up from the page and showing us a sketch of a serpent says, "I think that Phillip might have carved this symbol of the serpent somewhere outside the entrance to the ruins." I comment that it reminds me of an Anaconda, one of the largest snakes of South America.

Serge nods his head and said, "That makes sense, because Julio had mentioned there had been a sect of serpent worshippers known to have inhabited that area of the jungle."

Everything seems to be drawing together and our confidence in attempting to find the city is rising. As we put the journal and maps away, we realized that only a few days separated us from an adventure that could change our lives forever.

5
Arriving in Lima

The seat belt light had just come on, indicating we would be landing at Miami International Airport in a few minutes. Looking out the window, my mind wandered back to our short stay in West Virginia, and the morning that the three of us had poured over the maps and agreed that there seemed a good chance of success. The remaining days before leaving were spent in relaxing and preparing for our trip.

As the plane taxied to a stop, one of the attendants announced that there would be a 30-minute layover before leaving for Lima. Serge rose from his seat and told me he was going to place a call to Julio, to arrange for him to meet us at the airport in Lima. Jason and I decided to remain onboard, neither of us felt there was anything on the ground to attract us from the plane.

Turning to Jason I said, "I hope we have the time to visit the city of Cuzco before leaving for Trujillo."

With a distant look in his eyes Jason said, "Yeah... and I'd like to see Machu Picchu. We need to discuss this with Serge, it will give us some first-hand information on the Inca. We discussed this while we were in West Virginia and it seemed like a good idea at the time."

As Serge entered the plane, he could see we were deep in conversation and asked what we were discussing. I explained that we felt it would be very helpful to see some Inca ruins before traveling into the interior of the Amazon River Basin. He agreed and stated that he had asked Julio to try and schedule a few sites to visit.

Jason and I had spent many hours pouring through numerous books on the Inca Empire, but I felt we needed to physically see some ruins to be able to appreciate what the Inca people had accomplished. We continued evaluating the various sites we would like to visit, while passengers were boarding the plane for the continuation of the flight to South America.

As the plane taxied for takeoff, we settled back in our seats engrossed in our own thoughts of Inca sites we wanted to visit. I knew we would have to be careful to utilize our time carefully. The tourist cards we would be issued are valid for 90 days and had to be surrendered to immigration on our departure from Peru. Serge had informed us that you could get a 30-day extension, but it would not be something that we should plan on taking advantage of.

During the flight I must have fallen asleep because the next thing I knew, Serge was shaking my arm stating, "Wake up; we are landing in Lima." As I rubbed my eyes and looked out the window, all I could see were low clouds of fog. I wondered where the city of Lima might be. Within a few minutes we were landing at the Jorge Chavez International Airport, and the flight attendants were announcing that we should gather all bags and exit the plane.

We joined in the crowd of passengers heading towards customs and spent the next half-hour showing our passports, getting our entry stamps and tourist cards. My understanding of the tourist cards was confirmed as we were told of the 90-day time limit. After leaving these proceedings, I heard Serge's name called out. Looking about I noticed a Peruvian gentleman waving at us and calling out Serge's name. As Serge responded to his name, he turns and says, "Hello, Julio."

I watched as Serge shakes hands with an individual of medium height with an athletic build who seems very pleased to see Serge. Jason and I walk over, and Serge says, "My friends, this is Julio Garcia, the individual who will help us during our stay in Peru." After introductions are made, Julio suggests that we get his car and proceed to the hotel.

We walk to a parking area, where Julio unlocks a late model Toyota and we start loading our bags in the trunk. With items in our arms, we squeeze into the car and Julio takes off weaving thru traffic to gain access to Faucett Avenue.

Serge turns to Julio and said, "It is so good to see you again. Have your preparations for the trip been successful?"

Never taking his eyes from the road, Julio smiles and said, "Things are going very well. I have made reservations at the Miraflores Park Plaza, which has a very good restaurant on the premises named the Ambrosia. I think you will enjoy your stay in Lima, it is a very nice hotel. Shall I travel through town on the way to the hotel? The city is beautiful at this time of the day."

Suppressing a yawn, Serge said, "I would appreciate your taking the shortest route to the hotel. I need to rest and get a shower before visiting your beautiful city."

Smiling, Julio says, "Sit back and relax, I know you're tired from the flight. We'll be at the Plaza very shortly. There is plenty of time to visit the attractions in the city."

Julio had indicated that the Park Plaza was very luxurious; that was an understatement. I had never stayed at a hotel as grand as this anywhere in the world, and I certainly planned on enjoying our short stay. As we were shown to our rooms, I commented to Serge that I hoped we had the funds to stay in such a beautiful place. Opening the window curtains, I discovered we could enjoy a view of the Pacific Ocean.

I heard a knock at the door and opened it; Julio enters enquiring if we are pleased with the accommodations. He received a very hearty affirmative response to his question. He stated he had made reservations for 8:00 P.M. that evening at the Ambrosia. He suggested we get some rest, and he would meet us in the hotel lobby at 8:00. We all gladly accepted the opportunity to relax from our day of travel, and proceeded to our rooms.

That evening as we got off the elevator, Julio was waiting for us in the lobby. He said to follow him and led us to the restaurant, where we were seated. Within moments, a waiter greeted us and asked what we would like to drink. Jason said he would like a beer, which was greeted by all with enthusiasm. Julio suggested that we should try one of the local beers, such as Cristal or Arequipena. We placed our orders for the beer, and I asked Julio if he would be willing to interpret the menu for me, since I could not read Spanish.

Smiling, Julio says, "My friends, please let me order this meal for your first night in Peru." Everyone seemed more than willing to accept his generous offer. When the beers were served, Julio requested an appetizer be served. Julio asked if we liked avocados; we all indicated we did. He requested the waiter bring some *Palta a la reina* for the table. He explained that this is a very popular appetizer consisting of an avocado stuffed with chicken salad.

While enjoying the appetizer and beer, the conversation turned to archeology. Serge asked if Julio was having any success in acquiring the items that they had discussed for the trip into the interior.

Julio leaned his elbows on the table and lowering his voice said, "I have been storing items at the museum in Trujillo; the director had put a storage room at my disposal. Also, the director wanted to have a meeting with the team before we travel to Iquitos. I have also been able to acquire three 9mm Echeverria Model B Spanish pistols and a case of the powerful 9mm Parabellum cartridges." Turning his head, Julio paused and said, "The waiter is returning, we should speak of other things."

The waiter had noticed the appetizer had been finished and the beers needed refilling. We indicated that we were ready for another round of beers, and Julio asked for the menu to order the main course. Holding the menu,

Julio says, "I'll order several dishes, who would like seafood, and who would like lamb?" Serge and I indicate we would like the lamb and Jason says he would like seafood.

Julio motions the waiter to the table and speaking in Spanish, he orders our meals. He turns to Serge and states that the lamb he ordered is called *seco de cordero* lamb cooked with fermented *chicha* and served with rice. He then turns to Jason and says, "You and I will have fish. I've ordered *Ceviche* for you; it is white fish in a spicy marinade of lemon juice, onions, and hot peppers. It will be served with corn and yucca and sometimes with seaweed."

Nodding his head in appreciation of Julio's choice, Jason said, "What did you order for yourself?"

Julio, smiling and rubbing his hands together he says, "I ordered *Escabeche de Pescado*, it is cold fried fish covered in a sauce of onions, hot peppers, and garlic, with olives and hard-boiled eggs as a topping."

After Julio finished describing the meals, I asked if it would be possible to see some of the local sights before leaving for Trujillo. Julio made the mistake of asking what sights we were interested in visiting. I mentioned Machu Picchu and the fortress of Sacsayhuaman in the sacred valley. Serge spoke up and stated he would like to visit Cuzco, which would be in the vicinity of both the sights I had mentioned. Julio turns to Jason and asks him where he would like to visit. Jason smiles and says, "If we have time to visit those three areas, I can't ask for more."

Serge asks Julio how much time would be needed to visits these areas, without seeing everything, just the main items of special interest.

Julio finishes his beer and rubs his chin in thought, and says, "If we fly to Cuzco and spend a day in the city, the next day take a bus to the fortress of Sacsayhuaman, then we return to Cuzco in the bus. The next day we can board a train in Cuzco, which will take us to the Lost City of Machu Picchu. I feel we should be able to take in these three sites in a week. It will be a very full week of sightseeing."

We looked at each other and all agreed that the time would be well spent, and we would all enjoy seeing these areas of interest that reflect so heavily on the Inca Empire. I indicated we had come to Peru, not only to explore, but also to gather a better understanding of the Inca Empire.

As we finished our meals, Julio asked if anyone was interested in dessert, if so they had some very good rice pudding called *Arroz con leche*. I held up my hands and indicated I couldn't eat another thing; everyone else agreed with my sentiments. With the plates cleared from the table, everyone relaxed with light table conversation concerning Peru and its people. The evening passed quickly as lighthearted conversation circled the table. Julio must have noticed we were showing signs of fatigue because he suggested that we retire for the night and be ready to take an early morning flight to Cuzco.

Leaving the restaurant, Julio states he will make the flight and hotel arrangements for Cuzco. He suggests that we travel light with hand baggage for the trip and wear warm clothing and boots for sightseeing. Julio reminds us that we will be walking around in elevations exceeding 7000 feet, at this time of the year the temperatures can still be cool.

He said he would meet us in the lobby at 7:30 and not to worry about breakfast, he would have some *Churros* for us. He saw a puzzled look on my face, and stated, "Don't worry you'll enjoy them."

Entering the lobby I expected to be the first to arrive, but to my surprise, Serge and Jason were already seated and Julio was entering thru the hotel's front doors. As Julio came into the lobby he said, "I've got Churros in the car, grab your bags, and let's see some of the countryside." We needed no further encouragement to follow him out of the hotel and jump in his car.

After arriving at the airport in Cuzco, Julio led us outside the terminal explaining that he would get a cab to take us to the hotel. As we were leaving the terminal, Julio snapped his fingers and said, "I almost forgot, you will need to get Cuzco Visitor Tickets. They will cover the majority of the places where entrance charges are required." As we were walking he explained that we should let him get the cab because if you do not bargain for a reasonable rate, the drivers will charge sky-high prices. The term bargaining was an understatement for the exchange that took place between Julio and the cab driver. I thought for a few moments a fight would result from their exchange, but the driver produced a quick smile and opened the doors, we got in and proceeded into the city of Cuzco. During the drive into the city, the driver was talking and gesturing happily, while speaking with various individuals in the cab. At a time like this I felt the separation that comes from not knowing the language of the country. I kept nudging Jason asking what the driver was saying.

Julio had told the driver to take us to the Monasterio de Cuzco, the hotel we would be staying at while in Cuzco, located at the Plaza de las Nazarenas. It is an elegant colonial building that Julio indicates has very good service. After registering and dropping our things in the rooms, we met Julio in the lobby. He indicates that we should begin our tour of Cuzco from where the

Inca felt the center of their empire was located. It was known as Tahuantinsuyo – or The Four Quarters of the Earth. We know it today as the Plaza de Armas. The hotel had a shuttle service that was scheduled to leave in a few minutes, so we decided to take advantage of the service.

When the shuttle arrives at the Plaza de Armas, we disembark with other tourists, but Julio suggests that he will act as our guide. While walking in the plaza, Julio asks if we would like to hear of an old Inca legend. Without question we all quickly responded with a positive response. Julio begins, "Legend has it that Cuzco was founded by Manco Capac and his sister-consort Mama Ocllo, who were sent by the sun god Inti with the divine task of finding a spot where the gold staff they carried would sink easily into the ground. That place was Cuzco, and there Manco Capac taught the men to farm and Mama Ocllo taught the women to weave."

As Julio continues speaking he says, "Remember, the Inca Empire came into being during the reign of Inca Pachacutec Yupanqui, who began a great expansion, imposing Quechua as the common language, conquering other Indian nations, creating a state religion, and turning Cuzco into a glittering capital. It was Pachacutec who transformed Cuzco from a city of clay and straw into a thriving metropolis with grand stone buildings in the second half of the 15th century."

As we were crossing the plaza, Julio pointed across the street and said, "That is Cuzco's magnificent cathedral." Looking at his watch, he says, "It will remain open until 11:30 a.m. and be closed until 2:00 p.m. We still have time to visit the cathedral before it closes."

While crossing the street, we see a line of visitors entering the main doors of El Triunfo; Julio indicates not to follow them. He says when they are inside they just turn left into the cathedral, we will enter the cathedral by its main doors.

Upon entering the cathedral, Julio says, "The cathedral was built on what once was the palace of Inca Wiracocha and made in part from stones hauled from the fortress of Sacsayhuaman. It is a mixture of Spanish Renaissance architecture with the stone working skills of the Indians. It was begun in 1559, and took a century to build and an awesome investment of money."

We continue walking through the cathedral viewing examples of Escuela Cuzquena (School of Cuzco) paintings, including some by Diego Quispe Tito, a 17th century Indian painter, and other works by members of the Cuzco School. When they announce that they will be closing at 11:30, Julio suggests that we move on to other things.

Moving back to the plaza, Julio states that the site of the Temple of the Sun remains open all day from 9:30 a.m. till 6:00p.m. He suggests that we use this time when many points of interest are closed to investigate this important site. He leads us south on Loreto del Castillo until we come to Rosana Arrayan, to our left I'm able to see a church named Iglesia Santo Domingo. As Julio crosses the street he announces that there is a charge to enter the church, just remember to show you're Visitors Ticket. As we walk through the church, Julio tells of the fabulous wealth that had been in the Temple of the Sun at the time of the Spanish Conquest, examples of Inca architecture are still visible. Within the church I found a perfectly fitted curved stone wall that Julio explains had survived at least two major earthquakes. I have never seen such beautiful stone work, and so perfectly fitted to each other. Only in our imaginations can we try to picture what the Temple of the Sun must have looked like before the Spanish arrived.

Julio suggests that we retrace our steps back to the Plaza de Armas; he knows a place we can get some good home-cooked Peruvian food. As we return to the plaza I become acutely aware of a need for some food, I had been so preoccupied with so much to see that I had not given attention to my stomach. It decided it was time to reestablish contact with food.

Holding my stomach in exaggerated pain I said, "Julio is the restaurant nearby? I'm in need of food or I will be unable to enjoy your tour of this city."

Laughing, Julio points across the plaza and said, "The restaurant is located at the corner of Plateros, and it's called the Puca Pucara, I think you will like it. There will be plenty of food for young, healthy adventurers like you."

As we walked into the Puca Pucara, we felt immediately welcome. The atmosphere was friendly, and a middle-aged man welcomed us as if he knew us. He spoke to Julio for a moment and quickly led us to a table. As I sat down I realized how tired I was and mentioned it to the others. Julio reminded us that we had been walking and exerting ourselves at an altitude of 10,900 feet above sea level.

Smiling, Julio says, "My friends, you need to take your time to get adjusted to these elevations, relax and enjoy some delicious food. I would recommend the pink trout; it is succulent and melts in your mouth." Serge asked if these trout are the freshwater trout he had heard of from the mountain lakes and rivers. Julio indicated that these are those trout.

When the waiter arrives, Julio suggests that we order some Pisco sours. Everyone agrees.

When the waiter leaves, Serge turns to Julio and said, "I've never heard you mention Pisco sours. What do they put in them?"

Julio laughs and says, "A little of this and a little of that." When he sees the reaction of everyone, still laughing, he quickly raises his hands and says, "OK, OK, it has grape brandy, lemon juice, bitters, egg whites, sugar, and a dash of cinnamon, and I think everyone will enjoy it." While waiting for the sours to arrive, I watched Serge and Julio casually speaking in Spanish; I can see how Serge was able to develop a friendship with this relaxed Peruvian. I had only spent a small amount of time with him and already I felt like we had known each other for years. I found myself looking forward to the next few months with Julio as part of our team.

The waiter soon returned with our drinks and several bowls of *Cancha*. Julio could see that everyone was interested in what was in the bowls. As he grasped a few of the items he said, "Try some, this is *Cancha*, fried corn kernels. It's great for snacking on while drinking *Pisco*." He was right, they were very tasty and went well with the pisco. As we enjoyed the piscos and cancha, the conversations flowed from one side of the table to the other. Everyone was enjoying themselves and beginning to relax from the months of study and research that had occupied our lives so completely. I knew that in a couple weeks we would be traveling into the jungle and possibly facing dangers that I hoped we would be prepared for.

The waiter brought the trout for each of us and a large platter of *Ocopa* for all to enjoy. Julio spoke up and said, "Try this dish with your trout. It has sliced boiled potatoes, with a spicy peanut sauce." The *Ocopa* was served over a bed of rice and garnished with hard-boiled eggs and olives. As evidenced by the clean plates, everyone enjoyed the meal and thanked Julio for suggesting the Puca Pucara for lunch, and no one was ready to continue sightseeing.

Eventually, we knew we had to move on, but the atmosphere of the restaurant was so comfortable it made you feel at home. As Julio pushed his chair back, we all reluctantly rose from our chairs and began heading for the door. Leaving the restaurant we all said a heart-felt *Gracias* to the owner, for a good meal and an atmosphere that made us feel welcome.

As we entered the street, Julio suggested we circle behind the Plaza de Armas and on the corner of Calle Tucuman and Calle Ataud, we came upon the Museo de Arqueologia. He indicated that it was also known as the Admiral's Palace because it was once the home of Admiral Francisco Aldrete Maldonado. As we came to the entrance, we produced our Visitor Tickets and were allowed in at no additional fee. I asked Julio about the coat of arms over the doorway, and he indicated it belonged to a subsequent owner, an arrogant and self-important Count of Laguna, who died under mysterious circumstances. His body was found hanging in the courtyard shortly after he mistreated a priest who had complained about the count's behavior.

We enjoyed visiting the Admiral's Palace, but by 4:00 in the afternoon, Julio could see we were all lagging behind. He suggested that we should return to the hotel and get some rest. Walking about at 10,000 feet above sea level was having its effects upon us, such as fatigue and a couple of headaches. When we got to the hotel, Julio suggested we order some Coca tea, it is recommended for these symptoms.

While in the lobby preparing to go to our rooms, Julio said, "Get some rest and I will meet you here in the lobby at 8:00 this evening. I know of a good restaurant, where the food is good and they have one of the finest floor shows in the town."

As we gathered in the lobby a few minutes before 8:00, I could see everyone looked refreshed from their afternoon naps. I enjoyed the day's activities, but at this altitude I found my stamina wore down quickly. While relaxing in the lobby listening to the small talk from the others, I let my eyes take in the beautiful appointments of the hotel entrance. Someone had gone to great expense to provide an atmosphere that complemented the colonial exterior of the hotel. As I was quietly taking in the beauty of my surroundings, I heard Julio greeting everyone. "*Hola*! my friends. Are we ready to enjoy good food, some piscos, and first-rate music and dancers?" says Julio with a smile on his face, as he enters the lobby. I watch as he approaches us, realizing this man always has an up-beat attitude about him. I hope when times get tough, he will be able to keep that positive attitude; he'll be a great asset if things become difficult.

Leaving the hotel, Julio indicates we are going to the El Truco located at the Plaza Regocijo, a restaurant with good food and excellent entertainment. As we enter the Plaza, I can hear lively Andean music coming from a well-lit establishment. Julio points and says, "That is El Truco. Come my friends, let's enjoy the evening." We quickly crossed the plaza and walked into a colorfully decorated restaurant that was beckoning us to join the lively atmosphere of music and singing. Upon entering, a waiter came up to Julio and after a few words he led us to a table near the dance floor. The restaurant was very busy, with only a few tables available. I thought to myself, this place must be very popular with visitors and locals.

After we are seated, a waiter appears and asks what we would like to drink. Julio announces *pisco sours* for everyone, and is greeted with smiles from all of us. While waiting for our drinks, everyone turns to watch a beautiful woman singing a very lively song, but in a language that I don't understand. I ask, "What language is she using to sing that song?" Julio indicates she is singing in Quechua, the language of the Inca. As I watch her and the musicians dressed in traditional clothing and playing reed flutes, I could almost forget that the Incas had lost their country to the Spanish.

Within a few minutes the waiter returns with our drinks and a couple bowls of *Cancha*, which everyone quickly begins to enjoy with their piscos. As we relax with our drinks, some traditionally garbed performers enter the dance floor and the music begins a lively foot-stomping beat, which the dancers acknowledge by beginning to dance about the floor. There is much clapping from the audience and everyone joins in with singing and laughter.

After the second round of drinks, Julio suggests that we order something to eat. Everyone agrees with him, and he offers to order for everyone. It is agreed that Julio will order, so he waves the waiter to our table and places an order for Anticuchos, Paltas, and Rocoto Relleno, enough for everyone to enjoy. The waiter thanks Julio and quickly leaves to place our order in the kitchen.

Julio raises his hands and motions saying, "I think you will all enjoy this meal. I have ordered shish kebabs of beef heart, avocados stuffed with vegetables, and a hot red pepper stuffed with a mixture of meat, potatoes, and eggs."

The meal was as good as Julio had promised and the pisco sours packed a hefty punch, so as we began to mellow, so did the atmosphere in the El Truco. The foot-stomping dance songs were replaced by much quieter mountain music. The lights were dimmed and everyone seemed to enjoy the slower pace to the dancing and music. The hour was nearing midnight and as if a signal had been given, we all began to prepare to leave. Julio motioned the waiter to bring the bill, and after collecting the money from everyone, he paid the waiter. When we left I could still see the restaurant was half full and would probably continue that way for a couple hours more.

When we arrived at our hotel, Julio wished us a good night, and said he would see us early in the morning. He reminded us that we would be taking a bus to visit the fortress of Sacsayhuaman. We all wished Julio a *"Buenas noches,"* as we made our way to our rooms. It was agreed that the day had been a success and everyone was ready for a good night's rest.

CITY OF THE SUN

Hearing my phone ring I picked it up and heard, *"Buenos dias,"* Serge replies, "Julio's in the lobby, get a move on. I'll meet you there in a moment." As I enter the lobby everyone but Serge is there, and I can hear footsteps behind me. We greet each other and Julio states that he has a taxi waiting to take us to the buses, which are located near the Puno railway station. When we arrive at the buses, Julio indicates we should wait, while he determines which bus is going where. Julio returns in a few minutes and explains that he found a bus that will be visiting only two ruins, instead of several ruins in the valley. This bus would be stopping at Sacsayhuaman and four miles further on the same road it would stop at Qenko. He indicates the fee is reasonable and the bus will return to Cuzco this afternoon. Realizing that we hoped to visit Machu Picchu the next day, we agreed that the two ruins would be acceptable for visiting today.

Traveling on the bus was an experience in itself. It was anything but new and shook and rattled all the way to Sacsayhuaman. Conversation was limited due to the noise from the engine, so we resolved to hold any questions for Julio until we disembarked from the bus. As we came into view of the fortress, we were overwhelmed by the massive stones that have been used in the construction of the walls. When the bus stopped, we quickly followed other visitors and left the bus.

We begin walking towards the massive stone walls of the fortress, and as you near the walls, it's easy to be overwhelmed by the size of the stones. I tried to imagine the construction skills that must have been needed to not only cut the stones, but to move them. I realized that only by visiting this site could I appreciate the enormity of the task of building with such stones. As I continue walking along the outer walls, I can see they remain relatively intact, but the buildings that were part of the complex have been destroyed. Julio points out where the Inca sat upon his throne watching his troops parade on the flat plain before him.

I walked up to where the giant white statue of Christ with his arms outstretched has been placed, an amazing view presented itself to me. Standing on top of one of the rocks, I'm able to see the red-tiled roofs of Cuzco and the lush fields of the surrounding valley. The view is amazing in that it presents a startling contrast of Indian and Christian cultures, the city below and the fortress behind me.

After spending time walking among the ruins, we begin to slowly wander back towards the bus. As Serge comes near, I ask what his impression is of the construction effort that must have been spent to build these walls. He estimates that tens of thousands of workers labored on this massive structure for up to several decades, hauling the immense stone blocks that were used to build its double outside walls. Both of us stop and turn to look one last time at a true marvel of ancient construction.

Turning we see other tourists returning, so we continue walking towards the bus. After leaving we try to talk about Sacsayhuaman and what we saw, but as before it is almost impossible to carry a conversation. Julio indicates we only have about four miles to the next stop, so we decide to stop trying to converse with each other.

After leaving the bus, Julio tells us this is an Inca shrine called Qenko, which means "labyrinth." It was a ceremonial center dedicated to the worship of mother earth, known as *Pacha Mama*. As we enter the area of the shrine I see a circular amphitheater and an 18-foot stone block which is said to represent a puma. As at Sacsayhuaman, the stone work is beautiful and causes us to spend time marveling at the skill demonstrated by the workmanship. Julio points out that the limestone used on this shrine was cut from a huge formation found on this site, unlike Sacsayhuaman where the huge stone blocks had to be transported to the site and assembled.

While walking through the shrine, I see carved Inca style niches and alcoves that were used to display gold and holy items. Jason indicates that he found drawings etched into the stones depicting a puma, condor, and llamas.

After walking the site, and reflecting on yesterday's touring of Cuzco and its treasures, these sites seem less spectacular, but what I have seen today is the real ancient Peru. Gold and silver are beautiful and attract much attention, but it reminds me that people lived here that had the ability with limited tools to develop a great civilization.

We returned early enough to have the late afternoon to relax and rest. Julio suggested that we could stop at a local restaurant for pizza and garlic bread before ending the day. It was agreed and later that evening we went to the Pizerria Chez Maggy located on Plateros. Again Julio was a great guide, the pizza was great and the garlic bread was excellent. We were in bed by 10:00 that evening because Julio reminded us that he would pick us up at 7:00 a.m. to catch the train to Machu Picchu.

The next morning as I enter the lobby, I notice Serge and Julio are relaxing with glasses of juice. They see me and motion me to get a glass of juice and sit at their table. While getting the juice I hear the others entering the lobby and greeting everyone. While everyone is enjoying the juice Julio says, "Good morning everyone. I hope you had a restful night and am prepared for a full day. We'll leave in a few minutes for the railway station and travel through the Sacred Valley. If everyone agrees, I suggest that when the train stops at Chalcabamba, Km 104, we will be five miles from the lost city and only a few hours trek from the site. Would everyone enjoy walking to the site?" No one disagreed with Julio's suggestion of walking to the site.

After the train pulled out of Cuzco and began traveling through the Urubamba Valley, you begin to appreciate the lush subtropical vegetation that is so evident. As I watched the countryside pass by I'm reminded that Machu Picchu was a hidden world until Hiram Bingham came upon it in 1911. This Inca refuge hidden away in the mountains was never found by the Spanish and was unknown to the world until a little more than 60 years ago. As my thoughts dwelled on such things, I wondered if as Bingham had done, would we also find a hidden city unknown to modern man. As they say anything is possible. I remember at the time Bingham was actually searching for the ruins of Vilcabamba, a remote stronghold of the last Incas. Only by chance while traveling on a narrow mule trail in the Urubamba gorge did he meet a local *campesino* that led him to the jungle-covered ruins.

While I'm looking out the window with my thoughts wandering through ancient history, I feel a tap on my arm. Turning, I become aware of Serge asking me a question.

"I'm sorry, what did you say? I was dwelling on the history of this area," apologizing for my lack of attention to Serge. He indicates he also became caught by the same sense of history as we traveled through the valley. He comments about Hiram Bingham and his discoveries and with a smile I respond that I also was thinking of Bingham.

Then lowering my voice I say, "I was also thinking that we might get the chance as Bingham did, to find something no one knows exists." He smiles and nods his head in the agreement.

When we arrive at Km 104, we leave the train and follow a trail that Julio points out to us. I find the trail is not difficult and everyone seems to be able to set a comfortable pace, which still gives each of us time to appreciate the rainforest around us. Except for Julio, this is the first time any of us has ever been walking in a rainforest, and the beauty of such a lush environment easily distracts our attention from the trail. Jason points out several types of orchids and Julio indicates various palms and other flowers. As we continue walking towards the ruins, I begin to appreciate Julio's suggestion to walk these few miles to fully come in contact with our environment. Time seems to have no relationship to the present as we walk along the trail, it's very easy to imagine yourself walking this trail 400 years ago.

After walking several miles, I commented that we had continuously been climbing in elevation. Julio over heard my statement and agreed that we had been climbing and would soon arrive at the site. As we came within sight of Machu Picchu's outer walls and the terraces surrounding the site, we all paused to take in the mountainous grandeur before us.

The ruins above me overwhelmed me. Surrounded by the lush green mountains, a beautiful terraced city rose above me. I had seen pictures and read about the city, but to be within walking distance took my breath away. This was the reason I had traveled thousands of miles, I found myself walking quickly to enter this city within the mountains.

I could see people gathering and asked Julio if he knew what they were doing. He stated, "They are probably getting ready to take a walking tour of the ruins. If we hurry we could join them. It would be beneficial to hear what a trained guide has to say about the ruins." We all agreed and hurried to catch up with the other tourists.

As we entered a clearing overlooking the ruins, I could see fifteen or more people gathering around an individual who was speaking to them. He noticed us and called out, "If you would care to join us, please come over. I was just beginning to introduce everyone to Machu Picchu." We quickly did as he asked and joined the other visitors. The guide indicated a low wall and suggested that if everyone would find a seat, he would begin the tour. He paused a moment for everyone to find a place to relax, and when he had everyone's attention, he began to explain the recent history of Machu Picchu. He told of Hiram Bingham's discovery in 1911, when he arrived with a team of Yale University specialists. In 1914, Bingham returned to Machu Picchu with economic backing from Yale University and the U.S. Geographic Society to explore and map the site.

The guide gave a good presentation of the history of Machu Picchu and ended his introduction with a brief update. He stated in the years following Bingham's discovery the ruins were cleared of vegetation, excavations were made, and later a railroad was blasted out of the cliffs of the canyon. This opened the site to visitors. Pablo Neruda came in 1942 and was inspired to write his famous poem. In 1948 Hiram Bingham himself inaugurated a twisting 7-mile road from the riverbanks to the ruins.

During the last part of his introduction the guide had been giving out sketches outlining the points of interest in Machu Picchu. Returning to the center of the clearing, he states that Bingham had classified the ruins into sectors, naming some of the buildings. Over the years, others have disagreed with Bingham's conclusions of what some of the buildings were used for, but nobody has come up with a better system. So for the want of a better system, we use the names Bingham had used. The guide then asks everyone to follow him to the House of the Terrace Caretakers which flanks the Agricultural Sector.

Walking through the ruins I'm amazed at the stone work, without mortar the stones fit as if glued together. Following the guide through the Agricultural Sector, I marvel at the labor needed to fashion the terraces and how well laid out they are. The great area of terracing was undoubtedly for agricultural purposes and would have made the city self-sufficient in crops. We come to the end of the terraces, to what the guide calls the Dry Moat, beyond which lies the city itself.

Continuing to walk straight ahead we come to the Fountains, which are actually small waterfalls, in a chain of 16 spring-fed little water catchments, varying in the quality of their construction. They were probably used for religious purposes relating to the worship of water. The guide indicates that Bingham speculated that Machu Picchu might have been abandoned because this water supply dried up, or became inadequate to irrigate the terraces.

Turning back towards the Dry Moat, the guide leads us to the Main Fountain. He states it is so called because it has the finest stonework and the most important location, which is next to the Temple of the Sun. As we gather near the fountain, it is easy to agree with the guide that the stonework is beautiful. Near the Main Fountain stands a round tapering tower known as the Temple of the Sun, which the guide indicates features the most perfect stonework to be found in Machu Picchu. The guide indicates that the tower contains sacred niches for holding idols or offerings, and the centerpiece is a great rock, part of the actual outcrop on which the temple is built. The base of the rock forms a grotto, which some refer to as the Royal Tomb, but he states, no bones have ever been found there.

The guide indicates that recent archeo-astronomical studies have shown how this temple served as an astronomical observatory. He points to a rock in the center of the tower, which has a straight edge cut into it. The scientists have determined that it is precisely aligned through the adjacent window to the rising-point of the sun on the morning of the June solstice. He then points to the pegs on the outside of the window and states that they may have been used to support a shadow-casting device, which would have made observation simpler. As the guide begins to leave he points to the temple's entrance doorway and said, "Notice the holes drilled about the jamb; they are similar to the doorway at the Coricancha in Cuzco, but not as complex."

The guide brings us to an adjacent building, which has two stories, and was obviously the house of someone important. He calls it the Palace of the Princess. Turning to the Sun Temple, just above the main fountain, we see a three-walled house. The guide says this is called the Fountain Caretaker's House, but it's unlikely to have been a house, since it is open to the elements on one side. As we walk around the structure we see thick stone pegs fixed high up in the wall; the guide feels they were used as hangers for heavy objects.

As we gather at the front of the Fountain Caretaker's House, the guide points directly opposite the Sun Temple, across the staircase and said, "Those structures have been classified as the Royal Sector because of the roominess of the buildings, and also for the huge rock lintels which in Inca architecture generally indicated homes of the mighty." Someone asked if he knew the weight of the lintels, and he stated that they could be as much as three tons.

The guide turns and points to the top of the agricultural terraces, high above the city and says, "That is the Hut. After the tour you're welcome to walk to the top of the terraces, you will get a great overall view of the ruins. We have nothing specific on the hut, but just a few meters from the hut lies a curiously shaped carved rock called the Funeral Rock. Bingham speculated that the rock had been used as a place of laying-in-state for the dead, on which bodies were eviscerated and then left to be dried by the sun for mummification."

The guide leads the group to the staircase leading up from the fountains, where we come to a large jumble of rocks. He announces that this area served as a quarry for the Inca masons that worked on the city. He directs our attention to a partially split rock that seems to show precisely how the builders cut stone from the quarry. We see the rock bears a line of wedge shaped cuts where tools were hammered in to form a crack. After the group spends time looking the rock over and speculating on what the marks could mean, the guide says, "Now I'll tell you the rest of the story." After gaining our attention he states that a 20th-century archeologist named Dr. Manuel Chavez Ballon reportedly made the marks. He says he hates to disappoint everyone, but the marks are not very old.

He apologizes for misleading us and asks us to follow him across the ridge away from the quarry. As we are walking across the ridge, he indicates that the next temple is very interesting. With our backs to the staircase we follow the ridge to another structure. As we gather together, he indicates this is the Temple of the Three Windows. I slowly circle the temple and come to the east wall, which is built on a single huge rock. In this wall are three trapezoidal shaped windows, which are partly cut into the wall. Continuing to circle the building, where the fourth wall would be, it is empty except for a stone pillar, which once supported the roof. The guide points to a rock by the pillar which bears the sacred step motif and states that it is common to many other Inca and pre-Inca temples.

The guide moves a short distance and points to another three-walled structure. He states it is called the Principal Temple, indicating that it has been built with immense foundation rocks and artfully cut masonry. He then explains that it is so named for its size and quality, and also because it is the only temple with a kind of sub-temple attached to it. Walking a short distance he says this is the Sacristy because it seems a suitable place for the priests to have prepared themselves before sacred rites. He then draws our attention to the stone, which forms part of the left-hand doorjamb, it has no fewer than 32 corners in its separate faces.

The guide begins ascending the mound beyond the Principal Temple and states that we will now visit the most important of all the shrines at Machu Picchu. He states that it is called the Intihuatana, or as a 19th century traveler called it, the "Hitching Post of the Sun," turning, the guide faces us and says, "Nobody has ever unraveled the mystery of how this stone and others like it were used. Every major Inca center had one. Some have indicated that they served for making astronomical observations and calculating the passing seasons. Please gather closer and observe the beauty of the sculpture." The group responds to his request, and we all gather closer to be amazed by the fine detail shown on the stone.

The guide indicates that this is the only one in all Peru to have escaped the diligent attention of the Spanish "extirpators of idolatry" and luckily has survived in its original condition. While standing there I'm reminded that during my research I had come across several references to various Spanish religious leaders trying to eliminate all forms of idolatry from the Inca Empire. I feel very fortunate to be able to see something of a civilization that another culture had attempted to remove from the face of the earth.

The guide indicates a large grassy plaza, which the researchers feel was the utilitarian sector of the city. Walking towards the indicated area, the guide states this is the farthest point from the entrance to the ruins. As the group approaches the area I see two three-sided buildings opening onto a small plaza, which has a huge rock near them. The guide indicates the rock has been named the Sacred Rock.

He then motions everyone to gather at a particular point of the plaza and said, "Notice an intriguing aspect of this plaza, the outline of the great flat rock is shaped to form a visual tracing of the mountain skyline behind it." Everyone takes a turn to view the mountains behind the rock. As I step forward for my turn, I find myself impressed with the level of detail the craftsmen used to duplicate the mountains on the outline of the rock. When everyone has had a chance to view the rock, the guide informs us that the three-sided buildings are called *masma*, and if you step behind them to the southeast and look northeast, you will find another rock that depicts the skyline of the small outcrop named Una Huayna Picchu.

After waiting for everyone to observe the second rock formation, the guide states we will be walking back towards the main entrance along the east flank of the ridge. He announces that the crude structures that we are passing have been classified as the Common District. Everyone seems to agree with him. As I approach, it's obvious the stone work and formation of the buildings reflects less care to detail and arrangement of the structures. As we come to the end of the district, I see the guide is leading us to another building. The guide indicates we should enter the building, and after everyone has entered, he indicates two disk shaped cuts in the stone floor. He states they are about one foot in diameter, flat, and with a low rim carved around the edge. He states that Bingham thought they might be for grinding corn, since he did find pestle stones in the building.

The guide then tells us that the normal mortars used by the Quechua Indians today are much deeper and more rounded within; also they are portable, not fixed in one spot. However, he states nobody has suggested a more plausible explanation for these carvings. As Serge and I look at the mortar holes, we also have a difficult time coming up with a reasonable explanation for what we see in front of us.

Following the guide, we come to another staircase, with a deep hollow beyond, surrounded by walls and niches. He indicates that this is known as the Temple of the Condor. The guide leads us into the hollow and indicates a rock with a stylized carving. The carving is of a condor, with the shape of the head and the ruff at the neck clearly discernible. Continuing to walk through the temple grounds, the guide points out that there are vaults below ground, with man-sized niches with holes that some have suggested could have been used to bind wrists. Someone asks if they were prison cells, and the guide states that some have suggested this, but there does not seem any evidence of the Incas having prisons.

Walking towards the building with the mortar holes, the guide points out a small cave known as Intimachay. The building is located above and to the east of the Condor Temple; it has been identified as a solar observatory for marking the December solstice. Walking through the cave, I see it is faced with coursed masonry and has a window carved out of a boulder that forms part of the front wall. The guide says the window is precisely aligned with the winter solstice sunrise, so that morning light falls on the back wall of the cave for ten days before and after that date.

The guide announces that the walking tour of Machu Picchu is finished, and he hoped everyone enjoyed it and asked if there were any questions. There were several questions from the group and then he states we are free to wander the ruins, and if anyone needs anything he will be in the area of the House of the Terrace Caretakers.

As the group breaks up, the four of us begin to wander for more detailed inspections of some of the structures. While walking, Julio asks if we are pleased with the tour. We are so engrossed in our surroundings, that it took a moment to give Julio a proper response. We all assured Julio that the tour was a success and we greatly enjoyed it.

Later that afternoon, we walked back to Km 104 to catch the afternoon train returning to Cuzco. While waiting for the train Serge said, "The guide mentioned to one of the tourists that all parts of the city were connected together by alleys, side streets, and more than 100 stairways carved into the rock. It must have been a beautiful place before the city was abandoned."

I turned to Serge and said, "I overheard someone state that a narrow watercourse about four inches wide carried water from springs on Machu Picchu mountain and spread throughout the city. These people certainly understood the basic engineering practices of construction and infrastructure."

We caught the train back to Cuzco and safely arrived at the hotel. Julio could see we were exhausted from the day's activities and suggested we could order room service if we did not care to go out to eat. I suggested we return to the Puca Pucara for a final meal before leaving for Lima in the morning. Though everyone was dirty and tired, it was suggested that after a shower and a short rest we would be ready for the Puca Pucara.

Julio smiled and said, "That is wonderful. I will pick you up at 7:30, now get some rest."

The shower and a couple hours rest was all that was needed for everyone to find they were ready for a good meal. As usual, Julio was on time and within a short time we were entering the restaurant with the familiar dance music. Everyone ordered Pisco Sours and cancha and proceeded to relax and enjoy the music and dancing.

When the time came to order the main meal, Jason asked if there was something he could get that did not have hot peppers as the main ingredient. Julio laughed and indicated he would order *Sancochado*; it usually consists of beer, onions, potatoes, yams, corn, and carrots, boiled together and finished with a cup of consomme.

Julio raises his hand and says, "Before ordering, be advised the servings are generous, and one Sancochado usually is enough for at least two or three people."

I indicate that it sounds delicious and to include me as one of those eating the Sancochado. The evening was a success and as before we left filled and relaxed. We returned to the hotel, and Julio indicated he would pick us up at 8:30 for our flight to Lima.

Our return flight to Lima was without incident, and we returned to the Park Plaza, thanks to Julio having the foresight to schedule reservations for our return from Cuzco. After registering for our rooms, Julio indicates he would like to get together at the Ambrosia that evening. We all agree with his suggestion, and Serge asks if 8:00 is workable. Julio states he will make the reservations, and he will be bringing someone special to introduce to the group.

As we turn to go to our rooms, I ask Serge if he has any idea what Julio is up to. He indicates that Julio may have someone that may know about the City of the Sun. With these thoughts in our minds, we continue to our rooms for a couple hours rest.

I awoke at 6:30, showered and shaved and by 7:15 I proceeded to the lobby. Entering the lobby, I knew I was the first to arrive, so I decided to enjoy a bottle of Cristal and watch the people entering and leaving the hotel. You get to see many interesting people when quietly sitting in a hotel lobby. The only drawback to my people watching was my inability to understand what was being said by the people I was watching.

"Mind a little company?" said Serge as he sat in a chair next to me. I was happy to see a familiar face and indicated I was pleased to have some company. I told Serge that I was people watching, which brought a smile to his face. Before he could comment further, Jason said hello and joined us. While we were talking, Jason indicated we should look towards the front entrance.

Julio was holding the doors open for a very attractive lady to enter the hotel. After she entered, she took his arm. At that point our mouths must have fallen open, but we closed them quickly as they began walking towards us.

Smiling Julio says, "*Buenas tardes* gentlemen. I would like to introduce Dr. Maria Seminario, a very good friend of mine." We immediately stood and Julio introduced each of us to Maria, who, with a beautiful smile, indicates she is very happy to meet us. Julio suggests that if everyone is ready, we should go to the restaurant. Julio then takes Maria's arm and leads the way with the three of us following behind.

Having seen the look on my face Serge said, "I'm as surprised as you are. Let's wait until we are seated. Julio will fill us in."

After being seated and ordering Piscos, it was evident that Julio had something to say. I could see he was waiting for the opportunity to address everyone at the table. I decided to give him the opening he was looking for.

Setting my menu down on the table I said, "Julio, please tell us more about this beautiful lady that has joined us this evening."

With a quick nod of his head acknowledging that he appreciated my turning the conversation to him Julio said, "I've known Maria since we were youngsters in Trujillo, and our friendship has grown over the years. Maria is related to the director of the museum in Trujillo and while I was doing research at the museum, we became reacquainted again. Maria had decided to get a medical degree at the Universidad National de San Marcos in Lima, which she did with honors, but her interest in archeology drew her back to the museum quite often. As the years passed we spent our vacations on archeological excavations and Maria's skills have become quite good in research and in the field."

Julio turned and smiled at Maria and said, "At the present, Maria works at the Arzobispo Loayza Hospital also located in Lima. I have asked Maria if she would care to accompany us on our forthcoming trek, but I have only given her a basic understanding of what we are after. I hope after this evening you will agree that having Maria with us would be beneficial to the success of our venture."

After Julio finished speaking, there was silence at the table for several moments. Before anyone could speak, the waiter arrived inquiring if we were ready to order. Julio must have realized that we needed a few moments to reorganize our thoughts, so he quickly ordered for everyone.

With a grin on his face Serge said, "Julio, you sure know how to surprise someone. I remember you mentioned having a companion to excavate with, but I never imagined it would be a beautiful woman." Sometimes Serge has the ability to say the right thing at the right time. This was one of those times; his statement caused everyone to relax and laughter prevailed. Julio apologized for not saying anything to Serge before our arrival, but he wanted us to meet Maria before making up our minds.

I noticed Maria touch Julio's hand and he smiled and nodded his head.

Maria turned from Julio and said, "Gentlemen, I would appreciate your giving me a few minutes to explain why I would like to be a part of your group. I have known Julio for a number of years and think very highly of him. Yes, I am related to the director of the museum in Trujillo, but I would never use that as a way to pressure Julio into including me in the group. I was born in Chimbote, which is south of Trujillo on the coast. I have always been interested in the Inca Empire and in ancient cultures; my interest led me to the museum many times, as new finds came to the museum. As Julio has mentioned, I met him after many years at the museum, and over a period of time, we formed a friendship through archeology. I am a practicing physician, as Julio has also mentioned, and I feel that my medical abilities could be very useful if your expedition takes you into dangerous areas of Peru. My hobbies include hiking, backpacking, and archeology; I feel I'm in good condition and could handle the rigors of field research."

Julio seemed very pleased with what Maria had said, and turned to Serge and said, "We really could use her help."

I wanted to say it was a good idea, but I could see that Julio needed Serge's approval of what he had done. Serge leaned across the table looking at Julio and said, "My friend, I think we need to include Maria in the group. I can't thank you enough for bringing her tonight." All tension at the table disappeared and everyone was welcoming Maria as a member of the group. At that moment the waiter brought the meal, and for the next few minutes very little was said as everyone enjoyed the seafood.

After the dishes were cleared and our drinks were refilled, Serge began to explain in more details about what was involved in the expedition. Realizing that we were in a public setting, Serge still withheld some details that would be revealed in a more secure environment. Serge asked if she would have any problems with getting a leave-of-absence for two or three months? Maria indicated Julio had already informed her of the possibility of this happening, and she had prepared the hospital of the possibility of her coming absence.

"I'm sorry to interrupt," says Julio, "but I also have some potentially bad news." Julio informs us that he has a friend at the Jorge Chavez Airport in the customs division. He had requested him to keep an eye out for a French national entering the country by the name of Marcel Segault. Julio indicates that when they had returned to Lima, he had called his friend and was informed that Marcel Segault had entered the country. His friend also stated there were several other French nationals who entered the country at the same time.

With a worried look on his face Julio said, "My friends, I think we need to leave for Trujillo within a day. The professor will begin to search for us, and he has been in Lima for two days."

I asked Serge if it was possible for the professor to be this close behind us. With a look of resignation on his face Serge said, "Don't underestimate the professor; he is a very determined man. I would suspect he has many contacts around the world that deal in stolen artifacts. It's possible we have a very dangerous enemy, who will be stalking our every move, so we must move quickly, as Julio has suggested. Maria, this expedition could be quite dangerous, so we will understand if you would prefer not to join us."

With a determined look on her face, Maria states she has traveled in the jungles and knows how to take care of herself. As I watch her, I find myself fully believing what she has said. I have a feeling in a tight spot, Maria could be someone you could depend upon.

Realizing that Julio's last bit of information has put a new perspective on when we should leave for Trujillo; it is agreed that we will leave in the morning. Julio says he will pick us up in the morning, and we will catch the first flight to Trujillo. Leaving the restaurant and saying goodnight to Julio and Maria, I realize that the relaxed atmosphere we have experienced for the last few days have ended. With the rising of the sun, the serious business of research would begin, but with an element of danger that could cost some of us our lives.

6
North to Trujillo

True to his words, Julio and Maria were in the lobby of our hotel before any of us had left our rooms. Using the phone in the lobby he called Serge and said we should be ready to leave in ten minutes, and requested that the others be notified. Within ten minutes the three of us, with bags packed, met in the lobby. After paying our bills, we loaded Julio's car and proceeded to the airport. Julio informed us he had purchased tickets for an early flight to Trujillo on Aero Continente. He warned us that Peruvian airlines are not very reliable in meeting their flight schedules, but hopefully our luck will hold and the flight will not be cancelled.

Serge inquired if there were any extra expenses we needed to be aware of, when flying from city to city. Julio stated that on domestic flights there is Security Tax and a Municipal Tax at all airports except Lima.

Upon arriving at the airport, we discovered our flight was still scheduled to leave at its appointed time. Julio assisted everyone in checking our bags and finding the boarding area. Within 30 minutes our flight was called and we were ushered onboard with a number of other passengers.

Our flight was uneventful and before noon we were landing at the airport in Trujillo. After locating our luggage, Julio informed us that we were registered at the Hotel Libertador Trujillo, and he announced they have a shuttle at this airport. He said he was going to the museum and he would meet us at the hotel in a few hours. We followed Julio to where the shuttle was waiting for passengers and he and Maria indicated they would see us shortly. We boarded the shuttle with other tourists and within 20 minutes we were proceeding down Mansiche Ave. into the city of Trujillo.

One of the first shuttle stops was the Libertador Trujillo hotel, where we retrieved our luggage and left the bus. I noticed we were standing on the northeast corner of the Plaza de Armas, a huge, beautiful square. The hotel we were registered at was an attractive colonial style building; I notice that many of the buildings surrounding the square are beautifully decorated and painted. While looking around the square I notice the statue of a running winged figure – Liberty – holding a torch, standing in the center of the plaza.

Jason taps my arm and said, "Look at that statue, I can't put my finger on it but something about it is wrong."

After a few moments of studying the statue, I replied, "Yeah, check the legs, they seem disproportionately short for the size of the statue. I'll have to ask Julio if he knows why the statue was made with short legs."

Serge reminded us that we better register, and get settled in our rooms before Julio and Maria return. While we are registering, we are informed that the hotel restaurant has an excellent Sunday buffet lunch. Thanking the young man, we take our bags to our rooms, and decide to return to the restaurant for drinks until Julio arrives.

Arriving in the lobby within a few moments of each other, we enter a small, but very pleasant dining room. Serge proceeds towards a table next to the window, which look out onto the plaza. We order Cristal and while Serge and Jason are discussing plans for that evening, I found myself watching the people in the square. I can see life in Trujillo moves at a slower pace, several elderly men are sitting on shady benches reading their newspapers and a couple young mothers are carrying their market baskets, with toddlers in tow. There are vehicles parked around the square, and some traffic, but much less than in Lima.

Our drinks arrive with a bowl of *cancha,* which we all begin to enjoy. After a few moments Serge states he has asked Julio to arrange for us to visit some ruins about 6 miles from Trujillo. He indicates that it is known as Las Huacas del Sol y de la Luna, which stands for the Temples of the Sun and the Moon.

"That sounds interesting, but what makes them special?" I asked.

Resting his elbows on the table and leaning forward Serge said, "Julio mentioned that they were probably built be the Moche people around 700 A.D. These temples are pyramids and they might have some relevance to what we might encounter in the jungle."

As we were finishing our second round of beers, Julio and Maria enter the dining room and join us at the table. Julio asks if our rooms are acceptable and if there were any problems. We all thanked him for the pleasant accommodations and invited the two of them to share our table for something to drink. While their drinks were being prepared, Julio states the director of the museum would like to meet everyone at 10:00 a.m. the following morning. Serge indicates this would not be a problem, and asks where the museum is located. Julio states it is only two blocks away, and with a pleasant walk across the Plaza de Armas.

The waiter arrives with their drinks, and Serge inquires if it would be possible to see the ruins of the temples of the sun and moon that afternoon. Smiling Julio says, "Well, if you're ready to see the sites, let us finish our drinks and I'll get the car. The director feels that these pyramids could give us some understanding of what we might see in the jungle. He mentioned the murals that are at these temples; he's curious if murals like these could be in the City of the Sun."

As we gather outside the hotel, Julio leads the way to a van, which he proceeds to unlock. Opening the doors to the van Julio said, "Please take a seat, we only have a few miles to travel to the ruins."

I sit back and enjoy observing the colonial city of Trujillo, with its colorful buildings and architecture that appeals to my engineering senses. Letting my thoughts wander I realize that if we were not pressed for time I would like to wander the streets of this interesting city.

Shortly, we are entering an area with many tourists who have arrived in several minibuses; Julio parks near one of the buses and indicates we can proceed from this area. Julio takes the lead as we weave around a number of tourists and proceed down a trail through some thick vegetation. Coming into a clearing I see two pyramids, one larger than the other. Julio guides us off the main path the tourists are using and as we gather around him he indicates the larger pyramid is the Temple of the Sun, and the smaller pyramid is the Temple of the Moon.

I found myself listening to Julio, but the pyramids had my full attention. The Temple of the Sun is an adobe four-tiered pyramid that rises 130 feet above the valley floor, it fills my imagination as to what it must have looked like centuries before. Serge taps my arm to get my attention, and indicates we are to keep moving towards the pyramids. As we approach the pyramids I can see evidence of erosion from centuries of rain and wind. Where sharp corners had once been, they are now rounded from the elements, but their beauty still remains. Millions of adobe bricks must have been used to build the structure, whose summit was reached by a ramp on its northern side.

Julio states the Moche people built these structures probably around 700 A.D., and that the site had become the leading ceremonial and political center of the southern Moche realm. As we near the Temple of the Sun, Julio indicates the murals on the walls. He says, "The director would like us to sketch some of the murals from the temple, on the chance that we might find murals in the city within the jungle. He hopes that there will be some resemblance between the murals of the two cities."

Jason takes pad and pencil from his backpack and begins to sketch some of the murals, while commenting that many of the murals are in very good condition.

After Jason had copied a number of murals from the Temple of the Sun, Julio indicates we should proceed to the three-tiered Temple of the Moon, which is located on the other side of a large open area. Julio indicates the open area was once filled with domestic buildings and workshops, he also states the open area is over 1600 feet across. We find the temple is decorated with a rich and varied array of friezes and murals. Jason proceeds to copy some of these murals, stating that several resemble figures from the Temple of the Sun. After spending several hours walking the site, and admiring the ruins, Julio suggests that we should return to Trujillo. He states there is still much to be accomplished before leaving for Iquitos.

While driving back to Trujillo, Julio says, "I wish we had the time to visit the ruins of Chan Chan located northwest of Trujillo. The ruins are possibly the largest adobe city in the world." I asked if he knew the area of the city, and he indicated that it encompassed more than 7 square miles.

Driving back to the city, the van was filled with a lively discussion of early Peruvian Archeology and the influences of early cultures on the Inca Empire. As we neared the city Julio suggested that we get some rest, and he and Maria would meet us at 7:30 for an evening meal. Maria suggested we go to the De Marco located on Francisco Pizarro, Julio agreed and with a smile he said, "The ice cream and desserts are very popular." Serge indicated he wanted to try the freshwater trout again, and Julio indicated it would be on the menu where they were going.

After arriving at the hotel, I decided to relax in the plaza instead of resting in my room. The weather was pleasant as the evening was approaching and as the others went to their rooms I walked into the plaza. There were several vacant benches within the plaza with an unobstructed view of the surrounding buildings of the plaza. Earlier in the day I had noticed that many of the buildings had very ornate balconies, which I wanted to view at my leisure. As I relaxed and slowly let my eyes wander from building to building, I became aware of a number of intricately carved wooden balconies and very detailed window grilles. The window grilles seemed to be purely decorative and not for purposes of security. The balconies looked sturdy enough that the owners of the homes could use them. While enjoying the variations of balconies and window grilles, I'm resolved to ask Julio if there was a reason for their construction. The designs seem very elaborate, but other than the balconies, they seemed to have been for decoration only.

I returned to the hotel and requested the desk clerk to call my room at 7:00. I had a short period of time to make some notes concerning the ruins we had seen that day and my perspective on the murals. I doubted that the Moche had ever lived deep in the Amazon Basin, but I would keep my mind open. I also knew that a contemporary culture with the Chimu was the Chachapoyas culture, which flourished in the northern highlands. They made large fortified structures, which would indicate they felt threatened, but there seems very little information on their culture. I put down my note pad realizing I was impatient to meet the museum director, and discover what he knew about our intended area of investigation. I removed my shoes and decided I would lie on the bed till the desk clerk called.

The call came waking me from a light sleep. I washed and changed my clothes, and met Jason walking towards the lobby. Walking into the lobby, I noticed everyone was waiting, and Julio said we should follow him. The van was parked nearby and after everyone was seated, Julio drove around the plaza and proceeded east.

We arrived at the De Marco restaurant, which was brightly lit and with traditional music greeting us as we entered. It had a pleasant atmosphere and we quickly felt comfortable in our surroundings. As a smiling waiter arrived at the table, we ordered pisco sours and *Anticuchos*. The conversation at the table was light and flowed easily from person to person. It was evident that we were beginning to relax with each other. Serge was listening to Maria as she animatedly described some of the sites she and Julio had researched in Peru. Jason and Julio were discussing something in Quechua, and the conversation was becoming very animated, with hands moving and voices raised. I was concerned that an argument seemed inevitable, so I asked if there was a problem.

They both paused and began laughing, Julio turned to me saying, "Relax, there's nothing wrong, we're discussing the murals we saw today and the possibility of finding something like them in the jungle."

The waiter must have noticed the drinks were disappearing quickly and came to see about refills. Everyone indicated refills were in order, and Julio asked if we were ready to order the main meal. As everyone indicated they were ready, Julio suggested some hardy traditional foods. Everyone requested he order the meal, so he ordered *Corvina* and *lomo saltado*, indicating that they should bring enough for everyone.

Maria motioned Julio and said, "I'm glad you ordered the Corvina," and turning to me she continued, "The sea bass is delicious when cooked *a la plancha*, you will enjoy it."

Serge asked Julio what was in the *lomo saltado*. Julio indicated they took french fried potatoes and combined them with strips of steak, onions and tomatoes, which makes a spicy dish. It was easy to see everyone was anticipating the coming meal.

After the waiter had taken the order, everyone began relaxing and small conversations began around the table. Serge asked Julio a question concerning the ruins we had seen that day, and Jason was speaking with Maria about Lima. While not involved in either conversation I had the opportunity to let my mind dwell on several questions I had for Julio. After a few minutes the conversation between Serge and Julio came to an end.

I turned to Julio and said, "I have a couple questions I would like you to answer for me. While the others went to their rooms to rest, I decided to relax in the plaza. I found a shady bench where I could relax and noticed the beautiful balconies and window grilles on many of the buildings around the plaza. They are very ornate, but seem to be for decoration only. The statue in the center of the square also intrigued me; its legs are very short for the height of the statue."

Julio smiled and said, "I'm glad someone was observant enough to notice these things. First, the houses around the plaza have many detailed window grilles and they are purely for decoration; over the centuries their simple designs became increasingly elaborate as the colonial Trujillanos tried to outdo one another. The balconies, on the other hand, had a practical purpose; they allowed upper-class women to look down onto the street, but prevented interested men folk from looking up. As for the statue in the Plaza de Armas, the short legs were designed to appease officials who feared the monument would end up taller than the cathedral facing it."

I thanked Julio for answering my questions and said, "If you don't mind I have one more question to ask. I would like to know more about the director of the museum, and why he is interested in our attempts to find the city." After speaking I realized that all conversation at the table had ceased, and everyone was waiting for Julio to respond to my question.

Julio turned to Maria and said, "Would you care to say anything about Dr. Seminario before I explain his interest in our venture?"

Smiling, Maria nodded her head and said, "Yes, I would like to say something. I have spent several days with you gentlemen and you have indicated your willingness to allow me to accompany your group into the jungle. I appreciate the trust you have placed in me, and I want to assure you of my complete loyalty to this venture. Because of your trust in me I would do nothing to endanger the success of the venture. I say this to assure you that Dr. Jorge Seminario, who is my uncle, is a very honorable man. He is a highly respected individual in the scientific community, and I would trust him to deal honestly and fairly with you."

Julio turned towards Maria and said, "*Gracias* Maria; I appreciate your willingness to openly speak about your uncle."

With a final smile directed towards Maria, Julio said, "My friends, I consider Dr. Seminario a highly trained professional and a man well respected by his peers. I have worked for the museum full-time since 1976 and on a part-time basis for several years. The director and I have been involved in several research projects and he has impressed me with his knowledge of archeology and of ancient Indian civilizations of the Central Andes. He was involved in the excavations in the central highlands where pottery dated at 3,800 years old was unearthed. This pottery represents the oldest yet found in the high country. He was in Guanape on the northern coast of Peru, where the oldest pottery dated 4,300 years ago was found. Dr. Seminario has earned his position as director, I remember him mentioning that he had been involved with the excavations at the Lauricocha caves. They had found percussion chipped artifacts, such as scrapers, projectile points and other artifacts made by hunters 9,500 years ago."

Julio paused for a moment as if considering his next statement and said, "You've also asked why he was interested in our venture. After the Spanish had taken control of the empire, there was a large Inca population that fled into the jungles. Dr. Seminario believes that the only Inca City built in or near the jungles of the Amazon was near the old city of Lagima. The Spanish would have been able to find this city without much difficulty. He suspects that they might have fled to a city much deeper in the jungle, a city built not by the Inca, but by an earlier civilization. He has spent a great deal of time studying the Chimu culture, which you can see evidence of at Chan Chan not far from this city. He has also visited the remains of a huge stone city in the northern highlands, which stands above the Rio Utcubamba. The Chachapoyas were a culture that was contemporary with the Chimu, they built massive fortified structures, but little else is known about them. Dr. Seminario has always wondered if the Chachapoyas or the Moche had ever built cities in the jungles of the Amazon River Basin."

As Julio finished speaking, the waiter arrived with our food, and the aromas from the food ended all conversation. The meal was a complete success, the sea bass was delicious and the steak and potatoes was filling.

Within a few minutes, Julio sets his fork down and says, "Dr. Seminario has had several conversations with me concerning the possibility of a hidden city in the jungles. When I made him aware of the information Serge had found he was very interested in getting further information on our research. He has found evidence that there was a very powerful sect that worshipped a large serpent, which was considered a guardian, that mother earth had put upon the earth. I feel he strongly suspects that we may have a good chance of finding the city, if it is to be found."

After the dishes were cleared from the table, the waiter returned to refill our glasses, and inquire if anyone desired dessert. As was expected, everyone was full, so dessert was declined. With the dishes removed and everyone relaxing from a filling meal, Serge thanks Julio and Maria for their comments concerning Dr. Seminario.

Turning to me Serge said, "I appreciate your concerns about Dr. Seminario, and the comments that have been made at this table certainly indicate we are dealing with a man of principals."

Looking towards Julio, Serge continued saying, "Julio, I have also wondered why the director had decided to back our endeavors. He has never seen the journal, and has only my word for what it contains. What did you say to him that made him a believer in our venture?"

After setting his glass on the table, Julio slowly looks at all of us, and stops at Serge. He slowly turns towards me and says, "You have known Serge longer than any of us, and I feel you would agree with me when I say that he is a very honest man. I spent several years in France studying ancient cultures, during that time I met Serge Gaston. While in France I had observed Serge both as a student and as a researcher in archeology. I consider him a professional and a gentlemen, he is someone I would trust to always deal with me in an honest fashion. When Serge told me of the journal and some of what it contained, I suggested that it could be beneficial to the expedition to include the director in our planning. Before speaking with the director, I had received permission from Serge to reveal some of the information that is contained in the journal. I hope our meeting tomorrow with the director will be of benefit to our group and the museum."

As Julio concluded, there was silence at the table for several moments. I could sense that there had been a level of tension surrounding the table while Julio and Maria had spoken. Turning to Julio I said, "I appreciate your candid response to my questions. We have only known each other for a short time, and I have come to respect your honesty and professional knowledge of your country. I personally feel reassured in our success since Serge made us aware of your participation in our venture."

Turning to Maria I said, "I hope you haven't taken offense to my being cautious concerning the proposed members of this team. I would like to welcome you to our trip into the jungle, I feel you will be a great asset to the success of our venture."

As I turned back to the table, I could feel the tensions leave the group and light conversation began to take over. Julio ordered another round of drinks and as the musicians played a selection of *Musica Criolla*, I could hear laughter and see easy smiles around the table. I realized my question to Julio would be an uncomfortable one, but a question that I felt had to be brought to the table. I trust Serge implicitly, but Julio I did not know, and for my own peace of mind I had to ask about the director before our meeting.

The evening ended after midnight with everyone feeling no pain and looking forward to a comfortable bed to rest until the morning. Julio drove us to the hotel and indicated he would meet us in the lobby about 9:30 in the morning, and then we would visit the director.

Sleep came easy that night, my mind felt at ease with the people involved in the expedition, except for professor Segault everything was going like clockwork. As I slipped off to sleep, my mind kept toying with the idea of a city in the jungle that might have been built by someone other than the Incas. Could there have been another civilization that had built grand structures and cities, which have remained, lost in time? Could Diego and Phillip have discovered a culture that has remained lost to modern science? My last thought before sleep overcame me was, could we find this city in the jungle of the Amazon?

Serge called my room at 7:30 and suggested the three of us have breakfast in the restaurant before Julio and Maria arrived. I agreed and said I could be ready by 8:00 and I would meet them in the restaurant. Entering the restaurant I indicated to the waiter that I would like a table by the windows, which he was happy to provide. While waiting for the others, I enjoyed watching the elderly men secure their shady benches to read their morning papers. It was pleasant to watch the comings and goings of the people and the children playing in the plaza.

"May we join you?" asked Jason, as he pulled a chair out for himself. I was so engrossed in observing the people within the plaza that I was startled by Jason's question. I quickly turned and indicated that they should sit and relax. Jason asked what I was watching when they arrived.

With a last glance at the window I said, "I enjoy watching the peace and tranquility of the plaza and the people within it. I come from such a busy part of the world, that to have the ability to relax in a beautiful square like this, just causes me to want to forget the rest of the world."

After the waiter had taken our orders, I noticed Serge rest his right elbow on the table and begin to rub his chin with his right thumb and forefinger. Over the years I had observed this mannerism when he was giving thought as to how to address a situation or problem. I had also discovered that it was best to give him the time he needed to bring his concerns out in the open, if I tried to find out the problem, he would usually indicate it was nothing. Once his fingers stopped moving, I knew he was about to speak.

Serge slowly lowered his right hand and folded his hands in his lap. Looking from Jason to myself Serge said, "I need to know if there is a problem with Julio as a member of this team?" Lifting his eyes to mine, he says, "Do you have any concerns that I need to be aware of? I have known Julio for a few years and have never had a reason to doubt his honesty. If he feels the director will be fair and honest with us, I have every reason to believe Julio has given much thought to involving the director."

I realized Serge was very concerned that I had questioned Julio about the director, and I knew he needed to know if there was a problem. "Serge, believe me, I have more confidence in Julio now than I ever had. He and Maria spoke very openly concerning the director, and I have no hesitancy in you disclosing whatever is necessary for the director to believe in our venture. I think we have the makings of a very good team, and with some hard work, we will find the city. I'm sorry, I didn't give you any forward notice that I would put Julio on the spot, but I felt it was necessary to receive a spontaneous answer to an unexpected question. I fully believe both Julio and Maria answered my questions concerning the director in an honest and truthful manner." I could see Serge was pleased with my answer, and with a sudden smile, he rose and greeted Julio and Maria as they entered the restaurant.

We all rose as they walked to our table, and Julio looking at the dishes on the table asked, "Are we ready to leave?"

"Yes," answered Serge, "let's go meet Dr. Seminario, and start planning our trip to the interior."

The five of us walked out of the hotel and Julio suggested that we walk to the museum, he indicated it was only two blocks away. We walked around the plaza and a block away from the plaza, on Jiron Pizarro, lies the Museo de Arqueologia. Pointing to the museum Julio states, "This is the museum of the National University of Trujillo, I have spent many enjoyable hours within this building. If we have time I would like to show you some beautiful pieces of Moche and Chima pottery and copies of some of the wall paintings found at La Huaca de la Luna."

We entered the museum through the main doors and our progress was immediately slowed by the displays of pottery along the main entrance hall. We all found our attention drawn to the beautiful displays on either side of the walkway and Julio motioned we should keep moving. While the artifacts on display captivated our attention, Julio reminded us that out appointment was for 10:00, and we only had five more minutes before we were late.

Julio led us to the administrative section of the museum, and shortly we were approaching a middle-aged woman whose desk was stacked with books and papers. She seemed very busy, but when she glanced up and saw Julio, she smiled and said, "*Buenos Dias*, Julio, it is good to see you again. Dr. Seminario informed me that you had a meeting with him, I will announce you and your friends." She quickly rose from behind her desk and knocked on the door behind her desk. Waiting a moment, she opened the door and entered, speaking to someone we could not see. At that moment we heard a voice from within the room say, "Julio, my friend, please bring your friends into my office. I've been looking forward to meeting with these friends of yours."

I felt immediately at ease in the office of Dr. Seminario, this was a working office, not a place to impress people. He was standing behind a large wooden desk, which had several stacks of books and papers, which seemed to be in use at that time. The director of the museum of the University of Trujillo, was a man of average height, with slightly graying hair. He appeared to be in his late fifties, but with the physical appearance of a man twenty years younger. He seemed genuinely pleased to see Julio and produced a wide smile of happiness upon seeing Maria. He came from behind his desk and embraced Maria and warmly grabbed Julio's hand.

After a few moments he said, "Where are my manners? Julio, please introduce your friends. I was so pleased to see you and Maria, I forgot my manners." Julio stepped aside and quickly introduced each of us to Dr. Seminario, who requested we all be seated so we could get to know each other. As Dr. Seminario turned to sit behind his desk, he asked, "Julio, one of these gentlemen does not speak Spanish, is this correct?" Julio indicated that

I did not speak Spanish, but he would be pleased to interpret for me. Raising his hands, Dr. Seminario said, "I would like everyone to have a full understanding of what transpires here today, so we will conduct this meeting in English. I hope this meets with everyone's approval? Also, I would like to dispense with formalities during our meeting, please refer to me by my Christian name, Jorge, instead of formal titles. If this meets with your approval, I would like to order some refreshments before we get to work." The director picks up the phone, and requests bottled water and *Cocadas* be brought to his office for his guests.

Setting the phone down, the director folds his hands on the desk top, and looking at the group he says, "I don't know how much Julio has told you concerning me, and why I have such an interest in your intended venture. The information Julio has given me concerning your trip into the jungle has generated many questions that I would like to ask. Before doing so, I would like to give you a brief introduction of who I am and what caused my interest in your trip."

As the director finished speaking there was a knock at the door, and the lady we had seen earlier came into the room, followed by a young woman carrying a tray of water and cookies. The director asked to have the refreshments set on the conference table, which was located to the right of his desk. As they were leaving, the director said, "Marta, please wait a moment." The older woman stopped and closed the door and stood with her hands clasped in front of her, looking expectantly at Dr. Seminario. Looking from Marta to the seated group he says, "I would like to introduce my right hand and my left hand. This lady guards my door to allow me time to work and provides the assistance I need to accomplish my many tasks."

The men in the group stood and turned to face Marta, and the director introduced the group. He then said, "Marta Garcia has been with me for many years, both here in Trujillo and Chiclayo. Her knowledge of archeology and the artifacts of our ancient ancestors will astound you as it has me. If you need anything, and I am not available, please contact Marta and she will help you find what you require." The director then turns to face Marta and says, "Marta, I know you know Julio and Maria, but these other gentlemen are to be considered as friends. Please provide any assistance they may need for the task they are about to undertake for the museum." Marta acknowledged Dr. Seminarios request and with a smile, wished us a good trip, and asked the director to call if he needed anything. She quickly turned and opened the door to leave, but the director called to her asking that he not be disturbed for at least an hour. She responded, "Yes sir, as you wish."

Remaining behind his desk, Dr. Seminario says, "Please join me at the conference table for some refreshments, and we can continue our discussion of your forthcoming venture." Except for Maria, we were all standing, and followed the director to the table. Dr. Seminario removed a few books, and indicated we should be seated. There were ten chairs around the table, so we had more than enough room to be comfortable.

After everyone had helped themselves to the refreshments, the director says, "I would like to continue with my earlier statement, by introducing myself and explaining my interest in your venture. I was born and raised in Chiclayo, a very busy port city approximately 125 miles north of Trujillo. The city is a major commercial hub for northern Peru and a city with many different cultures intermingling together. This vitality is reflected in the architecture of the city center, which incorporates modern structures and colonial winding streets. Growing up in such a city contributed to my interest in the many cultures of our country. I have studied Archeology both in Peru and abroad, and have been involved in several excavations in this country." Dr. Seminario pauses and pours some water into a glass while asking, "Does anyone have any questions so far?"

Everyone remained silent and waited on the director to continue. After eating a cookie and drinking some water he says, "Beginning in 1970 I began to compile documents pertaining to a culture that in many ways differed from any known culture that had previously been discovered. I have kept this knowledge to myself, until I could verify my findings with actual archeological evidence. The first time I had found something out of the ordinary was at the Olmec site at La Venta. This was a large planned religious center with the homes of the elite groups that presided over the center. This was not a city, but a site that included temple mounds, monumental stone carvings, sacrificial altars and vertical stone slabs sculptured in relief with images of chiefs, priests, and warriors. I had seen several of these stelae at other Olmec sites, so at first I paid little attention to it. During the research at the site, a young researcher asked for my opinion of something he had found. He led me to the stelae located at the western edge of the site, and indicated I should look at some markings he had found. At first I saw what I expected to see engraved on the stone, but as I began to closely inspect the markings, I realized something was wrong. Around the base of the stone had been carved symbols not typical of Olmec art or symbology. I sketched the symbols from around the base of the stone for further study, even at that time I knew I was looking at something not from the Olmec culture." Dr. Seminario paused for a drink of water and Serge took the opportunity to ask, "Have you found these symbols at other sites not related to the Olmec culture?"

Nodding his head, Dr. Seminario states, "Yes, I've found markings at sites in the northern highlands and near Tarapoto. I have also found markings in Chan Chan and Las Huacas del Sol y de la Luna, that is why I requested Julio to take you to that site so you would have some familiarity with the murals. Before you leave for the interior I will have Marta make copies of relevant markings that you can compare with any markings you might find. What I have been able to reveal from the symbols indicates the Olmec and possibly other cultures have been influenced by another unknown culture. I have found markings of celestial bodies that these early people should not have known of, or of their very existence. There is a well-known site by the name of Chavin de Huantar in the Peruvian highlands. It appears to have been an important ceremonial center to which pilgrims came from other parts of the country. This location contains a number of impressive structures, including a large temple over 50 feet high and with a stone base of over 200 square feet. The temple has numerous rooms and interior passages with many decorations. While at this site, investigating within this temple I came across a room that had Chavin style artwork, but with Olmec influences. This intrigued me, and I began to study the markings in more detail. I copied many of the markings and saved them for later study. Some of those markings have shown up in other sites, all with markings that reflect an unknown influence."

After speaking Dr. Seminario relaxed in his chair, saying, "I must apologize for such a long explanation, but I felt it was necessary to give you some background for what I'm about to reveal. I hope you will hear me out. I feel I have found evidence that at some time in the past, the early people of these lands came in contact with individuals of a far superior and advanced intelligence. The knowledge that was given, was not given to the people, but accepted and used by a few individuals for religious purposes. I'm not saying who these visitors were, not until physical evidence can be obtained that demonstrates a technology that was not available to the people of that time or region."

"Sir, are you suggesting visitors from space?" I asked, with a look that revealed my lack of belief in such a possibility. I was aware of the mysterious line drawings of Nazca, a small city along the coast south of Lima. The line drawings are of animals, geometrical figures and birds ranging up to 1,000 feet in size. These lines have been scratched into the crust of the desert and preserved for an estimated 2,000 years. Due to a lack of rain and winds, they were never erased from the surface of the desert.

Smiling Dr. Seminario turns to me and says, "Have you read Mr. Erich von Daniken's theories about the lines, which he published in 1968, entitled *Chariots of the Gods*? I have, but I'm not ready to accept that extra-terrestrial space ships had landing strips in the desert. I've spoken to Maria Reiche who lives at the Hotel Turistas, who gives an hour-long talk on the lines every evening. No one really knows the origin or meaning of the lines, but Reiche has concluded that they corresponded to the constellations, and that they might be part of an astronomical calendar. Have we had visitors from the stars, I don't know, but I will not discount all possibilities of contact."

Reaching for another cookie, Dr. Seminario turns to Serge and said, "Mr. Gaston, I'm sorry, this is to be informal. Serge, would you be so kind as to reveal in more detail, what evidence you have to support the effort you are about to embark on? I recognize that we have only just met and only time will develop a level of trust between us, but if you could reveal a few facts, without compromising the knowledge you have obtained it could be beneficial in my support of the group's efforts."

I had noticed that Serge had not brought the journal for this meeting, which corresponded with our agreement not to divulge too much information to the director. We recognized that to have Dr. Seminario on our side could be a great asset, but we felt that proper caution called for withholding some critical segments of the journal.

Serge nodded and said, "I appreciate your willingness to be open with us, and your candid explanation for your interest in our research. I would be willing to disclose further details to you, but as you have stated, I will withhold certain knowledge that we feel is critical to our ability to discover the city. Not knowing what Julio has told you, and I feel that he must have given you information of some quality that caused you to send us the cash advance. With this in mind, I will state that I have acquired the journal of a 16th century Spanish adventurer, who left a record of finding a city in the jungles. A 19th century relative of mine found his journal, and that gentleman used the journal to travel to Peru. This ancestor of mine also wrote a journal of his travels, and of his finding the city that the Spanish gentlemen had found. My ancestor not only had kept a record of his travels, but also had made a crude map of his travels. With the help of a 19th century map and modern day maps, we feel we have a good chance of finding this city. In my ancestors journal he refers to a secret sect of serpent worshippers, and cautions anyone who follows him to look for signs of these people."

I noticed Dr. Seminario's eyes reacted to Serge's last statement concerning the serpent worshippers. He raised his hand and motioned Serge stating, "I'm sorry to interrupt, but you have mentioned a very important item that interests me greatly. You referred to a sect of serpent worshippers; did your ancestor indicate more about them?"

Serge realized he had hit a nerve, so he proceeded cautiously, "Yes he did, he stated that they were connected with the temple of the mother earth, and they had a gold statue representing a snake coiled around a branch. He indicated that there were many murals depicting snakes and they were used as guardians for the temple sent by the goddess, mother earth."

Dr. Seminario did not attempt to hide the excitement that showed on his face as he said, "You cannot imagine what this information means to me, it confirms years of research. I have found many references to this society of the snake, but never have I found evidence to prove its existence. The journal you mention, does it indicate the eyes of the serpent are fashioned of emeralds?"

Smiling, Serge says, "Yes, emeralds represent the eyes. It is evident from your reaction to this information that the worship of a serpent did take place. Has any evidence ever surfaced concerning this group outside of the jungle?"

"No, I have only found references to them from the Amazon Basin areas. I have seen sketches of a golden statue, but never have I heard of anyone finding one," stated Dr. Seminario as he rose from his seat and walked to a bookcase nearby. Within a few minutes he retrieved a leather-bound book, and turned to the table, while turning pages. He exclaimed, "There it is, I knew a picture of the serpent was in this book. Is it possible that your ancestor drew a sketch of the serpent, and if so did it look something like that?" Dr. Seminario had laid the book in the middle of the table, and was pointing to a picture.

Serge rose and leaned over the table to look at the page and said, "Yes, the sketch he made does resemble that picture."

The excitement Dr. Seminario felt was contagious as he paced from one end of the table to the other; he was rubbing his hands and repeating, "Wonderful, wonderful." As he took his seat he looked up and realized he had our full attention, "I'm sorry for this reaction, but this is one piece of evidence that confirms for me that no hoax is being played on this museum. My friends, I will do anything in my power to assist you in this endeavor.

Also, as I had requested Julio to inform you, the museum would offer a sizable finder's fee for the return of the golden serpent. I have placed a room at Julio's disposal for the storage of anything he felt was needed for your research. If after reviewing what has been stored, you find that something else is needed, please do not hesitate to ask Marta to assist you in acquiring those items."

Dr. Seminario rose from his seat behind the desk and shook hands with each of us and embraced Maria saying, "My best wishes go with you, and may God protect you. You will be entering some very dangerous country, where the danger can come from man or beast. I have authorized Julio to be a part of this expedition, so it has official approval from the university. This may come in handy if minor government officials get involved in what you are doing in the jungle. Thank you again for accepting my invitation to visit me today, and for revealing this new information. You have encouraged an old archeologist to always continue looking for the unknown, though it may seem out of reach." Dr. Seminario walked us to the door, and as he opened it, he wished us a good day and a successful trip.

Leaving Dr. Seminario's office we said our farewells to Marta, indicating we would see her before we left for the jungles. I assumed she had some knowledge of where we were going, due to the look of concern on her face.

Walking away from the director's office, Julio led us towards a set of stairs, which he indicated led to the storage rooms below. After arriving at the floor below, Julio turned left and approached the second door on the left. He produced a key, and unlocking the door he turned on the overhead lights to reveal a sizable storage room. As he walked in he said, "Please come in and the last to enter please shut the door behind you." Julio continued into the room, which at first glance contained several boxes and a large table in the middle of the room. I noticed Julio approaching some folding chairs stacked in a corner, which he asked if we could take one and sit at the table.

After everyone had taken a seat, Julio took a chair and sat at the table. With a look of success Julio said, "I hope all of you feel as good as I do. We have just received the blessing of approval from the director, and with that we can go far. He has also made my presence with the group official business of the university, which will be of great help with any government officials that decide to intrude in our affairs. The director has also approved a budget that I have permission to access if it is needed. My friends, we are on our way, and I hope things run as smooth as they have so far."

Julio reaches for a box sitting on the table and removes several papers, and spreads them out on the table. He looks about the table and said, "I would like to give you some further information about our travel plans. I have contacted a friend of mine who lives in Iquitos who owns several motorized canoes. I have contracted with him to guide us into the jungle using two boats and I authorized him to hire five men to help with the boats and setting up camp. My friend's name is Juan and I requested he hire another individual to guide the other canoe, someone he felt comfortable with if things get difficult. The other hired help may not be too dependable, so we must take precautions while on this trip. Now if I could have your attention, I would like to show you some of the things I have been able to acquire for the trip."

Julio rises from his chair and walks towards some boxes located next to the wall; he lifts one and sets it on the table. Opening the box he retrieves a pistol and says, "These are the Spanish Echeverria Star Model B pistols I had mentioned I would get for everyone. They are currently in use by the Spanish armed forces, so ammunition is readily available. I also have several boxes of ammunition; this 9mm cartridge should be sufficient as a sidearm for all of us. I see the look on your face Maria; no I did not forget you. Here is your Walther PPK with several spare clips and extra ammunition. I hope these weapons meet with everyone's approval."

Looking at me and indicating I should follow him, Julio says, "Serge informed me that you served several years in the United States Army, and were trained with several foreign weapons." I indicated I had been in the army and I did have some experience with a few foreign weapons. He led me to a wooden crate and proceeded to pry it open with a pry bar lying nearby. As he lifted the lid he said, "Have you ever used one of these?"

Peering over his shoulder I saw two 7.62mm SKS Carbines, that look to be in very good condition. I reached into the crate and lifted one of the carbines out, noticing that it was stamped with the Soviet star. Holding the weapon and pulling the bolt back I said, "Yes, I've used this weapon before. The SKS was adopted before the AK; they are very reliable weapons. I see you have the 30 round clips, they work well with this weapon, because of its light recoil you can achieve 35 r.p.m. of aimed fire. Who removed the 10-round fixed box magazines?"

Smiling Julio says, "I hope you approve of the modification, you never know what you might meet in the jungle. We need side arms, but real firepower sometimes has to be present to persuade someone or something to leave you alone."

"I hope we will not have to confront anything or anyone with these weapons," I stated as I returned the rifle to the crate. I knew from experience that the 7.62mm round could be very deadly in experienced hands. I would prefer that these weapons were never needed during the expedition, but I was not ready to suggest leaving them behind.

After closing the crate of rifles, Julio turned and said, "I will have the pistols and rifles shipped to Iquitos on the plane we will be flying upon. The crate will be marked as property of the university that will keep inspectors from becoming too curious about what is inside. I have acquired several items that I will ship, including knives, compasses, some canned rations, rope and various other items. I have asked Maria to put together a full field first aid kit that hopefully will not be needed. Marta has been of great help in purchasing equipment for our trip, and also keeping its existence from prying eyes."

Serge leaned forward and asked, "Julio, have you had problems with keeping these preparations secret?"

As Julio was seating himself he said, "Marta has told me that one of the workers in the museum has shown an inordinate amount of interest in what I have been doing. He has asked her why this room was locked, and if it needed cleaning. She told him that the director was storing personal items in the room, and they were not to be disturbed. I know of this individual, and I would not be surprised if he is working for someone outside the museum. He has been employed here for several years, but shows very little loyalty to anything but himself. He is certainly someone who would be motivated by money. Also, Marta indicated that he was seen in the plaza speaking with a stranger several weeks ago."

I turned to Serge and said, "It's very possible that professor Segault, realizing that Julio is from Trujillo has contacted someone he knows in this area to watch Julio's actions. He knows enough about the journal that he would expect Serge to contact Julio to begin his expedition from Trujillo. We know that the professor has arrived in Lima, and word will travel quickly to him that we were at the museum today. I would suggest that we acquire our tickets for Iquitos immediately and be ready to leave on a flight tomorrow."

Serge asked if the supplies were ready to be shipped to the airport, and if so they should be moved that afternoon. He requested Julio to purchase the tickets for the first flight he could get.

With a serious look on his face, Julio said, "I will have the supplies moved within the hour, by men who I will personally pick. I will have Maria purchase the tickets in her name; this might delay their tracking us for a short period of time. I will also contact my friend in Iquitos to prepare for our arrival, and have everything ready for a quick departure. We must put some distance between the professor's party and ourselves."

Within the hour we had finalized our plans for leaving Trujillo, hopefully without attracting any attention to ourselves. It was agreed not to cancel our rooms until the following morning, just in case someone was reporting on our movements. The three of us left the museum trying to act as tourists, while Julio and Maria stayed behind to finalize their duties. Returning to the hotel, we realized that the time was fast approaching for us to depart the city of Trujillo and to begin the task we had come to Peru to accomplish. We had enjoyed the beauty and grandeur of the country, but our time as tourists had come to an end.

We had spent many months preparing for this moment, and now that the time had arrived it seemed a daunting accomplishment to attempt. Three young men from highly civilized areas of the world, within a few hours would be entering an environment totally alien to them. We would be traveling by riverboats through the Amazon River Basin, into a world we knew very little about.

7
Iquitos – Gateway to the Amazon

After gathering our bags, Julio requested we wait for him in the waiting area. He said he was going to have our equipment taken to the hotel. We had arrived with a number of tourists who were in the process of locating their guides. I tried to shut out the volume of noise generated by the confusion of a busy airport. My thoughts were still dwelling on the past 24 hours.

We left Trujillo as quietly as possible, hoping that very few people were aware of our departure. Julio had requested that Marta if asked about the group she should indicate, that he and a group of Americans had decided to visit the Moche ruins at Sipan. He felt this would give the group some time to disappear into the jungle, before their absence was noticed. We knew professor Segault was behind us, and probably by only a few days. Julio agreed with Serge that the curious employee of the museum might have been paid to report any unusual activity concerning Julio and foreigners.

Within a short period of time Julio returned stating that the equipment would be sent to the hotel. We gathered our belongings and following Julio we entered the bright sunlight of a frontier jungle city. While flying to Iquitos, Julio had mentioned that Iquitos was only accessible by air and water. The population was a mix of indigenous tribes with European and Chinese immigrants, which provided a rich diversity of lifestyles. Maria mentioned that the people are generally warm and friendly, and unlike many larger cities, the streets are safe with very little violence.

Upon leaving the airport, I noticed a number of three-wheeled taxis used as rickshaws. While I was looking about, Julio approached a driver and began to speak excitedly. Within a few moments we were told to board several of the vehicles and we proceeded into the city. As we merged with other rickshaws, taxis and buses, I could see the streets were quite lively, but totally unlike Lima or Trujillo. I quickly realized why Julio called this a frontier city; most of the buildings we traveled past were a blend of European and Asian influences. I knew that in past years Iquitos was the clearinghouse for millions of tons of rubber shipped to Europe, I could still see vestiges of its former status as one of the most important rubber capitals in the world. We passed many homes on our way to the Plaza de Armas which were still faced with glazed tiles, which had been shipped from Italy and Portugal. While still trying to take everything in, our driver turned and entered the driveway to the El Dorado Hotel.

Julio paid the drivers and we entered the hotel, immediately sensing a difference from the accommodations we had previously had. Noticing our reaction to our surroundings, Julio motioned us to one side of the lobby. "I saw the reactions on your faces when you entered the hotel," stated Julio, "this is one of the better hotels in the city. Remember we are not in one of the modern coastal cities, so please be understanding of the type of accommodations we can get here. Except for Maria, we will have to share rooms while in Iquitos; they are very busy this time of the year."

Everyone quickly assured Julio that we were not disappointed in our lodging, it was just a natural reaction due to some of the hotels he had previously selected. Serge grasped his arm and said, "My friend, please do not take offense at our reactions. You have always provided the best for us, and we greatly appreciate your help. If we are going into the jungle, we better prepare ourselves for many adjustments to what we are familiar with. Let's get registered and find a place to get something to eat."

Serge and I were to share a room on the first floor, and Jason and Julio were given a room on the second floor. Maria was given a room two doors from Julio's room so after registering, Julio suggested we meet in the lobby in 15 minutes and get something to eat.

The room was clean and neat, with two double beds and a bath. Setting my luggage on one of the beds I turned to Serge and said, "Can you believe we are finally here? How long have we dreamed of attempting to discover something unknown to the world."

Serge slowly sat on his bed with his luggage next to him, looking at me he said, "I also find it hard to accept that we are really here. I've noticed that since we left Lima, the importance of the journals safety has truly impacted me. Without that book, this venture would be impossible. I find myself wanting to keep it on my person at all times for safekeeping. Knowing Segault is behind us only causes me to be more protective of it. I've debated carrying a weapon whenever we go out, I'll ask Julio if it is permissible."

I also was concerned for the safety of the journal; it was our only guide to finding the city within the jungle. We were all aware that we were being followed, and at some time in the future, we would be forced to safeguard the journal. Professor Segault had been given enough information by Serge, that he would determine Iquitos would be a logical stepping-off point to enter the jungle.

Rising from the bed, I said, "I'll ask Julio to get the Walther PPK from the weapons crate, it's small enough to carry without attracting much attention. I completely agree with you, the safety of the journal is of utmost importance. Get your backpack and put the journal in it, and I'll speak with Julio about the pistol. Our 15 minutes are about over, let's go to the lobby and meet the others."

Serge locked the room as we began walking to the lobby and said, "Help me with this pack; I want to make sure it's securely fastened."

Entering the lobby, I motioned to Julio to follow me where we could speak privately. Julio asked if there was a problem and I said, "Serge is very concerned about the safety of the journal, now that we are so near our goal. Before we leave for the restaurant, would you be able to get me the Walther and a belt holster? I can conceal it under my shirt at my back."

With a concerned look on his face he said, "I'm also concerned for its safety, come with me, and we will see the manager." Turning to the others Julio requests everyone relax in the lobby for a few moments, stating that we would be back in a minute.

I followed Julio to the desk, and waited while he spoke to the clerk. Within moments a middle-aged gentleman arrives and begins speaking with Julio, and motions us to follow.

The manager opens a door to an office and indicates that we should enter. He quickly follows and shuts the door behind him and approaches an old desk. He opens the desk drawer and produces a ring of keys, and says something to Julio. The manager motions us to follow him, and as we leave the office, Julio informs me that the manager is taking us to a storage room, where our equipment was stored after transport from the airport. The manager takes us to a steel fire door, and proceeds to use one of the keys on the ring to open the door. He turns the light switch on and says something to Julio, pointing to our crates stacked against the left wall. The manager begins to leave and turns to Julio and makes a final statement. Julio shakes the manager's hand and he leaves the room.

Julio turns to me and says, "I'm sorry about the language, but the manager speaks only Spanish. He told me our equipment is here and when we are finished, we should turn off the lights and lock the door." While speaking, Julio proceeds to the crates and produces a key to unlock a large crate. As I near the crates I see he has opened the crate containing the weapons and ammunition. Julio removes the Walther, two clips and a holster saying, "I hope we will not need this while in Iquitos, it would only draw attention to us." I agree with him, but I indicate a bit of caution now could prevent a major problem in the future. Handing the holster to me, he says, "I know you're right, our success depends on the journal."

I attach the holster to my belt and pull my shirt out of my trousers to cover it. Taking the weapon I insert a clip and place it in the holster, with the other clip in my pocket. I slowly turn asking Julio if the weapon is visible. He indicates it is practically invisible, and should go unnoticed. He locks the crate and he opens the door, asking me to shut off the lights.

As we enter the lobby, everyone greets us with questioning looks, and Julio states, "All is well, let's get something to eat."

I walk towards Serge and as we leave the hotel, I say in a low voice, "Julio was able to get me a pistol. Relax, if there is any trouble, we have something to defend the journal and ourselves." Proceeding out onto the street, Serge turned to me and thanked me for taking this precaution.

We gathered in front of the hotel and Julio suggested we walk to the waterfront district instead of taking a taxi. As we begin walking around the Plaza de Armas, Julio points towards a house located on one of the corners and say, "That is the famed *'casa de hierro.'* Gustav Eiffel designed it for the Paris exhibition in 1898. It was later purchased by a wealthy Iquitos rubber baron, dismantled and shipped to Iquitos and re-assembled." Jason commented that the house sounded more impressive than it looks, but he could see that it would be a symbol of the town's short lived affluence rather than as a piece of architecture.

Continuing around the plaza, Julio points out the house of Carlos Fitzcarraldo, the Peruvian rubber baron who dragged a steamship over the pass that bears his name. He states that by doing this he opened up the department of Madre de Dios. We continued walking around the plaza with Julio pointing out different items of interest, and all the time I'm aware of the motor scooters as they are moving through the plaza. The volume of noise produced by these vehicles is a constant din that adds to the everyday sounds of a thriving city. Iquitos is a colorful, friendly city, which must explain the vibrant atmosphere I felt as we walked around the plaza. Julio announces that we are going into the Belen district of the town, which is the waterfront area, where many houses float on rafts in the water.

As we near the waterfront, I begin to see boats of all shapes and sizes being rowed about in Venetian-style canals. Julio's statement concerning the houses built on rafts is truly amazing. Many houses are built on balsa logs, which float as movable homes. After passing a canal, we come to a market that Julio states has an incredible variety of products from the Amazon. As we pass through the market I see many stalls with many varieties of fruits, fish, turtles, frogs and waterfowl. Julio leads us through the market, and I see him approaching a two-story structure that resembles a restaurant.

There are several tables and chairs arranged outside the restaurant, and as we approach a dark complexioned man with a straw hat, rises from a chair and greets Julio. After greeting the man, Julio says, "I would like to introduce Juan Montegro, a friend of many years." Julio introduces Juan to each of us, and states, "Juan will be providing the boats for our expedition, and he will be our guide for the trip. I have invited Juan to share this meal with us so we can get acquainted before leaving for the jungle." Juan indicates that he had held a large table for us if we would care to sit outside. Everyone agreed that they would like to eat at the outdoor tables.

While we were seating ourselves, a waiter arrived and Juan spoke quickly to him. After the waiter left, I asked Juan what he had told the waiter. With a large smile he says, "He wanted to know what we would like to drink, I told him to bring Masato for everyone. I hope you will enjoy our local beverage?" Jason asked if this was the drink made from fermented yucca? Juan acknowledged that it was the same drink.

I had taken a chair facing the market, with my back to the restaurant. While several of the others were talking about food and native drinks, I let my attention wander through the market. It was late in the afternoon, and many people were about. There was a constant murmur of conversation from the market, and shouts of excitement from running children. I turned to Maria and asked if she could describe some of what was being said in the market by the various people.

She said she would be happy to help me have an understanding of life in the market. Then she looked at the market and laughingly said, "The stall owners were calling out their produce and women were berating them for the quality of their produce. The children are playing games and enjoying themselves, but this causes their mothers to constantly call their names. I have never been to Iquitos, but I find the city very charming. The people seem very warm and friendly, in spite of much material poverty. Life in these floating homes cannot be very easy."

While Maria and I were talking drinks were served and Julio announced a toast. Lifting his glass he said, "My friends, I would like to make a toast to the success of our venture. Please lift your glasses together to bond our friendship for the adventures we are about to experience." At that, he lifted his glass as we all did, and with several clinks of glasses lightly hitting each other, we toasted the success of our venture.

As Julio sat his glass down, he said, "I would like to give all of you a little more information concerning Juan and why I selected him to lead us into the jungle. I have known Juan for many years; he has guided tourists and several groups of researchers for the museum into the jungles. His jungle knowledge is excellent and he speaks many of the local dialects of tribes we may come in contact with. He also has a wide range of experience with time honored folk remedies for a wide range of ailments. Juan has informed me that he has already purchased a number of items from the medicinal plant market right here in the Belen. This knowledge may come in handy if one of us contracts a sickness in the jungle. Juan has selected the men that will handle the boats and carry our gear."

Turning to Juan, Julio says, "Juan, would you care to say a few words? Also, if you would, please use English, as some of us do not speak Spanish."

Juan looked about the table with a slight smile, and said, "I would like to welcome all of you to the city of Iquitos, a pleasant little city on the edge of the jungle. I was born in a small town south of here called Requena; it is located where the Ucayali and the Blanco Rivers come together. I have traveled through much of this country and much of that travel has been in river canoes. Julio has mentioned my experience with natural remedies for ailments contracted in the jungles. I have studied with several tribes such as the Bora, Witoto and the Ashininga, who have great knowledge of natural herb remedies for jungle sicknesses."

Juan paused for a moment and looking at Maria says, "I understand from Julio that you are a physician, I would like to discuss some of these remedies with you at your leisure." Maria indicated she would be happy to compare notes with him, whenever they have some free time.

Juan thanked Maria and said, "Except for Julio, I don't think any of you have ever traveled in the riverboats that we use. We call them canoes, but they will comfortably hold seven people, with some limited room for equipment. They are equipped with small outboard motors, which are sufficient to get us anywhere we are going, but I would like to remind everyone that we can only carry a small amount of gasoline for each boat. The boats will have sufficient paddles for everyone to help row the boats when the current is not strong enough to keep us moving. By taking advantage of the current of the Amazon River, it will take us about three days to reach the Napo River. I would suggest that you discuss how you would like to separate your group between the two boats for river travel. I have hired other men to help with the boats and to act as porters when needed. One of the men I hired is named Esteban; he is related to me on my mother's side of the family. He will be the lead boatman for the second boat; I have great confidence in his abilities both on land and on the river."

Juan paused for a moment as the waiter approached, requesting if we were ready to order our meal. Julio asked if Juan could suggest a local dish for everyone to try. Juan turned to the waiter and said, "Bring enough *paiche a la loretana* for everyone, and more Masato."

After the waiter had returned to the restaurant, Juan said "I have ordered a local dish I hope everyone enjoys, it is a fillet of a huge primitive fish found in these waters. It is served with fried manioc and vegetables; it is a very filling meal. To continue with what I was saying about the men I hired, other than Esteban, the other five men are individuals I normally would not hire. In the past few years we have had an increasing number of tourists coming to Iquitos for trips into the jungle. This has generated such interest that several companies have been formed that provide excursions into the jungles and the companies have started to build lodges for the tourists to stay overnight. These companies have hired many of the good river men to work for them and have caused a shortage of dependable help. I have had to hire men to help with the boats that I barely know and do not completely trust. Hopefully having offered above average wages will help to keep their loyalty as we leave civilization."

Julio leaned forward and said, "This will be a difficult journey, I hope these men will not abandon us as we enter unfamiliar country. I would suggest that you and Estaban split the men between the two boats, with an eye to who might be troublemakers, and keep them apart from each other. I also feel it would be a good idea for everyone to be armed at all times. This might help keep the troublemakers from feeling to bold to take any action against the group."

Nodding his head, Juan says, "I agree with you, let them see everyone armed, it might cause them to think twice before taking any action against us. These men are experienced jungle travelers, but they lack the courage that is needed to be guides. They are lazy and would prefer to steal what they need, so be very watchful of your belongings."

Julio spoke up and said, "The food has arrived, let's try this jungle delicacy that Juan has ordered." I watched the waiter approach the table with a large tray, which held several large platters, piled high with food. He set the platters on the table and two bowls, one containing vegetables and another of rice. Plates were set in front of each of us and Juan indicated we should proceed to fill our plates.

Silence fell upon the table as everyone helped themselves to the food. The fish was delicious and combined with the fried manioc was very enjoyable. After a few minutes, Juan paused in his eating and asked, "Other than Julio, do any of you have any experience in the jungle?"

Juan looked around the table at each of us, receiving the same negative response. "I was afraid of that," said Juan with a slight frown. "This trip will be dangerous, and the more prepared you are the better your chances of survival. I hope Julio has advised you to wear long-sleeved shirts and pants of close-woven materials. I would also suggest that everyone wears a hat and I will provide mosquito nets for everyone."

Jason stopped eating for a moment and asked Julio if he had provided bottled water for the trip. Julio nodded his head and said, "Yes, I've provided several cases of water and fruit juices. The last thing we need is intestinal problems from drinking the water. We also have to be careful not to eat foods prepared with river water, this will also cause problems."

After several moments of silence, Juan leaned back in his chair and said, "If you don't mind, I would like to give you a brief idea of the terrain you will be traveling into. Julio has informed me that you will be traveling along the Amazon River and going north on the Napo River. That country is made up of jungle known as a rain forest, a very primitive environment with tribes such as the Yagua that still use blowguns to hunt small birds. A rain forest is a very special place, with trees as tall as 200 feet. Then the tops of other trees will be 100 to 150 feet above the ground, with another layer between these trees and the ground. This layering of trees are known as canopies. We will be traveling in a triple canopy forest, as I have described, which means that the canopies shade the forest floor so that it receives very little sunlight. As a result of this shading, we will be able to walk without too much difficulty through many parts of the rain forest. There will be areas of dense growth where more sunlight has been able to reach the ground and generate more growth. Does anyone have any questions so far?"

Juan had our full attention, as he asked for questions, no one responded. Julio stated that it would be a good idea if he would continue, since he had not had a chance to review the basics of traveling in this country.

Juan nodded and said, "I realize some of you may have studied about this type of country, but the reality of traveling in the rain forest can be totally different. Our rainy season is just about over, so it's the best time to be traveling in this country. The average temperature will be in the upper 80s, and the air below the lower canopy is almost always humid. A tropical rain forest is always green because of continuous growth, and with the reduced sunlight, we will be traveling in a damp, semi-dark environment. There are a great variety of animals that live in the rain forest. Many of these animals spend their lives in the trees and never descend to the ground. Due to the amount of wildlife, there is a constant volume of noise that you will learn to adapt to and soon ignore. I have given you a brief description of the terrain you will be traveling into, but never forget this is wild and dangerous country. I will do everything I can to make this a safe and successful trip. Julio has not told me your ultimate destination, but I understand you want to travel up the Napo River. Is it possible to tell me what you are searching for, I may be of some help in locating what your looking for? I'm also concerned if you need to travel the Napo River north into Ecuador; this could be very dangerous."

Serge spoke first and said, "I appreciate your approach to this trip and your willingness to provide a safe trip. I don't want to act mysterious, but I would prefer not disclosing our destination or why we are here at the present time. When we arrive at the Napo River, I will reveal to you alone what we are trying to do. I hope you can accept this arrangement and work with us on this research project. Julio speaks very highly of you and we would like to have your assistance in this endeavor. To address your last question, we will not be entering Ecuador."

Juan indicated that he could accept the arrangement, because he knew and trusted Julio. He stated Julio was a good friend and if he vouched for us, that was good enough for him. The meal ended in silence as the last of the fish was enjoyed by all. Julio motioned the waiter to bring refills for our glasses, and we relaxed as the dishes were cleared from the table. Julio told Juan that this expedition was approved of by the museum in Trujillo and as Serge had stated, he would be given more information as their journey progressed. The evening ended pleasantly with Juan stating that we could leave at first light in two days. He had a few items that he had to acquire before leaving for the jungle.

After finishing his drink, Juan says, "I will say *buenas noches*, have a good night's rest. I would also suggest you check your gear and coordinate with Julio for anything you might not have for the trip. Once we leave Iquitos, we will be on our own and we will have to be self-sufficient. There are a few tribes in the interior, but very few are friendly, because of the intrusion of outsiders into their country. We will be passing two settlements as we travel, but I would suggest that we not stop at them. They are Mazan on the Amazon River and Sta. Clotilde on the Napo River; it could be a mistake to stop, as we would attract the wrong type of attention. There are individuals who live along the river that would not hesitate to steal from us or worse. You mentioned bringing weapons, remember to bring a good supply of gun oil, weapons rust very easily in the jungle."

Juan stood and shook hands with everyone, and thanked us for accepting him as our guide. He told Julio where we should meet him for departure in two days. He thanked Julio again and as he was leaving, he said he would see us soon. I watched as he easily moved through the market and slowly disappeared from sight. He seemed a man very confident in his own abilities and someone who would comfortably accept the position of expedition guide. I felt that Julio had selected an individual who was qualified to guide us into the jungle.

As relaxed conversation resumed, Julio asked if anyone had any reservations concerning Juan as our guide. There was a general agreement among all of us, that Juan seemed very qualified to fulfill the position of expedition guide.

After a moment Julio says, "I would like to make another suggestion concerning our travel arrangements. As Juan has stated, the help he has hired will not be very dependable, so I think we need to take a few precautions. I would suggest that Jason travel with Esteban in boat two, and I will travel in boat one with Juan. I make this suggestion because both Jason and myself speak Quechua, and if the men Juan has hired decide to use this language to plot anything we will be able to anticipate any sudden problems."

"I think that's a good idea," indicated Serge. "I would also like to suggest the arrangement of the rest of the party. Unless anyone disagrees, I will travel with Julio and Maria in boat one." Looking at me he says, "If you would accompany Jason in boat two, I feel this would provide adequate mutual protection for each of us. Jason will be able to translate any Spanish that is spoken, but he will pretend not to understand Quechua if it is used. I hope this arrangement meets with the approval of everyone?"

After finishing our drinks, it was agreed that we should return to the hotel and get some rest. The walk back to the hotel was pleasant and unhurried, as the streets were still busy with many people strolling through the plaza enjoying the evening environment of the city. Upon arriving at the hotel, it was obvious that everyone was ready to return to his or her rooms for a night's rest. It was agreed that we would meet in the lobby by 8:00 the following morning and we would get breakfast together.

After saying goodnight to everyone, Serge and I went to our room. I noticed he was still wearing the backpack, and had kept it with him through the meal. Entering the room, I said, "I think we had better get a waterproof bag so we can protect the journal while we are traveling. You must always remember that when you need to refer to the journal, that you do it in a private setting. If the help Juan has hired realizes the value of the book, you can be sure they will try to steal it. Have you made any notes to refer to while we are traveling so you can keep the journal hidden for as long as possible?"

Without saying a word, Serge reaches into his shirt pocket, and produces a small black notebook. Smiling Serge states, "I'm way ahead of you. I figured that I better make some notations separate from the journal, so it would not be so evident to everyone that the journal existed. I have a waterproof bag I've used for camping; it will serve very well as protection for the journal." He reaches behind himself and removes the backpack setting it beside the bed. With a sigh he kicks off his shoes and pushes his pillows up to the headboard. As he sits back against the pillows, he opens the black notebook and says, "Let me give you an idea of what I've written. I've tried to keep my notes as general as possible, without being too specific as to area or landmark. My first notation states that we should travel east past the Nanay River and then past the Mazan River. Then I indicate we are to travel upstream on the Napo River past Sta. Clotilde. What I have failed to mention is that I have placed false statements concerning landmarks that don't exist in among these references, so hopefully if someone finds these directions they will be confused."

While Serge had been speaking, I had also removed my shoes and relaxed upon my bed. "Have you considered how much you will reveal to Juan?" I asked with concern evident in my tone of voice. "And will you reveal the existence of the journal? I know you trust Julio, but Juan is unknown to us and I would suggest not giving him everything we know." I could not help myself, we had spent many years preparing for this trip, and preserving our source materials was of great importance to me.

Serge agreed with me that Juan was to be given only enough information to provide guidance for the party. We agreed that if the journal fell into the wrong hands, whether professor Segault or Peruvian boat handlers, we could forget ever finding the city. We spent the next half-hour getting ready for bed and securing the door for possible intruders. As we relaxed in our beds, Serge says, "Do you remember the many conversations we had while in France? Discussing the possibilities of searching for lost treasure and lost civilizations, look at us now. If this is a successful venture and we can return with enough to finance future research projects, I would like to continue what we have started and look for other items to discover."

As I reached towards the nightstand to turn the light out, I said, "That's one of the things about you that have always impressed me. Here we are in the middle of the Peruvian Amazon River Basin, preparing to sail into a jungle we know nothing about, and you're already thinking of our next adventure. I truly hope you're right and we can come out of this alive and with some money to show for our efforts. I also agree with you, if we were successful, I would be the first to join you in another adventure."

We said goodnight to each other, and tried to relax our minds enough to get some rest. I knew it was going to be difficult for me to get to sleep, as my mind was moving from one subject to another. What would we find in the jungle, or would we find anything at all? Would we find the remains of one of the lost cities the Spanish had searched for, such as El Dorado? Would we find a hidden city stacked with gold, and its streets paved with gold? With thoughts such as these, I finally fell into a restless sleep, as thoughts of the unknown moved through my dreams.

The next day passed quickly as everyone made a final check of his or her equipment, and discarded items that were not necessary. It quickly became evident that available room and weight would be the primary guideline for what would be taken and what would be left behind. Julio indicated we would be taking canned food, but Juan had stated he would provide food for the group from the jungle. Julio confirmed that the manager had agreed to rent us the storage room for the next few months, so everyone was encouraged to store items that would not be needed on the trip. We took a break from our packing to eat a morning and early evening meal, and towards the end of the day everyone was ready for their final night's rest in a bed. Juan came to the hotel in the early evening and informed Julio that we should meet him at the boat docks by 6:00 in the morning. He wanted to get an early start, before the tourist boats began moving on the river.

The early morning air had a faint chill to it, but the sky was clear with small white clouds above the treetops. As we approached the waterfront, Julio led us to the boat docks. I noticed Juan waving to us and motioning for the group to hurry. I looked at my watch and confirmed that we still had a few minutes before 6:00, but Juan indicated he was ready to load our gear in the boats and get on the river. While Juan directed his laborers to transfer our gear to the boats, I had an opportunity to observe the two boats we would be using to enter the jungle. They were well-used wooden boats, with an outboard motor attached to the rear of each boat. I noticed long poles attached to the side of each boat, I gathered they were to be used to push the boat off sandbars if we became grounded. As I looked across the brown waters of the river before me, I began to realize how small these boats were and the reality of the distance we would be traveling seemed quite daunting.

After everyone was settled aboard their assigned boat, Juan gave the signal to start the motors. After settling myself next to Jason I noticed paddles at my feet, and several more towards the bow of the boat. Juan proceeded into the swirling waters of the Amazon and signaled Esteban to follow in his boat. As I watched the city of Iquitos slowly fall behind us, I was reminded of an item I had found in my research of the area. In the early 1850's Iquitos was a fishing village of approximately 225 inhabitants, with a considerable part of them being whites and Mestizos. It was incredible how 150 years could make such a difference in such a remote part of the world. Leaving Iquitos I noticed the shores of the river were of white clay. I had not noticed this until I was upon the river and able to view the city from this vantage point.

Jason had taken a seat and turning he said, "It's a strange feeling watching the city fade away behind us. I heard Juan explaining to Julio that we may not be able to sail much further than Sta. Clotilde before having to continue on foot. He stated that where the Napo River and the Curaray come together travel becomes very dangerous."

Speaking in a low voice I reply, "Juan knows we want to travel the Napo, but he is not aware of how far up the river we plan on going. I agree with Serge, we should keep our destination to ourselves for the present time."

Jason stated he agreed and then made himself as comfortable as possible as he watched the shoreline slowly passing. I also watched the shoreline passing and estimated the river was about 120 yards wide at this point, and moving about three miles per hour. I noticed the shoreline was covered with tall grass, much like a species of cane. Behind the grass the trees seem so thick that it would be impossible to penetrate into the interior.

I ask Jason if Esteban could sail closer to the shore, I would like to get a better view of the growth along the shore. After speaking with Esteban for a few moments Jason says, "Esteban is sorry, but he and Juan must keep their boats in the middle of the river since they are going downstream. He says the rules of the river are that boats traveling upstream hug the banks, and those going downstream are to stay in the middle. He indicated that we would be stopping for a short period of time after passing the Nanay River."

Once we had attained our position within the current of the river, Esteban shut the motor off and proceeded to let the boat drift with the current. The next few hours pass without incident and I find myself loosing track of time until Jason motions to the left.

"What river is that?" asks Jason as he turns to look past my shoulder.

Without looking at Jason I say, "I believe that is the Nanay River, and it appears to be at least 150 yards across where it empties into the Amazon. Ask Esteban if he knows the depth of the Amazon at this point, where the two rivers meet?"

Jason turns and speaks for a moment to Esteban, and suddenly Esteban speaking in English says, "I would be happy to speak English since one of you does not speak Spanish. I'm happy to see you are interested in our country and ask questions about the land and river. I will try to answer any questions you have about my country. As for the depth of the river at this point, I believe it is about 50 feet deep."

I thanked Esteban for the information and his willingness to accommodate my inability to speak Spanish. After passing the mouth of the Nanay River, the Amazon seemed to widen by at least 30 yards and the current moved with a stronger force. Within a half-hour Esteban said, "Gentlemen, look towards the left shore and you will see one of the local boats bringing produce to Iquitos."

Both Jason and I turned to see a long boat, whose sides were barely above the water. The boat must have been 50 feet long with a thatched roof, which was providing shade for the people and produce it was carrying. I could see several people relaxing from front to rear, and numerous stacks of bananas and other produce. These were the first humans we had seen since leaving Iquitos, and I commented to Jason that I was happy to see other human beings. While traveling the river I had adjusted to the sounds from the jungle, but it still gave me a strange feeling not to be able to see what made the sounds. When asked about the sounds, Esteban had commented that he had heard monkeys and a variety of birds. Most of the birdcalls were from parrots, which he stated were constantly calling one another.

With the additional water from the Nanay River, I noticed the Amazon was moving several miles per hour faster than when we entered the river at Iquitos. Though the river had widened, I could still see the jungle was so thick and tangled with undergrowth that only an Indian could possibly penetrate the forest. I recalled Esteban stating that we would be making a short landing after passing the Nanay River, with the foliage so heavy I found it very difficult to imagine landing anywhere.

We spent the next 30 minutes quietly traveling with the current of the river, with only the sounds of the jungle to keep us company. I mentioned to Jason that I expected to see more river traffic this near to Iquitos. He agreed that he was also surprised to see so few signs of mankind. While we were talking, I became aware of the boat slowly turning towards the right shore. Turning from Jason I can see the river has formed a pocket in the shoreline and with a small beach. I watch as Juan's boat entered the shallows and approaches the beach, two of his men jump into the water and pull the boat up on the beach. Esteban follows the lead of the first boat and he also runs his boat upon the beach, with two of his men jumping out and pulling the boat ashore.

As Esteban jumps over the side he said, "Come my friends, we will take a break from the river and have something to eat." He continues walking through the water onto the beach, at the same time speaking to his men.

I hear Serge call our names and turning I see him approaching with a smile upon his face. His excitement is quite evident as he walks towards us and says, "We have arrived in the jungle, and can you believe it?"

I replied that I could also feel his excitement, and asked if he had noticed how impenetrable the jungle appeared to be. Turning he says, "Yes, I've noticed while traveling the river and even here where we have stopped. Juan has mentioned that once you penetrate the jungle that borders the river, traveling will be easier." The three of us stood looking at the jungle, and I would guess each of us was wondering how we would ever penetrate the forest we could see.

While we were talking, Julio called for us to join him. As we turned to join him and Maria, I could see the men gathering driftwood that was lying about the beach. As we approach Julio he says, "Juan is having the men gather wood and making a fire to cook a meal. We are welcome to join them if we care to; they will be roasting sweet potatoes and yuccas. It would be a good idea to accept their invitation for this meal. It would help to get things started on the right footing, a friendly footing." We all agreed, and began to make ourselves comfortable while waiting for the food to be cooked.

After the sweet potatoes and yuccas were cooked, Juan tells one of his men to bring some beer for everyone to have with their meal. Everyone greeted this with smiles and when he returned with cups and several bottles of Cristal, we all demonstrated a great need to quench our thirsts.

Though the meal was simple, it was also filling and with a couple cups of beer, I found the thought of a hammock very agreeable. Looking about I could see the same effect had taken over the majority of the party. Juan asked Julio a question and Julio answered him, after which Juan clapped his hands and directed the men to begin cleaning the camp and preparing to leave. It was evident that they would have preferred to remain for a mid-afternoon rest before continuing down the river. Within 20 minutes the camp had been cleaned and everyone was directed to board the boats.

Juan's boat took the lead and shortly we were traveling near the center of the river with a good current to help keep us moving. After a few minutes of travel and everyone had settled in their places, I said to Jason, "Serge told me that Juan is planning to slip by Mazan in the early morning hours. He hopes our passing will go unnoticed by the town's people, if not, it could bring unwelcome attention to us. He told Serge he knew of a small island a couple miles above the town where we could camp for the night." Jason agreed that we did not need to bring attention to ourselves.

Esteban occupied the last seat of the boat, which indicated he was responsible for steering the boat. Jason and I were sitting on the seat just before him so our conversation was not too difficult to hear. After a moment Esteban leaned forward stating, "It is a good thing that Juan has suggested. There are many people on the river that would not hesitate to attack us for what we carry. Many are fishermen, but they are always armed and willing to work together if they feel the prize is worth the danger. I believe the island Juan has selected for the night is well suited for a hidden camp. He may suggest that guards be posted for added security."

Though the sounds of the jungle were constantly with us, my mind seemed to be dulled by the steady motion of the boat. Only when Esteban spoke to one of his men, did I come out of my stupor, realizing that I had almost dozed off. I watched as one of the men opened a box under his seat and proceeded to rummage around for something. Within moments he produced a hook and a stout roll of fishing line. He spoke to the individual beside him and he took something from his pocket, which he proceeded to attach to the hook. I asked Jason if Esteban had told him to catch a fish. Jason turned to me and with a smile said, "Esteban told him to get a hook and line and catch something for our evening meal. As you can see, he is more than willing to attempt to catch something."

I could see he was slowly letting the line trail behind the boat as we traveled down the river. He had no sinker, so I did not expect the line to sink very deep. I had not seen any signs of fish while traveling the river, but I suspected many species of fish were to be found in the river. After several minutes without anything happening to his line we all began to slowly forget what he was attempting to do. The calls of the wildlife from the nearby jungle were a constant source of noise, but I was adjusting to not looking into the jungle for the sources of all the sounds. It seemed the animals remained out of sight within the jungle, at least while we were traveling in the vicinity.

Without warning, the fisherman gave a shout as his fishing line snapped taunt beside the boat. He began shouting to the others and one of the men helped to hold the line while he wrapped it around a stick he had on the seat. Esteban swung the boat so the line would not hit anyone, but only enough so we could remain within the current. I could see the fish was putting up quite a fight and he had his hands full just trying to hold his stick. Every time he attempted to twist the stick to take in some line, the fish would continue fighting with such strength that he was unable to shorten the line. The tug-of-war went on for 15 minutes, before the fish began to show signs of tiring. As he began pulling the fish near the boat, one of the men approached the side of the boat to assist in pulling the fish within the boat. With a great shout he fell back over his seat as the fish jumped into the boat. He still held the line as the fish jumped about in the bottom of the boat, trying to snap at anything nearby.

I quickly pulled my feet away from a dolphin shaped fish of about 30 inches long. It had two curved sharp teeth, like those of a serpent, in the lower jaw. It thrashed about for several minutes before giving up the fight and gasping its last. He held the fish up and said something, which caused everyone to laugh and congratulate him on his catch. As things quieted down, Esteban said, "Everyone is happy with what he has caught, the fish is very good to eat. We will roast it tonight with some plantains, and drink some beer. It will be a very good meal you will enjoy." I could see from the pleasure on his face that he was looking forward to enjoying our stay on the island. I also hoped it would be a safe and quiet evening, without any visitors.

The excitement of catching the fish gave everyone something to talk about while the boat continued down the river. While the men were talking among themselves, Jason turned to me and said, "Have you had a chance to observe the jungle and how it grows to the edge of the river. If we had to make a sudden stop it could be very difficult, I have seen very few places where we could land. I see now why they indicated Iquitos was a frontier city, once you leave the city you will be in the jungle. It's beautiful, but for the unwary it can be very deadly."

I agreed with Jason that there were many dangers waiting for the untrained traveler in this country. I pointed to the right side of the river and said, "Look, I believe those are Jabiru Storks. You were mentioning the dangers of the jungle and there are many, but I'm glad to see a few creatures not so deadly. When we go ashore, we must be always on the alert, from what I have read there are many deadly spiders and snakes waiting for the unwary traveler."

"You are right to be cautious," says Esteban. "I'm sorry to have listened to your conversation, but you must be very careful when traveling in this country. There are dangers in the waters around us, such as the piranha and several poisonous water snakes. There is a little red and black streaked frog that will kill you if it bites you, it's known as the poison dart frog. If you see one of them, turn quickly and go the other way. If you quickly look to your left you will see a beautiful sight; those are pink river dolphins."

After hearing of all the dangers we could encounter on this trip, it was a pleasure to view these creatures of the river. I continued watching the dolphins until they disappeared up river behind us. When I turned back towards the front of the boat, I saw three more river craft loaded with many forms of fruit traveling west towards the markets of Iquitos. I felt a tap on my shoulder and turned to see what Esteban needed. Motioning behind us he says, "I see another boat approaching on our side of the river, can you see what it looks like? They seem to be moving faster then we are, as they get closer let me know what you see."

I turned around on my seat and began watching the craft slowly gaining upon us. Within 20 minutes I could see a boat much larger than ours, with an awning stretched over the boat. I informed Esteban of what I could see of the boat and its passengers. Esteban turned and stated, "That is one of the new tour boats that take people to jungle lodges to visit in the jungle. These tours are becoming very popular with tourists who want to experience what life in the jungle is like. Most of these lodges are 25 or more miles from the city, at that distance they will have a better chance of seeing wildlife." I asked Esteban where the tour boat might be going, he stated that it could be going to a lodge on the Mazan River. The people onboard the boat waved and shouted greetings to us as they pulled ahead of us. It was a strange sight to see people on vacation, while we were traveling in the same direction on a much more serious venture.

I saw several more river craft carrying goods to Iquitos or beyond as the afternoon came to an end. Esteban mentioned that the island Juan would be stopping at would be in sight within the hour. Having spent the majority of the day in the boat, I was impatient to get to the island. I needed to stretch my legs and move about, the boat provided very cramped quarters for six people, equipment, and one dead fish.

I noticed Jason was also trying to find a comfortable position to place his legs, as he twisted one way and another. Turning I said, "If I saw the island from here I would jump overboard and swim to it."

Jason laughed saying, "I know what you mean, after a short time in this boat your legs want to cramp from lack of use. I plan on walking around as soon as we make shore; hopefully it will work out some of the cramps I've been feeling. Imagine traveling these rivers for weeks as Phillip must have done, I would assume they had to land periodically to release cramps and the monotonous routine of river travel. I'm glad we have the motor and the current seems steady, we should be able to travel 25 to 30 miles a day."

Before I could respond Esteban announced that the island was in sight. Looking up I could see a dark strip upon the river ahead, as we continued approaching it began to take shape. At this time in the early evening, the trees on the island blended with the trees along the sides of the river. I watched as Juan's boat began to slow and turn towards the right side of the island. I saw Juan shut his motor off and he motioned Esteban to do the same. The men used poles to guide the boats, as the current provided plenty of headway to maneuver along the shoreline.

Traveling slowly beside the island I began to wonder where we would be able to land. The shoreline was nearly covered with tall grass, several times we began to enter it only to be faced with an impenetrable wall of grass. After 15 minutes of weaving in and out of the tall grass, I saw Juan direct his men to turn towards the island. I could see Esteban was following the other boat, and as we turned towards the island I noticed the grasses seemed to close behind us. Within moments the lead boat came to a stop, and as we approached I could see a small clearing under the branches of nearby trees. The men jumped overboard and pulled the boat onto the small beach, while Esteban was directing them towards several tasks.

Jason and I stepped out of the boat and made our way to the others who were already on shore. As I approached Serge he said, "Look behind you, I doubt if we could be seen from the river. Juan has suggested we have an early meal and not have a fire during the night. The light from a fire can be seen for a long distance upon the river, and it could attract unwanted attention to us." We agreed and told the others about the fish that had been caught for the evening meal.

"Esteban says the fish is good to eat," Jason said as his stomach growled, announcing its need of food.

Julio laughed saying, "From the sounds of your stomach, I hope the fish is a large one. You may need a double portion to quiet that stomach of yours." Julio motioned everyone to follow him to a nearby tree and said, "Let's step over here while the men gather driftwood and prepare the fire. I spoke with Juan while we were traveling about any concerns he might have about the river or the men. He stated again that it would not be advisable to attract the attention of the people in the nearby village of Mazan. He has heard that there are several groups that will raid unprepared parties traveling the river, and some of the travelers have been lucky to survive the incident. I also will remind everyone to keep your weapons in good shape, if we need to use them it will be at a moment's notice. Juan mentioned that he had brought his personal weapon, which had been his father's, it's a 1907 Peruvian model Mauser 7.62mm. A very dependable rifle to have if trouble comes upon us suddenly."

I motioned Julio and said, "If possible I would like to get the SKS and several clips, so I will have it if I need it. From what you know of this area, do you also feel that we are traveling in potentially dangerous country?"

Nodding his head, with a serious look upon his face he said, "I do not doubt Juan in the least, this is still considered the frontier and as you recall your American frontier of the last century, it was considered dangerous for the unwary traveler. There are many small villages scattered along the rivers, and the people of these villages are very poor. Many of these people live in poorly made cane huts and their living conditions are terrible. The men fish when they feel like doing something and the rest of the time is spent drinking masato. The women do most of the work and are treated badly by their husbands. As you can imagine this type of environment will only produce trouble for the innocent traveler who happens upon these people. Juan's suggestion of taking precautions while traveling in the jungles should be heeded by all of us. If they see a party of travelers who are armed, it may be enough to convince them that they should wait for a group less prepared to defend themselves."

Julio puts his hand on Serge's arm and says, "Enough of this depressing conversation, let's get something to eat and discuss our next days travel. I believe we will see the Napo River within a day and a half and then we will be turning north. I hope the fish Efrain caught is tasty, I also think my stomach has forgotten what food is."

As we returned to the beach, I could see a fire burning with the fish spitted above the flames. Placed upon a grille under the fish I could see yuccas and plantains cooking over coals. The aromas of the cooking food were also causing my stomach to remind me of its empty condition. While waiting for the food, I noticed everyone was finding the mosquitoes very troublesome. We had attempted to spray ourselves with a repellent, but to no avail, the attack was continuous. I hoped the mosquito netting would help to protect us while we slept, if not, sleep would be very difficult to attain.

Approaching the fire, I could see Juan and his men were preparing to remove the fish from the spit. Juan noticed our return, and calls out, "Come my friends, try the fish that was caught earlier today. Sit near the fire it will help keep some of the mosquitoes from biting you. We must eat quickly and put the fire out, so it does not attract attention to ourselves. There is little traffic on the river at night, but you never know when someone might be returning late from some errand."

The fish was evenly split between everyone and with the addition of the yuccas and plantains, we were comfortably filled for the night. Juan directed the camp grounds be cleared for sleeping and the fire was extinguished. There was enough daylight to prepare the grounds for sleeping, and everyone began to arrange ground mats and spread their netting for later use.

While we were occupied with these tasks, Serge called to Juan saying, "Juan can I talk with you for a moment?" Juan finished speaking with one of the men and said he would be over in a moment.

Turning from his men, Juan proceeded through the camp to where Serge was standing. "Please sit with us for a moment," asked Serge as he settled himself on his sleeping mat. Juan accepted the offer and made himself comfortable on the mat. "I would like to thank you for a very successful first day of travel." stated Serge with a smile that reflected his appreciation. "I think I speak for everyone, when I say that you have given us a great deal of confidence in your abilities as a leader. The decision to spend the night on this island, instead of attempting to pass the village of Mazan before dark demonstrates the decision making we need. I have a question in regards to our safety that I would like to ask. Will you be having your men standing guard during the night?"

Juan, with a serious look upon his face said, "As you have noticed safety is foremost in my mind. When we left Iquitos, I left with the intention of returning to Iquitos with the whole party at the end of this expedition. Until we return, there will always be guards posted every night for the safety of the group. If any of your party would care to contribute their time for this duty, it would be appreciated. I hope this relieves any worries you might have had concerning the safety of the group while camping."

Smiling Serge said, "I appreciate your concern for the group and your professional approach to traveling in this country. Speaking for myself, I would like to contribute some of my time to providing security for the camp." After Serge finished speaking, we all responded that we would be willing to share in these duties.

Julio spoke up with a pleased look on his face, "This trip has begun in a very positive atmosphere of teamwork. I'm glad to see that everyone is willing to work together, but I would like to make one suggestion concerning guard duty. Realizing that three of our group has no experience with the jungle, I would suggest that they pair up with someone knowledgeable with this country." Turning to Juan, Julio asks, "Do you agree with that suggestion?"

Juan said he totally agreed with Julio, and then thanked everyone for their willingness to participate with this duty. Asking if there was anything else that Serge needed, he indicated he would like to settle the camp down for the night, and assign who would stand guard first. As he rose from the blanket he said, "I plan to have three-hour shifts, for the first night, I will use my men. If you care to, starting tomorrow you men can begin helping with this duty." Juan wished us a good night, and reminded everyone, that once the sun had set night would come upon us quickly. He indicated the night would be very dark, so be aware of where you are in reference to others around you. He warned that if we left our sleeping mats during the night we could be lost very quickly, so if you need to relieve yourselves, do so before the sun sets.

I asked Serge if he would care to look the area over a little bit before the sun had fully set. He agreed and as we walked towards the trees, I mentioned to Jason that we would only be gone for a few minutes. Nearing the trees I realized that evening had progressed enough that within the tree line the forest had become quite dark and visibility was very limited.

Serge turned to me and said, "I think we better wait until another time to venture into the forest, it's so dark we would be lost quickly."

"I agree completely," stated Julio from behind us, "the forest is very deceiving in the evening light. I saw the two of you walking towards the forest and I was concerned for your safety. When the sun sets in the jungle, it can drop a veil of darkness over everything in a very few minutes."

We agreed that returning to the camp was the prudent thing to do, and we would explore the forest another time. Upon reaching my sleeping mat I became aware of how quickly the evening sunlight had disappeared and darkness was quickly over taking our little camp. I noticed the fire had been completely extinguished and everyone was preparing their sleeping mats and netting for the night. Juan was stationing two of his men for the first watch and giving them their orders for the night. As instructed by Juan earlier, I could see Maria settled under her netting between Julio and myself. Turning to my right I could see Jason was completely covered by his netting, and his breathing indicated that he was close to sleep.

Using the last bit of light I positioned my netting as tightly as possible around me, as I could hear the constant buzzing of mosquitoes around my body. I had rolled a shirt for a pillow and tried to settle my mind to attempt to get some sleep. I had never slept in the jungle and as the night darkness settled over the camp, I realized that the jungle at night would be very different from the forests of North America. I became aware of a multitude of night sounds, from mellow sounding calls, to screeches resounding through the night. As my eyes began to adjust to darkness, I became aware of a multitude of flying creatures constantly flying around us. I could not see them, but their wings produced a constant droning sound that began to blend into the overall sounds of the night.

After adapting to the sights and sounds of the night, I became aware of the night sky. The sky was beautiful, a velvety black sky filled with bright twinkling lights. The sight was overwhelming and also calming, I began to dwell on the beauty of the sky and slowly the sounds of the night began to be replaced with the quiet beauty of the heavens. My last thoughts were of how great the maker of the universe must be to provide such a spectacular sight as what I had been able to see this night.

I awoke to Jason shaking my arm and telling me to begin rising and packing. I sat up with the netting hanging over my head and became aware of movement around me. The camp was stirring and I realized I better prepare to move when the word was given to enter the boats. While rolling my sleeping mat and netting together, I noticed there was just enough light to see what I was doing, but not enough to move about freely. Within a few moments Juan approached us and stated we will be leaving within 15 minutes, he said there would be enough light, so be ready to leave. As my eyes continue adjusting to the gradual light of dawn, I see Juan motioning the men to gather the equipment and he quietly tells everyone to begin moving to the boats.

Jason moves beside me and says Juan wants everyone to move as quietly as possible to the boats. I can hear whispered instructions being given, as everyone moves quickly towards the boats. As I approach the area where the boats had been pulled ashore, I notice several of the men pushing the boats into the water. I watch Julio approach the group and announce that we are to board the same boats we had traveled in the previous day. I notice Esteban seated in one of the boats and Jason and I move towards that boat. As I near the boat one of the men takes my gear and indicates I should move to the back of the boat. Jason quickly follows, and we are quickly seated and our gear stowed quietly. I notice the men have poles handy to push off from the beach, which I notice Juan has directed his crew to proceed doing.

Our progress seems to take forever through the tall grasses as we slowly weave in and out looking for a passage through the grass. As if by magic, the grasses seem to part as I watch Juan's boat slip through the grasses, and Esteban is quick to follow his lead. After Esteban clears the grasses he turns and starts the motor, which comes to life quickly. The sudden sound of the motor seems deafening, but I also become aware of the motor of the other boat coming to life.

Esteban leans towards us and says, "Don't be concerned about the noise of the motors, we are still several miles from the village of Mazan. Juan has directed that the motors be used to enter the current of the river and then they will be shutdown, from that point we will all paddle quietly. Try to relax, we will stop for something to eat after passing Mazan."

Thanking Esteban for the information he had given us, I turned and began to notice I could see a short distance from the boat. I could see a low fog shrouding the river, and the sounds from the jungle seemed to be muffled as from a distance. The river seemed to be moving at 2 to 3 miles per hour, which helped our boats to continue down river as swiftly as possible. Jason whispered that orders had been given that there was to be no talking except for emergencies, and movement within the boats was to be kept to a minimum. Within ten minutes Juan slowed his boat and as our boat came within 15 feet of each other he spoke to Esteban who immediately shut off his motor. As silence returned to the river, Juan gave Esteban some instructions and then turned to his people and spoke in a low voice. Esteban says something in a hushed voice and the men begin using the paddles within the boat to continue moving with the current.

After having drifted with the current for several minutes, Esteban leans towards us and said, "Juan wants us to drift with the current until we pass Mazan, I hope the people have not begun to move about within the village. Please watch Juan, he said he would signal by waving his arms, if our passing attracts attention. If we are seen he wants me to immediately start the motor and to move as quickly as possible down river. He will stay behind to cover our boat, and if we get separated he told me of a place that we will meet. I hope we can all slip by the village without being noticed."

While drifting upon the quiet river, I notice the visibility has gotten better and the fog has almost lifted. The silence encloses us like an envelope; it's as if we are the only people existing in this part of the world. I begin to notice sounds from the jungle, they seem to be more easily located and the animal calls have more clarity. The sounds of howler monkeys seemed very clear from the left side of the river, I knew our passage was not going undetected by the local wildlife.

After traveling for 30 minutes, I began to see small spots of light on the shore to our right. I could also make out the shape of several structures and the sound of a dog barking, hopefully not at us. Someone shouted something, and the dog quieted, but it still barked once or twice as we passed the village. We gradually passed Juan's boat, and he waved for us to continue down the river. It seemed to take an eternity to leave Mazan behind us, but eventually the river turned and we lost sight of the village. As we were starting to feel we had passed the dangers that had been waiting for us, I heard Efrain whisper something to Esteban.

Esteban had positioned one of the men in the bow of the boat as a lookout for any possibility of danger. Looking up I could see him pointing towards a small boat between the shore and us. I could hear an individual calling out to us saying, "*Quien va?*" and I noticed he had raised a rifle across his chest. Esteban said something in a low voice and slowly began turning the boat towards the small craft. Esteban had the men using their poles to guide our craft, not wanting to start the motor this close to the village. Esteban whispered something, and his man in the bow immediately called out to the other craft saying, "*Somos pescadores.*" I noticed the other man seemed to be uneasy and with little patience in his voice said, "*Traiga su bote para aqui se tiene que pagar impuestos por derechos al uso del rio,*" while shifting his legs and slowly moving the rifle to cover our approach. When we had approached within thirty feet, I noticed our man slowly move his arm towards his lower back and withdraw a knife from under his shirt. With great speed he threw the knife at the man. The guard staggered backwards clutching the knife that had suddenly appeared in his heart, dropping his rifle he fell overboard with a resounding splash. Esteban quickly turned the boat towards the center of the river, and the men began to use their paddles to quickly enter the main current. Once within the current, everyone seemed to take a deep breath and continued watching for any other witnesses to our passing.

Within a few minutes I asked Esteban why he attacked the fisherman? Leaning over he said, "That was no fisherman, he was a lookout for a group of river pirates. No fisherman carries a rifle like that man or speaks in such a commanding voice. He wanted to know who we were. We told him we were fishermen. I don't think he believed us. He ordered us to approach him, he said we had to pay a river tax. There is no river tax and if we had declined his order he would have shot at us. This would have brought many of his friends to investigate what the shot was all about. I told my man I would get him within knife throwing distance, and he was to remove the guard. He said he is very good with a knife, and can throw very accurately. I hope Juan passes that area before they decide to check on the guard."

Within a short period of time, daylight was sufficient to see the full extent of the river, and I could see Juan's boat behind us. Esteban must have heard Juan start his motor, because he proceeded to start our motor, which caught quickly as if anticipating a need to escape the area. Within a few minutes Juan passed our boat and together we continued down the river. Everyone seemed to relax with the village of Mazan behind us and with the prospect of seeing the Napo River the following day.

The river was its usual brown in color and the current seemed to move us east at a considerable speed, it soon became evident that we had escaped undetected and the motors were shutdown. With the sun rising above the treetops, our surroundings came into full view. Much as the previous day, the river was at least 150 yards across and the jungle grew up to the waters edge. I saw very few possible areas to beach the boats, as the terrain was heavily overgrown. Jason brought me back to reality by indicating river traffic to our left. I watched as three boats filled with produce were slowly moving west to Iquitos or beyond.

We had been traveling about an hour, when I noticed Juan turn and call out to Esteban. With a short laugh, Esteban says, "Jose has caught our breakfast, Juan wants us to follow his boat to shore." Looking towards Juan's boat, I see he is slowly turning towards the right shoreline. We approach within 50 yards of the shore waiting for Juan to decide were we would come ashore. Suddenly, Juan turns his boat to the right and as we follow I see a strip of beach approximately 50 feet long, with thick brush within 20 feet of the water. Our boats come ashore within moments of each other, and the men jump ashore accompanied by commands from Juan and Esteban. Jason and I step out of the boat into the warm brown water of the Amazon and walk up to the beach. I use the word beach, but there is no sand here, only a reddish-brown soil with scattered vegetation.

Turning I see Serge, Julio and Maria approaching up the beach, but I could see Julio wanted to speak with us. Julio greeted us and in a low voice said, "I saw an empty boat as we passed down the river in the darkness, did you have trouble? I heard no gun shots, but an abandoned boat is unusual to find on the river."

I stood in a position that would give me the ability to observe what was going on about us; I did not want to be overheard by the workmen. Keeping my voice low I said, "We came upon an individual in a small craft, which demanded we pay a river tax. He was carrying a rifle and seemed ready to enforce his demands. At first I thought he was a fisherman asking for help. Esteban later explained that fishermen are not armed as he was, and that there is no river tax. He felt he was a river pirate and was stationed as a lookout for others camped upon the nearby shore. Esteban had the men pole the boat towards the guard and when we were within range; one of the men threw a knife and killed the man. We proceeded as quickly as possible down river and we never heard anything from the shore."

Julio explained he and Juan had been concerned when they saw the empty boat, but since there was no activity-taking place in the area, we quickly moved towards the east. He was sorry that we had to take deadly action to remain undetected, but he felt Esteban's quick thinking probably saved all our lives. While Julio was speaking, I noticed the men had started a small fire and small red-headed fish were being hung above the flames. I caught Julio's attention and told him Juan was approaching our group.

"Julio bring your friends, the food will be ready shortly," calls Juan as he walks towards us, "I hope everyone is ready to eat? Jose has caught some pan fish that are very good, I hope you will enjoy them." As we began walking towards the fire, I noticed Juan ask Julio something and they remained in conversation for several minutes. I could see concern on Juan's face, but as he nodded his head, he seemed pleased with what he had been told.

Approaching the fire I could see green plantains and yuccas roasting upon the fire, with the fish hung from a rod above the flames. With the excitement of the morning I had forgotten about breakfast, but the aromas of the cooking food was quickly bringing my stomach back to life. Everyone was sitting around the fire and there was a lively conversation taking place between our brave knife welder and the other boatmen.

I asked Jason what the excitement was all about. Jason leaned next to me and said, "They are asking numerous questions about the actions their friend had taken this morning. They want to know what type of knife was used and how much distance was there between him and the pirate. Everyone wants an action report, and he is trying to answer all their questions, but as you can see with some difficulty. Juan calling everyone to breakfast rescued his man from the barrage of questions.

As predicted by Juan, the pan fish were delicious and I was already beginning to substitute the plantains for bread in my meals. I was resolved to try to eat foods from the land as much as possible, and leave the canned foods for emergencies. Julio opened several bottles of fruit juice, which were greeted with smiles by everyone. Within the hour we had finished our meal and the temporary campsite had been cleaned and the boats prepared to leave. Serge had explained to Juan, that there was a possibility that we could be followed, so whenever we come ashore, we must by very cautious not to leave evidence of our having been there.

With breakfast over, and the boats having been returned to the river, everyone settled themselves into the routine of river travel. It was becoming evident that you could travel for miles and not meet another human being, and the only sounds you would hear were from the jungle. The forest is as thick as usual, with the constant calling of birds and monkeys, which creates quite a volume of noise. The river maintains a consistent width of 150 yards and periodically we pass small islands, some with very little vegetation. During the morning hours we pass two more boats laden with produce, heading west. I also noticed that signs of human habitation were never evident, though we were a day and a half's travel from Iquitos, it felt like we were traveling in totally unexplored territory.

Later in the afternoon I noticed the shores to our right had become ten or fifteen feet high very abruptly. I had become so accustomed to the low flat shoreline, that it took several minutes to realize that the shoreline had changed. I could see the current was taking us closer to this shore and I could see that many trees along the small cliffs seemed ready to fall into the river. Within

15 minutes the shoreline had returned to what I was beginning to call normal, tall grasses or jungle growth touching the river.

Late in the afternoon I noticed Juan's boat begin to pick up speed, and within moments one of the men said something to Esteban. Our boat also begins to accelerate and stay within a short distance from Juan's boat. I turn to Esteban and ask if there is a problem, and he says, "No problem, he has heard the call of some monkeys, and the men want to go ashore and kill one for their evening meal." I said I had not heard anything, but he stated the men had heard their calls down river. I think we must have traveled a mile before I heard the sounds they spoke of. When we came around a gradual bend in the river, I saw a large group of large red monkeys leaping from tree to tree, making a noise like the grunting of a herd of enraged hogs. I could see the sight of the monkeys excited the men and within minutes the boats had been brought upon the shore.

With rifles in hand, the men ran into the undergrowth hunting the monkeys. As we came ashore, everyone but Juan and Esteban had disappeared from sight. I could hear their progress as they thrashed there way through the thick growth, and the slowly diminishing calls of the monkeys. Juan called us together and informed us that the men considered these red monkeys a delicacy, so they will be gone until they get one. At that moment we heard a couple of gun shots and then silence. Esteban suggested we open some beer while waiting for the men to return, his suggestion was quickly agreed upon by all. We were relaxing by the boats enjoying our beer, when the sounds of people moving through the underbrush could be heard. Turning I could see the men returning from the hunt carrying two monkeys. They called out with great excitement and brought the animals for everyone to see. The monkeys were about 18 inches long and covered with long, soft, maroon-colored hair, and they had a large goiter under their jaws. I was informed that this apparatus gave the monkeys the means of making their peculiar noise. I noticed one of the monkeys had a long red beard, I was informed that it was the male.

The men quickly began to gather driftwood and prepare a fire to roast the monkeys. I suggested to Serge that I would prefer eating something from a can for my evening meal, he fully agreed. Watching the men dress out the animals confirmed my desire not to share their meal this evening. Later that evening while the men enjoyed their feast, our group dined on beans and franks, and several bottles of Cristal.

As evening approached, Juan began directing the men to begin setting up camp and to prepare a fire that would be kept burning during the night. It was considered safe to have a small fire throughout the night, as long as sentries were posted. Juan indicated that he did not expect problems with any of the local people, but once we had entered the area north of Sta. Clotilde the situation would change. During the next half-hour everyone was occupied with setting up sleeping mats and netting and collecting wood for the fire.

I was sitting on my mat when Juan walked up to me and asked if I would be willing to join Esteban for the first watch. I told him I would be happy to help with this duty, and proceeded to rise from my mat. He said I should go talk to Esteban and coordinate where we would station ourselves. Jason had prepared his sleeping mat next to mine and I informed him that I would be on the first guard watch. I had kept my SKS in the boat, but had kept the clips in my pack. After retrieving my weapon from the boat I returned to my pack and removed a 30 round clip and inserted it into the weapon. I would chamber a round only after occupying my guard station.

I noticed Esteban had a rifle in his hands as I walked over to speak with him. I noticed he was nodding his head as I approached him, saying, "With that weapon, I feel sorry for anyone getting caught entering the camp unannounced. I appreciate your willingness to help with this duty; it means a lot to the men to have you share in some of the responsibilities of running the camp. I have selected two positions that should serve to protect the camp; I would appreciate your opinion on these positions." As he finished speaking, he led me away from the firelight and into the shadows of the camp. In a low voice, Esteban says, "I suggest we stay out of the light of the fire and position ourselves at each end of the shoreline. We should be able to hear anything that might come through the underbrush, with the majority of our attention centered on the river. An enemy could approach us from the river without our being aware of them until the last moment. I will take responsibility for keeping the fire burning, that way I will be the only person giving their position away. You will be in the shadows and not easily seen." I told him I agreed with him completely and said I would take the other end of the camp if that were acceptable with him. He thanked me again for my help, and said he would relieve me in four hours. I wished him good luck and walked around the camp to take up my position at the other end of the camp.

As I selected my position, I chambered a round in my rifle and placed the safety on. A box of canned goods was nearby, which I positioned so I could sit upon it when not walking. The camp had not fully settled down, I could hear low conversations taking place and the sounds of last minute decisions to move items. Within 20 minutes the camp had quieted down to the snoring of several sleepers, with only the night sounds of the jungle to disturb the quiet of the night.

When the sun has completely set and full darkness has settled upon the land, its enormity can be overwhelming. The jungle can be daunting in its danger and the mysteries that are hidden within its green carpeted terrain, but at night its dangers are hidden to the naked eye. There is a constant volume of sounds coming from all around you, and this becomes very unsettling as you stand by yourself in the darkness.

Though the camp was only 25 feet away, I felt very alone and vulnerable to the dangers around me. The night sounds of the jungle can be very frightening; especially to someone who has never spent time in this type of environment. I looked back at the camp to reassure myself that the rest of the party was still with me. While watching the river before me I became aware of movement to my right, turning I watched Esteban place some wood on the fire and quickly return to the darkness. I found Esteban's presence reassuring, which gave me the ability to relax and do my job. Turning back towards the river, I reflected on Esteban's presence of mind not to look towards me as he was placing wood on the fire.

I soon found myself becoming more attuned with my environment, and I noticed my senses seemed more alert to the sounds around me. I became aware of small sounds from the river, but as I let my senses adjust to the night, the sounds seemed less intimidating. As I relaxed and let myself become part of the night, a new feeling of appreciation for this new world I had stepped into began to surface within me. I had discovered beauty during the daylight hours, but I began to recognize there was a beauty to appreciate during the night. Looking at the night sky was breathtaking, a velvet black dome with bright diamonds shining through. The sight was so overwhelming that I had to pull myself away from dwelling on the majesty of such a sight.

My first tour of guard duty passed quickly without incident, and before I was aware of it, Esteban quietly told me to get some sleep. I returned to my sleeping mat and rolled the netting over me, the protection was welcomed after having been feasted upon while on guard duty. Sleep came quickly and I vaguely remember Serge and Juan taking the next four-hour shift. My last thoughts were of the drone of mosquitoes and wondering if the next day would bring the Napo River into sight.

I awoke to the smell of frying eggs and plantains. Sitting up I was aware that I had over slept, and everyone was eating or waiting for the next helping to be served. I looked up to see Maria walking towards me saying, "You must have been very tired after your time on guard duty. How do you feel?"

"I feel pretty good, but I was quite tired," I said as I rose from my mat. Pointing towards the cooking fire, I said, "Where did the eggs come from?"

Laughing Maria says, "The men went into the forest and returned with the eggs. I'm not sure what type of bird they come from, but everyone likes them."

I rolled my bedding up and placed it in the boat with Maria keeping me company. Together we walked over to the fire and watched one of the men put peppers, onions and eggs in the pan and scrambles them together. I had to admit, what was in the pan looked good enough to eat, and my stomach was ready.

While eating, Julio pointed to the dishes and said, "Take a plate and enjoy the omelet, it's very tasty. We will be leaving soon after breakfast. Juan states that we should make the Napo today, possibly by the middle of the afternoon."

The eggs were good and I never asked what kind of bird was responsible for the eggs. Within a half-hour, everyone was packed and the boats were loaded. Juan had detailed two of the men to clean the campgrounds so only a close check would reveal that someone had camped there. It was best to take these precautions, because professor Segault was always on our minds. Julio had indicated that once we had left Trujillo, there was no one to watch for curious strangers, asking about North American adventurers going into the jungle.

Juan pointed out that there were a number of clouds in the sky, and unless the winds picked up from the west, we could have rain later in the day. The Amazon was as brown as ever, and the current quickly took our boats into the river. We passed several boats going west laden with produce, and the people onboard waved in a friendly manner. As the morning progressed, the wind from the west that Juan had mentioned began to make itself felt, and before long the clouds had disappeared. The morning hours passed without incident, and around noon we passed between two islands. As I looked towards the right shore I could see a pleasant shoreline of green banks slowly rising up to the forest. I pointed to the area and asked Esteban if people had ever lived there.

Nodding his head he said, "Yes, many years ago. They say there was a small village located upon the upper banks, but raiders from Pebas attacked the village and burned it to the ground. It is said that the people from the village were taken to Pebas and were never heard from again. That is one story, but I have heard another story that is more believable. I have heard that the villagers left freely to follow a priest to Pebas who wanted to establish a new town. The town was to be located near a stream known as the Ambiyacu, which entered the Amazon two miles above Pebas. I have never been to Pebas, so I cannot verify which of the stories are true."

Passing the snug little harbor formed by the islands and shoreline, I found it hard to believe that anyone would freely leave such a beautiful area. Esteban said that Juan had instructed him to have everyone eat on the boat today, he did not want to stop for a meal until the Napo was sighted. Esteban instructed Efrain to get crackers, cheese and beer for everyone. The next two hours were spent watching the jungle pass quietly, with only one more produce boat going west.

Without warning, Esteban taps me on the shoulder and points to the left saying, "There is the Napo." At first I don't see anything different about the jungle, but as we continue down river, I begin to notice a finger of land disappearing into the Amazon. Within 10 minutes the mouth of the Napo River is revealed, it is at least 200 yards across. It is truly a beautiful sight to watch a large river merge with a mighty river like the Amazon.

While watching the Napo, I become aware of Juan turning his boat towards the left shore and as quickly Esteban follows his lead. Esteban states, "Juan is planning to spend the night at the mouth of the Napo. The Napo River can be a dangerous river to travel upon, so I think Juan wants to discuss the best way for traveling up the river. I have only traveled as far as Sta. Clotilde, Juan is more familiar with this country, but I know it is dangerous."

As we continued towards the northern shore, I couldn't help wonder if the professor was behind us. Serge had indicated that the professor could be a very determined man, and someone who would probably stop at nothing to attain what he wanted. If we found the city, would the professor attempt to take whatever we found, and if necessary by force? I was determined that if it came to that, he would have a fight on his hands. We had spent too much time and effort to timidly hand anything over without a fight.

8
Into the Interior

After landing on the northern shore of the Amazon, Juan directed the men to set up camp. It became evident that after traveling for only three days, the men had developed a routine in setting up camp quickly. The grounds were cleared and the firewood was gathered and stacked, all in a short period of time. After the initial setting up of the camp, Juan called two of his men, and discussed something, which involved their taking the rifles with them. I assumed they were going into the jungle to hunt for the evening meal.

I gathered my gear from the boat and found a level spot that I would use for my sleeping area. Shortly after setting my sleeping mat on the ground, and putting my pack on top of it, Serge called out, "Could everyone come over here. I would like to coordinate the next leg of our journey." As we gathered around Serge, he suggested we find a location where we could talk privately. Julio indicated we should follow him, and he led us along the shore about 90 feet from the camp. Serge asked everyone to relax, he felt it was necessary to discuss the next stage of our journey and answer any questions anyone might have.

Turning to Julio, Serge says, "I will talk with Juan after this discussion is finished, but I felt we should discuss any concerns that anyone has about the next segment of the trip. Traveling in two boats, presents a small problem in daily communication between all members of the party, and by the time we stop for the evening there is little time to talk. We also have very little private time as a group to discuss our concerns between ourselves. I will also be discussing the next leg of the journey with Juan as I had promised him, but I will only indicate we are searching for signs of ancient Inca remains. I will also indicate that we will be traveling northwest on the Curaray River, and I will remind him that we are not entering Ecuador. Are there any questions concerning the trip so far, or on the rest of the journey?"

Maria raised her right hand motioning Serge that she wanted to speak. "Yes Maria, what are you concerned about?" responded Serge.

Maria slowly looked around the small group and said, "As you know I am trained in the medical field, and because of that training I have some concerns I would like to mention. We have now traveled many miles into the jungle, and I would like to remind everyone of some basic precautions to practice while in this environment. Please remember that river water is dangerous for drinking, you may wash in it, but do not drink it without boiling the water. I know you have been vaccinated for malaria, but there are many infectious plants and insects in the jungle, so be aware of any cuts or bites that show signs of infection. That is all I have at this time." After speaking Maria put her hands in her lap and visibly relaxed. Serge thanked her for her advice and stated that he appreciated her concerns about these matters.

Serge asked if there were any further questions before he revealed further information to Juan. Everyone seemed encouraged with the progress the group had made since leaving Iquitos, and they looked forward to the next segment of the trip. Turning to Julio, Serge said, "I would appreciate it if you would join me while I explain to Juan further details about our journey."

"I would be pleased to join you."

Serge turns to the rest of the group and says, "If there are no further questions, Julio and I will find Juan and discuss the trip."

I followed Maria and Jason as we returned to the campsite, where we continued arranging our sleeping areas. I watched Serge and Julio walking towards the camp, they were deep in conversation. As they were passing our sleeping area, Serge leans towards me and says, "Would you mind joining us?" I turn and follow them as they approach Juan, who is stacking wood next to the fire.

Juan turns as he notices our approach, and said, "I saw you had a private talk. I hope there are no problems with our progress or the men?"

Serge smiles and said, "No, there are no problems. I had promised that once we had reached the Napo River, I would give you further details about the trip. If you have a few minutes, we would like to make you aware of further details about our destination."

Juan motions for us to relax around the fire, and says, "I am pleased you would like to confide further information to me. I hope you are pleased with our progress and with the way things are organized?"

Nodding his head, Serge said, "You are doing a good job, and we appreciate how you have things organized. We have arrived at the Napo River and as I had indicated several days ago, we need to travel up river to the Curaray River. You had mentioned that we would need to pass Sta. Clotilde without being observed, could you give us more details about the area north of here?"

Juan reached into the pile of firewood and selected a slender stick, without saying a word he began to make several marks in the soil at his feet. After making his sketch, he points with the stick at one of the lines and says, "This is the Amazon River, and this is where we are." Moving the stick to a line that connects with the line representing the Amazon River, Juan says, "This is the Napo River, and this mark represents Sta. Clotilde. As we travel north on the Napo you will see several smaller rivers feeding into the Napo. Also, the river will gradually decrease in width, as you can see, here the river is almost 200 yards wide. When we pass Sta. Clotilde, the river will be approximately 80 yards wide, which will make our traveling by the village very risky. Another problem we will encounter as we travel up river, will be the current. The average velocity of the river south of Sta. Clotilde will be three to four miles an hour; we will be traveling against a strong current. This is wild country, and the travel will progressively be more demanding on everyone. The majority of the shorelines will be covered with trees, bushes, and wild cane. I anticipate that there will be times when we will have to carry the boats around difficult areas of the river. During these times we must be on the alert for wild animals and renegades, we will be very vulnerable to attack while carrying the boats."

As Juan paused, Julio states, "I see why you mentioned that we should be armed while traveling in this country. Do you expect trouble with people along the river?"

Moving the stick above the mark for Sta. Clotilde, Juan says, "I have heard of attacks on small groups north of Sta. Clotilde, in this area. You have mentioned traveling on the Curaray River; there are no settlements in that part of the country. I have heard of Indians attacking outsiders who they feel are trespassing in their country. This line represents the Curaray River where it meets the Napo River and this is the Napo River continuing north to Pantoja, a small village near the border of Ecuador. We will be traveling in unexplored territory, and if we are attacked, no one will be coming to our rescue. Please remember my precaution concerning your weapons keep them well oiled. I also suggest that it would be best not to mention the Curaray River around the men. They would fear going into that part of the country, and would attempt to steal one of our boats and return to Iquitos. Could you tell me what you are looking for that is worth putting your lives in such danger?"

Looking at the marks in the soil that Juan had made, Serge says, "Could I borrow your stick for a moment?" Juan hands the stick to Serge. Serge then proceeds to circle an area west of the line, which represents the Curaray River. After completing his circle, Serge says, "We hope to find evidence of

Inca ruins in this area, which is why we are traveling into this country. Due to security reasons, I will give you further directions as we travel up the Curaray River. I hope this arrangement is still agreeable with you?"

Juan leans forward and removes the marks he and Serge had made in the soil, after satisfying himself that everything had been removed, he raises his eyes to look at Serge. "Yes, I can accept the arrangement," says Juan as he takes his hat off and wipes the sweat from his forehead. Putting his hat back on his head, he says, "I hope these precautions have nothing to do with your trusting me as your guide. I will not reveal anything you have told me in confidence, and I will only tell Esteban what he needs to know."

Serge reassured Juan that he had our full trust, but we felt more secure in keeping our final destination a secret for the time being. He reminded Juan of the untrustworthy situation with the help he had been able to hire in Iquitos.

Nodding his head, Juan says, "I cannot find fault with your reasoning. The men I had to hire are not dependable, especially if danger threatens. If they knew we were going deep into the interior, they would surely return to Iquitos at the first opportunity."

"How long will it take to get to the Curaray River?" asked Julio, as he was wiping his face with a scarf he had taken from his pocket.

Juan began to rub his chin in thought saying, "I would estimate six or more days, if the river is not too difficult to travel. We will travel up the west side of the Napo River for several days, and as we near Sta. Clotilde, we will cross to the east side of the river. We must be very careful traveling near the village; our passage must go unnoticed." I spoke up and said, "We appreciate the precautions you are taking to protect everyone, but I would like to remind you of the danger that might be following us. Serge has indicated that Professor Segault is a determined man, and he may only be a few days behind us. I would suggest you inform Esteban of this danger, so he can also be prepared if problems present themselves."

Juan nods his head in agreement and said, "Serge has informed me of the professor, and the possibility of his attacking our group. You have not told me what you are searching for, but it must be very important to attract this much attention. I have never heard of Inca ruins this deep in the jungle, but Julio has reassured me that you have spent many months researching for this expedition. I will do everything possible to make this trip a success, and I will be watchful for any danger following us."

We thanked Juan for speaking with us, and as we were beginning to rise from the ground, a shot rang out from the forest. Juan says, "I hope the men were successful in getting something good for the evening meal. I sent two men to try and kill a deer, I hope they were lucky." Juan also rises and says he will begin sharpening a knife for skinning the animal, and proceeds to walk towards his equipment.

Noticing the looks of concern from Maria and Jason, we inform them of the possibility of venison for our evening meal. Everyone continued cleaning gear or writing in personal notebooks as we waited for the return of the hunters. Within a half-hour, I could hear the men returning, they shouted a greeting as they neared the camp. I was sitting on my sleeping mat and turned as the hunters enter the camp from the forest. Each man was carrying a hindquarter over his shoulder and a rifle in his other hand.

While watching them enter the camp, Jason turns to me and said, "They are very happy with their kill. It looks like it was a young animal, and should be good eating. Juan asked if they had seen any signs of other people, and they indicate they saw no one in the jungle. Did Serge give Juan more details concerning our route of travel?"

While reaching for my backpack, I turned towards Jason and said, "Yes, but only enough to get us north of Sta. Clotilde. We will fill him in after passing the village; it is a precaution we need to take." I pause for a moment and remove the cleaning kit for my pistol from my backpack saying, "It might be a good idea to clean your pistol while we have some free time, the humidity will cause rust to appear quickly." Jason agreed and proceeded to follow my example by cleaning his pistol. I had a feeling that Juan's warnings concerning the danger of traveling north on the Napo River should be taken seriously, and it would be best to be prepared if danger threatened.

Cleaning our weapons gave us the opportunity to talk in a relaxed manner about the jungle and what we had seen for the last three days. Our conversation flowed easily while we worked on the pistols, each of us commenting on the insects, food, and the countryside we had seen.

"Do you mind a little company?" asked Serge as he sat next to me on my mat. He was carrying his cleaning kit and proceeded to open it and begin removing his cleaning tools. After arranging his cleaning tools from the box, he says, "I noticed what you two were doing, and realized that I had better do the same. Also, you appeared so relaxed over here, that I just had to join you. I hope you don't mind a little company?"

I laughed and said, "Your more than welcome. We were just comparing notes concerning our travels so far and what possibly could be waiting for us as we travel up the Napo River. I find it relaxing to keep busy, especially doing things that need to be done." Turning to Serge I ask, "How is everything going for you, is the trip progressing as you had hoped?"

Serge had broken his pistol down and laid the parts on the mat for ease of cleaning. While running a patch down the barrel he says, "So far I feel confident in our ability to find the ruins. Julio and I have had the ability to privately share our thoughts concerning our progress and we both feel that we are making good time. Julio continues to assure me that Juan can be trusted, and I must admit so far I have no reason to doubt that trust." We continued a light conversation while cleaning our pistols, until Jason remarked that something smelled very good. We all looked up to observe what was cooking.

"That's an interesting way to cook over a fire," remarked Serge. "He has that stick so he can rotate the roast for even cooking."

Looking towards the fire, I see one of the men had placed a roast on the end of a stick and propped the stick upon three sticks that had been tied together to form a vertical brace to hold the stick. He had also taken a branch and removed the 'Y' that formed the joining of two branches and placed the 'Y' upside down in the ground. The stick holding the roast was wedged under the inverted 'Y' and rested upon the tied three sticks. This arrangement gave him the ability to slowly rotate the roast for even cooking.

We watched him for a few minutes and then returned to cleaning our weapons. As we were putting our cleaning tools away, and returning our pistols to our holsters, I heard Julio say, "Could I interest anyone in a beer?" Turning I see Julio and Maria smiling as they handed each of us a beer. Julio says, "I wish they were cold, but at least they are wet. This heat will drain you of fluids quickly, so drink up. Juan says the food will be ready soon, and they are cooking rice and black beans. This will be a treat to have fresh meat, most of the time we will be eating fish or canned foods."

The evening was approaching as the food was ready to serve, and everyone enjoyed the venison. The only problem during the meal was as the evening breeze stopped that was when the mosquitoes arrived. We quickly grabbed repellent from our packs and passed it around to each other. The tiny insects were quick and moved to the attack before we could cover ourselves with repellent.

Juan must have noticed our discomfort and spoke quickly to Esteban, who ran towards the boats. As he was running he said something to two of the men, who quickly put their food down and went towards a nearby tree. They proceeded to pick a hand full of leaves and place them on the ground near the fire. Esteban returned with three small clay pots, he removed some matches and proceeded to light the small candles in each of the pots. The men took the leaves, which had begun to dry near the fire, and they crumbled the leaves and gave them to Esteban. Esteban placed the leaf fragments in the clay pots and placed the pots around the group.

After Esteban had finished placing the pots among the group, Juan says, "The leaves from that tree will help keep the mosquitoes away. Try to sit near the pots and let the smoke pass over you. The mosquitoes do not like the smoke and will keep their distance. I will have the men collect some leaves and dry them for future use during our trip."

The smoke helped keep the mosquitoes at a distance, but everyone still felt the bite of a determined insect every few minutes. Everyone enjoyed the meal and as the sun was beginning to settle behind the jungle trees, everyone slowly began to make their way to their sleeping mats. The mosquito netting would be welcomed tonight by all, as the insects moved among us in small black clouds. As I was settling under my netting, Jason commented he had guard duty that night. I wished him well, and told him to wake me if there were any problems. Before closing my eyes, I made a final check of my netting to confirm that there were no openings for insects to attack me during the night.

The last of the evening light was fading quickly as everyone in the camp was making his or her final arrangements for the night. I noticed several of Juan's men sitting around the fire, quietly conversing and passing several bottles of beer from man to man. Juan and Esteban were sitting in Juan's sleeping area, and seemed to be deeply involved in their own conversation. I had traveled three days with these men, and only as I rested beneath my netting, did I become aware of their appearance. The five men sitting around the fire were dressed in old tee shirts, old gym shorts, and sandals. Only now did I become aware that Juan and Esteban wore trousers instead of shorts and they both had well cared for boots. The physical appearance of all seven men was much the same, black hair and dark eyes, semi-Caucasian features, and various shades of brown skin. They all were about 5' 6" tall with slender body structures, and with a tendency towards moving at a slow pace. I was quickly coming to the realization that in the jungle time has no meaning, these people had no understanding of time schedules.

As I watched the men talking around the fire, I realized my eyes wanted to close. The sounds of the jungle seemed to blend in with the low conversations of the men and as I listened to the drone of the insects, I slowly fell asleep to the soothing sounds all about me.

I awoke to the sounds of monkeys howling in the jungle. Removing my netting from my head, I could see one of the men stirring the fire and placing a pot above it. The camp was coming to life, so I proceeded to gather my sleeping gear and prepare for another day. While walking towards the boat to stow my gear I notice there is a light breeze blowing from the west with a few small clouds slowly rising above the trees across the Amazon River. After placing my gear aboard the boat, I notice Juan speaking with Serge.

While walking towards Serge, I hear Juan say, "I would suggest that we eat a quick breakfast and begin our journey up the Napo. These early morning clouds and the breeze from the west could be announcing a storm later in the day. We are entering the dry season, but storms are not unheard of this time of the year."

With some concern on his face, Serge said, "We will have our equipment packed and on the boats whenever you are ready to leave. I will let my people know that we are to leave after everyone eats." Juan thanked Serge for his assistance, and turning shouted something to one of his men.

Serge must have heard me approaching, as he was turning towards me he said, "I guess you heard what Juan was saying, he suspects a storm may hit us later today. Let's tell the others, and make sure they will be ready to leave when Juan gives the word to board the boats."

We had rice and beans for breakfast and within an hour everything had been cleaned and packed aboard the boats. During breakfast Juan had informed Esteban that they would use the motors to enter the Napo River and they would remain within 50 yards of the western shoreline. He said he would indicate when they would shut off the motors and everyone would help with the paddling.

After everyone had settled themselves aboard their boats, Juan made a last inspection of the campsite. He had told Serge that he did not want to help the professor to find us, so a clean campsite would benefit our trying to stay out of sight. Juan returned to the group and signaled Esteban to proceed into the river, starting the motor he immediately turned into the river. Within a few minutes Juan had taken the lead, and Esteban fell in behind Juan's boat. We followed the finger of land that separated the Amazon and the Napo River's until the opportunity presented itself to turn into the Napo River. The current was not as strong as the Amazon was, so entering the river was not too difficult and we soon began moving north towards Sta. Clotilde. We used the motors for almost a half-hour and Juan signaled that they should be shutdown. Esteban followed Juan's example and shut his motor off. Everyone picked up a paddle and a steady pace was soon set that over came the current that was confronting us.

The morning progressed quietly as we traveled up the river, with only an occasional animal call from the forest. The shoreline resembled what we had grown accustomed to while traveling east on the Amazon with very little change in jungle growth. The jungle grew down to the shoreline and very few open areas were available for landing.

Around noon we passed a small island with several trees and undergrowth covering the land. Nearing the island I could hear the calls of many birds. Esteban tapped my shoulder and said, "Look, up in the trees. The noise you hear is coming from the parrots, they are all over the trees."

Looking up into the trees I could see many parrots of various kinds with brilliant plumage. The majority of the birds were the yellow-headed, green bodied variety, and they could be heard a 100 yards from the island. As we were passing the island the upstream end of the land ended in a large area of tall grasses. In among the grasses could be seen a large gathering of black river ducks, who seemed unconcerned about our presence, and paid little attention to our passing.

Within an hour, Juan motioned that he was going to land on a small shelf of ground projecting from the river. Esteban steered towards the shore and as we neared the land two of the men jumped over the side and pulled the boat ashore.

Juan called out saying, "We will take a short break for a quick lunch, and nothing will be cooked. Esteban open some cans of sardines and a box of crackers. We will eat that and drink some beer and return to the river."

As I made my way through the water towards the shore, I felt exhausted and ready to drop. I thought about the sardines and crackers and felt at that moment I would much rather enjoy a steak and baked potato. My hands and wrists were sore and painful from rowing and they were beginning to show signs of sunburn. The realization that traveling up the Napo River would be quite different from traveling on the Amazon River was settling in quickly. Jason and I had discussed the need to get our bodies ready for the ordeals of traveling in the jungle, but as reality set in, it was evident that my body needed more conditioning.

I located a patch of ground that seemed clear of snakes and other deadly creatures, and set my weary body down. "I could hear you moaning from 20 feet away," says Serge as he walks toward me. With a smile on his face he says, "Do you mind a little company?" as he slowly lowers his body to the ground.

I wait until he is sitting and said, "Please have a seat. I was not aware that I was moaning, but rowing this morning just about did me in. At this moment I am feeling all of my 35 years, my body is aching from muscles I didn't know I had."

Serge laughs and says, "I know what you mean. The last time I rowed a boat, I had a young lady with me in the moonlight, and I was not rowing very much."

As I was about to ask about the young lady, I began to feel something biting my legs. I jumped up and pulled my pant leg up and saw small red marks on my legs. Serge had also risen and as we were brushing our legs, I heard Juan say, "You have just met some Peruvian sand flies, their bites will itch for a while, but it is best not to sit on the ground. Come over to the boats and get something to eat, before we continue up the river."

The insects seemed to find us quickly and swarmed around us as we tried to eat without swallowing a mouth full of bugs, which seemed determined to eat our food. Everyone quickly finished their food, and without any encouragement from Juan the men indicated they were ready to continue up river. As we were leaving the shore, I noticed the clouds from the morning had cleared away and the sky was a brilliant blue with a blazing sun beating down on the jungle.

Once we had returned to our position upon the river, and the motors were shut-off, I became aware that the bugs seemed to have remained on shore. Before the motor was shut down, Jason had given me a bottle of sunscreen, suggesting I cover the exposed parts of my body. I quickly applied a coating to the backs of my hands and on my neck. Jason doesn't say much, but his mind is always working.

The afternoon passed quietly as we rowed up the Napo River. We had traveled many miles and had not seen a single human being. I mentioned to Jason that it felt like we had slipped into another world, a place where the only human beings that inhabited it were the twelve of us.

He agreed, saying, "This was the first day of travel that I truly felt we had left all forms of civilization behind us."

Esteban had rotated the rowing, so there was always one person resting in the bow of the boat. This individual was given the opportunity to rest, but also he was to be on the lookout for any obstructions in the water. My turn had arrived to rest in the bow of the boat, and while resting I notified Esteban that I could see a large island up ahead. We could see Juan was turning his boat towards the island, and Esteban proceeded to do the same. The island was covered with trees and undergrowth and seemed to have no cleared area to land. I could see Juan was slowly circling to the west side of the island looking for an opportunity to go ashore. The island seemed to be shaped like a teardrop, with the largest area facing downstream. As we continued along the shoreline, Juan suddenly turned towards the island. I could feel Esteban turning our boat to follow in the direction Juan had taken.

The grasses near the shore were only four feet tall and Juan's boat passed through them with ease. As our boat entered the grass, I could see a small cleared area under some low hanging branches. Juan had his boat pulled ashore, and we quickly ran our boat alongside his boat.

I was starting to rise from my seat, when Esteban said, "Please stay in the boat for a few minutes. Juan will have the men clear an area for camp, just sit and watch how quickly they remove the undergrowth." Looking towards Juan's boat, three of his men were taking large machetes from the boat and began walking through the water towards the shore. The machetes have long handles, which the men swing with both hands and quickly cleared a large area for the evening camp.

Within 15 minutes, Juan gives the signal for everyone to come ashore. It's obvious everyone is tired and sore from a day of rowing up the river and Juan suggests that we have a quick meal. A fire is prepared as one of the men prepares rice and beans for everyone, and Jason removes a box of crackers from his pack to be shared with the group.

I feel exhausted and every muscle in my body is complaining. I thought I was in good shape, but a day of rowing against the current of a river will reveal muscles unprepared for such exertion. I quickly found a spot for my sleeping mat and was determined to relax after eating. As I was clearing the ground, Serge approached saying, "I feel like I could sleep for a week. How do you feel?"

"I may be asleep before the sun goes down," I respond as I turned rubbing my arms. "Rowing is an exercise I had never spent much time practicing. This trip will sure prepare me for any future requirements for rowing anywhere in the world. I just hope that I never have to use the experience in the future."

Serge smiles and said, "I asked Juan if we could use the motors for a few hours each day. He said he was concerned with the amount of gasoline that would be used, but he agreed that he would use the motors. Juan mentioned that there was an old trading post north of Sta. Clotilde near the Curaray

River. He had visited the store several times over the past few years, and remembered that they sold gasoline. He also suggested that if we used the motors we could save a couple days travel time. I told him we would be willing to take the chance of finding gasoline at the country store. He agreed to use the motors for several hours starting tomorrow."

With a relieved look on my face, I said, "Thanks; I appreciate you saying something to him. How are Julio and Maria holding up?"

Smiling, Serge says, "They seem to be doing fine. Maria has told me to remind you and Jason to use your sunscreen." Looking at my hands he says, "I'm glad I said something. You got quite a dose of sun today, I hope you're not burned too bad." I indicate that I'm sore, but I'll be all right after a good night's rest. During our conversation Juan calls everyone to get some food, and the reaction of everyone indicates he won't have to make a second call for dinner.

As everyone finishes their meal, Juan says, "I would like to caution everyone about staying near the camp tonight. I have seen signs of alligators, and they grow very large in this country. Also, those on guard duty tonight, must be especially careful of alligators coming ashore. They have been known to come ashore and drag a sleeping man into the river." It was evident that these words of caution had a great impact on everyone, as several of use began eyeing the shoreline for attacking alligators.

With the setting of the sun, and dusk quickly setting over the land, everyone began settling their sleeping gear for the night. I had already pulled my netting over my head, and was prepared to get a good night's rest, when Esteban approaches and says, "How are you doing?" I immediately became suspicious of his concerns about my well being.

Pulling the netting from my head, I said, "I'm fine. It's been a long day and I'm ready to get some rest." His next words caused all thoughts of sleep to flee into the night.

With a smile and chuckle he says, "You have guard duty. You ate such a good meal I know you would prefer not going to bed on a full stomach."

Rising from my sleeping mat, and releasing a moan of resignation, I proceed to take the SKS and load a clip. "Where would you like me to be stationed?" I ask, as I begin to follow Esteban towards the fire.

He motions towards the boats and says, "Stay near the boats and watch the shoreline. Juan was very serious about the alligators. Do not hesitate to shoot if you see one come ashore, they are very fast, and can attack before you are aware of their presence." I indicate that I had taken Juan's warning very serious and would be on my guard for any uninvited guests from the river.

I decided to make myself comfortable in one of the boats, but realizing how exhausted I was from the days' travels, I kept myself in a sitting position. The sky was darkening quickly and I could hear the camp settling down for the night. The sounds from the jungle indicated the wildlife was preparing itself for the coming night. I watched birds fly low over the water, looking for one more fish for the night. The sights and sounds of the jungle were calming, and only the sound of a splash from the river brought me back to full wakefulness. I realized I had begun to doze off and the sound could be an alligator moving into the river, and this thought kept me fully awake.

A slight breeze began, which helped keep the mosquitoes from completely covering me. The repellent helped, but I was painfully aware that nothing would keep all the biting insects from enjoying a taste of my body.

Within a half-hour darkness had fallen upon the jungle and only the night sounds could be heard. Everyone had made his or her final preparations for the night and the camp had become quiet, with only the occasional snap of wood from the fire. My four hours passed without incident, and only when Esteban approached was I aware that my time was over.

"Did you see anything while you were here?" said Esteban as he approached the boat.

"No, everything was quiet, only the sounds of the night. Was everything quiet for you?"

"Only a few alligators, but nothing that threatened the camp," said Esteban. "Did you see any alligators?"

Getting out of the boat, I said, "No, I don't think they came near this area."

I could hear Esteban chuckle, as he pulled a flashlight from his pocket. Turning on the flashlight he says, "Let's see if the area is clear."

As Esteban pointed the light towards the water, I could see two little red dots glowing just above the surface. He slowly moved the light back and forth and several more sets of red dots became visible. I realized that several alligators were just off shore and had been watching me for a period of time.

Turning I said, "I never heard a sound. How did they get so close?"

"Once they enter the water, they can move as quietly as a shadow upon the water," said Esteban. Putting the flashlight away he says, "I will warn the next sentry to stay on guard for them. I can see they are very curious about us." Esteban pats my arm and says, "Get some sleep, Juan wants to leave at first light. We have several more days of travel before we reach Sta. Clotilde."

I wished him a good night, and went to find my sleeping mat. I was bone tired and my shoulders and hands ached from the days rowing. A good night rest was something I was ready to take advantage of, if only I could get my mind off the alligators. Rolling out my bedding I checked for any uninvited snakes or other guests, and quickly wrapped the mosquito netting around me. I fell asleep to the sounds of flying insects around my head, and the thoughts of an alligator wanting to drag me off into the river.

We traveled up the Napo River for the next two days without seeing any signs of other people. The river gradually narrowed to 120 yards in width, and the current became stronger as we continued upriver. Juan estimated we had come half the distance to Sta. Clotilde, and warned everyone to be on guard for unexpected encounters with local people.

Our fourth day on the river dawned with gray clouds gathering from the west. A strong breeze was helping to move the clouds towards the east and Juan said he could feel rain in the air. Juan suggested we could continue moving up the river and if the storm did not blow away, we would come ashore and wait it out. Expecting the worse, everyone packed quickly and pushed the boats into the river. Juan said he would use the motors until the rains came, to gain as much distance as he could get with the threat of a storm ending out travels for the day.

Once we had moved into the river, I asked Esteban if he thought the clouds would pass without any problems. Looking up at the sky, he shook his head, and said, "No, this time we will have some rain. The season for storms is almost over, but some still come in from the west. Juan will keep a watch, if the rain begins he will head for the shore."

Turning to Jason, I ask, "How are you doing so far? Has the journey been anything like you had expected?"

Smiling, he said, "I'll be honest with you. I didn't know what to expect, but so far I'm doing fine. The heat and insects were expected, but the reality of living in this environment is a real eye opener. This country is as wild as anything you could have imagined." Looking towards the gathering clouds, he says, "I hope Juan turns to the shore shortly. Have you noticed how rough the river has become?"

I had noticed the surface of the river had become very rough with small white caps flying with the stiffening breeze. Using my hands to brace myself I said, "Yes, the wind is really picking up and I can see Juan is guiding his boat closer to the shore. This could be quite a storm." I also found myself holding onto my seat, due to the rocking of the boat within the rough waters of the river.

Within an hour the rain began to fall, and Juan directed the boats towards the shoreline.

He had found a clear shelf of land where the boats could be pulled ashore. We made the shore before the storm hit with its full fury, and Juan had the boats tied to trees for safe keeping. As we gathered near the boats, I looked up to the sky and noticed that it had changed quickly from gray to black.

"Take cover near the boats," shouted Juan, "This storm will be very violent."

I could feel the air become very heavy and suddenly a drenching rain began to fall. Huddling next to the boats left most of us completely exposed. There was nowhere to hide or take cover. It seemed as if there was nothing but water all about us. After a few minutes of drenching rain, the winds began. The rain was being driven with such force that if I had stepped out of the limited cover of the boat, I would have been driven to the ground.

With my hat pulled down to keep some of the rain off my face, I attempted to see how everyone was handling the storm. All I could see was a huddled group of soaking wet people looking as miserable as anyone could possibly be. The wind was driving the rain with such force as to keep everyone holding onto something for safety purposes. The storm continued for over an hour, and then the lightning came streaking through the sky giving us the ability to see for only a few moments.

After two hours the rain slackened, but everyone stayed where they were as if they were afraid to move. I could see the storm was slowly leaving and within 30 minutes the rain had stopped. As the rain came to an end, everyone slowly began to move about, as if they were shell-shocked. The storm had hit with such force that everyone seemed to be slowly recovering from its effect.

I noticed Juan was speaking to his men, and directing them to gather equipment and untie the boats. He seemed the least effected by the storm and was quickly organizing his people.

After speaking with his men, Juan turned and said something to Serge. Serge nodded his head, and turning said, "Could everyone gather around. Juan would like to speak with everyone about something."

As we gathered around Juan, it was evident from everyone's appearance that they had taken a complete soaking from the storm. Juan waited until we had gathered around him and said, "That was a very severe storm, and as I can see everyone is soaked. I would suggest that you change into dry clothes, if you have any. I have directed Esteban to check the river, and see if we will be able to continue up-river at this time. It could be dangerous for traveling due to fallen trees and debris. The storm that just passed is unusual at this time of year, but not unheard of. Hopefully that will be the only storm we will have to endure during your journey in the jungle. Does anyone have any questions?"

Maria said, "I would like to change my clothes if I can find something dry. Could you provide something so I can have a little privacy?"

Juan nodded and said, "Yes, I can give you a little privacy, but first everyone check and see if you have dry clothing." The men had removed our gear from the boats and set our packs on the ground. We found those packs with zippers, provided the best protection from the weather. Maria discovered much of her equipment had become soaked and so she would have to remain in her wet clothing. Julio pulled a shirt out of his pack and told her to remove her wet top.

Taking Maria by the hand, and carrying his shirt he said to Serge, "We will be right back," and proceeded into the forest. Serge called out as they disappeared out of sight, "Don't go too far. The jungle seems very thick in this area."

"We'll only be a minute. Please keep watch while we are in here," said Julio from within the forest. I could not see them, and his voice seemed to come from various directions. The jungle has a way of confusing sound and the direction it is coming from. By the time we had changed into whatever dry clothes we wanted to wear, Julio and Maria had returned. Maria was rolling up the sleeves of the shirt and wearing the shirt outside of her shorts. As they walked towards us, I could sense something had happened between them. Maria seemed to be walking close enough to Julio to constantly touch him in little ways. Julio looked a little uncomfortable, but seemed to be walking very light on his feet. Our Peruvian friends were having a hard time hiding their feelings for each other.

"If everyone's ready, let's try to continue up the river," said Juan as he walked towards our group. Turning to Serge he says, "Esteban indicated he had seen some debris in the river, but we should be able to continue. We will take the precaution of placing a man in the bow of each boat to watch for floating debris." Serge indicated we were ready and everyone followed Juan towards the river.

The storm had passed, but its effects could be seen everywhere. Water was dripping from the trees above and the ground felt saturated. When we came to the river, I could see limbs and debris floating downstream. The air was saturated with moisture and the dry shirt I had just put on, was quickly becoming damp. Travel this day would be very uncomfortable unless a breeze came up to blow the moist air to the east.

Esteban stated that Juan wanted to use the motors for the rest of the day. He felt we might need them if we had to evade something in the water. Watching the debris floating downstream, I fully agreed with Juan's precautions.

I felt a tap on my arm and Esteban said, "Would you move to the bow? I would appreciate it if you would be on guard for large debris floating towards us. If you see anything, just signal which way I should go to avoid it. I will have the men ready with poles to push things away from us."

Rising from my seat, I said, "Sure, just watch for my signals, some of the floating debris is moving pretty quickly." I continued towards the front of the boat and signaled Esteban that I was ready. Waiting for the motors to be started, I began to take in the view before me. The brown water of the Napo River was moving with renewed strength, and was cluttered with floating branches and debris from fallen trees. I also became aware of the attacks of numerous mosquitoes while we were waiting to leave the shoreline. The insects were ready for a meal after the storm and they had discovered us, and were wasting no time in attacking.

With the motors propelling the boats we quickly entered the river and proceeded upstream. The next few hours were spent dodging branches and the occasional uprooted tree. Juan maintained a course close to the western shore, which seemed to have less floating debris than in mid-stream. Esteban and I worked well in keeping the boat from running into floating debris, and the men were always ready with their poles to direct branches out of our path.

Late in the afternoon, Juan motioned for Esteban to follow him. I could see a tree covered island towards the eastern shore of the river, and Juan was turning his boat towards the island. I could see tall grasses along the shoreline and hoped we would find a cleared area for our camp. An area that would have no alligators.

Within a few minutes Juan directed his boat into the grasses and slowly began to disappear from view. We followed and discovered a cleared area large enough for a camp to be set up. There seemed very little storm damage upon the island and the men quickly found dry wood for a fire. Juan sent two of his men to catch fish for the evening meal and the rest of the group prepared their sleeping areas.

"If you have wet clothing, now is the time to let it dry," stated Juan, walking towards Serge. Looking from Juan towards the rest of us, Serge says, "That's a good idea. Do we need to unpack any of the provisions? I never thought to ask if any of the food was damaged."

Nodding his head, Juan says, "I've directed two of the men to unpack the supplies and check everything. This environment will cause things to rot quickly, and if storm damaged, it will go even quicker. Another thing, after we eat I would like to discuss the next part of the trip. We will be circling Sta. Clotilde early tomorrow morning, and we should consider the best way of doing that without being seen. Also, make sure your weapons are cleaned and oiled. We may need them in working order if strangers confront us tomorrow."

With a look of concern Serge says, "We'll have all weapons serviced and ready if needed. Let me know when you are ready to talk and we can discuss getting around Sta. Clotilde. I will let the others know what will be happening later this evening."

Serge called the four of us together and informed us of Juan's proposed get-together later in the day. He suggested we all clean our weapons, due to the possibility that we might run into trouble circling the village. Jason and I pulled our sleeping mats together, and the five of us sat together exchanging thoughts and cleaning our weapons. I noticed Julio and Maria sat next to each other on Jason's mat while cleaning their pistols. It was possible their relationship was growing much closer as the trip progressed. Conversation flowed among the group, with such topics as the storm and river travel.

As Jason slid the clip into his pistol, he said, "Serge, do you know what Juan wants to talk about? I know we have to be getting close to Sta. Clotilde, and he seemed very concerned about passing the village without being seen."

Serge put his pistol down and said, "That's exactly what he wants to discuss. He mentioned we would be passing the village tomorrow, and he wanted to discuss his plans for circling the area without being seen."

As I reloaded my pistol, I said, "Julio, what are your thoughts about this village we have to pass? You have not had much to say about Sta. Clotilde and the people that live there."

Julio seemed uncomfortable with my question and glanced at Maria before speaking. As he began speaking, he seemed to be selecting his words with great care. "I have been concerned about this part of the trip since Serge had disclosed the route he intended to follow in hopes of finding the city. I have never traveled this far into the interior, but I have heard tales of bandits and Indians who will attack strangers in this part of the country. We have traveled seven days from Iquitos, and in the jungle there is no established law enforcement. If we are attacked, we will have no one to turn to for assistance but ourselves. That is the reason Juan has suggested we have our weapons ready to defend ourselves."

With concern in his voice, Serge says, "What type of weapons could we expect the bandits to have access to? Also, could the Indians have firearms?"

Before responding to Serge, Julio reached over and held Maria's hand. "The bandits will have firearms, but very few Indians will have access to modern weapons. They will have spears, machetes, and blowguns. Please don't underestimate the ability of the Indians because they have no firearms. They can move through the jungle as the puma and strike as the eagle. Never forget the Indians know the jungle and are familiar with poisons derived from many plants growing in the jungle. The small arrow that is fired from their blowguns is usually dipped in a poison, and will kill quickly."

"Do they still use blowguns?" asked Jason. "I thought that was a weapon used by the Indians more than a century ago. I never expected that it would still be in use at this time."

With a knowing expression, Julio says, "Our modern weapons would soon become useless in this moist climate. Within a day, a careful inspection of your weapons will show signs of rust, but the weapons of the Indians are not effected as quickly as ours. Believe me, if they attack we will not know it until someone is hurt or killed."

Turning towards Maria, Julio squeezed her hand, as if to reassure her. "My friends, please take this information to heart. I know we have spoken of the dangers of the jungle, but remember the most dangerous animal of the jungle is man. We are traveling with limited supplies, but in this part of the country our equipment is worth a lot of money." As Julio finished speaking, he looked at Maria and squeezed her hand as if to reassure her.

Julio's words seemed to hang in the air, causing everyone to pause and consider his words of warning. Slowly weapons were reassembled and prepared for what might await us upriver. We were a very sober group when Juan announced that the men had returned with fish for the evening meal.

Jason was sitting on his mat with his back turned from the camp and his head in his hands. Hearing me approach he slowly turned and looking at me said, "I don't think I ever told you when my birthday is. I'll be 33 this June.

As far back as I can remember, searching for the unknown has always intrigued me. When I met you at the university, I was fascinated by the tales you told of the exploring you and Serge had done in Europe. I had never taken part in any field research projects, and when you seemed willing to include me in the group I was overwhelmed. I have never been a very brave person, and you two seem to be so confident in everything you do."

I knew Jason was a quiet person, but this was a side I had never seen. Sitting on the mat next to him and speaking in a hushed voice I said, "Hey, who said we were brave? We are a team, and as a team we stick together. Serge and I are no braver than the next man is. Believe me, our next day of travel could be dangerous, and I'm plenty scared. Anyone who says he's not worried would be lying."

With a small smile, Jason says, "I appreciate your words of encouragement, but I've known you long enough to recognize a brave man when I meet one." After a short pause with his eyes cast down, he raises his eyes and says, "Would you do me a favor?"

"Sure, anything."

I could see he was having great difficulty in choosing his words. He kept rubbing his hands together and little beads of sweat were forming on his forehead. My concern for my friend was growing as I suspected the pressures of the trip were having an adverse affect on him. After rubbing his hands on his pants legs, he raised his head and looked me in the eyes.

"I realized that we would be facing many dangers on this trip, but I had never given much thought to the possibility that I might not live through this adventure," said Jason with a look of determination on his face. "If something happens to me, I would appreciate your telling my parents about this trip, and what we were trying to do. I know I surprised them when I announced my intentions of traveling to South America."

"Sure, I'll notify your parents if something happens to you," I said, in a tone of voice that indicated that the thought of his dying was the last thing on my mind. "Jason, we all face the possibility of mortal danger in this jungle, but we must keep a positive attitude that we will succeed. I've known you a number of years, and you're a strong individual, both physically and mentally." I crossed my legs and leaned forward saying, "Remember the time we were rock climbing in the mountains west of Harrisburg, Virginia? We had been backpacking south of Rawley Springs not to far from Reddish Knob. You had found a small stream and we set up camp for the night in a clearing nearby. We were sitting around the fire and you pointed above me and said let's climb that in the morning. I remember turning and looking at a shear wall of rock extending several hundred feet above our camp. Do you remember what I said?"

He was trying to keep a serious look on his face, but with a smile he said, "Yes, you wondered if I had lost my mind. I still look back and wonder what I could have been thinking of at the time."

Encouraged by his reaction to the story, I continued, "That's right. I looked up at this wall of rock behind me, and hoped you were pulling my leg. Realizing you were serious. I remember saying I would climb it if you would. The next morning you were up early and had your climbing gear ready before I had climbed out of my sleeping bag. Realizing that you were serious about the climb, I prepared my gear, and we proceeded to challenge the cliff. After several hours of climbing we found a small shelf mid-way up, where we could sit and rest. We were having a great time and you never mentioned the danger that was constantly with us at every finger and toehold. We climbed further and came to an overhang that projected five feet out from the face of the cliff. I remember saying that we should turn back, but you insisted that you could place a piton above the overhang and lower a rope to me. You checked your pitons and immediately began climbing up until you could grasp the rock shelf above. When you released your feet from the cliff face and hung from the shelf above your head by your hands, I knew if you fell I couldn't catch you. I must have held my breath the whole time you hung there. You slowly pulled yourself up and disappeared over the edge. I could hear you hammering the piton into place and within a minute you dropped a rope to me. We made the top of the cliff in a couple hours, and I remember we celebrated with a bottle of fruit juice."

I paused for a moment, and then said, "Do you realize how brave you were that day? A lot of people would never hang by their fingertips hundreds of feet above the ground. They would have given up and turned back. That was a very dangerous climb we made that day. Believe me, I would never hesitate having you guard my back."

Jason had an embarrassed look on his face as he said, "I had forgotten that climb."

"That is one climb I will never forget, and you shouldn't either." Wiping my hands together and rising from the mat, I continued saying, "Let's keep this conversation between us. Is that all right with you?"

With a relieved look on his face, Jason said, "Thanks; I appreciate your discussing this with me."

"Forget it. Let's check the food," I said. "I'm hungry enough to eat the fish raw."

We walked towards the fire as Juan was announcing that the food was ready. Waiting our turn to get some food, my thoughts wandered back over my conversation with Jason. I knew this was a dangerous venture, and some lives could be lost. I hoped Jason and all of us would survive this journey, and would be able to plan another trip in the future.

Conversation flowed easily during the meal, and I could see that a level of comfort had settled within the group. Julio and Maria were sitting together sharing some quiet time as they ate their meals. Juan was having an animated conversation with several of his men, which I enjoyed watching. I asked Jason what they were talking about, and he indicated they were joking about how much trouble the men had catching the fish.

With a puzzled look on my face, I asked, "What kind of trouble did they have?"

Jason laughed and said, "A local alligator was trying to chase them away from the fish. I guess he felt it was his fishing hole."

With the late-afternoon sun filtering through the trees, and a full stomach, I found myself ready to set my bedding out for a nap. I felt so tired that the insects flying about my head seemed to be a minor irritation. Just as the mosquitoes began to be a nuisance, a wind came in from the west driving them away. The wind also brought the scents of the jungle that surrounded us. The smell of growing things dominated my senses; scents of water and moist earth, which contained strange plants and creatures unknown to me. Times like this reminded me of how alien this environment was to what I was accustomed to.

As conversation came to an end around the fire, Juan stood and directed his men to various duties. He then turned to us and resumed his seat, saying, "If you were finished with your meal, I would like to discuss what we have to do tomorrow. I have given the men various chores to keep them busy, so we can talk freely about traveling up river. It would be best if we were in the boats before first light; this would give us enough time to pass Sta. Clotilde before the sun rises."

Looking at Jason, Juan said, "I have asked Esteban to place you in the bow of his boat with your rifle. If you run into trouble do not hesitate to use your weapons. We are entering very dangerous country and we must take every precaution to protect ourselves."

With his arms folded across his chest, and a concerned look on his face,

Jason nodded and said, "I'll coordinate everything with Esteban."

I was encouraged to see Jason still had a positive attitude after our earlier conversation. He knew he would be putting himself in danger tomorrow, but he still agreed to help in whatever way he could be used. Juan asked Serge if he would place himself in the bow of their boat with his rifle, which Serge agreed to do.

"If everything goes as planned," said Juan. "We should pass the village quietly and not be discovered. I have warned my men to row carefully, and I also ask those of you who will be rowing tomorrow to be aware noise travels over water very clearly. I have also warned the men to remain silent until we are beyond the village. We must all remain silent as ghosts and move as ghosts."

Looking towards the sky, Juan says, "We only have about an hour before the sunsets. I suggest we get some rest, we will be rising early."

I awoke to Jason tapping my arm and saying, "It's time to get up. Juan wants us to have our things packed and in the boats within 15 minutes. He said we would worry about eating later today. Do you need help with anything?"

As I was pulling the netting from over my head, I said, "No, I can see well enough to get everything together. Thanks for the offer." I could see the camp gear was quickly being packed and the boats were almost packed. There was a level of tension in the air as everyone hurried about their chores, very little was said as everyone quickly gathered their things.

Juan moved through the people, speaking in a low voice, encouraging individuals to hurry and not to leave anything behind. He seemed to be everywhere, and within his 15-minute schedule, we had all assembled at the boats.

He waited until everyone had gathered near the boats and said, "Remember what I said last night. Silence for the next few hours is important if we are to pass the village unnoticed." Looking at Serge and Jason he said, "I will depend on the two of you to keep a watchful eye for anything that might threaten our travel upriver. Now lets board the boats and pray that they are sleeping late in the village. We will use the motors for a short distance and then we will row, as quietly as possible."

With the help of the motors, we were able to move quickly upriver against the steadily strengthening current. This was our fifth day on the Napo River and I had noticed the width of the river had progressively diminished as we traveled north. As I took my position in the boat, it was evident that the current of the river had also increased with the dwindling width of the river. Our progress would be greatly decreased once the motors were shut down, and the paddles were to be used. I quickly glanced towards the sky and noticed that there was the lightest shade of gray beginning to show. The sun would be fully risen within two hours, and the people of the village would be up and about. I hoped Juan had calculated our travel time correctly, if not we could be in trouble.

I had begun to relax with the motion of the boat and the droning sound of the motor. When suddenly, Juan's motor shutdown and just as quickly Esteban followed his lead. The sudden silence seemed overwhelming, as if my ability to hear had been greatly decreased. I heard Esteban whisper to the men, and I could hear them taking the paddles and begin to row. Our progress had been cut in half without the motors, but we also moved through the water with very little noise.

Within 45 minutes we were passing the village of Sta. Clotilde. Juan kept his boat near the eastern shoreline and Esteban followed his example. I could see two wooden docks projecting out into the river, with several canoes tied to the pilings. Sunrise was still a half-hour away, but I could see there were lights shining from several dwellings. From what I could see the village of Sta. Clotilde could have a population of 200 or more people. Juan's suggestion of slipping by unnoticed seemed a precaution that may have been in the best interest of us all.

I watched the sun rise above the treetops, and bring the jungle into its full beauty. We had passed the village safely and Juan had decided to start the motors. I could hear the monkeys calling from the jungle, and once in a while I could see a few swinging from tree to tree. I found myself at times like this, having difficulty accepting that death waited for the unwary only yards away.

We continued traveling upriver for the next three hours without incident. Times like this reinforced the fact that we were in an unexplored wilderness. Except for the village of Sta. Clotilde, I had not seen any signs of civilization during our trip up the Napo. The width of the river had decreased to eighty yards and Esteban had said that it was about eighteen feet deep in the middle. The color was a lighter brown than the Amazon was, and the men drank the water with no ill effects. Juan insisted that the water is fit for drinking if allowed to settle before using. I still continue using bottled water and juices.

I noticed Juan motioning and said, "Esteban, Juan seems to be motioning about something. He's pointing towards the shore to our right."

Nodding his head, Esteban said, "He is ready to go ashore and have a quick meal. We had agreed that if we had a safe passage, we could stop for a quick meal."

We followed Juan's boat towards a low shelf of land that seemed quite clear. Scattered piles of driftwood were lying along the shore with thin growths of tall grasses. Nearing the shore I heard several alligators quickly move into the water, and disappear with only their eyes watching our progress towards the shore. I was becoming accustomed to seeing these reptiles on a daily basis, so their presence caused me very little disturbance.

Once we were ashore, Juan announced that the meal would consist of canned fruit, sardines, and crackers. He wanted to put as much distance between Sta. Clotilde and our group as possible.

During the meal, Juan turned to me and said, "I told Serge about a small store located north of here where the Curaray and the Napo Rivers come together. It's nothing fancy, but they sell gasoline. I think it would be a good idea to fill our fuel cans before continuing up the Curaray. You may see some Indians around the store, stay away from them. If we didn't need the gasoline, I would not take the chance of stopping. Word will spread that a group is traveling upriver, so we must not stay for any period of time."

The meal was quickly eaten and Juan had the men prepare the boats to continue up the river. After making sure that nothing was left on the ground to indicate that we had been there, Juan boarded his boat and proceeded upriver with the help of the motors. Jason had resumed his seat next to me and Esteban thanked him for his help during the morning.

Jason turned on his seat and said, "I was happy to help. As we passed the village I could see a number of houses and other structures. I estimated that Sta. Clotilde had about 200 or more people living in or around the village, do you know if that is correct?"

"At least 200," stated Esteban. "I would not be surprised if it was double that number. That village may be on the outskirts of civilization, but the government has been trying to encourage people to move into this area. They are trying to get families to relocate into this part of the country and start farming."

"Farming?" asked Jason as he frowned. "This is the jungle, how could people farm in this environment? What kind of crops could they grow?"

Smiling, Esteban says, "The Indians in this part of the country grow cotton, maize, ground peas, yuccas, sweet potatoes, and plantains. There are many crops that can be grown, but it requires a lot of work. The average man in this country would rather watch his woman work and he would relax in a hammock with a jug of Masato. They are very lazy, but this country is easy to live in if your lazy. Many of the everyday foods that people eat grow in great abundance, so why work when you can get food so easily."

"I hope Juan didn't bring any Masato on this trip?" I said with concern evident in my voice.

Raising his eyes to the heavens, Esteban says, "Absolutely not. If Juan had brought Masato on this trip, he would have a difficult time keeping it away from the men. They enjoy it, but do not know when to stop drinking it. If it is made correctly, it can be very powerful. Masato is a common drink among the Indians, it is made from the yucca. I will tell you how the Indians make this drink. The women used the yucca root and would grind it into a white pulp, and then boil it. During the boiling the women take the mash in their mouths, chew it, and spit it into a pot. After it has been cooked, it is put into large jars, covered, and allowed to ferment. When you want some Masato, it is taken out of the jar, mixed with water, and drunk. Do you think you would like to try it sometime?"

Laughing Jason says, "It didn't sound to bad, until you mentioned the women chewing and spitting it into a jar. I think I'll stick with the beer."

"The beer sounds good," said Esteban smiling, "I'll get one of the men to get a few bottles out for us," Esteban said something to one of the men, who produced a smile, and he quickly produced three bottles of beer. As the bottles were opened, he passed two of them to the back of the boat. Esteban said he had told him to open one bottle to be shared between two men. Jason and I shared our beer and relaxed watching the jungle pass quickly by. I noticed that every ten or fifteen minutes an alligator would slide into the water, as if anticipating a potential meal.

In the late afternoon we passed a small stream entering the Napo from the west. Esteban stated we were only a few miles from the store, which is near the point where the Curaray River merges with the Napo River. Esteban seemed a little nervous when speaking about the store. It dawned on me, if Esteban was concerned about this part of the country, I better be very careful.

With just a couple hours of daylight left, Esteban suddenly pointed and said, "That is the store. Remember Juan's words of caution. Stay near the boats, and be ready to leave at a moment's notice."

To call what I saw a country store, was being very generous. The building that we were approaching seemed ready to collapse if a light breeze struck it. It was a tiny building, made of unpainted rough-cut boards, with a tin roof that sagged in several places. A small dock projected into the river, with a boat tied to one of the piers. The jungle seemed to grow all about the building, as if at any minute, the building would slip back into the forest.

Our boats were run up to the dock and tied to piers green with water growth. Juan assigned a man to stay with each boat while the rest of us investigated the store. Walking on the dock was a test of fortitude, it seemed to have a life of its own. It had never been built to hold ten people moving at one time. The dock was in constant motion until the group had moved to the shore.

Turning to Jason, I said, "I never thought we would make it to shore, that dock felt like it would fall apart at any minute. Do you think it's safe to enter that building? Look at the roof its ready to collapse, this place must have been here for many years." Jason just nodded his head, and kept looking around as if he could sense something was wrong.

The building was set back from the river about twenty yards, and was built on stilts. A precaution which seemed to make a lot of sense, what with the rising and falling of the waters of the river during the wet and dry seasons. A narrow porch covered the front of the building, and as expected, an individual was sitting on a box smoking. Juan approached the man and spoke for a few minutes. As the man stood, I could see he was taller than the average Peruvian, but with a body that belied the years his lined face inferred. He continued speaking with Juan, and pointed to the left side of the building.

Serge was standing near Juan, and as I approached I said, "Serge, what's going on? Who is the man talking with Juan?"

Turning Serge says, "Juan asked if he has any gasoline, and the owner said he had a fuel tank on the side of the building. We are allowed to fill our fuel cans, but the price is high. I told Juan to pay whatever he could bargain for, we need the fuel. Let's go in the store and look around."

The porch creaked as we walked across the sagging boards towards the open doorway. As I crossed the threshold of the doorway I had to wait for my eyes to adjust to the dimly lit interior of the store. After a few minutes my eyes began to wander around a small room with two small windows. The windows were the only source of light that could enter the room, but it was enough to confirm that we were alone. I slowly turned around trying to absorb the assortment of goods before my eyes. Nothing seemed to be arranged in any type of order, boxes of shoes, axes, buckets, ropes, shovels, canned goods, and books were piled on shelves or on the floor along the walls. Towards the far right corner sat an old desk and chair, with boxes of papers stacked beside it on the floor.

Looking at Serge I said, "From the looks of this place, I don't think he has many customers. Is there anything you can think of that we need?"

Shaking his head from side to side, Serge said, "No, I think the gasoline is all we need." Serge continued walking around the store, and motioned for my attention. Pointing towards a box with several earthen jugs he said, "What do you think is in those jugs?"

I bent over and picked one up and shook it. I could hear a liquid moving inside, and I said, "I bet this is Masato. An alcoholic drink that Esteban was talking about earlier today, it's supposed to be very powerful. I bet he sells a lot of this to the local people."

We spent a few more minutes wandering through the store, and finding nothing of interest, we turned to leave. Approaching the door, I could see three barefoot men in loose clothing walking towards the dock. One of the men was carrying a jug similar to those I had seen in the store. I called Serge and told him we might have some trouble. When he saw the men, he said he was going to get Juan, and quickly walked out onto the porch. As I came out on the porch, I saw Esteban and Juan with a couple of our men carrying fuel cans. Serge approached them and began talking to Juan, whose reactions indicated his concern. He quickly set his cans down and said something to Esteban, who quickly looked at me standing in the doorway.

Esteban motioned me over to the edge of the porch, and as I approached he said, "Listen quickly, but do not react. Those three men are Indians from this area, and they have been drinking. They can be very mean when drinking, and could attack anyone that upsets them. I want you to move behind us and quietly get down to the shoreline, and if things get ugly don't hesitate to shoot. Juan is going to try and get them to move on, but he may not be successful. They may have friends nearby, so we need to get away from here quickly."

I nodded to Esteban, acknowledging his instructions, I began moving behind Esteban and Juan towards the shore. I noticed two of our men coming from the rear of the store carrying fuel cans. I motioned them to move towards the side of the building, they acknowledged my directions and stepped to the side of the building lowering their cans to the ground. Julio had been talking with Maria while carrying a fuel can. When Juan came to a sudden stop, Julio almost ran into him. That was when he noticed there was a potential problem at the dock. I continued circling behind Juan, Julio and Maria as I slowly headed for the beach 50 feet away. Passing Julio I paused long enough to whisper, "Have your pistol ready if there is trouble." Without looking at him I continued moving towards the shore.

After watching my approach towards the beach, Juan began walking towards the dock, motioning Serge to follow him. I noticed Serge remove his pistol and hold it behind his back while continuing to follow Juan. Our eyes met for a moment, and I could sense that Serge knew what I was trying to do.

Keeping my eyes constantly on the Indians, and hoping nothing would develop that would lead to violence. They seemed very upset, and were talking to our man who was sitting in one of the boats. The Indians resembled our men in many ways, they were of average height, black hair and eyes. As I closed the distance between them and myself I could hear them speaking in a series of grunts and arm waving. The guard kept trying to say something, but the Indian with the jug set it down and looked as if would leap into the boat at any moment. With his hand on the knife at his side, one of the Indians advanced to the edge of the dock. Looking down at the guard, he lowered his voice and spoke in a menacing manner.

While slowly moving, I noticed Juan out of the corner on my eye, he raised his hand and called out to the Indians. The Indians turned around upon hearing Juan call out to them and seemed to hesitate in what they were saying. One of the Indians began to speak to Juan in an excited voice and with his arms swinging from side to side, he kept pointing downriver. I had approached to within 30 feet of the dock, when one of the Indians turned his head and looked straight at me. I came to a complete stop, I had never felt such power in another human beings eyes. I had never felt such hatred emanate from one human being, and have it directed at me. His coal black eyes held mine with a look that acknowledged that he knew why I was moving towards the dock, and if we met, only one of us would walk away. He never blinked while watching me, but he slowly placed his hand on the knife at his waist, his intention was clear.

I finally broke contact with those black eyes and noticed one of our men moving towards the shore from the opposite side of the dock. He acknowledged my look by nodding his head. At that very moment Juan stepped up on the dock continuing to talk to the Indians. The Indian that had been staring at me turned his head as Juan came near. I took the opportunity to turn my body slightly to the right and at the same time draw my pistol, and place it behind my back. I could not chamber a round without exposing the weapon, but at least I felt more prepared if our people were attacked.

Juan's action of stepping upon the dock, caused the Indians to advance a couple steps towards him. Their action must have felt like a threat to Serge, who immediately advanced to Juan's side. The Indian in front of Serge lowered his hand to his waist and withdrew a knife, and at the same time said something to Serge. Juan quickly stepped forward and placed his left arm in front of Serge, and at the same time said something to the Indian with the knife. At the first sight of the knife, Serge had stepped back, and I imagine only with the greatest of self-control kept from swinging his pistol from behind his back.

As the knife was drawn threatening Serge, I almost swung my pistol into the open, but Juan's actions kept me from exposing my weapon. At the same time I heard a strange voice saying something from the area of the store. I turned my head enough to see the owner approaching with Esteban following a few feet behind. At the same time I noticed Juan stepping back from the dock and motioning with his arm for Serge to do the same thing. The owner was motioning the Indians towards him as he approached them, and while speaking to them he seemed to keep a friendly tone in his voice.

I continued to walk slowly along the shore towards Juan, all the time keeping an eye on the Indians. They seemed to be listening to the owner, and every few moments one of them would look towards one of us. There was an unspoken statement that they were not afraid of us, and we better watch our backs. Within another five minutes it seemed the owner had calmed the situation enough for the conversation to end on a quiet note. The owner turned towards our man and motioned him to return to the store, and at the same time he started to walk towards the forest with the Indians. The four of them spoke for another minute and before I could register their disappearance, the three Indians had disappeared into the forest. The owner turned and quickly approached Juan speaking quickly with a lot of concern in his voice.

Juan nods his head and turning says, "Listen everyone, the owner has warned me that they could return at anytime. If they return they could have more men with them, and he feels they would attack us."

Putting his pistol in his holster, Serge says, "What was the problem? Why were they so upset?"

Shaking his head, Juan says, "We didn't do anything, but the owner states the Indians fear the government coming into this country. When they saw us, they thought we were with the government. They know the government is encouraging people to bring their families into this country to farm, this is something they fear. We may not have much time, let's load the fuel cans and leave this place. I must tell you that the Indians told the owner to warn us not to travel up the Curaray River. They say it is their country, and they will not allow outsiders in their country. The owner feels that there is a very good chance that they would attack us."

Juan called to his men to begin loading the fuel cans in both boats, and then motioned Serge and I to his side. Lowering his voice, Juan says, "Several of the men heard the Indian speaking with the owner, and his threats of attacking us. I must warn you that they may abandon us at any time, these men fear the forest Indians. They are a very superstitious people, and if they think we could be attacked they will abandon us. Their fear of the forest people is greater than their fear of us. If you are having second thoughts about continuing into the jungle, now is the time to turn around. Once we start traveling up the Curaray River, we will be invading their country. The Indians will not hesitate to attack us, and it will come when we least expect it."

Looking at Serge, I said, "I've come too far to turn around now, how do you feel about it?"

With no hesitation, Serge says, "Let's get moving. We need to find a safe place for our camp tonight."

The boats had been loaded, and as Serge and I parted to enter our own boats, we shared a glance of encouragement. I knew this trip would be dangerous, and that there was always the threat of attack from man or beast. The possibility of that attack had now presented itself, and I for one was not ready to back away from our goal.

With very little time left before sundown, Juan led the group up the Curaray River. Esteban stated Juan would be looking for a campsite on the western shore, he was hoping to put some distance between the Indians and us. The river was about 60 yards wide as we entered the Curaray River, and its current was strong enough to keep our small motors working to maintain headway.

The sun was beginning to settle behind the trees as Juan turned his boat towards the shore. It had been a day of great stress on all of us, and with the decision to continue into the interior I couldn't help feeling some responsibility for the others. This trip was a dream that Serge and I had been following, but now it could involve the safety of others. After camp had been set up, I would suggest to Serge that we have a meeting between the five of us. I felt that a vote to continue should be agreed upon by all, even Juan's men. If some of them wanted to turn back, I felt we had to allow them to leave. I knew the threat of an attack was real, but the possibility of finding the city was to great to turn back now. My vote was to continue into the interior.

9
Where Danger Lurks

Laughter and the bustling of individuals busy with preparing the food for the evening meal usually marked the setting up of camp at the end of the day. Juan's men would be clearing an area for the group to arrange sleeping mats and generally removing brush and undergrowth from the area. It was a time for sharing the events of the day and speculating what the next day's travels would hold in store for the group. The evening meal served as a social gathering for the men and also for our group to share time together. This was the first evening meal since leaving Iquitos that seemed to have a shadow of gloom hanging over it. Wood was gathered and a meal of beans and rice were prepared, but many nervous glances were cast into the jungle as the sun set and darkness spread across the land.

The effects of the encounter at the store had cast a shroud of fear and gloom over the entire party. The meal was eaten in silence with only the evening sounds from the jungle, which seemed to hold a certain sense of foreboding as darkness covered the land. I also noticed Juan's men had taken their food away from the fire and sat in the shadows, as if to make themselves less visible to lurking eyes from within the jungle.

I had taken my plate and sat beside Serge, motioning with my fork towards the group I asked in a low voice, "What do you make of this?"

"Our confrontation with the Indians at the store has made quite an impact on the men. They seem ready to bolt for cover at the slightest sound."

"I like your use of the word 'impact.' We have seen snakes, alligators, and piranha and they have shown no fear, but the Indians have certainly made an impact on them." Finishing my food I said, "I think we better have a get together with Juan and discuss our next move, one more incident and the men would be ready to return to Iquitos."

Nodding his head in agreement, Serge says, "I agree. I have overheard much grumbling and complaining between the men, and several have suggested we turn back to Iquitos. I will say something to Juan after the meal."

As we finished our meal, Serge said, "While I speak with Juan, get the others together so we can discuss our next days travel." I quickly finished the last of my rice and returned my plate to the wash bucket for cleaning. I found Julio and Maria sitting together speaking in low tones, they looked up as I approached and greeted me. "*Buenas noches, como se llama?*"

I knelt next to Julio and said, "I'm doing fine. I mentioned to Serge that the men seem very intimidated by the Indians and that we should speak with Juan concerning their dependability. He agreed with me, and he is asking Juan to have a quick meeting with our group. If you have finished your meal, please meet me at my sleeping mat. I will get Jason and meet you in a minute."

"Do you have a few minutes to talk?" I asked as I neared Jason. He nodded, and taking his plate he rose and followed me. As we walked towards my sleeping mat, I mentioned we were going to have a quick meeting with Juan about the day's events. He agreed that it was a good idea, he also mentioned the men had been talking among themselves about the Indians. Approaching my sleeping area, I could see Julio and Maria had already made themselves as comfortable as the conditions would allow. I greeted them and turned to see if Serge and Juan were ready to join us. I could see Juan was giving instructions to the men who seemed to show very little response to his orders. He then motioned Esteban to him and said something, which caused Esteban to turn on the men and begin giving orders in a commanding tone of voice. Juan nodding his head turned and indicated Serge should follow him. As they were approaching, I could overhear the last of Juan's statement, "Don't worry, Esteban will keep them busy while we talk. I'm glad to have this chance to speak with your people before we continue upriver."

As Serge and Juan approached the group I asked Serge, "Should we sit here, or move to another area?"

As Juan began to lower himself to the ground, he said, "I have directed Esteban to keep the men busy while we talk." Juan waited until we had all seated ourselves and turning to Serge he said, "Serge has asked me to spend a few minutes with you to answer any questions you may have concerning events of the day. I had hoped to avoid encountering any Indians while traveling in this country. They feel we are intruders in their country, and we are unwelcome to say the least." Looking towards the sky, Juan says, "Darkness will be here very soon, I would like to have the camp settled and quiet before total darkness. I will try to answer your questions as quickly as possible. Who would care to speak first?"

Jason spoke first, saying, "Will the men continue upriver in the morning with us? I have heard several men talking about returning to Iquitos."

Juan folded his arms across his chest and said, "You have asked a good question. If we are not attacked tonight, they will probably continue upriver in the morning. You must try to understand these men, they are very superstitious. Especially when it comes to the Indians. They feel the Indians are very close to the spirits of the forest and if angered they could turn the animals of the forest against us. I hope we have no further contact with the Indians, it will be very difficult to keep the men from turning back."

"You mean to say," asks Jason, "if the men see another Indian they will demand that we turn around?"

"Yes, they realize that if we see an Indian it is because they want us to see them. These Indians are only seen when they want to be seen. The men fear the Indians, and they will want to turn back to Iquitos immediately."

Juan turned from Jason and asked if there were any further questions.

With a concerned look on his face, Julio says, "If some of the men decide to return to Iquitos, is there anyway to persuade them to stay?"

Juan's head slowly moves from left to right, as he says, "These men will face many dangers, but they fear the unknown of the forest. I know Esteban will remain, and possibly a couple more, but the majority will want to leave. These men are not loyal to me, and I know they were frightened by the incident at the store. You know enough about the people in this part of the country, they can be very superstitious. To answer your question, we will be lucky if we loose only three men. There will be no way to persuade them to stay, threats or money will not matter."

"If some of the men want to leave," I asked, "Would you give them one of the boats to return to Iquitos?"

"No, the boats are mine, and I will not lend them to these men. I do not trust them; I would never see my boat again." Looking from me to the others, Juan says, "If they decide to leave be prepared to defend your belongings. Their fear of the Indians will give them courage to attempt almost anything to escape from the people of the forest. I expect they will try to steal one of the boats, so we must guard them at all times."

After a short silence, Serge says, "If the majority of the men leave, do you feel we will be able to continue the expedition?"

Juan slowly turns to Serge and says, "For your own reasons, you have kept your destination a secret from me. I respect your reasons for taking precautions with the knowledge that you have acquired, but to fully answer your question I must know your destination. The Curaray River is a dangerous river, which travels through unexplored country. I know of no villages located along the river, not even in Ecuador. Julio had explained that we would be traveling up the Napo River, but he never indicated where your destination was located. If I am to answer your question you must trust me with the knowledge of our final destination."

I turned towards Serge and could see the turmoil on his face. Should he reveal our destination to Juan? Could he truly trust this man from another world, a world so different from his own? We had spent years preparing for this trip, if he revealed the knowledge of the city to this man, would he use it for his own gain? Would he mislead us, by taking us in circles and eventually stating the city does not exist? I could imagine all these questions flashing through his mind as he slowly began to nod his head.

"You're right," stated Serge. "You have every right to know our destination. The dangers we could be entering will also involve you. My friends and I have information that indicates that the ruins of an ancient Inca city could be located west of the Curaray River. We are to travel north on the Curaray River beyond the second waterfall and then turn west on the second tributary. It is possible we might have to travel by foot after the first waterfall, early records indicate the river is very treacherous as you travel north beyond the first waterfall. I hope this information is helpful in determining our ability to continue the trip?"

With a determined look on his face, Juan says, "I appreciate your trust in me. I have never traveled up the Curaray River, or entered the country west of the river. As I said, it is unexplored territory and considered very dangerous for travelers. If your group is willing to continue, Esteban and I will do our best to get you to your city." Looking at the night sky, Juan states, "We only have a few minutes before darkness covers the jungle. We can continue this conversation in the morning, if anyone has further questions." Rising from the ground he shakes Serge's hand and turning to the group says, *"Buenas noches, amigos."*

Watching Juan return to his men, I said, "I think one of us should be on guard duty for each change of the guard. Keeping these boats in our possession could mean the difference of life or death for each of us." It was agreed that one of the men would stand guard for each of the nightly watches.

Juan had everyone up and moving by five in the morning, with instructions that there would be no fire for cooking. He said we could have crackers and canned fruit for breakfast before continuing upriver. I noticed that Juan's men were moving to his orders, but their attentions were directed towards the jungle.

Within 30 minutes the boats were loaded and with our weapons close at hand we entered the Curaray River. As the hours passed and the routine of river travel began to settle the nerves of the men, a sense of relaxation began to settle over the men. I noticed the river had begun to change in subtle ways from what I had become accustomed to seeing. The breadth of the river was constantly varying, but steadily decreasing as we traveled upriver. Also, the river began to twist and turn, unlike the Napo that flowed in a more lazy manner. There were hills on each side of the river, but their size was deceiving due to the height of the trees.

I turned to Esteban and asked, "This river seems to be different from the Amazon or the Napo Rivers. Do you think we will be entering rough water today?"

Keeping his eyes on the river he said, "The Curaray River is much different from the other rivers we have traveled. The current will get stronger as we travel north and it will steadily decrease in width. I have heard that we will see rough water before we get to the first waterfall. Please remember that I have never traveled this river, I have only heard about it. Do you or Jason have experience with rough river travel?"

"Yes we do," I said with a smile, remembering a few rafting trips we had taken.

With a look of reassurance, Esteban said, "I'm happy to hear that. As you can see the river has begun to twist and turn. This will give me problems with sandbars when the river bends. I would like the two of you to take turns in the bow and let me know if you see debris in the water or sandbars. The current is strong and it will want to drag us towards the outside of each bend, but if I go into the inside of the bend we will see sandbars or shallow water. I will need your help to navigate this river."

Jason said he would take the first turn in the bow, and proceeded to move carefully towards the front of the boat. We spent the next two hours without incident, making good progress up the river. The tension of the previous day had begun to slip away from our thoughts as I noticed the men becoming livelier in their conversations with each other. I also found myself relaxing and not trying to see an Indian behind each tree or shrub at the edge of the river. With the width of the river decreasing, I became aware of the trees growing on both sides of the river. They must have reached a hundred feet from the ground, with their branches and leaves reaching over the river's edge. I wondered how soon it would be before the trees formed a canopy over the river, it would certainly filter much of the sun before it touched the ground.

A tap on my shoulder brought me out of my reverie of the jungle. "It is your turn," said Esteban. "Your friend called you and you did not answer him."

I motioned to Jason to return to his seat and thanked Esteban for getting my attention. Moving towards the bow of the boat, I could see the men were chatting and laughing with each other. If the Indians would leave us alone, we should be able to make good time up the river.

Jason and I exchanged places in the bow of the boat a couple times before Juan's boat turned towards the shore. As we were nearing the shore Esteban told us that Juan had said he would only stop once during the day.

Turning to Esteban I said, "Did he do that to put distance between the Indians and us?"

"Yes, the men fear the Indians greatly."

I could see that we were turning towards the western shore of the river, which was covered with wild cane. The forest was thick in all directions and the chatter of monkeys could be heard over the roar of the river. I could imagine this camp would be difficult to clear as the brush and cane seemed to cover the shore. Juan kept his boat near the cane and with a sudden swing of his arm, he turned towards the shore. Esteban followed after Juan's boat and shortly Juan and his men came into view.

Turning on my seat, I could see the cane closing behind us, as if a curtain had hidden us from the river. Esteban ran our boat through the cane and up onto the shore. Two of our men jumped out and pulled the boat further out of the water.

As I stepped out of the boat Juan said, "We will camp here tonight. I will have the men clear an area for sleeping, but it will be cramped. We will eat early and there will be no fire tonight. I do not need unfriendly people aware of our presence. Let's move quickly and quietly with what you have to do. We must be settled and quiet before the sunsets." After making his statement, he turned and began giving orders to his men. They immediately responded and began moving towards their assigned duties.

Serge, Julio, and Maria joined us as we were taking our gear from the boat. Serge approached Jason and I and said, "I spoke with Juan while on the boat. He stated that he wanted to find a sheltered place for an early camp. He's hoping the Indians are not aware of our presence and he wants to be sure we don't make ourselves obvious to them. From the looks of this place, I would say he has certainly found an isolated spot for a camp." We all agreed with his assessment of our surroundings and proceeded to make ourselves as comfortable as possible.

The men had killed a turtle for the evening meal and with fried plantains and beer we enjoy a meal that was quite good. The fire was quickly extinguished after the meal and all remains of the meal were buried away from the camp. Juan indicated who would have guard duty and encouraged everyone to be settled before the sunset.

I motioned to Juan and he turned towards me saying, "What can I do for you?"

"Could we talk for a few minutes?"

Juan squatted next to my mat and said, "We only have a few minutes. What's on your mind?"

Keeping my voice low, I said, "I have a strong feeling that we are being watched from the jungle. I have seen subtle movements along the shoreline as we traveled today."

He was nodding his head as he said, "You are correct. I have also seen movement within the jungle, and I suspect that the Indians are watching us. If they attack it will be a surprise attack, we will not see them before they attack. Their ability to blend with the jungle growth is incredible. I have heard they can be a couple feet from you and if they do not move you could not see them."

"Is there any way to prepare us for such an attack?"

Folding his arms and putting his chin in his left hand, he said, "If they attack it would be when our defenses are down. Tomorrow we should arrive at the first waterfall, it will require us to carry our boats around the falls. It would be a perfect time to attack us. We must be very careful during that time, if you see someone do not hesitate to shoot." He quickly stood and said, "I will mention our conversation to Serge. Get some rest, you have guard duty tonight."

I thanked him for his time and turned to find Jason lying on his mat fully covered by his netting. "Did you overhear our conversation?"

Turning his head, Jason said, "Yes. I've been wondering if the Indians had been watching us. I noticed several times during the day that you seemed to be watching the jungle very intently. I wondered if you had seen Indians, but I did not want to say anything to scare the men."

I proceeded to get under my netting and rolled over to continue speaking with Jason, "I'm not sure I saw anything, but I was concerned enough to mention it to Juan. I have grown used to the movement of monkeys, but they usually remain in the upper canopy. I noticed that several times today the monkeys would stop moving and stare at the ground below. They never seemed overly alarmed, but would pause as if curious about something below them. That was when I began to pay more attention to the shoreline. I'm glad I said something to Juan, he also stated he had noticed movement within the jungle that could suggest Indians."

With concern in his voice, Jason said, "I heard Juan mention the waterfall and the possibility that we could be attacked when we come ashore."

"Keep your weapon ready, my friend. I have guard duty tonight, so I better get some sleep. See you in the morning," I said as I settled myself under my netting for a few hours sleep. Try as I would, sleep would not come easy. My short conversations with Juan and Jason continued moving through my thoughts. I knew that the waterfall was near, and the journal had mentioned that we would have to carry the boats around the falls. This would present a perfect opportunity for the Indians to attack, because many of the men would be needed to carry the boats and equipment. As I fell into a troubled sleep, I wondered if all of us would be together at the end of the next day.

The following morning dawned clear with only the usual sounds from the jungle to greet us. The men seemed to be less concerned with the threat of Indians as they prepared a breakfast of fried plantains, yucca, and sweet coffee. I could see there was less tension among the men as they went about their morning chores.

Juan announced breakfast was ready, which produced an immediate reaction from everyone. The meal was quickly consumed with light conversation taking place among the majority of the group. I noticed Juan seemed less talkative and more contemplative while eating his meal. When spoken to, his answers were short and abrupt as if his mind were occupied with other thoughts. I realized our conversation of the previous night was still occupying his thoughts.

The boats were loaded and the campsite cleared within an hour. Juan spent more time then usual inspecting the campsite and after he was satisfied we proceeded upriver. The next few hours of the morning passed without incident, with the only recognizable change being the width of the river. I estimated that the width had steadily decreased to 30 yards across and the current was becoming more difficult to move against. I noticed Esteban had very little time to relax as he struggled to keep our boat clear of objects in the river. I saw Juan pointing towards the shore and made Esteban aware of his signals. Juan began turning his boat towards the left shore and Esteban turned to follow. Within fifteen minutes Juan had found some still water and Esteban ran his boat along side Juan's boat. Juan and Esteban spoke for a few minutes, and then Juan proceeded to reenter the river and continue north against the current. Esteban followed the other boat and within minutes we were also heading north.

I turned to Esteban and asked, "What did Juan want to discuss?"

Glancing quickly at me he said, "He told me that we should be nearing the waterfall and to be prepared to follow him towards the shore. We will have to carry the boats and equipment above the waterfalls, before we can continue upriver."

Before the hour had passed, a final turn in the river revealed a beautiful waterfall ahead of us. I remembered that Phillip had written that the first waterfall was twenty feet tall, as we approached the waterfall his estimation seemed very close. The terrain on either side of the river was covered with heavy growth and trees reaching sixty or more feet into the sky. I could also sense the grade was gradually becoming more uneven which could make carrying the boats quite difficult. I could see numerous rocks along the shorelines and cane growing thickly along the banks of the river. The water at the foot of the waterfall formed a large pool of deceptively quiet water. I anticipated several alligators waiting within the canes for the unwary traveler, but to my surprise we made shore without seeing the dangerous beasts.

The boats were pulled out of the water and Juan began giving the men orders to empty the supplies from the boats. I watched Juan walk over to Serge and speak for a minute.

Serge nodded his head and turned towards me saying, "Could you get Jason and come here for a minute, Juan wants to organize our move above the waterfall."

Juan waited until we arrived and said, "We must move as quietly and quickly as possible. I suspect Indians could be watching this area, because they know we are going upriver and must carry our boats around the waterfall. This will be very dangerous, so we must have our weapons ready for immediate use."

I was the first to speak saying, "How would you like to have the boats and supplies moved?"

Juan acknowledged my question by nodding his head and saying, "I would suggest we move one boat at a time, with half of the supplies from that boat. We can carry the boat and half of the supplies within the boat with six men. I would suggest Serge and Jason accompany that boat as guards, they will also remain with the boat to guard it while five of us return to get the second boat. I will assign one of the men to remain with them to help guard the boat and supplies."

Turning towards me, Juan said, "I would like you, Esteban, and Maria to remain with the second boat and the remaining supplies. I also think it would be a good idea to bury some of the canned goods and extra camping gear after I take the men with me. The additional supplies will be difficult to carry once we begin our travels on land, and they may be needed on our return trip. Esteban will locate a good hiding place after I take the rest of the men with me."

Juan removed his hat and rubbed his left hand through his hair saying, "I know I'm splitting the party, but it is the only way I can think of moving the boats and supplies. This way there will always be three people guarding a boat and supplies while the party is split. Does anyone have any suggestions how to do this in a better way?"

Silence greeted his question, as several individuals slowly shook their heads.

Placing his hat back on his head, Juan said, "I will take Julio and four men to help carry the boat. Esteban you know what to do, as soon as we are out of sight, bury the extra supplies. There is a path beside the river we will use to carry the boat, I will return as quickly as possible." Juan turned quickly and walked towards the men telling them what to do.

Serge lifted his rifle to his shoulder and said, "Jason and I will be all right. Just don't take too long to join us, it gets lonely in the jungle when you're alone." He gave a short nervous laugh and turned towards the boat.

Jason patted my shoulder as he began to follow Serge and said over his shoulder, "Be careful and watch your back."

"You do the same."

As they began to carry the boat up the path, Esteban lowered his voice and said, "Juan is worried that the men are getting scared and will want to turn back to Iquitos. He wants the supplies buried without the men knowing where they are. Get two shovels and lets bury some of these cases. Maria keep your eyes open and your ears alert. Juan has seen signs of Indians in the area, and they could attack at any time."

We quickly selected several cases of canned goods and other gear and Esteban selected a spot to dig. Within fifteen minutes we had buried the goods and covered them with ground debris. I knew they could be found if someone made a determined effort to find them, but unless the spot was stumbled upon, they should remain hidden. It was another fifteen minutes before we noticed Juan and his men walking down the path.

He quickly joined us and said, "I left Serge, Jason, and one of the men to guard the boat and supplies. Let's quickly get this boat and supplies moving. I will use three men to carry the boat. Esteban if you and Julio will carry the supplies, we should be able to move quickly."

Juan turned to me and said, "I would like you and Maria to guard us as we move up the path, it is rough and steep in some places. Keep your eyes open for trouble."

I nodded my head in acknowledgement of his request, Maria and I took our rifles and proceeded to walk ahead of the boat. The path led into the fringe of the jungle as it bordered the river, and as Juan had stated it was rough climbing. I could hear the men struggling behind us as we continued climbing the path, all the while mosquitoes circled my head trying for a meal. I was concentrating on my surroundings when the first shots were fired. The firing seemed to be in controlled bursts, and I could hear yelling from ahead.

I quickly turned to Julio and said, "Put down your supplies, take Maria's weapon and follow me. They must be under attack and if we can surprise the attackers we might be able to drive them away. Be sure to chamber a round, but keep your safety on. I will enter the clearing first, don't fire unless you have a target."

Julio quickly did as I requested and with the sounds of sporadic firing from ahead we proceeded up the path. The undergrowth was thick to either side of the path and visibility was very limited. While moving up the path, I motioned Julio to come close to me. As he approached my left side, I said in a low voice, "We must move quickly, but try to describe what I will see when we come to the end of this path. I must try to be prepared for what could be waiting for us."

Julio nodding his head and said, "We must continue climbing for a short distance and the path winds through this type of jungle growth. The path will end about twenty feet from the river's edge in a small clearing. The clearing might be forty feet wide and seventy feet long beside the river. The jungle is very thick around the clearing. I would suspect the attackers would be within the jungle to your left when you enter the clearing." Julio was having difficulty speaking due to the arduous climb up the path. With sweat running down our foreheads and our shirts sticking to our backs Julio begins motioning me to slow down. I also noticed that the shooting had come to an end and there was a deathly silence from the path ahead.

Breathing heavily Julio said, "The path will turn to the right and then opens into the clearing. I don't hear anything, be careful as you enter the clearing. I will try to cover your back as you continue into the clearing."

Moving slowly to also catch my breath, I said, "Stay to my right and a little behind me. If the attackers are still there they may be on my left, and I will need a clear field of fire."

Julio nodded his understanding of my request, and moved to my right side. As Julio had warned the path began turning to the right and just as suddenly the clearing was before me. The first thing I noticed as I entered the clearing was Jason backing slowly towards the edge of the river. He seemed to be watching for something to attack from the jungle. He must have noticed my approach, because he immediately began turning his rifle towards me. I quickly called out to him, and continued entering the clearing. With my eyes on the jungle for any signs of further attacks I approached Jason, who seemed ready to attack anything that moved.

I continued moving carefully towards Jason and called out to Julio saying, "Julio, watch the jungle while I see to Jason. Make sure the safety is off on your weapon, if you see anything out of the ordinary do not hesitate to fire."

"Cover me," says Jason, as he leans his weapon against the boat and turns towards the river. Taking a few steps into the water he immediately begins to assist Serge in rising from the river.

As I near Jason and Serge I see an Indian lying partially in the water with a large exit wound in his chest. Another Indian is lying near the edge of the jungle, and one of Juan's men is lying near the boat with an arrow in his chest. Turning to assist Jason I notice blood streaming down Serge's left arm.

Realizing Serge is wounded I say to Jason, "Move Serge to the cover of the boat. I'll guard you while you try to stop the bleeding. Maria should be here shortly."

Turning from Jason I see Julio has taken a position near the shore to have a better view of the jungle. I tell Julio to watch for any movement from the jungle while I check on Serge. With a final glance at the surrounding undergrowth to confirm that nothing is about to attack, I slowly move towards Jason and Serge.

"How is he doing?" I ask, noticing Jason helping Serge to lie on the ground with his arm elevated.

Jason glances at me and says, "He should be all right. I'm applying pressure to the wound until Maria gets here. He dropped his rifle in the water, try to find it." Looking beyond me he says, "Are they very far behind you? Serge really needs to be cared for."

Just as I'm about to speak, Julio announces that the rest of the party has entered the clearing. Turning I see Juan and his men carrying the boat out of the jungle. I call Maria to join us and tell her to bring the medical bag.

Juan quickly has the boat placed in the shallow water and has the men loading the supplies. He says something to Esteban and he proceeds to move the second boat into the water. While preparations are quickly proceeding to continue up river, Juan joins Maria as she works on Serge's wound.

With concern on his face, Juan says, "How bad is his arm? We must leave this place quickly. The Indians will want revenge for their dead, they could return at any time."

Without raising her eyes from what she is doing, Maria says, "The wound looks worse than it is. I have taped the wound together and applied a dressing. He will be ready to travel as soon as I finish wrapping his arm."

Juan seemed satisfied with her answer, and without saying a word, turned and began giving orders to his men. The men were responding to Juan's orders, but their attention was constantly on the jungle. Their fear of the Indians was all the incentive they needed to comply with Juan's orders without any hesitancy.

I returned to Julio and asked if he had seen or heard anything from the jungle. With his eyes never leaving the impenetrable undergrowth, he shakes his head saying, "Everything is quiet. I hope we can leave this place very soon. I keep imagining an arrow flying from the jungle straight for me."

While standing beside him with my eyes also scanning the undergrowth, I could also feel the threat of an imminent attack. Without moving my eyes, I said, "Juan has the men loading the boats, he also feels the Indians could return at any time. Maria will have Serge ready to travel, so be ready when I call you to get in your boat. Keep watch, I'm going to help with loading supplies." I took one last glance at the jungle and turned to find the men loading the last of the supplies.

Juan motioned me to get Jason and return to the boats. I could see we would be ready to leave as soon as we had boarded our boat. With our attention on the jungle and the shoreline, we slowly backed towards the boats. After helping to push the boat into the water, we jumped aboard. Esteban quickly started the motor and we proceeded to follow Juan's boat into the turbulent water of the Curaray River.

As we enter the river the current begins to buffet the boat violently causing Esteban to use all his skills to keep the boat headed upriver. I notice the river has decreased in width, and the current has gained in strength. I quickly realize our time on the river will soon come to an end.

I turned for a last look at the receding shore where we had our first casualty. The impact of his loss causes me to realize that I'm not sure what his name was. He had spent a couple weeks with us, but suddenly his life has ended. The adventure of a lifetime had turned very deadly. I slowly turned around to face the front of the boat, with my thoughts dwelling on how quickly death could come to any of us.

The sudden jolt of the boat hitting rough water wakes me from my state of reverie. I realized that I had become so concerned for the dead that I had failed to check on the living. Turning to Jason, I said, "I'm sorry, losing that man caused me to forget to ask how you're doing. Were you wounded during the fight?"

Jason slowly turned, and with a haunting look in his eyes said, "I killed two men today. It happened so fast...there was nothing I could do."

The turmoil within Jason was quite evident by the shaking of his voice and hands, which he kept clasping and unclasping. I could see he had not suffered any visible wounds, but he had been wounded deep within his soul. I grasped his left arm and said, "You did what you had to do. Do you feel like telling me what happened? It might help to talk about it."

He nodded his head, and taking a deep breath said, "It happened so fast. One minute we were talking and looking around the clearing, and suddenly Pablo is clutching at an arrow embedded in his chest." He pauses for a moment and continues, "I think his name was Pablo. I never had a chance to get to know him." Jason sighs as if his thoughts are causing him great pain.

I squeeze his arm to reassure him saying, "Take your time. Try to start at the beginning. After Juan left the three of you in the clearing, what happened?"

Again he takes a deep breath, and in a voice barely audible above the sounds of the river says, "Serge said we should take positions facing the jungle. He told Pablo to take cover near the boat, and he indicated we should find cover behind the supplies." He paused for a minute and seemed to be considering his next words.

Suddenly as if he had found the resolve to continue, Jason began speaking in a stronger voice saying, "Pablo said he heard the call of an owl. He pulls his machete from his belt and says the owl is not from this part of the jungle. In the next instant Pablo is struck by an arrow in his chest, he screams and falls to the ground grasping the arrow. It happened so fast, one minute it was peaceful, and the next a man lays dying on the ground." He looks at me and says, "It happened so fast. I just stood there without moving."

I didn't want to interrupt him, but I could see he needed my acceptance of what he was relating. Looking at him, and getting good eye contact, I said, "Don't beat yourself down. The attack was totally unexpected, and most people would have frozen during the initial moments of the attack. There were two dead Indians in the clearing, you and Serge must have done something right. Tell me what happened after Pablo was hit."

I could see he was starting to open up, as he said, "After a moment Serge and I took cover, and suddenly arrows are coming at us from the jungle. Hoping to scare the Indians away, we fired several rounds into the jungle. The attackers were well hidden, so I fired a few rounds in different directions, not expecting to hit anything just hoping to scare them away. There was silence for thirty seconds and then I see a screaming Indian waving a machete above his head coming out of the jungle. He was charging straight at me, and I could also hear screaming from my left. Without thinking I fired several rounds in his direction, and he seemed to crumble like a rag doll. It all happened so fast I found myself just standing there looking at his broken body, not able to move."

I could see Jason was reliving the fight as he kept nervously rubbing his hands together while relating his story. I had seen this man face many challenging situations in his life, but today's actions had brought him face to face with violent death. My estimation of my friend's inner strengths had greatly increased as I watched him contend within himself with the events of the last hour.

"The screaming of the Indian attacking Serge brought me out of the daze I was in," stated Jason. "I turned to see an Indian swinging a machete at Serge, and striking him in the arm. He was trying to defend himself and while stepping back, lost his footing and fell into the water. The Indian raised his machete preparing to kill Serge, and that is when I fired and killed him. I quickly turned towards the jungle expecting further attacks, but there was only silence. While keeping my eyes on the jungle I began moving towards Serge when you entered the clearing." Relief was evident as he slowly relaxed and turned towards me saying, "Damn, that scared the hell out of me. I hope that's the last time we have to fight anyone on this trip."

With as much reassurance in my voice as I could muster, I said, "I hope you're right." Remembering the looks the Indians had given us as they left the store, I doubted if this was the last we would see of them. I knew this was not the time to remind Jason of that first confrontation, but I felt we would have more trouble before reaching our goal.

As the hours slowly passed, and the events of the morning fell further behind us, a sense of relaxation started to be felt by all. In the beginning only a few words would be spoken by the men, and then only with nervous glances towards the jungle. The river provided enough diversion to keep the men occupied with watching for driftwood and water covered rocks.

Esteban was constantly shouting orders and directing individuals to keep a sharp lookout for anything that might damage the boat.

The river had continued to narrow as we progressed upriver, and in the early afternoon, I felt Esteban turning our boat towards the left shoreline. I had failed to notice that there was a large waterfall a short distance from us. It presented a beautiful site within the emerald green walls of the nearby jungle. As our boat turned towards the shore, I found myself wondering if this could be the second waterfall Phillip had written about.

Jason must have had the same thoughts as I did. He turned and with excitement in his voice said, "This could be the second waterfall. It has to be thirty feet high or more. This could be where Phillip began traveling through the jungle."

I nodded and said, "I think your right. I'll check with Serge when we get ashore, but I have a feeling this is where we also begin to travel overland."

Approaching the shore I became aware of a subtle change in the jungle and the surrounding terrain. The shoreline was covered with cane, but the jungle growth seemed to grow down to the river's edge. The trees which grew within a stones throw from the river rose more than a hundred feet into the air. Their branches and leaves seemed to intertwine to form a canopy that filtered much of the sunlight that tried to penetrate to the ground below. Staring at the world that was fast approaching, I wondered what could be awaiting us during the next part of our adventure.

Juan soon found a place to penetrate the cane and our boats were pulled ashore. Juan asked Jason and myself to stand guard while the men prepared the area for our camp. While the men were clearing the area, I became aware of the sounds of breaking branches overhead. I began studying the nearby trees, and after nearly a minute I began distinguishing shapes moving from branch to branch. They seemed to be chasing each other and completely ignoring our presence below. We remained on guard duty for the next hour as the camp was prepared and food was cooked. The smell of roasted plantains and yucca awakened my need for food, realizing we had last eaten many hours before.

"Are you ready to eat something?" asked Serge, as he carefully made his way towards my position at the edge of the encampment. The undergrowth was thick and walking was difficult, especially trying to carry two plates of food.

Waiting until Serge neared my position, keeping my voice low, I said, "I didn't realize how hungry I was until the smell of the food reached me." As I took the plate Serge offered, he stated he would keep watch while I ate. Thanking him I immediately proceeded to take advantage of the opportunity to enjoy a hot meal. While I was eating Serge informed me that Juan wanted to meet with the group to discuss the next part of our trip.

As I finished my meal and resumed my sentry duty, I said, "Finish your meal, I'll keep watch while you eat." While looking around I said, "Did Juan indicate what he wants to talk about?"

While eating Serge says, "He plans on taking a couple of the men after they finish eating and walk upriver beyond this waterfall. He wants to see if traveling by boat is possible beyond this waterfall. I told him that my information stated that boat travel was very dangerous further upriver."

It was several hours before sunset when Juan and a couple men left the camp moving along the shoreline. I could hear Esteban giving orders to the men and soon after that I noticed he was making his way slowly towards my position.

Esteban smiled as he approached the tree I was leaning against and said, "How was the food? I hope Serge brought you enough."

Smiling I said, "It was fine, I enjoyed it. I see Juan has left the camp. Have you two talked about the next part of this trip?"

His smile quickly disappeared from his face, as he said, "Yes, we have discussed the next part of the trip. We both agree that either tonight or in the morning the men will demand we return to Iquitos. They are very fearful of the Indians, and the last attack caused the death of one of their companions. I must caution you to sleep tonight with your pistol. We also feel that it will be to dangerous to continue upriver by boat, we must continue on foot keeping the river nearby. Juan has gone ahead to check the conditions of the river and look for trails along the river."

I also had felt some tension among the men, especially after the attack, but I had assumed it was due to the death of one of their number. Turning towards Esteban I said, "Do you plan on hiding the boats and extra supplies?"

"Yes, we can not take everything with us."

Nodding my head, I agreed with him, and suggested we hide our supplies well enough so the Indians would not find them.

He shrugged his shoulders saying, "The Indians are very good, but Juan feels he can disguise the goods so they will not find them." Rising he says, "I must return to the camp and check on the men. I will send one of the men to relieve you in half an hour."

I thanked him for stopping by and spending time with me. I enjoyed the times Esteban and I had been able to spend together. He reminded me of men I had met in the military that I would not hesitate to ask to cover my back if we were in danger. He was a quiet man, but he always seemed aware of what was going on around him. I would certainly rely on his words of caution, and keep my pistol loaded and at hand.

An hour before sundown, Juan returned with his two men. He spoke with Esteban, and proceeded to get himself a beer. Esteban walked over to Jason and I and said, "Juan would like you to get the others and come over to the fire. He wants to discuss the next part of the trip."

I had noticed Serge, Julio, and Maria relaxing near the boats. I told Jason I would get them, and we would meet him at the fire.

Walking towards the fire I could hear Juan speaking with Esteban, who proceeded to direct the men to care for several chores. I assumed he wanted to keep them busy while he talked with us. I still wondered if any of his men could speak English.

Finishing his beer, Juan set the bottle down and said, "I have followed a faint trail beside the river for several miles. The river above this waterfall is very rough and I would advise not trying to take the boats any further. If we are to continue, it will have to be by foot. I suggest we hide the boats and extra supplies in this area, and hopefully they will be here when we are ready to return to Iquitos." Looking around the group, he says, "Does this meet with your approval?"

As we all nodded our heads in agreement, I said, "I would say we all agree. How do you plan on hiding the boats and supplies?"

He smiled saying, "I discovered a small cave behind the waterfall. We must be very careful not to leave any signs that we went behind the waterfall, but it would be a good hiding place." Turning towards Serge, he said, "As I remember, you indicated that we would have to walk about three days from the river to find the lost city. With this in mind we must carry only what is necessary for seven to ten days. The rest of the supplies must be left in the cave." I noticed Juan pausing for a moment, as if trying to select his next words, "I have one more concern I must share with all of you." At this point he looked around, as if to confirm our privacy and said, "I suspect we will have trouble with the men. With the death of Pablo, they are very frightened and want to return to Iquitos. I have overheard them discussing their fears, and I expect they will confront me tonight or in the morning. We must keep all weapons secured and out of their reach. They have their machetes, but no firearms. If there is trouble do not underestimate their abilities to use the machete as a weapon. Are there any questions?"

We were so preoccupied with our thoughts that no one responded to Juan's question. After a period of silence, Serge spoke for all of us when he said that there would be very little sleep for the group tonight. We all agreed and Juan suggested that we partner with someone and take turns sleeping during the night. We broke up the meeting as the sun was slowly setting into the west. The jungle seemed unnaturally quiet that evening as we settled onto our sleeping mats.

The men had returned after our meeting and I could see Juan assigning various tasks to the men. After they were dismissed, they moved towards the boats and settled upon the ground talking among themselves. I had a very uncomfortable feeling about that little group, as every few minutes one after another would raise his head and quickly confirm they were alone.

I turned to Jason and said, "Would you care to flip a coin to see who takes first watch?"

"No, You were on guard duty while we ate. Get some rest, and I'll wake you in a few hours."

I thanked Jason and proceeded to cover myself with the netting. The mosquitoes were already trying to find a way inside my netting for an evening meal. Rolling over to face Jason I said, "If you start to feel sleepy, wake me up. Also try to keep an eye on the men without them noticing." Jason acknowledged my advice and tried to make himself as comfortable as he could, but still remain awake.

I tried to relax, but between the insects and the thoughts of possible danger whirling through my mind, sleep did not come easy. I remember placing my hand on my pistol and feeling comforted by its touch, and the next thing I knew my arm was being shaken.

I heard Jason saying in a low voice, "It's almost midnight, are you able to take over?"

I quickly rubbed the sleep from my eyes, and turning over said, "Yeah,

I'm awake. Is everything quiet?"

"It's quiet," said Jason with a hint of concern in his voice. Leaning towards me he said, "The men went to their mats about an hour ago, but they remained in deep conversation for several hours. When they broke up it seemed as if they had come to a decision. We could have trouble very soon. If you're ready, I'll try to get some sleep."

I told him to get some rest, and I sat up to look about the camp. The fire was just a bed of coals and several of the men were snoring loud enough to keep the alligators away. I could just make out the form of Esteban leaning against a tree at the edge of the camp. Seeing Esteban on guard gave me a feeling of reassurance as I turned to try and find the other guard. After several minutes of trying to find the guard, I gave up, whoever the other guard was I could not see him.

Dawn crept slowly upon the jungle, with the trees and undergrowth slowly taking form. The animals were also waking with their usual cacophony of calls and shrieks. The camp also came alive before the sun had risen above the trees, I could see Juan and Esteban moving among the men assigning tasks to be done. I woke Jason and told him to get prepared to move when Juan gives the signal. Before waking Jason I had rolled my mat and had my pack ready to load on the boat.

"I'll be right back," I said to Jason, "I'm going to see Serge for a few minutes."

Moving across the camp, I could see Maria putting a new dressing on Serge's arm. He looked rested and seemed to be moving the arm without to much trouble. Squatting next to Serge I said, "How's the arm this morning?"

He was about to answer when he winced as Maria tightened the bandage around his arm. "I'm doing fine," he said, with a slight grimace, "The doctor says I'm ready to tackle the jungle single-handed."

As Maria was packing her medical case, she grinned and said, "If I were you, I would not pick a large jungle to tackle. That is a nasty wound, and we must keep it clean. This environment is very dangerous for people with open wounds. I checked on you during the night and noticed you had a low fever, but you are back to normal this morning." As she rose from Serge's side, she said, "Try not to over exert yourself today." Chuckling she said, "That's the doctor speaking, I realize where we are. Just be as careful as you can as we move through the jungle."

After Maria left I moved closer to Serge and asked how he was feeling. He indicated he was sore, but he would be able to keep up with the group.

Looking about he said, "Have you noticed Juan's men, they do as they are told, but very reluctantly. I suspect we will have trouble this morning, you and Jason be ready to cover Juan if they confront him. I've already spoken to Julio, just be alert."

As I was preparing to return to gather my gear, I heard Juan calling our group to gather around him. He was also speaking with one of his men, who seemed very agitated. I stood near Jason, and I said, "They are speaking Spanish, interpret what they are saying. If there is a problem I want to be ready for what might happen."

He acknowledged my request and said, "That is Manuel, and he wants Juan to give him one of the boats to return to Iquitos. He says the men are afraid of the Indians, and want to leave the jungle."

Juan shakes his head from side to side saying, *"No, los botes se quedan con nosotros. Tu conoces la selva sigue el rio hasta la Sta. Clotilde, deahi tu consigues un bote para Iquitos."*

Manuel looks at the men around him and says, *"Sin bote, nosotros morimos."*

Juan changes his tone of voice, and in a reassuring manner says, *"Lo mejor es que se queden con nosotros."*

Manuel turns to the men around him and begins speaking with them. They seem to be unsure of what to do, and while they are debating what has been said, I turn to Jason.

Keeping my voice low, I said, "Fill me in on what's going on."

Jason leans towards me and says, "Juan told Manuel that the boats remain here. He said if they want to leave they know the jungle, and could follow the river to Sta. Clotilde and get a boat to Iquitos. Manuel said they would die without a boat. Juan said that it would be better to stay with us. They are discussing what they should do. I think they are afraid of Juan and they are aware of our weapons."

I had kept my eyes on Manuel and his men while Jason interpreted what had been said. I saw one of the other men step forward and say, *"Los indios nos van a matar. Ellos tienen el apoyo de le gente de la selva."*

In the same reassuring voice, Juan said, *"No, ellos son gente buena. Es tu decision si te quedas con nosotros o caminas hasta le Sta. Clotilde."*

Manuel pulled the other man to his side and said something to him, and then he spoke with Juan for a few moments. Juan nodded his head, and the men moved to the other side of the camp.

Leaning towards Jason, I said, "Now what's happening?"

Jason took a deep breath, and said, "Whew, that was close. Efrain stepped forward and told Juan that the Indians would attack and kill all of them. He also said that the Indians have the powers of the forest people. I could see Juan was trying to calm them down. He said that the Indians are just people, and they have no special powers. He gave them the ability to choose between staying with us or walking back to Sta. Clotilde. He reminded them that we are safer if we stay together. They have decided to talk it over between themselves, and Manuel will let Juan know what their decision will be."

The four men were standing near the underbrush at the edge of the camp, and I could see there was disagreement between them as to what they would do. If all four of the men left, it would almost cut our group in half. Juan had indicated the men were not very dependable, but a group of eleven is much more formidable than a group of seven. Serge had walked over to Juan and was speaking when the four men approached them.

I leaned towards Jason and said, "Listen carefully, if there is trouble, let me know."

Serge remained at Juan's side as Manuel began speaking, after a few minutes I could see Serge's head nodding in agreement. When Manuel finished speaking, Juan asked them a question, and they all responded. Juan responded, "*Muy bien.*" He then turned to Serge and said something and Serge turned towards our group.

We gathered around Serge as he said, "It looks like Juan has everything under control for the time being. The men are very frightened of the Indians, but Juan has assured them that there is more protection for them with the group than on their own. He also reminded them that we have modern weapons to protect ourselves. He told the men to help hide the boats and extra supplies, for our return trip." At this point I noticed Serge seem to hesitate in his telling of the confrontation.

"Why the hesitation?" I said. "What else was said that you don't want to reveal?"

Looking at me with concern evident on his face, Serge says, "Juan promised the men that if we don't find what we are looking for, we would turn around and return here. I think Juan is also becoming worried being this deep in unexplored country."

Julio put his hand on Serge's shoulder and said, "Juan is a good man, he will stay with us to the end. He knows the men are needed, and I suspect he is trying to do what is necessary to keep the group together." Turning to the rest of the group Julio says, "I have known Juan for a while, we must trust in his judgment. We have worked together on some very dangerous trips, and he always covered my back. If he made that promise to the men, he has good reasons for doing it."

We all agreed to follow Juan's leadership on this matter. The boats and extra supplies were carried behind the waterfall, and great care was taken to hide any signs of our passage to the hiding place. Juan assigned each one of his men various supplies that they would carry, while we carried full packs and our weapons. Serge had informed Juan that we needed to travel upriver crossing two tributaries entering from the west into the Curaray River. When we reach the second tributary we should turn inland, and continue for three days travel.

It was decided to leave the area as soon as the equipment had been hidden. The morning progressed well, with a short break for a quick uncooked meal, and then the march continued. In the early afternoon light gray colored monkeys that seemed very interested in what we were doing in their territory accompanied us for several miles. I had grown accustomed to their chatter and playfulness in the upper limbs of the trees, so when unexpected silence descended upon the jungle I was stunned.

I tapped Juan on the arm and said, "Have you noticed the sudden silence? The gray monkeys had been with us for some distance, now they are gone. Could there be Indians in the area?"

Juan motioned for the group to stop and remain silent. I watched him slowly begin to scan the surrounding thick foliage of the jungle, with hand signs he indicated we should do the same. The silence was so complete that I could hear the low roar of the river that was some distance to the east of our position.

With so many eyes on the surrounding jungle, I let my eyes begin to wander up into the trees. They rose more than a hundred feet from the ground, and their branches and leaves seemed to filter out the majority of the sunlight. The enormity of the trees and vines made me feel like a small child, it was truly an overwhelming experience. While studying the branches overhead, I began to distinguish shapes and shadows moving from branch to branch.

I turned to Juan saying, "Are those monkeys? I can just barely see some movement in the upper branches."

Looking up, Juan said, "There's the reason for the silence of the jungle. They scared the small gray monkeys away, these are much more aggressive monkeys." As he said this one of the large monkeys rushed down several branches and began screeching and barring his teeth. "They feel we have invaded their territory. Let's move on so they will quiet down. This could bring some unwanted attention to our group."

Within an hour we came upon a small tributary flowing from the west. Juan suggested we travel upstream and look for a safe place to cross to the other side. The stream was about thirty feet wide, but its depth was unknown. The forest was thick on both sides of the stream, where trees hung low over the water. While standing next to the water I found myself looking into a tunnel formed by the low hanging branches of the trees. Much of the light was blocked out by these trees, which provided a dark eerie atmosphere surrounding the stream flowing out of the jungle.

Juan led the group through thick undergrowth for some distance, periodically stopping to investigate the stream. Within an hour he had found a suitable crossing and without incident we were able to safely continue downstream towards the Curaray River.

I could hear the river before it came into sight as we broke through the undergrowth of dense shrubs and thick grasses. Juan had the men get some beer, and several bottles were shared between all of us. Juan indicated that we had a couple hours of daylight and we should take advantage of this time to continue upstream. I had a feeling he wanted to get as much distance as he could from the boats before setting up camp. It might help to discourage the men from slipping away during the night to return to the supplies.

Juan continued to follow the faint path through the jungle, which seemed to run parallel to the river. I noticed the path would disappear frequently only to reappear as a faint discoloration of the vegetation that grew upon the jungle floor. I quickly realized that without Juan's ability to move through this type of terrain, our progress would be greatly affected.

We had traveled for about an hour when Juan stopped the group and motioned Esteban to his side. After a quick discussion with Esteban, Juan and one of the men quickly left the group and disappeared into the jungle. As the rest of the party slowly formed around Esteban, he indicated for us to relax and wait.

I approached Esteban and said, "I noticed Juan took one of the men and continued up the path, is there a problem?"

With a smile and a negative shake of his head, he said, "Juan felt he could locate a campsite for the night much easier without the group following him. He can move very quickly and quietly in the jungle. He will return shortly. It has been a long day, enjoy this chance to rest."

Esteban's words were sufficient to quell any fears of the unknown and the group began finding comfortable places to sit and wait on the return of Juan.

The evening shadows were beginning to lengthen as Juan appeared out of the jungle. He paused for a moment to observe the group and then approached Esteban. They spoke for a few moments and then he turned and spoke to his men. Several of them quickly rose from the ground and taking some of the equipment, they proceeded to follow Juan into the jungle.

Esteban spoke to the rest of his men, and then turning to our group said, "Juan has found a good campsite. He has taken a few men to clear the area and have some food prepared. We are to bring the rest of the supplies to the campsite."

As he was picking up his pack, Serge asked, "How far away is the site? The sun will be setting in a little more than an hour."

Esteban was moving among the men and encouraging them to quickly organize the equipment and prepare to leave. While tending to his duties, he said, "It is not far. Maybe 20 minutes up the trail. Juan wanted to find a location that would be safe for the night."

Shouldering my pack I moved near Esteban saying, "Does Juan anticipate trouble tonight?"

"No, he is trying to keep our presence hidden from the Indians." Esteban continued to get the group organized and as we proceeded north along the path he said, "I hope he is successful."

Esteban proceeded to take the lead and guide the group into the jungle. I couldn't help reflect on his last words. I to hoped Juan would be successful in keeping our presence hidden from the Indians, but I suspected they knew where we were. With these thoughts occupying most of my attention, I almost walked into Jason as he came to an abrupt stop.

"Why have we stopped?" I asked Jason. He turned slightly and said, "Esteban seems to be looking for something."

Suddenly an individual stepped out of the jungle and motioned us to approach. Esteban quickly got the group moving, and as we approached I realized that one of Juan's men had been waiting for us to appear. He led the group into the jungle away from the path, which quickly disappeared behind us. Juan had selected a campsite that was out of sight of the trail. Within minutes we entered a small clearing that the men had prepared for the night, and a small fire had been started.

Juan gathered his men together and gave his instructions for the evening. He then approached our group and said, "If I can have your attention for a few minutes. I have tried to select a campsite for tonight that is off the path we have been following. I will have the men prepare a quick meal and then the fire will be put out for the night. While traveling in this country, we must try to follow a few basic rules. Silence is critical for us to remain hidden from our enemies. We must also be very aware of leaving any evidence of our passing this way. This country belongs to the Indians and we are the trespassers. Understand, we will be shot on sight by the people who live in this land, so take every precaution necessary for your survival."

Juan paused for a moment and wiped his forehead with his sleeve. Making eye contact with each of us he said, "This has been a dangerous adventure thus far, but from here on, it is deadly. Have your weapons ready for immediate use, and always keep your eyes on the jungle around you. The Indians of this forest are masters of disguise and will blend in with the undergrowth so well that you could walk into one of them without realizing their presence. Once the sun has set, you must be settled for the night. There will be no talking unless absolutely necessary. Sound carries very well at night in the jungle." With a reassuring smile, Juan turned and motioned Esteban to follow him.

Serge motioned me to his side and speaking in a hushed voice said, "I think we will find the second tributary tomorrow. If you remember the journal stated that Phillip traveled three days from the river to the city." He paused for a moment and slowly turned his head, saying, "Did you hear that call? It had a strange honking sound. I don't recall hearing a sound like that before."

After looking around the area, I said, "I heard the sounds, but it is evening and this part of the jungle has changed much from the jungle near the Amazon. Listen to the sounds of this area, even the monkeys are calling to each other. Remember the jungle is never quiet until the sun has set and then many of the sounds are deadly."

Juan walked through the camp encouraging the group to eat quickly so the fire could be extinguished. With a final crescendo of sounds from the jungle, we finished our meal and prepared to make our final preparations for sleeping.

I remember waking to the screeching sounds of many brilliantly colored parrots flying above our campsite. Looking about I could see others of the group were rising from their sleeping mats and preparing for another day. The jungle was alive with the sounds of monkeys howling and birds calling to each other. I realized I had grown accustomed to the sounds of the jungle in a very short time. It truly was a world that had to be experienced to be appreciated.

Juan instructed his men to pack the gear and he informed us to be ready to leave in ten minutes. We were to clean our sleeping areas and leave no evidence of our ever being here. Esteban said Juan felt uneasy as if we were being watched from the jungle. The group took very little encouraging complying with his orders, and we were ready to leave in his allotted ten minutes.

Juan led the group back to the path we had been following north beside the Curaray River. As we neared the river I could hear the rushing sounds of water, but the dense undergrowth made it impossible to see the river. We continued following the faint path north constantly looking for the second tributary.

We almost stumbled into the water of a slow moving stream flowing from the west. Juan stopped the group and indicated we would rest long enough to eat and drink, but no fires were allowed. He spoke to Esteban and then to Serge, who motioned the group to his side.

As we approached Serge he said, "Juan feels this is the second tributary we have been looking for. I also feel this could be the tributary that is described in the journal. I asked Juan to remain on this side of the stream and to proceed west. If the journal is correct, we should begin entering a mountainous region by late tomorrow."

It was agreed that we should change our direction of travel and follow the stream west. After a quick meal of crackers and water Juan led the group into the jungle, but this time with no path to follow. It soon became evident that without the path to follow our progress would be slowed considerably.

The following two days passed slowly with my only memories being the insects and the heat. The jungle never seemed to be silent with the overpowering sounds of millions of insects and the heat of the jungle draining the fluids quickly from our bodies. As Serge had indicated when we left the Curaray River, the terrain had steadily begun to climb in elevation. Juan kept us moving parallel with the stream, but at a distance that would keep us away from the heavy underbrush. We were an exhausted group that made camp on the second day of travel. Juan continued to insist that the fire be extinguished after the evening meal and no unnecessary talking was permitted. He had indicated to Serge that he felt the Indians were following and could attack at any time.

I had finished eating and was lying on my mat with my eyes closed, when Serge said, "Are you asleep yet?"

I slowly opened my eyes, but without moving said, "No, but it won't be long. Have a seat if you want to talk."

I watched him slowly sit beside my mat and rolling to face him asked, "What's on your mind?"

"Juan has told me that he feels the presence of the Indians all about us, and is greatly concerned for our safety. If the journal is correct, we could be in the area of the city some time tomorrow." Looking towards the surrounding jungle, his concern was very evident and his next words spoke volumes.

"We may not come out of this alive." He paused and slowly wiped sweat from his forehead saying, "We have traveled more than three weeks into a world that is very unforgiving. I never dreamed death could be waiting for you in so many ways. Juan stated the men would turn around, but they also feel that safety in numbers and our weapons could keep them alive."

I sat up stretching and said, "We knew this would be dangerous, but I agree it does seem to be more than we had bargained for. Remember we have trained for years for just this chance, and we could be within reach of our dreams."

Nodding he said, "I know, I guess I just needed to hear some reassuring words. We have been traveling in total silence and it just makes our isolation that much greater."

The sounds of some monkeys moving through the tree tops seemed to provide a familiar sound that had a calming effect on Serge as he looked up with a smile saying, "I guess they must be getting ready for bed."

Wanting to keep his mind occupied with other things, I asked, "It would be best to remind the others to keep their eyes open for the symbol of the coiled serpent. We don't know where Phillip has placed his markings, but tomorrow will be the third day."

As expected Serge's whole demeanor changed, and with excitement in his voice he said, "That is a good idea. I will spend a few minutes with the others before the sun has set." Rising he smiled and said, "Thanks for letting me bend your ear." Smiling he said, "It was like old times."

As he turned to go I said, "Sleep well my friend. Tomorrow may be a day of discovery."

Pulling my netting over my head, and settling myself for the night I thought of our conversation. This was a very dangerous trip, and his statement of not living through the adventure was a possibility. Just this day we saw a fourteen-foot-long python draped along a branch. We were close enough to see its tongue flickering in and out. The group seemed to move more warily as we continued deeper into the jungle. Though danger is all about us, things of great interest are also to be found.

After the noon meal, one of Juan's men said he had found some black wax. Julio said that a small bee no larger than an ant, builds its home in the ground. The bees produce a white wax and deposit it in the branches of a small tree, which is hollow, and divided into compartments like the joints of a cane. The wood of the tree is soft and the deposited wax slowly absorbs the color of the sap of the tree, changing the color of the wax.

As the night sounds of the jungle slowly drifted into a soft lullaby of tiny twitters and little chirps my mind drifts away with the thoughts of how marvelous this land really is.

I awoke to the sounds of parrots and other birds greeting the world with their calls. I could see the camp was stirring and Juan had his men packing. After a quick breakfast of fried plantains Juan directed Esteban to have the men clean the campsite. He then called our group together and informed us that he expected trouble from the Indians today.

Julio was the first to speak, saying, "What have you seen?"

With his eyes constantly moving around the camp he said, "We are being followed, and I have seen at least four people moving in the shadows. They are Indians, and if I see four, I know there are more. They will not confront us, but they will attack from the jungle."

Turning to Serge, he said, "Is it possible we will see the city today?"

Serge shrugged his shoulders saying, "The journal indicated three days' travel. This is our third day of travel, it is possible we could be in the area this afternoon. We can only wait and see."

Nodding his head in agreement, Juan said, "I hope it is today. The Indians are very superstitious, and the ruins might scare them away. Keep your weapons ready for use, I expect we will be attacked today."

Looking around the camp, Juan said, "The men have everything packed, get your packs and let's get moving."

The morning passed without incident and progress was good considering the rugged terrain we were traveling through. Juan kept the stream to our right, and periodically we were able to see how the quiet stream had changed into a swiftly moving body of water.

At mid day we came to a clearing where the stream had formed a pool of water at the bottom of a small waterfall. Juan cautioned the group to wait within the jungle's edge until he and a couple men could confirm that we were alone. Esteban set up a quick location for the guards and we watched Juan move cautiously into the clearing.

The clearing consisted of an area of approximately 100 square yards with an imposing tree covered cliff before us. A small waterfall magically appeared out of the underbrush of the cliff and fell 30 feet to a bubbling pool of water. The ground around the pool and stream were heavily strewn with rocks of various sizes, and the water of the stream was tumbling over numerous pale colored rocks. The surrounding jungle was thickly covered with undergrowth and towering trees were reaching for the welcomed sunlight. I could see Juan directing each of his men to move to either side of the pool and he continued toward the stream. Juan seemed to be looking for tracks as he continually kept his eyes on the ground swinging his head from side-to-side. I knew he was worried about an ambush in such an open area, but Juan had mentioned we needed to refill our water containers.

I moved slowly to Serge's side and said, "Have you noticed the quantity of rocks in this area, and the height of the cliff before us? I bet we are looking at a cliff formed of limestone. Remember Phillip noted that there were limestone cliffs near the entrance to the city. This may be the area we should spend time investigating."

With a slight smile he said, "You must be reading my mind. I think we need to get on the other side of the stream and begin looking for evidence that Phillip was here. The terrain has been steadily climbing and that cliff could be surrounding the city. Remember he said the city was in a valley surrounded by cliffs."

Before we could say more, Esteban indicated Juan wanted the group to approach the pool. With weapons ready we stepped out into the sunlight and with eyes half shut from the brightness of the sun, we quickly moved to the pool. Crossing the brush covered clearing caused the skin of my back to tingle in anticipation of an arrow from the surrounding undergrowth. I had forgotten how unprotected it felt to be out in the open after traveling for days in the jungle.

Juan motioned us to him saying, "Quickly fill your water containers, I do not like being out in the open."

While the group filled their containers and resumed their positions to guard the others, I noticed Jason stop filling his canteen and look towards the trees.

I moved next to Jason and asked, "What's the matter? Did you see or hear something?"

"Listen, did you hear the call of an owl?"

Shaking my head, I said, "No, but I really was not paying attention."

While reattaching his canteen, Jason said, "I think that was the call I heard before we were attacked at the boats." Suddenly his head lifted and he said, "Did you hear that?"

I also heard the call of an owl and nodded that I also heard the call. I told Jason to mention this to Serge and Julio and I would warn Juan of a possible attack.

Turning away from Jason I noticed Juan looking at us and then looking at the jungle. He also must have suspected that something was not right. Walking towards Juan I said, "Jason thinks he heard the call of an owl, it could be the same call he heard when he was attacked at the boats."

As I neared Juan, I noticed he never moved his eyes away from the jungle surrounding us. Without moving his body he said, "I also heard the call, and that owl does not live in this area. I knew it was possible that we were being watched, but they might attack at any time. I would suggest we move to the other side of the stream, it would be easier to defend ourselves with the cliff to our backs. Please tell the others to slowly move to the stream. I will have Esteban lead the way across the stream, will you help me cover our move across?"

Nodding my willingness to help I said, "Sure, I'll tell Serge to get the others moving behind Esteban."

Serge had been observing our conversation and when I approached he said, "Do we have trouble?"

"Yes," I said, trying not to show the apprehension I felt for our safety. Keeping my voice low, I said, "Jason heard the call of an owl, he thinks it was the same call that he had heard when he was attacked a couple days ago. Juan heard the call also, and suggests we get to the other side of the stream. I will stay behind with Juan to cover our crossing. Tell Julio and Jason to be prepared to cover our backs when our turn comes to cross over."

While we were speaking, the call of an owl could be heard from the jungle behind us.

Turning away from Serge I said, "Get the others moving, I see Esteban has his men preparing to cross now."

Juan was turning from Esteban when an arrow flew between them and struck the ground. I heard screams from the jungle surrounding us, and then more arrows arched out of the undergrowth striking all around us. The screams were a great motivator for hurrying the party across the stream, but crossing on the rocks was treacherous. They were slick with slim and water covered making the footing very dangerous.

Juan and I took cover behind the largest rocks we could find, but so far I had not seen a single attacker. I decided to fire a couple rounds into the undergrowth in hopes of driving our attackers away. Juan must have had the same idea, as he also fired some shots into the jungle. While firing I heard a scream behind us, and quickly turning my head I saw one of Juan's men fall in the stream. I could not tell if he had been hit or had lost his footing. As I turned back to face the jungle I saw four Indians running towards our position and firing arrows as they ran. I rose from behind my rock to fire and felt my hat snatched from my head by one of the arrows that had been fired at us. I quickly fired a three round burst not knowing if I had hit anyone and moved to another position.

Rising to fire I saw one of the men lying on the ground and another clutching his chest after Juan had fired a couple rounds. The remaining two attackers had grabbed their machetes and were running as fast as they could to close the distance between us. Leaping from behind the rock I had used for cover, I fired a quick shot, which I could see never hit my attacker. A green painted Indian was screaming at me as he ran straight towards me swinging his weapon. I braced for his attack holding my SKS across my chest hoping to block his first swing. The machete hit my rifle with such force that it almost flew from my hands. The vibrations from the force of the strike against the rifle ran up my arms and it took all I had not to step back from his attack. He kept screaming in my face as he prepared to swing another time.

I knew I had to close the distance between us if I was going to survive this attack. I could try to use my rifle as a club or drop it and grab my knife. I stepped inside his next swing and dropped the rifle with my left hand and with my right hand reached for my belt knife. I grabbed for his right hand to hold the machete away while trying to drive my knife into his body. As we struggled I tripped and we fell to the ground, striking my head on a rock. I felt dazed and I realized he would soon over power me as my head was ringing from the fall and my sight was blurring. He twisted his hand from my grasp and rose with the machete to strike when a shot rang out near my head. A look of astonishment crossed my attackers face as the bullet threw him to the ground.

I turned my head to the right and saw Juan holding his rifle and looking for further attackers. He reached for my arm saying, "Are you able to rise? We must cross the stream while we are not being attacked. I can hear the others firing their weapons, they must be under attack. Where have you been injured?"

My vision was slowly clearing as Juan helped me rise. My head was pounding as I said, "I hit my head on a rock when we fell, but I should be able to cross the stream. Give me a second to clear my head before we move."

My head felt like it had been split in two, and reaching behind my left ear I could feel blood running down my neck. I suspected I had a slight concussion from the fall, but my vision had cleared and I felt it best to get moving. Juan handed my rifle to me and asked if I was ready to try and cross the stream. I told him that I was ready and together we crossed to the other side without incident.

As we came to the opposite shore I saw the body of one of Juan's men lying among the rocks. Juan turned him over and I could see an arrow sticking out of his neck.

Juan took my arm and said, "Quickly, we must help the others. It sounds like they are still under attack." Looking at the body he said, "If we can, we will come back for Manuel's body."

I could hear yelling from the jungle to our right, and occasional shots were being fired from within the jungle. As we approached the sounds of battle, I spotted Serge and Jason firing into the jungle. Juan moved to Esteban's side and they began speaking rapidly. I could see Maria placing a bandage on Julio's left arm which was slick with blood.

"Serge, how are you doing?" I called as I knelt next to him. He had taken cover behind a large tree, which was sufficient protection for the both of us.

He fired into the jungle and turning his head said, "I think we are in trouble. I saw you fall to the ground when you were attacked. Are you all right?"

I turned to show him where I had struck my head saying, "You tell me."

I could feel his fingers moving the matted hair behind my ear when he said, "You have a nasty split in your scalp, and it's bleeding bad. See Maria as soon as she is finished with Julio. He took an arrow to his upper arm, there seems to be no sign of poison."

I started to rise when Serge said, "Before seeing Maria, ask Juan to come over for a minute. I think it would be a good idea to start moving to higher ground. If we wait to long our attackers will have us surrounded."

I agreed with his assessment of the situation and told him I would ask Juan to visit him as soon as he could. Keeping my head low, I turned and noticed Julio returning with his weapon to assist in defending our position.

As Julio passed me I asked, "How is the arm?"

He ducked behind the tree and said, "Maria said the wound was not too bad. There was no evidence of poison." Looking at the side of my head, he said, "I think you should see Maria. That head wound is bleeding and could get infected."

I thanked him for the advice and turned to find Juan and Maria. I found Juan and Esteban in an animated discussion behind some heavy underbrush. They turned as I approached and Juan said, "I think we better get out of this area. The Indians seem to have a large force and they could surround us in this position."

Taking advantage of the shelter given by the heavy undergrowth I joined them saying, "I just left Serge, and he suggested we move towards the cliff. It would give us the ability to keep the Indians from surrounding us."

Juan nodded his agreement saying, "We will get everyone ready to move toward the cliff. You better see Maria and get that wound cared for."

Juan and Esteban quickly separated and moved through the group, while I located Maria for some quick first aid. During the next ten minutes several arrows were fired at our group and we responded with a couple shots. It was agreed not to waste our ammunition firing into the jungle at shadows. The Indians were masters at camouflage and were only visible when they stepped into the open to attack.

Juan told us to keep the Indians occupied while he took one of his men to find a safe way toward the cliff. We all took turns firing several shots into the jungle hoping the Indians would not notice two of our group had left. It seemed to take ages, but within ten minutes Juan had returned and joined Serge and myself behind the large tree.

"I have found a dry creek bed," stated Juan, wiping the sweat from his face with his shirtsleeve. "It looks like during the rainy season the creek flows from high on the cliff face. We might be able to find a place to defend ourselves by following the creek. I think it offers a good chance to escape this area we are trying to defend."

I turned to Serge saying, "It sounds good to me. I don't think we have much time before the next attack."

Serge agreed and Juan suggested Esteban and Jason cover our retreat. I said I would ask Jason if he would be willing to join Esteban in providing the rear guard. Juan said he would return after checking with Esteban. Within a couple minutes the group were prepared to follow Juan towards the creek bed, and Esteban and Jason took positions to protect our retreat.

We had been moving as quietly as possible along the creek bed when shots were fired from our rear guards. It didn't take the Indians long to discover that we were moving and they were determined to not let us escape. The next several minutes were consumed in a wild race for the cliff hoping to find some place to provide shelter from our attackers. The old creek bed was covered in small rocks and was treacherous to run on. It soon became evident that we were climbing in elevation as the effort to run up hill was taking its toll on each of us.

After what seemed an eternity, with my head pounding and sweat stinging my eyes. Juan stopped the group and said to take cover behind the rocks. We had followed the creek to a point where it leveled out as it wound between large trees and rocks. Within moments we had all found something to hide behind and also realized we were on a narrow strip of land on the face of the cliff.

Esteban and Jason came running into our position with several arrows following their flight.

"Man, that was close," said Jason as he fell to the ground beside me. With a grin on his face he looked up saying, "I think those people are serious about kicking our asses. Esteban and I were running and shooting and all the time arrows were flying all around us."

Rising from the ground and looking around Jason said, "I don't think we can hold this position very long, those Indians will get above us. These are very determined people."

Before he could say more several arrows flew over our heads and we could hear yelling from below our position. I motioned for Serge to join me and I asked him to get Juan to continue upstream looking for a better place to defend ourselves. Serge nodded his agreement and quickly moved on.

I was so absorbed in staying low and firing at the enemy that the tap on my shoulder caused me to jump and yell. I swung my rifle to fire just as Serge said, "It's me, don't shoot." It took several seconds to slow my heartbeat and be able to respond.

"You almost caused me a heart attack." I took a deep breath and said, "Did Juan find a better place for the group?"

With a big grin on his face Serge said, "Yes, we found a great place. I also found the symbol left by Phillip carved in the cliff face, it was at the entrance to a cave."

It took me a moment for Serge's words to register with my mind. I grabbed his arm and said, "You found the symbol of the coiled serpent around a limb? The same one that was sketched in the journal?"

With the grin still on his face, Serge said, "Yes, just like the sketch. Juan wants to move the group into the cave. Tell the others to get their gear and move up the creek bed, it turns to the left and disappears into the cliff."

Serge's description of the path of the creek was accurate and within a short period of time I saw the entrance to a small cave disappearing into the cliff. The entrance to the cave was a little less than five feet square, but Serge said it opened into a large chamber within ten feet from the entrance.

Approaching the cave I could see several large shrubs had been pulled from the ground exposing the entrance to the cave. Serge was standing next to the entrance pointing to a carving of a coiled serpent.

"This has to be the sign Phillip left for us," stated Serge with evident excitement. "It's possible this cave leads to the lost city."

As I ran my hands over the carving, as if to verify that our search had actually discovered where Phillip had been over a hundred years ago, I also noticed something else. "What do you make of these other symbols?" I said.

Before more could be said Esteban ran by firing a shot down hill. Standing beside a large rock he said, "They don't seem to be following us. I don't know why they are holding back." Esteban then turned and looked at the cave, pointed and said, "That is the reason, those carvings must be taboo to these people. I noticed they seemed reluctant to follow us up the cliff as we retreated further up the hill."

I turned to Serge saying, "When you and Juan were following the creek and you came to this rock face, did you see those carvings?"

Without turning his head from studying the carvings, Serge said, "Yes, we were able to see some of the carvings, but when we pulled the shrubs out of the way the cave entrance was revealed. That was when I saw the carving left by Phillip."

Taking one last look down the cliff, I suggested we find Juan and coordinate our next move. The cave would provide some shelter, but it could also be a death trap. If there was no rear entrance and the Indians were not frightened to continue the attack, we could be trapped within the cave. The narrow entrance would only allow two men to hold off a determined attack. I hoped we would find that the cave had a rear exit or we would be in serious trouble.

Esteban said he would stay at the entrance to guard against a surprise attack. Serge and I entered the cave and found Juan arranging our supplies and gathering flashlights.

Juan turned as we approached and said, "Did you see the symbols at the entrance to the cave? I do not believe that the Indians will dare enter this cave. I recognized several symbols that indicate evil beings are living in this cave, but I also suggest we search for another way out of this cave. If they overcome their fears and attack, we will be in great danger."

We agreed with Juan and stated that it would be best to leave immediately. After confirming that all flashlights were working, we notified Esteban that it was time to join us in the cave.

As we moved into the silent darkness of the cave, my thoughts were occupied with the strange occurrences that lead us to locating Phillip's carving. If the Indians had not selected this particular area to attack us, we would have continued following the stream for many miles before sundown. I marveled at the impossible odds of traveling thousands of miles and finding an old carving left by an adventurous Frenchmen. Was it possible that the city we searched for was at the end of this cave.

Following the lights before me, my thoughts continued to dwell on what dangers awaited us as we penetrated deeper into the earth.

**10
City of the Sun**

Moving deeper into the cave it soon became evident that time and distance were items that had very little meaning. We quickly left the small amount of daylight filtering through the cave entrance and found ourselves moving through a dark world void of sounds. Except for the occasional scrape of a boot on the pebbles of the floor of the cave, only silence greeted us as we slowly moved deeper into the cave. I marveled at how quickly circumstances could change what we accept as normal. We had been traveling in the jungle for more than two weeks in a world teeming with the calls of a myriad of different jungle creatures. Within moments we had entered a world of total silence and devoid of light.

Juan had formed the group in a single file and using our flashlights we were able to move without any difficulty. Esteban and Jason had volunteered to stay at the rear of our slowly moving group as we penetrated deeper into the cave. Juan placed me in the middle of the group behind Maria, due to my head injury. I suspected he was worried I might loose consciousness and did not want me far from medical help.

The cave continued to remain about six feet high and four to five feet wide. The floor showed signs of water erosion with numerous small pebbles covering our path. It also became evident from the excavation marks on the walls that this was a man-made cave. I found this encouraging considering that Phillip's sign for the lost city was at the entrance to this cave.

Suddenly I heard Juan announce that we would stop for a few minutes rest. Maria turned and suggested that I lean against the wall and rest. I willingly accepted her advice and was preparing to open my water bottle when Serge approached saying, "How are you doing?"

After a quick swallow I said, "O.K. I noticed the floor of the cave has been rising steadily, it would explain the water marks on the walls. During the wet season a small stream passes through this cave to the cliff behind us, it's possible a sinkhole or gorge is open to the ground above. Your tone of voice indicates you came back here for more than a health report. What else is on your mind?"

Keeping his voice low, Serge says, "We have come to a Y in the cave, and I would like you to give me your opinion on which way we should go. I know you have some experience with caving and Juan says he has no idea which passage to take."

I put my water bottle away and said, "Let's see what you found."

We moved to the front of the group and as Serge had indicated there were two passages, one rising to the left and one slopping down to the right. It was evident that the main flow of water was from the left passage and some of that flow went into the right passage. Both passages showed signs of human shaping of the ceiling and walls.

After shining my light into both passages, I turned to Juan and said, "I want to check the right passage, will you come with me?" Juan nodded his willingness to accompany me. I turned to Serge saying, "We will not go far. Keep the group here and we will return shortly."

With our lights pointing down the gently sloping passage, Juan and I slowly moved into the silent world of caves. The floor of the passage was also covered with small stones and gravel as evidence of water erosion. After traveling about 120 feet the passage made an abrupt right turn and as I directed my light into the passage it continued straight into the darkness. As I shone my light into the passage I noticed the ceiling was also gradually rising in height.

Juan tapped my arm and said, "What should we do? If we continue down this passage we will be out of the sight of the group. This could be very dangerous."

Turning I could see the lights of the group dimly lighting the passage we had recently left. I still needed to see a little more, so I told Juan to remain where he was and wait for me. I continued walking down the gravel-strewn passage and after a distance of 70 feet I could see the width of the passage was widening. I also became aware of a slightly different smell to the air. While I was trying to sort through the signals my senses were sending me I heard Juan calling to me.

"Señor, please do not go much farther. We must return to the group."

As I turned I realized I was detecting moisture in the air. It was quite possible there was a large body of water underground. While returning to Juan, I decided it would be best to take the left passage that indicated it was rising in elevation.

Returning to the group I said to Serge, "The passage to the right slopes down gradually, and I think it will widen into a much larger passage. I also detected traces of moisture, unlike this passage that shows no signs of moisture, except for seasonal rains. There could be a sizable body of water somewhere below. I would suggest that Juan lead us up the left passage. I think it is our best bet to reach the surface."

It was agreed to take the left passage and Juan led the way with the group following single file. The passage continued to gradually climb with the floor clearly showing evidence of water erosion. It was evident that during the rainy season this passage could be very difficult to move through.

We were slowly walking up a slight grade when I noticed those in front of me coming to a stop. I tapped Maria on the shoulder and asked, "Why have we stopped?"

Turning she said, "I have no idea, but I can hear several people speaking."

I noticed one of Juan's men turn to Julio, they spoke for a moment and Julio turned towards me saying, "Serge wants you to see something that they have found."

I quickly left my place in line and moved up the passage where I could see Serge and Juan looking at the wall. They seemed to be excited about their discovery and Juan was pointing further into the passage as I approached them.

Keeping my light out of their eyes as I approached their position I said, "What's all the excitement? Julio said you needed me up here."

Turning as I approached, Serge said, "Look at these inscriptions on the wall. Juan feels they are warning visitors that they will soon be within the Earth Mothers City." Turning Serge points to another inscription and says, "This is describing the city of the Earth Mother, which is protected by the Sun god." His excitement was evident as he quickly turned to Juan and indicated that we should continue up the winding passage.

I decided to remain with Serge as we continued up the passage and within a short period of time Juan announced he could see daylight. That announcement removed all interest in the inscriptions on the walls as we hurried towards the possible source of daylight. The anticipated daylight that Juan had seen was soon apparent to all as the passage made a sharp right turn and the end of the passage came into view.

The passage had gradually been widening since we had left the Y in the cave, and as I turned into the last part of the passage I was amazed at the beauty before me. Juan and Serge had also come to an abrupt stop in front of me as they tried to absorb the sudden change in their surroundings. The passage had been widened to twelve feet and the ceiling was almost eight feet high. The walls were covered in murals from floor to ceiling, and some of the murals still had color that had withstood time and the elements. The floor of the passage was strewn will small pebbles and debris that had blown into the cave entrance, but my attention was drawn to the intricate depiction of paving blocks that had been carved into the passage floor. Ancient craftsmen had spent many days carving and chiseling the floor to resemble large paving blocks with finely cut mortar joints.

While studying the floor I heard Serge say, "Look at that. We have found the city."

Looking up from the floor I saw Serge pointing towards the mouth of the cave. I moved to his side and stood in awe of the scene before me. The cave entrance presented a view into the distant past of another civilization. I found myself slowly walking towards the mouth of the cave as if in slow motion. Stepping out of the cave onto a wide ledge, I realized that the lost city was a reality and we had found it.

The view from the ledge presented an endless carpet of undulating shades of green, stretching in all directions to the far distant mountains. Three man made objects protruded above the carpet of green piercing the thick umbrella of trees. Two step pyramids protruded twenty feet or more above the canopy of trees, but a strange structure stood between them which was even higher.

"Is that a tower?"

I turned recognizing Serge's voice and said, "I have never seen anything like that. The two step pyramids are typical of fifteenth century Inca construction, but the cylindrical structure in the middle is unknown to me."

Serge's question had pulled me out of the revere I had entered upon walking out onto the ledge. I also became aware of the presence of the rest of the research team as they silently stared at the beauty and mystery before us. We had spent weeks traveling through an environment that was made to discourage all but the committed. I knew our adventure had only begun, but as I looked at the team the fatigue of the last three weeks of travel was evident in their faces. Also a resolve to complete what we had begun several weeks ago in Lima could be clearly seen as they slowly accepted the reality of the scene before us.

Standing beside Serge Julio said, "I always had a little doubt in my mind that the journal might not be true." He spoke in a hushed, almost reverent voice, saying, "When you told me of the city, it seemed too good to be true. I never imagined such an isolated valley existed. This would explain why the city had never been found."

After a moment of silence, Serge said, "I must admit while researching the information in the journal I also developed some doubts as to the existence of the city. The journal was very convincing, but it was hard to imagine the city really existed."

As we gazed upon the mystery in the valley I noticed Juan approach Serge saying, "Señor, I suggest we spend the night in the cave. The sun will be setting soon, and the path to the floor of the valley could be dangerous."

It was agreed that it would be best to remain within the mouth of the cave for the night. I had noticed the ledge we were standing on proceeded along the face of the cliff with a steady decline into the distance. Also its width decreased as it seemed to cling precariously to the brush covered cliff.

As Juan turned to leave, I said, "Serge, let's take a closer look at the ledge. It seems to be the only way to reach the floor of the valley."

Before leaving the group Juan said, "Do not go far, we will lose the sun light quickly because of the mountains. I do not want a fire during the night its light could be seen for miles. The light would announce our presence to anyone in the valley."

I thanked Juan for his precautions and then Serge and I proceeded along the ledge as it quickly decreased in width to only three feet wide. I could see the ledge disappearing into the distance as it wound along the face of the cliff. It was evident that the ledge would be dangerous to travel during full daylight, but almost impossible at night.

While standing beside each other with our backs to the cliff face, Serge said, "How far can you see the ledge? It seems to disappear around a bend further down the cliff."

"In this light it's hard to see clearly," I stated. Carefully leaning forward I said, "We would have to be very careful going down this path. I hope Juan will be able to get the men to follow us into the valley. They seemed very frightened of the murals within the cave."

We stood in silence for several minutes each lost in our own thoughts. As dusk began to settle within the valley I suggested we return to the cave before all light had disappeared. Approaching the cave I could hear the voices of several of the team and the excitement they felt was evident as we entered the cave.

"Have we found the city?" asked Jason as he motioned me to his side.

I accepted the cheese and crackers he handed me and said, "I think we have, but we won't be sure until we reach the floor of the valley. The ledge seems to be the only means of entering the valley and it could be very dangerous to travel upon. Serge and I could see only a short distance and its width is only two to three feet wide with plenty of brush obstructing our travel."

Before more could be said, Juan announced that it would be dark very soon and we should all prepare our sleeping areas. I quickly finished my food and laid out my sleeping mat. As darkness settled over the valley there was a steady murmur of excited voices within the cave discussing the events of the day. Jason and I continued to speculate on what was waiting for us as we entered the valley in the morning. Juan's estimate for the setting of the sun was quickly realized as darkness settled over the valley and our cave was plunged into darkness.

After settling onto my sleeping mat I turned to Jason saying, "Did you see the strange tower between the pyramids? I don't recall seeing anything like that in our research of the Inca."

I could hear Jason settling himself and then he said, "That tower must be over a hundred feet in diameter and its height will only be determined when we reach the base. I also overheard Maria telling Julio that the murals inside this cave are quite different from anything she has seen before. She said they remind her of the murals in Chan Chan, but in many subtle ways they show evidence of other influences. She suggested that the Chibchas from the central highlands of central Colombia had symbols that resembled some of the symbols in this cave."

With all thoughts of sleep forgotten I said, "I remember reading about the Chibchas of Columbia, one of their largest sites are near present-day Bogota. They also honored the sun as a god and sacrificed children as did the Aztecs. Unlike many peoples their women would accompany their warriors into battle and participate in the fighting. It's possible they were influenced by several other civilizations. Do you recall reading anything about the Chibchas having a snake god?"

"No, I don't recall any references to a snake god, but remember many chiefdoms possessed both shamans and priests. The Chibchas considered many natural objects, animals, and sites as sacred. Also unlike state priests, the shamans served individuals, interceding with the supernatural. Its possible that a particular chief honored a snake god and the religious practice spread into this area."

With Jason's words resounding through my mind, I said, "This discovery could generate more questions than answers to who built this city. The journal mentioned a strange mixture of cultures would be found here. I hope we can come away from here with a few answers that will tell us who the original occupants of the city might have been."

With thoughts of the city and what we would find in the coming days swirling through my mind, I drifted off into sleep.

I awoke to the sounds of the team moving about in the cave with just enough light to keep from stepping on each other. I realized that the excitement of the unknown had everyone packing his or her gear for the descent into the valley. The atmosphere within the cave almost crackled with excitement as ideas were passed from one to another about what was to be found in the valley.

I started to roll my sleeping mat together and gather the rest of my gear, when I heard Maria say, "How is your head today?"

Rising from the floor of the cave I said, "I slept well, and there is only a slight headache." I felt the back of my head and felt a very tender spot, and winced. I also felt a bit unsteady as if the cave walls were moving.

In her most professional voice Maria said, "Sit down and let me examine your head. I can see you are in some pain, but you also seem to be unsteady on your feet. You should not have risen to your feet so quickly. Your head injury is serious and you must give yourself time to regain your balance and strength." Maria continued to inspect my injury as she spoke and after a moment stated, "There is a scab forming on the wound and you should heal with no problems, but you will have a scar for the rest of your life. I would suggest that you remain in the cave today and rest, but I know you would not listen to me. Please use caution today as we climb down the cliff to the valley, if you feel dizzy let me know."

Remaining on my mat I said, "You're right, I could never remain up here while the team travels to the valley. I will take my time and use caution as we descend down the cliff ledge. If you have a few aspirin I could use them for my headache."

After taking the aspirin, I remained on my mat for the next half-hour while a quick breakfast of crackers and sardines was served. Juan stated that he would prefer waiting until full light before attempting to descend the cliff. It was agreed, and I for one was more than willing to rest and wait for the sun to rise above the mountains.

While lying on the floor I saw the first rays of light striking the interior of the cave, and at the same time I heard Julio announce that we should come to the ledge. Rising from the floor I followed the rest of the group towards the ledge and noticed Julio standing on the ledge pointing towards the east.

"Julio, what have you found?" I asked as I stepped to his side.

With his left hand shading his eyes he said, "Notice how the sun is rising directly behind the cylindrical tower." He quickly turned towards the entrance to the cave and said, "The sun rises behind the tower and shines directly into the cave. This did not happen by accident, these people were very advanced in astrological observations to have accomplished this feat."

I noticed the others were also mesmerized by the sight before them as we stood on the brink of a city that had been lost to the world for over 400 hundred years. After the sun had risen above the tower and the valley began to fill with the early morning sun, it was Juan's voice that brought us out of our reverie.

Turning from the spectacle before him, Juan said, "The sun has risen, get your gear, there is much to discover today." He then spoke to his men and turned towards the cave.

As I turned I saw Serge slowly shaking his head from side-to-side while looking into the valley. I stepped to his side saying, "It's hard to believe that we are really here isn't it?"

With a slight smile he turned and said, "I've dreamt of this day for years, really for all of my life. To be standing here with this marvel at my feet is breath taking. I can't wait to get to the city, but I want to remember this moment for the rest of my life."

We stood in silence trying to indelibly print the image of the valley into our memories for several minutes and without a word we turned and entered the cave. I also found it difficult to express my feelings while standing upon the ledge looking into that mysterious valley.

We arrived at the valley floor without incident to find one of many marvels that would present itself during our stay in the valley. Upon reaching the floor of the valley a stone road was evident disappearing into the jungle. It measured 12 feet wide and though covered by undergrowth, it was easy to follow.

Juan quickly organized the group, and proceeded into the jungle using the road as the best means of reaching the ruins. We soon lost sight of the cliff we had used to descend into the valley as the jungle growth seemed to shut out everything but the road. The jungle was alive with sounds of monkeys and birds, but our attention was constantly drawn to the road.

I had lost sight of the ruins once we had reached the valley floor. Serge had taken a compass reading before we left the ledge to assist our travels once we reached the floor. It soon became evident that the stone road was not going to take us to the city in a straight line as it twisted and turned through the jungle.

Turning towards Serge I said, "Serge, are we still heading east? The road has twisted several times and the jungle has closed in upon us so completely that I've lost my bearings."

Checking his compass again, and looking down the road, he said, "Yes, we are still heading east." Putting the compass in his shirt pocket, and pointing to the road, he said, "Have you noticed the size of the stones used for the road? This was a major engineering feat to lay the stones for this road. Have you ever seen roads like these in any of your studies of the Inca?"

"No, these stones seem to have been laid so perfectly that they have formed an almost flat surface."

Juan continued leading us deeper into the jungle with the road always visible enough to follow. The undergrowth was thick and grew up to the edge of the road, but only small ground cover grew within the stones. Suddenly, Juan stopped the group and called Serge to his side. Juan was excitedly pointing to the right side of the road. Serge turned towards me and motioned me forward.

"Look what Juan has found," stated Serge turning and moving into the jungle.

As I followed Serge into the jungle I kept looking for what had excited Juan. Suddenly the jungle seemed to peal itself open to reveal a stone stele covered with carvings. It must have been twelve feet tall and four feet wide. The most astounding thing was that the carvings were in brilliant color, as if they had just been painted. As the rest of the group surrounded the stone pillar, astonishment was written across all their faces.

"It's beautiful," stated Maria as she reverently ran her hands over the carvings.

Serge turned to Julio saying, "Julio have you ever seen anything like this? The stone work is beautiful, but the painting is magnificent. It shows no signs of deterioration from the elements, it's as if the work was completed recently."

Julio walked slowly around the stone marvel touching it in the same manner as Maria. After walking around the pillar several times, in a soft voice he said, "This is an ancient work of art, not something that was recently made." He reached for Maria's hand and turning towards the stone spoke quickly in Spanish. She pointed at something and nodded her head as if to agree with what Julio had said.

Turning towards the rest of us, Julio said, "Please forgive my rudeness, but this is a momentous find. Maria and I noticed several carvings relating to the snake cult, which confirms that we may have found what we have been looking for. It's possible this column announces to the traveler that they are entering a sacred city. We have also noticed the surface of the stone, it is unnaturally smooth, and covered with some form of iridescent substance."

Upon hearing Julio's words we all began touching the stone, marveling at the unexpected feel of the stone. Whatever the substance was that covered the stone it would explain the lack of deterioration of the stone work and colors applied to the carvings. Jason also commented on how the play of sunlight on the stone generated lustrous colors that seemed to be ever changing on the surface of the pillar.

Turning to Juan, Serge says, "If this is a sample of what we will find in the city, I think we need to get moving."

It was evident from the excitement that was demonstrated by the group by the discovery of the stone pillar that we were ready to continue on to the city. Juan led the group back to the stone road and turned in the direction of the ruins we had seen from the cliff above. Within another fifteen minutes another stone pillar appeared to the left side of the road. It was also shaped as the first pillar with beautiful colored carvings coated with the same iridescent coating.

Continuing down the road we found six more pillars alternating from one side of the road to the other, each as beautiful as the first. We had been traveling west for an hour when Juan stopped the group saying, "*Señores*, you must see this."

The road had turned right and Juan was standing in the middle of the road, pointing into the jungle. As the group formed around him all conversation came to a halt. It was as if the sounds of the jungle seemed to be drowned out by the pounding of our hearts. Before us were the ruins of an ancient city, surrounded by dense jungle that was slowly enveloping the remains of an ancient civilization.

I slowly became aware of my surroundings and the sounds of the jungle seemed to lend a touch of reality to the moment. The road we had been following had doubled in width and led straight towards the jungle-covered city. In the distance I could see the mysterious cylindrical tower flanked by two step pyramids. Without a word, the group slowly began to move towards the city as if drawn by an invisible thread. Each individual was lost to his or hers own thoughts as we tried to comprehend the beauty and mystery of a city that had been lost to the world.

Walking next to Serge, I said, "Imagine how Phillip felt standing here looking at what we see before us."

"I always had a little doubt about the existence of this city," stated Serge in a hushed voice, as if worried that Phillip might over hear his lack of faith.

The group continued walking towards the city in total silence, as if in fear of waking the inhabitants of this long lost city. The stone road led into a plaza with three stone structures of approximately forty feet square. Beyond the three structures I could see the remains of the city walls extending to the left and right as they disappeared into the jungle. Nearing the city I became aware of the monkeys that called the city their home, and their displeasure with out uninvited presence.

"This plaza is enormous," stated Jason as he wandered past. Turning in a slow circle he said, "How large would you guess this to be?"

I stopped for a moment and slowly viewed the three stone structures and said, "Those three building seem to be an equal distance from each other. I would venture a guess that the plaza is approximately 200 feet square. Also, have you noticed the stone work that we are standing on?"

After hearing my words, Jason slowly knelt and ran his hands over the stones of the plaza. Looking up he said, "They are incredibly smooth, and the joints are almost invisible. How did they have the technology to produce such quality stone work?"

"You've noticed the stone work," stated Serge as he stopped by my side.

"Yes, I have never seen such beautiful work," I stated as I slowly ran my hands over the floor of the plaza.

"I have a feeling this is but the first of many unexplained things we will find in this city," stated Serge as he slowly turned gazing towards the city. As if talking to himself, Serge continued speaking, "From what I can see, a wall might surround the city. The jungle is thick, but I can see traces of the wall in the distance."

Rising from the plaza floor and brushing my hands I said, "I noticed the wall as we were nearing the city. These three structures were built outside the city walls for some reason, but notice there does not seem to be any evidence of a gate or closure at the entrance to the city."

"I've noticed that," said Serge as he continued staring at the city. "They must have felt very confident in their safety to not have a gate to close-up the city from uninvited guests."

Rising from the plaza floor, Jason said, "Should we investigate what we have found?"

Jason proceeded to move towards the middle stone building, with the rest of the group slowly spreading out across the plaza. Realizing this was a moment that needed to be recorded, I removed my pack and unpacked my 35mm camera. Waiting until the group had spread out before me, I took the opportunity to snap a picture that would record this momentous find.

Looking through the viewfinder I could see the three temples and the surrounding jungle as it tried to engulf the city within its arms of emerald growth. I saw the team moving towards the structures and Juan's people showing great hesitancy to advance on the city. With the click of the shutter the magic of the moment disappeared, and the reality of our discovery drew me towards the city.

Jason had taken the lead, and ran from behind the center structure calling for us to see what he had found. I quickly ran towards the building and as I turned the corner a scene was before me that I will never forget. The head of a giant serpent was protruding from the wall of the building and Jason was standing within its jaws. Nearing the building I could see that some early craftsmen had constructed the entrance to the building in the shape of a serpent with its mouth wide open.

Approaching the open jaws of the serpent, I said, "Can you see inside?"

"Yes, a passage leads inside," said Jason as he slowly moved deeper into the mouth.

"Jason, let's set up camp before exploring." said Serge, as he approached the open jaws. Turning to me, Serge said, "I think we better set up camp and see what is inside the city walls before exploring inside any of the buildings." I nodded my agreement with his suggestion and motioned Jason to leave the building.

"You're right, my friend," I said as I walked towards Serge. "The initial excitement of being here overshadowed the needs of everyday life."

Serge put his hand on my shoulder saying, "I also feel the excitement to drop my pack and see what is in these buildings, but first let's see what else is within these walls."

The group gathered at the front of the serpent building as Serge motioned everyone together. As Juan and his men gathered near, Serge said, "I would like to suggest that we continue moving through the grounds of the city, but refrain from entering any of the buildings for the time being. We need to set up camp and find a source of fresh water." Turning towards Juan, Serge said, "Would you and your men search for a suitable site for the camp while we try to map out the area within the city walls?"

Juan agreed and turned giving instructions to his men, who immediately responded by moving into the city.

Serge seemed to pause for a moment after Juan and his men moved away, then turned saying, "We have several hours of daylight left. I suggest that we try to map out the buildings within the walls of the city, this will give us a point of reference for when we begin moving in smaller groups."

Julio mentioned he had some graph paper marked off in grids scaled to one foot equaling ten feet. It was agreed that this would be of great help as we began searching the ruins of the city. After several hours a tired and exhausted group gathered at the campsite Juan had erected inside the city wall. The aroma of cooking meat seemed to attract the attention of the entire party as we gathered around the fire.

While sitting near the fire Juan says, "My friends, please relax and get something to eat. The men killed a small wild boar and it will be ready to eat by the time you get your plates."

The invitation was not ignored, as everyone scrambled to get their eating gear from their tents. Juan had our tents set up and the men had arranged the camp with the city wall providing a secure wall between the jungle and us.

The meal provided a special atmosphere for the ending of our first day in the city. Relaxed conversation easily moved around the fire as the day's discoveries were discussed.

"Julio, I see you are sketching," says Serge. "What did you find?"

We all moved closer to Julio to observe the sketch pad on his lap. He was carefully drawing lines and counting the squares on the pad to keep it to a predetermined scale. Looking around the fire Julio says, "The city walls measured 1900 feet by 1300 feet with an average height of 50 feet. The walls were in surprisingly good shape considering the potential for erosion in this climate. I found the remains of numerous stone buildings that must have been used by the craftsmen that worked and lived in the city. Much of the ground within the walls are stone covered, but not of the quality of stone work as seen outside the walls. As you have discovered there is much undergrowth growing throughout the grounds of the city."

The sun had set while the team sat around Julio's sketch pad making notations and adding small corrections from their own wanderings within the city.

Motioning to Serge, I say, "Do you have any suggestions on how to proceed with investigating the city?"

"Thanks for the invitation, but I bet you already have a suggestion on how to proceed."

Smiling and nodding my head, I say, "Well...I do have a proposal to suggest to everyone. I think we should split into three teams and investigate three separate temples at the same time."

Raising my arms and motioning for their attention, I say, "Hold on now. I see the skeptical looks on your faces; I'm not proposing an in-depth investigation into the temples. Just a preliminary search of the accessible interiors without going too far into the structures. I think it would be beneficial to have a general layout of the immediate interiors of the temples. Julio can compile our sketches on graph paper for everyone to become familiar with before proceeding with a more detailed search of the interiors."

Silence met my final words and for several minutes the group seemed to dwell on my proposal.

Smiling and nodding her head, Maria said, "I like that idea. It will give everyone the chance to know what the immediate interior of each temple looks like. After this preliminary search, we can decide which temple we will investigate first. Who would you suggest should be in each team?"

Rubbing my chin in thought, I say, "Well, since we are trying to gather information for Julio to sketch for our records, I would suggest that Jason and I form one team. Serge and Juan form the second team and you and Julio form the third team. I made those selections because Serge, Julio and myself have drafting experience. We can take dimensions and make sketches that Julio can readily transform into scaled drawings depicting what we find."

Rubbing his hands together with a grin across his face, Serge says, "My friend, I like your plan for investigating the city. This will help us to have a better understanding of what will be lying before us. The next question I have is which temple will each team search?"

Looking at me, Jason quickly said, "I would like to investigate the serpent temple if you don't have a problem with that?"

"No, I would like to see the inside of that building," I responded with a chuckle.

Julio pointed to the south and said, "Maria and I will investigate the temple to the right side of the city."

Serge raised his hands in resignation with a sad look on his face saying, "Well, I guess Juan and I can take a look in the temple to the left side of the city." Then with a smile he continued saying, "It will probably be filled with treasure, but don't worry, I will share all we find."

This last statement brought laughter from all the team members around the fire. The group seemed relaxed and in a good mood and ready to tackle the unknown.

Turning towards Serge I say, "We should call Juan over and discuss these plans with him, especially since he is invited to be a member of a search team."

Rising from the ground, Serge says, "I'll get Juan. Let's make this fast, it's getting late and we need to get our rest for the next day. Speaking for myself, I'm exhausted."

Waiting for Serge to return with Juan, I closed my eyes and tried to listen to the sounds of the jungle around us. The sun had set more than an hour ago and the monkeys within the city had finally settled into their nighttime lairs. As my head began to fall to my chest, I suddenly realized I had grown accustomed to the sounds of the jungle as I found myself being lulled into a drowsy state of consciousness by the sounds of the jungle. Raising my head I saw Serge and Juan walking towards our fire and quickly forced myself to keep alert for the final plans to be discussed.

As Serge and Juan made themselves comfortable by the fire, Serge brushes his hands together and says, "I have asked Juan to join me tomorrow to search one of the temples. He has agreed, but has a few suggestions to present to the group." Motioning to Juan, Serge says, "Please tell them of your concerns."

Juan reaches under his leg moving a stone as he makes himself comfortable. He looks around the fire and says, "As I promised, we have found the city. It has been a costly trip in lives and several of us are wounded. I like the idea of making small teams to search the temples, without going to deep within them. The early people of these cities made many traps in their temples and the unwary could lose their lives within these buildings. We must take every precaution that is possible to prevent further loss of life. With that in mind, I have suggested to Serge that a sentry be posted near the cliff. Serge has reminded me of the professor and the possibility of him following us into the valley. If we post a sentry near the path from the cliff he would be able to alert us before they get to near the city."

Silence answered Juan's comments as each of us was reminded of the possible threat that had shadowed our trip from the day we landed in Lima.

Nodding my head and running my fingers through my hair, I sighed and said, "You're right, I had almost forgotten about the professor and the threat he could pose to our research in the city. Now that we are here, we must keep our senses alert for possible danger."

"I agree," said Serge leaning forward to stress his point. "I have every reason to believe that he will try to follow us to this site. If he finds us, we must be ready to defend what we have found. He has a reputation for getting what he wants by using any means at his disposal. I would suggest that we heed Juan's suggestion of posting a sentry near the cliff. If he sees something he will be able to give us enough warning to be prepared to set a trap for unwelcome visitors. Do the rest of you agree?"

With no hesitation all members agreed to the suggestion of placing a sentry near the cliff's path.

Juan seeing our approval of his suggestion stated, "I would also suggest that we plan on how to defend ourselves in the event that we are attacked. My men will be taking care of the camp and preparing food, but the teams will be scattered around the city. We need a way to alert everyone that danger threatens the camp. I will instruct Esteban that at the first sign of trouble he is to send a man to warn the teams of danger."

Nodding his approval Serge says, "We shall do as you have suggested." Looking about the group Serge says, "I would suggest that we all remain armed as we move about the city. If danger threatens we should not be running for our weapons."

Conversation continued around the fire for several minutes as each individual gave his opinion of what had been discussed. Juan soon excused himself and returned to his men. I could see he was assigning sentry duty and asked if Jason could take first watch. Jason indicated his willingness to accept the duty as the rest of the party began moving towards their sleeping mats. Within minutes the fires had been banked and everyone began settling in for some much-needed sleep.

I found sleep to be an elusive element to come to grasps with, my mind was still actively anticipating the next days exploration of the serpent temple. I realized I was as excited as Jason to enter the serpent's mouth and see what was lying inside. With thoughts of what was waiting to be found in the city swirling through my head, I slowly drifted off to sleep.

11
The Golden Garden

As Jason and I sat leaning our backs against the city wall sketching the layout of the serpent temple we had just left, I looked up to see Julio and Maria descending the steps from the pyramid they had just searched. Jason and I had been the first to return from investigating the serpent temple and we had been recording the interior of the temple.

Turning to Jason I said, "Julio and Maria are returning, I wonder what they found."

With his head bent over the sketch, Jason says, "I'm looking forward to hearing what they have found, but wait till they hear about the serpent temple. It may be hard to decide which temple to concentrate on first."

With a chuckle I say, "You're right, I'm sure we are not the only ones that suspect there is more to find in the temples."

Looking towards Julio and Maria, I call out, "How did your investigations go? I hope as well as ours."

With smiles crossing their faces, Maria said, "It was a marvelous find. Wait till Julio sketches what we found and he will describe what we saw. Did you find anything in the serpent temple?"

Jason spoke quickly saying, "It's full of mysteries, I suspect hidden passageways are in the main room. The main room leads no where that is why I suspect hidden passages."

As Julio sat and prepared to sketch the temple they had searched, Maria asked if anyone would like something to drink. Maria's kindness was greatly appreciated as we all requested something to drink. Silence descended over the three of us as we concentrated on preparing our sketches for the group to review. The sketches and information that was discovered this morning would determine which temple to enter first. With the prospect of professor Segault following us into the valley, Serge and I felt that our stay in the city should be kept to a minimum.

"I see Serge and Juan coming from their pyramid," stated Maria as she stood and pointed towards the pyramid that they had entered several hours ago.

Jason and I had finished our sketch and stood to wait on Serge and Juan to approach the camp.

"They seem to be excited about what they found," stated Jason with excitement rising in his voice.

"Yes, they do seem excited about something." I only hope it is good news, I thought as they neared the camp.

As Serge came within range of my voice I asked, "How did it go?"

He waved and said, "Very well. How was your search of the serpent temple?"

"I have finished a sketch for everyone to review." Pointing to the mats I had laid on the ground I said, "Come relax, get something to drink and prepare your sketches. Julio should be finished soon and we can review what has been found." Serge and Juan willingly sat on the mats and Maria brought them something to drink. She received many words of thanks for her kindness.

Esteban approached me asking if the group would like to have something to eat. I told him we would be ready to eat in about a half-hour. He said he would have the men prepare a quick meal of beans and rice with fried plantains. I thanked him and returned to peek over Serge's shoulder as he prepared his sketch of the temple he and Juan had entered.

After a noon meal accompanied by much excited conversation about the different temples that had been entered that morning, we all prepared to compare notes with each other.

Brushing his hands together, Serge says, "If everyone has finished eating, I suggest that we move to the mats and let each team describe what they found in their temples."

Getting up I said, "That's a good idea. I'd like to know what the other teams have found this morning."

The six of us had made ourselves comfortable on the sleeping mats that Jason and I had arranged around the fire pit of the night before. I could see everyone was prepared to share their investigations with the group as the searchers reviewed sketches and looks of anticipation were circling the fire pit.

"Well, who will be first?" I asked as I looked from face to face.

Serge pointed to me and said, "You and Jason were the first to return to camp and everyone had a chance to see within the entrance to the temple yesterday. Please describe what you found in the serpent temple."

I pulled my backpack from behind me and laying our sketch on top of it I said, "Does everyone have the ability to see what we have put together?"

Looking up from the sketch I could see there were no complaints from the other four-team members.

"I will assume you can all see the sketch that Jason and I have prepared. You may all remember from yesterday that once within the mouth of the serpent head a passageway enters the temple. The passage is four feet wide and seven feet high, with a curved ceiling. Upon closer investigation we could see that the walls of the passage were carved to resemble the throat of a serpent. The passage is eight feet long and ends in a large chamber with a ceiling approximately 15 feet above the floor. The interior is dark as there is no natural light entering the temple except for the main passage from the mouth. The chamber is 15 feet wide and 24 feet long, with a flat ceiling. We could see evidence of monkeys using the room and some wind blown debris was evident."

Jason tapped my arm saying, "Tell them about the columns in the chamber."

With a short laugh, I slap Jason's back saying, "No, you tell them."

Jason was more than willing to enlighten everyone about the columns. Raising his arms into the air and with curving motions, Jason said, "They are beautiful, and very life-like. There are four columns rising from floor to ceiling about three feet in diameter, but they are carved to resemble serpents coiling up thru the floor and entering the ceiling. We only had our flashlights to see the columns, but they were in full color and very life-like." Turning to me Jason said, "I'm finished. I just had to tell about the columns, they reminded me of living creatures. Now I'll shut up and let you finish."

Putting my hand on his shoulder I said, "Hey, we went in there together and you speak up anytime you want to. An extra pair of eyes is always needed to recall what may lie before you."

Turning back to the other team members I said, "As Jason stated, those columns need to be seen to be appreciated and be sure to look at them when you enter the chamber. I will certainly be taking pictures inside that chamber. Another interesting thing about the serpent columns was the fact that the serpent is depicted as coiling around a wooden shaft. Serge, that should get your attention. The journal refers to the coiled serpent around a branch as an indicator that we should be looking for. In the center of the chamber is a hexagonal shaped depression in the floor. It measured two feet deep, but its purpose is difficult to ascertain at this time. Located at the rear of the chamber is a four foot wide stone seat, at the present time I suspect a monkey is using it for a nesting area. It could have been used as a seat for a person over looking a ceremony within the chamber. The walls are made of stone blocks of very high quality workmanship with a pale glistening substance applied to them. When the light from our flashlights shone on the walls, they seemed to shimmer. You would almost suspect that the walls were made of living substance. There were several niches in the walls with curved depressions about five feet above the floor. Located at both ends of the long chamber were four identical carvings of the coiled serpent engraved on the walls. These carvings are in full color and beautifully carved."

I paused for a moment and said, "I also agree with Jason that there has to be more to that temple then that small chamber. The snake cult was very powerful in this culture and such a small structure must hold more than the single chamber."

Looking at Serge I say, "Well, who is next?"

"Julio would you and Maria present your findings from this morning?" said Serge as he turned towards Julio.

"Thank you my friend, we would be glad to describe what we saw," stated Julio as he motioned to borrow my pack for a flat surface to lay his sketch.

After arranging his sketch, Julio smiled at Maria and said, "Maria and I entered what I suspect is a temple honoring their sun god. This pyramid is a three-step structure with a base of 400 feet and a height of approximately 90 feet. We climbed the entrance steps to the top floor, which I estimate is 60 feet above the ground. The sides of the pyramid show many signs of deterioration and are covered in many areas with shrubs. I could see where the sides of the pyramid were covered with limestone at one time. The stone work is good but not of the quality that can be seen in Cuzco." With a chuckle Julio continues saying, "The monkeys felt we were trespassing in their domain and proceeded to inform us of this fact. They were not happy to see us on the pyramid and tried to threaten us to leave." Turning to Maria, and placing his hand on hers Julio says, "I would like Maria to describe what we found inside the pyramid."

With a smile directed towards Julio, Maria began to speak with great excitement saying, "The interior is beautiful, but let me start from the beginning. There are four entrances to the inner chamber, each entrance is 12 feet wide and 6 foot high which tapers down to a 4-foot wide opening flush with the floor. The opening leads into a passage that is 24 feet long with walls that are as smooth as any modern surface made today. We noticed that half way through the passage the stone masons had cut a groove in the floor and walls of several inches deep. The other three identical passages all enter a beautiful domed chamber with a roof 25 feet above the floor. The walls of the chamber are of an iridescent material that is constantly reflecting incoming sunlight, which causes the light to be constantly dancing around the chamber. You get the feeling that the chamber is pulsating as if it was a living thing. In the center of the chamber is a 14-foot square by 12-foot high structure which has a highly polished disk attached to each face of the structure. The disks are covered with symbols depicting the Inca sun god, Inti, bestowing blessings upon his people. As Julio has indicated, this is a temple dedicated to the sun god. The chamber is 64 feet in diameter and is well lit by the sunlight that enters through the four passages. Another aspect of the lighting of the chamber is the effect that the iridescent walls provide an ever-changing display of colors."

Squeezing Julio's hand, Maria says, "I have said enough. I hope we have time to investigate this pyramid, I would suspect there is more to be found inside this structure."

Turning from Maria, Julio says, "I agree with Maria. The inner chamber is beautiful, but I would suspect that the pyramid holds secrets that are waiting to be found. After we are finished, I would be happy to help finish any sketches that need some final touches."

Serge had placed his backpack in front of him with his sketch placed upon it, looking at the group he said, "We seem to have our hands full with structures to investigate from what I hear everyone describing. Juan and I also investigated a three-step pyramid much like the one Julio and Maria visited. The exterior is in much the same state of deterioration and the monkeys also feel it is their territory. We also went up a set of steps to the main floor located approximately 60 feet above the ground. At that point our pyramids differ, we found only one entrance into the interior and that is a 20-foot square opening. The opening is on the west side of the pyramid and provides much sunlight into the interior. The square entrance passage is 16 feet long and opens into a large chamber with eight square columns from floor to roof. The inner chamber is 44 feet wide and 56 feet long with the underside of the roof 20 feet above the floor. Once we were in the chamber we discovered that the roof had a large square opening in the center of the chamber located above a three-foot deep depression in the floor. Upon closer investigation we discovered the floor of the depression had small round holes cut into the stones. The columns were of dressed stone and of high quality workmanship, but with a pale green finish that I could not identify. The south wall had a raised platform with a stone throne chair facing the depression in the floor and a passage leading to a set of steps going down into the pyramid."

Serge paused for effect and said, "Yes, we decided to see where the stairs led. Juan believes this is a temple to mother earth, he noticed several murals that depicted blessings from her. The steps led down to a lower floor with two large storage rooms and three smaller rooms, all the rooms were empty."

Slowly raising his hand for effect, he says, "We also found a stone slab that had been forced open at some time in the past. We were able to see an 8-foot wide passage beyond the door."

Jason could contain himself no longer and blurted out, "Did you go down the passage?"

We all began laughing at his sudden question and the look of anticipation on his face.

With a look of serious concern, Serge says, "No, I felt this should be done with you present incase we need help."

The expression of complete surprise on Jason's face caused all of us to fall over laughing. I lightly punched Jason's arm as I tried to control my laughter and said, "Relax buddy, this adventure will be shared by all. Plus it would be a good idea for all of us to keep in mind that safety is in numbers. In our preparations Jason and I found many references to traps and deadfalls that were used by the Inca in the building of their temples. They anticipated that there would be unwelcome quests trying to get into their temples."

"Your caution is well given," stated Julio with a very serious expression on his face. "I have seen several traps that were cleverly built and very well hidden." Turning to Maria, Julio says, "Do you remember visiting Chavin de Huantar in the northern highlands?"

The memory brought an expression of concern on her face as she said, "Yes I do. It was an important ceremonial center to which pilgrims traveled from all parts of the region to receive inspiration from the cat-god, possibly a puma. The location contains a number of impressive structures, including a large temple of stone masonry 250 feet square and more than 45 feet high with numerous rooms and interior passages. Julio and I were shown several ingenious traps that were constructed by the builders to stop the unwary intruder from entering to deep into the temple complex." Turning back to Julio she said, "We must take great care to enter these temples anticipating that the builders have prepared traps to stop us."

Julio nodded in agreement saying, "Maria's words speak for themselves. We must take great care as we move through these temples."

"These were my very thoughts," said Serge. Turning to Jason Serge said,

"I know what you are feeling, I wanted to continue down the passage and see where it would go. Caution made me turn back, Maria's words are a clear call to all of us to be preparing ourselves before entering these temples. I also suspect that individuals who searched these ruins in the last few centuries have sprung some of the traps. This will help to reveal what may lie ahead for us." Turning to the group Serge continued saying, "We have several hours of daylight left, I would suggest that we get our gear and go to the temple Juan and I searched. We can follow the passage that was revealed by the broken stone panel."

The suggestion met with a unanimous response from all assembled about the fire pit. Juan stated he would notify Esteban of our plans and give instructions for the evening meal.

As the others separated to arrange their gear, Jason and I turned to our sleeping area.

Kneeling next to my pack I turned to Jason saying, "It might be a good idea to bring your climbing gear it might come in handy. I hope you brought your piton hammer we may need it to drive pitons and bring some rope. It would probably be a good idea to bring horizontal and wafer pitons for this type of construction. Don't forget to unpack that large camp light, our flashlights might need some help."

With his head buried in his equipment, Jason mumbles, "Good point, and I'll check the batteries before we leave the camp. I don't want the lights to fail us just as we near the treasure that is waiting for us."

Jason's last statement ended with a chuckle as he kept pulling items from his pack.

"No, I hope our lights don't fail as we begin to gather the treasure," I stated as he slowly turned to me with a questioning look upon his face. Smiling I said, "Gotcha."

"Oh, man," said Jason, "you know what I mean."

"Yeah, I do," I stated as I finished getting my gear. "You could be right, there may be items to be found this very afternoon. Remember what was said about traps, if we rush into things it might cost us our lives."

With a serious look on his face Jason said, "You're right, but the excitement can be overwhelming. I'll use care as we move through the temples." Looking up Jason says, "Let's hurry, everybody is ready."

With the group assembled, Serge suggested that he and Juan would lead the way since they were familiar with the entrance to the temple. The entrance to the temple was as Serge had described with a large square opening leading into a large chamber. The walls were covered with murals in full color depicting the worship of mother earth and the blessings that would be bestowed upon her worshippers. Julio commented that he had seen many of the same types of murals in Chan Chan.

After spending a few minutes in the main chamber Serge directed everyone to follow him down the stairs to the lower level. The stairs were well made of dressed stone 8 feet wide and provided sufficient room for the group to spread out as they turned on their flashlights and proceeded down the stairs. With the last of the daylight fading with our continued descent into the temple the group began to form an unconscious arrangement of individuals. Serge and Juan were in the lead with Serge providing a sporadic commentary of our surroundings. Maria and Julio had moved into the middle of the group with Jason and myself bringing up the rear.

Serge had moved to the right side of the corridor and as we gathered around him he said, "This is the opening Juan and I found and as you can see a stone door has been forced open to reveal a passage." Serge stepped aside to allow the entrance to be investigated.

After a minute Serge said, "I would suggest that Juan and I lead the way into the passage and the rest of you follow, but keep ten or more feet between the couple in front of you. Also, keep your eyes open for anything that might suggest a trap. I'm hoping that by spreading the group out that we might not trigger a trap that responds to weight."

Everyone agreed to Serge's suggestions to proceed down the passage and with lights shining into the passageway I saw Serge and then Juan disappear beyond the leaning stone door. As Julio and Maria were moving thru the doorway, I heard Serge announce that they were moving down some steps.

Entering the passageway with Jason behind me I could see flashlights ahead of me. It was also very evident from the amount of cobwebs that we were the first intruders into this area in ages. The lights ahead of us were at two separate levels illuminating a four foot wide corridor with two short sets of steps descending to an opening at the end of the corridor that was illuminated by a source of light other than our flashlights. Within moments I heard Serge announce that he had found a large chamber beyond the opening.

As we gathered at the end of the corridor it was evident that we had come to a very large chamber which did not require the use of our flashlights to see within the chamber.

In a hushed voice Serge said, "This is beyond belief, I have never seen anything like this. It looks like a separate world from the one above." Turning towards the corridor Serge sees me and says, "Come look at this. I never imagined anything like this within one of these pyramids."

I carefully moved past Julio and Maria and stood next to Serge as Juan stepped to the rear. Before me was a small six-foot wide by four foot deep ledge overlooking a world that existed 50 or more feet below the ledge I stood on. I could see a ceiling 20 feet above the ledge with numerous holes providing for sunlight to penetrate into the underground chamber. I later found that the chamber measured 80 feet by 124 feet, and the pool of water in the center of the room was feed from the roof opening above and a small spring.

Serge grasps my left arm and said, "It looks like a garden, but look at the tree to your right. Is it my imagination or does it look like that tree is made of gold?"

With my astonishment under control I said, "Serge they made this a special garden to their earth goddess." Holding on to the edge of the wall and looking to the right I said, "Yes, the tree looks as if it is made of gold, but at this distance it's still hard to distinguish what is below." Stepping back and looking over the edge towards the garden below I remarked that the garden was heavily over grown and we would have to descend to investigate further.

"Have you got any ideas on how to get to the floor of the chamber?" asked Serge as he was looking over the edge towards the floor.

"Yes, but I don't like what I see," I stated as I pointed to Serge's left. "Look along the wall, see the stone projections descending from this ledge to the ground below. This won't be easy, but I think Jason and I can rope up and work our way to the bottom."

After a moment of looking at the wall projections, Serge says, "I can't see all the projections because of growth on the walls. I don't like this, there has to be a better way to the bottom."

"Let me get Jason up here and see what he says about our chances to climb down," I suggested to Serge with more confidence in my voice than I felt.

I asked Jason to move to the front and as he approached I made room for him to view the chamber below. I then pointed out the projections on the walls and suggested that they seemed to descend to the floor below.

Jason stepped back from the edge and said, "I think we can do it, but it will be tricky. The stone projections are small and many seem to be covered with some form of moss, which can be very slippery." After a moment as if Jason were talking to himself he says, "If we rope up and use pitons to anchor the rope we might be able to move down on the stone projections to the floor."

I gave him a few more moments and said, "Well, what do you think? Could we make it to the bottom?"

Continuing to inspect the wall next to the corridor entrance he said, "I think we can. Notice the stone work of the wall, it's not as finished as the exterior of the pyramids. We should be able to imbed our pitons securely into the walls." Turning to look at me with concern written across his face, Jason said, "It's no cakewalk. We'll anchor the rope in the corridor wall and thread it through the pitons as we descend. We've handled more dangerous climbs, remember?"

Nodding my head I said, "Let's get our gear together and see what is below." I also felt butterflies moving through my stomach as I calculated the effort to climb down into the chamber below. Jason's last words brought to mind our last climb in Virginia, a climb I would never forget.

While Jason set the piton in the corridor wall, I explained to Serge what we were going to attempt. He was concerned for our safety, but I reminded him that Jason and I had acquired much experience as climbers and finally that this is what we came thousands of miles to do. We had never considered that exploring the city would be without danger, it was accepted as part of the adventure.

Silence soon returned to the underground passageway as Jason confirmed the stability of the piton he had set in the wall by pulling a rope through it and pulling from side to side. Satisfied that the piton was well set he turned to me saying, "If you're ready, let's see what's below. I'll take the lead and set the pitons and you bring the rope up from the rear."

Coiling the rope over my left shoulder and under my right arm I turned to Serge saying, "It would be best to wait for our signal before allowing anyone to descend the rope. Let's wait and let us check out the floor before coming down and I would suggest two people remain up here. If we need help they can return to the camp for Esteban."

Serge agreed with my suggestion and assured me that no one would climb down until I gave the signal indicating all clear.

Turning from Serge I could hear Jason setting the next piton and for the next half-hour we carefully descended down the growth covered stepping-stones. Nearing the bottom we became aware of a heavy stench of rotting vegetation and mold. The ground was covered with various forms of growth of a sickly yellowish color. I suspected this was due to the lack of sufficient sunlight entering the chamber. Several stunted trees were struggling to climb towards the weak sunlight filtering through the floor above. I did not relish stepping into this realm of rot and decay. I also suspected that some very unfriendly things might be making their home in this chamber.

With these thoughts running through my mind Jason says, "Look at the size of that centipede, it must be six inches long. I wonder if it's poisonous?" Pointing above his head I see the largest centipede that I had ever seen scurrying across the wall to find safety from our intrusion into its world. Jason grasps the piton he had just set and turning to look below says, "We only have about 15 feet to go, but I sure don't like the look of this place. It gives me the creeps. I feel as if something has been watching us entering its world. Let's keep our guard up while we're down here."

Balancing myself on a slippery stone shelf I said, "I've had the same feeling. I wouldn't let one of those centipedes get too close to you, it looked big enough to take a finger off."

Our descent had taken us around the chamber to the opposite wall from the passageway entering the chamber. Carefully turning I could see Serge and Juan watching our every move as we made our way to the bottom. Holding on to a piton I call out saying, "We should be on the floor in a few minutes. It smells bad down here as if the place is rotting and I suspect that things live here that are not friendly."

Serge calls out saying, "What did you see on the wall?"

"A centipede, a very large, ugly looking centipede. This may be a dangerous place to spend much time investigating," I said and turned as Jason indicated that we should continue our descent. Nearing the floor we realized that we would be out of sight of those above due to the height of the thick shrubs covering the floor of the chamber. I watched Jason step to the floor and with a final stepping stone I also stepped onto the floor of the chamber. The shrubs varied in height from 4 to 6 feet in height and seemed to intertwine its branches to hinder passage into the room. The floor had a resilient feel with each step I took as we struggled to move forward through the thick shrubs.

Staying within reach of Jason and watching the ground I said, "Keep your eyes open, this place may not be to healthy for us."

"I agree," stated Jason as he forced the growth apart to proceed. "I think I see the pool of water that was visible from above." We soon stepped out of the shrubs and saw a pool of black water and a small stream that appeared from the foliage on the other side of the pool.

"I wondered if the pool was fed from the room above or if an underground water source provided the water," I stated as we stood beside the pool. "I wonder how deep it is?"

Without turning Jason says, "I don't know and I don't care. Let's keep moving and see if we can get to the tree. I can see the top of it from here, it could be 60 feet away. Wow...what was that?" shouted Jason as he jumped back pointing across the pool.

I turned quickly but only saw movement of a black creature the size of a large turtle scurry into the thick shrubs.

Turning to Jason I said, "I missed it. What did you see?"

"That thing moved so damn fast, but I think it was a spider," said Jason with a visible shudder moving through his body. "I hate spiders and that one was big enough to carry you away."

I heard Serge say something from above and looking up said, "Did you say something?"

Serge leaned over saying, "What's going on down there? Have you seen anything?"

After a final look around our position for unwelcome visitors I said, "The growth is very thick and hard to move through. I think we saw a very large spider, but it moved so fast that I'm still not sure what it was. Don't send anyone else down here until we confirm that its safe."

Serge acknowledged my information and cautioned us to be careful.

Turning to Jason I said, "Let's get going, and watch where you set your feet. Have you noticed the ground has a spongy feel to it?"

"I told you this place gives me the creeps," stated Jason as he turned to push through the growth near the pool.

Moving through the high shrubs made a rustling type of sound that was emphasized by the stillness of the chamber. Having moved about 20 feet from the pool I began hearing scuttling sounds behind me, as if hundreds of small clawed feet were moving all around us. I decided I would stop Jason and ask him if he had also heard the sounds or seen anything.

I reached forward and touched his shoulder, but before I could say anything Jason jumped at my touch and turning said, "Oh, man. You almost gave me a heart attack. If that tree didn't look like gold I would be out of here." With nervous glances to left and right Jason asked, "Why did you stop me?"

"O.K. relax, I'm sorry I made you jump, but have you heard the scratchy sounds in the shrubs around us? It sounds like a bunch of small creatures are moving all around us."

With a nervous grin Jason says, "I was afraid that it wasn't my imagination." Casting glances around us he continued, "I bet it's more of the spiders. I've heard there are some poisonous types that live in South America. With our luck we have a bunch in this room."

"If you're right, we better get moving," I said as I motioned Jason to keep moving in the direction of the tree.

After moving another 20 feet we came into a relatively cleared area with a sight before us that took my breath away. I stood mesmerized by the beauty before me. A golden tree almost 20 feet tall with golden fruit hanging from its branches stood in a garden of gold. Near the tree were two rows of golden corn stalks with golden ears of corn on the stalks.

Jason slightly turned towards me saying, "This reminds me of Cuzco and the garden that the Inca had made. Could the same people have made this?"

Hearing Jason's voice I quickly came back to reality and said, "In some ways it does remind me of the garden in Cuzco. Look at the detail of the tree and its leaves, they look real." I moved towards the tree and came within reach of one of the fruit hanging from a branch. It was cunningly hung from the branch by a finely wrought hook of gold placed on its top, which passed through a hole attached to the branch. Removing the fruit I turned to Jason saying, "Feel the weight of this fruit, it must be at least 5 pounds."

Taking the fruit from my hand Jason examined it saying, "This is beautiful, look at the detail of the stem where it attaches to the fruit." Holding the fruit in his hand he says, "You're right, this must weigh 5 or more pounds."

Our attention had been centered on the tree to the extent that we were unaware of the sounds about us. Only the sudden movement that I caught out of my right eye caused me to turn and I became aware of three large spiders boldly staring at us from the edge of the shrubs.

Slowly touching Jason's arm I said, "I think we have company. Don't move quickly, but three spiders are watching us from the edge of the shrubs. I think we better get out of here."

Jason slowly turned his head and said, "You're right, I think it's time to leave. Let's see if we can get a few more of these fruits before we leave. Put a couple in my pack and I'll put a couple in yours."

Attempting to move slowly and not startle the spiders, we gathered three more golden fruits. We each placed two of the fruits in each others pack and agreed it was time to get moving.

Turning to leave the garden we became aware of additional spiders that had boldly stepped out of the shrubs watching our every move. I could see the far wall where we had climbed down into the room and from the garden it seemed to be a hundred yards away. The spiders had taken an aggressive stance along the edge of the golden garden, as if they were guardians left by the ancients.

Without taking my eyes from the spiders I said, "Let's see if they will move as we advance towards the edge of the garden. Have your pistol ready if they charge." I started to slowly move forward never taking my eyes from the spiders that I suddenly realized had grown to a dozen or more. They resembled tarantulas, but were twice the normal size of 6 inches. I had a machete attached to the rear of my belt and removed it to use if they attacked. The spiders grudgingly moved back into the shrubs as we neared them, but never out of our sight. By the time we had reached the pool I was drenched in sweat and could feel spiders crawling up my back. They remained within the shrubs just out of reach and were constantly moving all about us as we moved.

Without looking at Jason I said, "When we get to the wall I'll watch your back as you start up the wall. When your ready I'll start up, just watch my back. Before we move I'm going to let Serge know what is going on down here. If they get aggressive don't hesitate to shoot."

I chanced a quick glance above to ascertain that Serge was still at the edge of the ledge. Seeing him looking down I called out saying, "We have a problem down here. Giant spiders surround us and they seem very aggressive. I'm not sure if they will try to follow us up the wall."

Leaning forward Serge says, "Is there anything we can do?"

With little hope in my voice I said, "If anyone up there is a good pistol shot, they could cover our retreat up the wall."

Turning to Jason I motioned him to begin moving towards the wall. The spiders kept just beyond our reach, but the sounds of their moving were all about us as we neared the wall. Jason holstered his pistol and climbed up on the first ledge and then indicated that I should follow him. Putting my machete back on my belt and backing towards the wall I could sense the spiders preparing for a charge, but it never materialized. We had climbed half way up the wall when a shot rang out and a thud sounded behind me. I quickly looked behind me to see a large furry spider spattered on the wall with body parts falling to the floor below. I turned to see Maria lying in a prone position on the ledge with her pistol grasped in her hands. My next thought was, women never cease to amaze me.

We were able to get to the ledge without further problems and to retrieve most of our pitons. While we were leaving the temple I informed Serge of the golden fruits we had taken from the garden and of the spiders that lived in the chamber. It was agreed that we would continue searching the other temples and leave the garden to the spiders.

12
The Serpent is Found

Our second day of investigation within the city dawned with the sun spreading her light upon a city that we had begun to awaken from a long sleep. During the previous evening's meal, it was agreed that no one should mention the golden fruit that had been discovered in the pyramid. Juan felt that it would be best not to let his men become aware of the amount of treasure that was found. He indicated that the men were not trustworthy and would be willing to steal from the group if given a chance. Before retiring to our sleeping mats it was agreed that the next temple to be investigated would be the serpent temple.

"How is everyone this morning?" said Serge as he knelt next to my mat. Looking over my shoulder at the sketch Jason and I were looking at he said, "Are you ready to enter the serpent?"

Jason was the first to respond saying, "We're ready to find what's in the belly of the serpent. We feel there is a hidden passage within the main chamber that will allow us to enter further into the temple."

I leaned back on the mat and turning to Serge said, "I agree, this temple is honoring the serpent god and it must hold more than what we have found. After breakfast let's see if the group can find a way into the inner chambers of the temple."

As if on cue, Juan announced that the food was ready. Grabbing his cup and plate, Jason rose from the ground saying, "Let's go guys. I'm starving and everyone else is gathering to get the food."

Realizing that Jason's observations were correct, Serge and I quickly gathered our eating utensils and followed Jason to the cooking fire. Esteban had prepared a meal of various jungle vegetables and yucca with a fiery sauce. The vegetables were served with a generous portion of pan fried fish which Esteban informed us that had been caught in a nearby stream. The stream also supplied our fresh drinking water, which was appreciated as the bottled water, and juices were running low.

After breakfast was finished and everyone had a chance to arrange their gear for the next temple to be searched, I called the group together. Looking from face to face I said, "Well if everyone is ready, Jason and I will lead the way. Keep your eyes peeled for anything that might hint of a hidden panel or entrance."

We soon found ourselves within the main chamber of the serpent temple and as we gathered near the basin in the center of the room I said, "Light your flashlights and search the walls for anything that might look out of the ordinary. Hopefully with the additional light we might find something that Jason and I were unable to find."

I noticed that unconsciously the group broke up into three teams as they slowly moved about the chamber. The next twenty minutes quietly passed as the six adventurers slowly searched the chamber for signs of a secret passage. The throne seat was searched for movable slabs or levers and Jason checked the basin for the possibility of anything that resembled a trip mechanism.

I noticed Serge and Juan investigating the carving of a serpent on the right-hand wall near the throne. Jason and I walked over and I said, "The detail is very well done, don't you think?"

Slowly nodding his head in a thoughtful manner Serge turned and looked towards the left wall saying, "Did you and Jason compare the four carvings in this room? I wonder if they are the same, it would be interesting to know if they have any differing markings."

Turning to Jason I said, "That's a good idea. Let's look at the other carvings." Jason followed as we moved to the carving at the end of the room on the right wall. The carving covered an area of 15 or more square feet, depicting a serpent coiling around a tree trunk. The body of the serpent was detailed with finely carved lines representing the scales of the snake's body. The tail was hidden behind the tree trunk as the body coiled up the trunk, but the head was twisted back towards the trunk looking into the room. The head of the serpent had been carved in such a manner that it projected beyond the surface of the stone slab. The detail of the carving was of such detail that the eyes seemed to follow me while I moved searching the carving.

Stepping back from the panel and leaning towards Jason I said, "Do you see anything about this carving that differs from the carving Serge was looking at? I know we looked at all four carvings, but Serge may be right about their being some hidden difference between them."

Jason was staring at the carving and slowly running his hand over the carved surface when he said, "There's something about this carving that is different from the one that Serge was looking at." Pausing for a moment he continued saying. "I can't put my finger on it, but something is different."

Turning to look at me Jason said, "Give me a minute to look at the other carving and I'll be right back." With one last glance at the carving in front of Jason he turned and proceeded towards the carving at the other end of the wall. I started to follow, but decided to let him work this out on his own. I saw Serge on the other side of the chamber and decided to see if he had found anything new.

Applying my light to the carving in front of Serge I said, "Have you had any luck?"

Stepping back from the wall Serge said, "No, this carving looks the same as the one across the room. Did you and Jason find anything different at the carving you were looking at?"

While continuing to study the wall carving I said, "Not really, but Jason feels there is a difference. He's not sure what it is, but he decided to compare the carvings on that side of the chamber."

Juan approached us saying, "He might be right in his suspicions. I will look closely at the carving Jason and you were looking at." Juan turned and proceeded to spend some time slowly looking at the carving in great detail.

I suddenly became aware of Jason quickly stepping back from the carving he had been viewing and glancing from his carving to the carving where Juan was standing. While shinning his light on the wall before him, he continued to look from one carving to the other. Suddenly Jason says, "Juan, how many eyes does the snake have that is in front of you?"

Juan takes a final look at his carving and says, "Two."

With excitement in his voice Jason turned towards Serge and myself saying, "Serge, how many eyes does your serpent have?"

Serge turns to confirm what his answer should be saying, "One."

The excitement in Jason's voice had risen with audible tremors as he said, "Julio how many eyes do you and Maria see on the carving before you?"

They also turned to confirm their answer as Julio says, "One."

By now Serge and I had realized that Jason might have discovered the secret to a possible secret passage into the temple. As if an invisible thread were pulling the group together the rest of the group quickly moved to the carving before Juan. As we gathered about Juan, silence prevailed for several minutes as each of us surveyed the wall carving.

Jason was the first to speak saying, "I knew there was something about the serpent's head that disturbed me." Pointing to the serpent's head he continued saying, "Two eyes, I knew something was different about the other carvings, but what is the significance of the two eyes?"

Juan reached forward and tried to rub each eye in hopes of some effect, but nothing happened. I moved beside Juan to examine the wall in more detail. I suspected that their was a hidden passage behind the carving, but how to open it was the next question. Turning my flashlight at a right angle to the wall and slowly moving the light up and down besides the carving revealed a fine line of separation in the wall. This confirmed my suspicions that the carving covered a movable partition.

"Have you found something?" asked Serge as he looked over my shoulder.

"I think there is a finely cut line in this wall surrounding the carving," I said as I traced my finger along the crack I had discovered. Turning to Serge I said, "Let's step back and study this puzzle. Where could this passage lead, and what would it be used for?"

Serge agreed with my suggestion and the group slowly retreated from the carving with their flashlights never leaving the carving of the serpent. Silence prevailed as each of us tried to picture how and when the passage would be used.

Julio was the first to speak saying, "The snake cult was a very secret and feared society. The chief priest would be a man of great power and his assistants would also be feared among the people. Many times the chief priest would be a man of noble birth, which would give him much power among the people. It was not unknown for the temple to house a giant serpent and at designated times a captive would be sacrificed to the serpent. I would expect that very few people would enter this temple without permission. I say this because he would have had the privacy to open this panel without the worry of being seen by unauthorized persons."

Maria stepped forward saying, "I see what Julio is saying. The chief priest would have the time to operate the panel without worrying about being seen."

Julio knelt on the floor looking at the panel and the floor before the carving and turning to Juan said, "Juan, step on the small rounded stone at the right side of the carving."

Juan did as Julio requested and stood on the small rounded paving stone. When nothing happened he turned his head to Julio saying, "Nothing has happened. What else would you like me to do?"

Julio slowly rose from his position on the floor and looked around the chamber. He began to slowly move to the left side of the carving and all the while he kept looking from the entrance to the chamber to the carving on the wall. Julio continued to move towards the wall until he stood with his back to the wall next to the carving.

As usual, Jason could contain himself no longer as he broke the silence saying, "Julio, what have you found? Is there a way of opening the panel?"

Smiling Julio slowly raised his left-hand saying, "Patience, my friend. It is possible I might have an idea. The chief priest would need to open the panel quickly so we need to look for a triggering mechanism that is hidden, but easily accessible."

Looking about the room Serge said, "I can see your mind is working on something. What do you suspect may trigger the movement of the panel?"

With the same smile that he had given Jason, Julio said, "I suspect that light will provide the means of opening the panel." Julio had remained at the wall next to the carving and pointing to the column nearest the carving he said, "Do you see the niches that have been carved into the body of the serpents? I investigated them earlier and they were used to provide light for the chamber. Jason, lift the oil bowl out of the niche to see if the bottom of the niche can be pushed down."

Jason proceeded as directed and lifting the bowl he inserted his right hand into the niche. "Hey, it's moving!" exclaimed Jason as his hand disappeared into the niche.

Satisfied that his suspicions were correct, Julio turned his head towards Juan and said, "Put your hand over the serpent's head and push."

Juan did as he was directed and immediately the stone he was standing on slowly rose a foot above the floor. At the same time the section of the wall with the carving receded and began to rise into a cavity that had been made for it in the wall above. Startled, Juan quickly jumped from the stone and looked into the passageway that was slowly being revealed.

Serge clapped his hands together saying, "Julio, you did it! That was a clever way of opening the panel. How did you suspect that the bottom of the niche was the trigger?"

Julio could barely contain the excitement he felt as he said, "I have visited the Olmec ruins of Tres Zapotes, which was a religious center. One of their principal cults was a serpent cult and the researchers found a hidden panel in one of the temples that was operated much as this one was. I just took a chance that this door would open by pushing down on the bottom of the niche."

After the panel had risen into the wall above revealing an opening 5 feet high and 3 feet wide, we could see a passage disappearing into the darkness. Shining our lights into the passage we could see a 4-foot wide corridor turning to the right twenty or more feet away.

Stepping forward I said, "Jason and I will take the lead in investigating this corridor. Before we proceed let's wedge something into the wall opening in case the panel starts to close."

Turning I looked for any disagreement with my suggestion and Serge says, "You two were the initial searchers of this temple so you have the right to take the lead." With a chuckle he continued saying, "I wouldn't think of trying to stop you, and keep an eye on Jason he looks like he's ready to run down the corridor." Serge turns to Juan and asks him to go outside and bring in a stone large enough to wedge into the wall opening. Juan quickly returned with a large stone that fit snuggly into the wall opening for the panel.

Acknowledging Serge's cautionary statement I said, "We'll be careful. Let's proceed as we did in the temple yesterday, in pairs. Jason and I will take the lead, with Julio and Maria several feet behind. Serge, if you and Juan could bring up the rear, I would appreciate it. I would like the two of you to remain outside the doorway until we have entered ten or more feet. If the builders set a trap to close the panel after we have entered the corridor, you would be able to trigger the panel open again. I hope."

With flashlights trained forward the group began to proceed down the dusty corridor. I could see cobwebs blocking our path at every step and the floor of the corridor was covered with a thick coating of dust. The corridor made a right turn and within 5 feet made another right turn ending at the top of a flight of steps descending into the darkness below. The flight of steps was 8 feet wide and was made from material that seemed to give off a green hue when our lights shone on it. The steps were steep and descended to a flat platform 25 feet below the corridor above.

As Jason and I stepped onto the platform Jason said, "This is interesting, a four way intersection." With a grin and chuckle he continued saying, "Which way shall we take?"

I could see Jason's quandary as I stood in what resembled an intersection of four corridors. The platform resembled a cross measuring 16 feet from corner to corner with an additional 8 feet of flat surface before leading to another set of descending steps. Standing with my back to the stairs we had just descended, I could see a set of steps to my left leading to a large chamber. The stairs before me descended to a blank wall and the stairs to my right descended into a corridor disappearing into the darkness.

"What do we have here?" asked Serge as he stepped out onto the platform. Looking from left to right he said, "This could be interesting, especially that blank wall it invites investigation."

As the team members gathered on the platform it was agreed that Serge and Juan would investigate the large chamber at the bottom of the stairs. Jason and I led the rest of the group to the corridor, leaving the blank wall to be investigated later. It was agreed that we would all meet back at the platform in 15 minutes.

Returning to the platform I could see Serge and Juan searching the walls of the platform and the niches that were in each side of the corners. Serge turned as we neared the platform saying, "What did you find down that corridor?"

"Nothing interesting," I stated as I reached the top of the platform. Shrugging my shoulders I continued saying, "The corridor continues for about 40 feet and makes a right turn continuing for an indefinite distance. The interesting thing that we found was the condition of the corridor. After turning into the corridor the floor, walls, and ceiling quickly return to excavated rock and earth. I'm not sure if they were still working on it or if they deliberately meant to leave it in that condition."

Serge grinned and said, "Well we found something better than an empty cave." Motioning to Juan he said, "Tell them what was in the room."

Lifting his arms and shrugging his shoulders Juan says, "Oil, four large urns of oil. They must have used it for the bowls placed at the corners of the walls. It would burn providing light for what ever they were doing."

Jason stepped forward saying, "Well I want to see what is at the bottom of the stairs that lead to the wall." Turning he started down the stairs moving his light slightly from left to right. Before reaching the bottom he exclaimed, "Come here, this could prove very important."

I could see Jason several steps above the small area before the wall, but what his light revealed caused all of us to begin moving down the steps. Jason's light had revealed a beautiful depiction of a large serpent coiled around the trunk of a tree. The colors were so lifelike that at first glance the serpent seemed alive. Its eyes reflected our lights and I waited to see if its tongue would quickly flick out to sense what was near.

Standing before the wall I wondered why I had missed seeing the carving as I turned I realized that we had descended more than 30 feet below the platform above. The space before the wall was to small for everyone to stand together which required giving each person the ability to view the carving.

"I think I will sit on the steps above," stated Maria with a nervous tremor in her voice. While moving up the stairs she said, "The area is to confined for me, I sense this could be a very dangerous area."

Julio began examining the walls saying, "Maria and I have seen traps where the designers have caused victims to gather in a predetermined place and than cause the ceiling to fall on them. Their accumulated weight in a small area caused hidden levers to release a suspended slab above them. I would suggest that we move up the stairs and let two people examine the wall at a time."

Nodding his head in agreement with Julio Serge said, "I think it would be best to take Julio and Maria's advice and move up the stairs." Turning to me Serge said, "Would you care to be the first to examine the wall?"

Looking about the confined area I said, "Yes, I'll stay here, but if any of you hear anything let me know." Turning to Jason I ask, "Do you want to stay with me?"

With a grin on his face he said, "You couldn't drag me out of here. I want to see what's behind that wall." With that said he turned and began shinning his light along the wall and floor.

In total silence Jason and I spent the next 15 minutes carefully examining the wall and where the wall met the floor of the small platform. It was evident that the wall must be able to move, but no visible lever or mechanism was evident that would trigger its movement. With frustration written across our faces I turned and started up the stairs saying, "If that wall moves it won't be because we did anything down there. I can see that the wall is separated from the floor by a small margin, but it must weight a ton. I can't see anyway for us to lift the wall up."

The group moved up to the upper platform and sat on the stairs rising to the next level above. Conversation flowed between the group with ideas for moving the wall and what could be behind it.

"Did anyone bring anything to eat?" asked Jason looking from one member of the group to another. With a grin he continued saying, "This temple exploring can generate an appetite in a young healthy guy like me. Also, let's get some of that oil and put it in the bowls and light it. We can conserve our batteries."

Jason's outburst brought laughter from several of the team and crackers and nuts began appearing from pockets and packs.

Serge opened a can of crackers saying, "Jason has a good idea, let's get some of the oil from the storage room and put it in these bowls. When Juan and I discovered the urns in the storage room I found a smaller urn with a pouring spout. Our batteries are taking a beating from the environment we have been traveling through."

While Serge, Julio and Juan went to get the oil I decided to investigate the bowls in the niches at each of the four corners. The niches were 15 or more inches in depth and circular in shape, with the walls of the niches as smooth as if finished with modern machinery. Lifting one of the bowls out of its niche I was amazed at the weightlessness of the bowl. It was as if the bowl was made of fine bone china, but I was further amazed that the base of the bowl was flat and fit into a perfectly round flat base in the bottom of the niche. The bowl seemed excessively deep to be used as an oil lamp, but their placement suggested that was the purpose they were designed for. I pressed on the bottom of the niche and it moved further into the wall.

Turning at the sound of Serge and the others returning from the storage room I saw Juan carrying a spouted urn that I assumed was filled with oil.

"I would suggest that you pour an equal amount of oil in each niche before lighting the oil," I stated as Juan began pouring some oil into one of the bowls.

Juan stopped pouring the oil and looking at me said, "What have you found?"

Relaxing on the steps I said, "While you went to get the oil I decided to check one of the niches to see if it functioned like the one in the main temple. I removed the bowl and pressed on the bottom of the niche and it slowly depressed into the wall. Let's try putting the same amounts of oil in each niche and see what happens."

After Juan finished pouring the oil into the bowls Serge struck a match and placed it near the edge of the bowl. The oil immediately ignited and the reflections of the light from within the niche produced sufficient light to see our surroundings. Serge proceeded to ignite the oil in each of the bowls.

Sitting on the steps and looking about the platform Julio pointed to the wall with the carving of the snake saying, "That wall is meant to move, but in a manner that is to mesmerize the unsuspecting victim. I can see a chief priest and his attendants leading a victim down these stairs for some ceremony. I have a feeling it was a one way trip for the victim." Looking at me he continued saying, "Remember, everything we found in our research of the cult of the serpent required human sacrifice to a large serpent. I have a feeling that the trip ended for the victim on the other side of that wall."

Jason was standing in the center of the platform as if anticipating something to happen. The silence was deafening as we all held our breath waiting for the wall to rise. Jason slowly turned facing the stairs leading to the wall with the carving of the serpent as if expecting it to rise at any moment.

Serge had begun to say something when Jason raised his arms motioning for silence. He turned and looked up pointing to the ceiling saying, "I think we might have triggered something, look at the ceiling."

We rushed to his side and looking up we could see a thin line separating a round slab of stone from the rest of the ceiling. The circular stone was slowly turning with the barest of sound to reveal that it was moving. While we were totally engrossed in the turning ceiling stone, Jason turned saying, "The wall is rising."

Jason had found the answer to how the wall was raised without letting the victim know what was happening. I could see that this would mystify the intended victim into believing that the gods had welcomed him to their world. As if drawn by an invisible thread the group slowly moved towards the top of the stairs leading to the rising wall. The opening that was slowly being revealed was dark and uninviting. As the group neared the opening flashlights were turned on trying to penetrate the chamber before us.

The wall had risen into a cavity above revealing a 6-foot square opening with a small stone platform projecting into the chamber. Jason had stepped up to the edge of the stone projection and was shinning his light from one side of the opening to the other.

Julio joined Jason at the entrance and shining his light into the room said, "Serge, we have found the golden statue of the serpent cult. Look at the far wall."

Directly across the chamber from the entrance platform was a smaller replica of the temple entrance depicting an open-mouthed serpent facing us with a statue of a golden serpent coiled around a tree in its mouth. Each member of the group stepped forward to view one of the goals of our trip into the Peruvian jungles.

Serge's voice brought everyone back to reality saying, "I think this is a very dangerous place to spend much time. It smells bad and I can't see the bottom."

Looking about the room I realized that Serge's words were well founded. The room had a rank evil smell that seemed to claw its way up from the darkness below. The walls to the left and right sides of the chamber had large golden masks attached to the walls. When my flashlight crossed over the masks their eyes seemed to reflect the light as if they were filled with gems. The walls of the room were made of roughly cut stone with a dark form of growth attached to the stones. The room was approximately 30 feet wide and

25 feet deep with a ceiling 15 feet above our heads. No visible way was evident for us to get to the masks or the statue.

Julio had approached the edge of the platform projecting into the room and turning said, "Jason, would you and Serge try shining your lights into the bottom of this room. I thought I heard something moving below."

Shining their lights into the darkness below revealed that the bottom was about 20 feet below. While holding his light pointed into the bottom Jason said, "Is it my imagination or is the floor of this room covered in water full of vegetation? I just saw the bottom move as if something were below whatever is covering the floor and the smell in this place is enough to make you give up treasure hunting."

Standing behind Serge I said, "Serge direct your light at the snake's head on the far wall, especially at the bottom of its mouth. It looks like a large space has been left between the teeth."

With the light from Serge's flashlight directed at the bottom of the mouth it was evident that the individual who fashioned the head had deliberately left a rounded gap between the teeth.

As if to himself Serge said, "I wonder." He paused and pointed his light at the edge of the platform near his feet. "Just as I thought," stated Serge. "They made a rounded impression into the end of the platform. I bet they laid a log between the platform and the snake's head to gain access to the golden statue. A person with good balance could walk across to the head and retrieve the statue."

Turning to me Serge says, "We must get that statue, it's worth $100,000, if we return it to the museum in Trujillo."

With complete agreement written across my face I said, "I agree, this is one of the items we have been searching for." I turn to Juan saying, "Would you get the men to cut a tree that would fit from the platform to the snakehead? We'll use it to cross over the chamber to the snakehead. I would guess that it has to be 20 feet long."

Nodding while looking at the distance and the impression in the platform slab he quickly left the platform and said he would return shortly. After Juan had left I suggested that Jason and I try to retrieve a few of the masks. It looked possible to use our climbing gear and slowly move along the walls.

Jason looked at me saying, "I knew learning to climb would get me into trouble. This room is worse than the spider room and the walls are twice as dangerous, but those masks are sure interesting. Well, while we're waiting for Juan to return with the pole let's see if we can get some of these masks."

Jason and I proceeded to get our gear and he prepared to position his first piton. The room was smaller than the spider room as Jason called it, but the walls were covered in dark slime. I could see very small projections in the stone walls for footing and realized that our ability to move was very limited. If we were attacked by something in the room we would have to depend on others to protect us, as our hands would be needed to hold ourselves to the wall. Jason and I had our backpacks on and it was agreed to put any masks we were able to get into each other's pack.

Jason had hammered his first piton into the wall and said, "Let's get moving. I keep hearing strange sounds from the floor below."

Before following Jason I turned to Maria saying, "I like your shooting, would you watch our backs while we're out on the wall?"

Smiling, Maria pulled her pistol and chambered a round saying, "If I see anything coming up from below I will make it disappear." Saying that she moved to the edge of the platform and proceeded to guard us from whatever was making the noise from below.

Jason and I had covered the distance from the platform to the first corner when I heard a distinct sound of splashing from below our position. We were roped from piton to piton and had our hands and feet balancing on slippery cracks and fissures. I tried to look between my feet at the floor below, but found that it threatened my ability to balance myself.

Jason turned his head towards me and said, "With my luck a very large snake is going to rise out of the muck below us. I hope Maria is ready to cover our butts, we are in a very nasty position to defend ourselves." Saying that he turned his head and proceeded to hammer another piton within arms reach of the first mask.

The hammering of the pitons was definitely disturbing something in the watery muck below us. I could hear an occasional sound of swishing water and the rustle of something moving through the growth covered water. I watched Jason fasten his line to the piton he had just inserted into the rock and move within arm's reach of a mask.

Taking great care to wedge his boots into a small ledge of rock he reached towards the mask saying, "It looks like solid gold and the eyes could be made of lapis lazuli. I better get closer just in case it's anchored to the wall and I have to struggle to remove it. I could loose my balance very easily on these slippery rocks."

Watching Jason inch towards the mask, I heard Serge ask if everything was all right. Without turning my head I said, "We're doing fine. Jason is within reach of the mask, but his footing is very slippery."

Jason had finely moved to another perch that gave him better balance. Without turning his head Jason said, "I'm ready to try for the mask. Hold the rope just incase I slip, my footing is still not good." With that said, he reached for the mask and with a few twists it came off the wall. Jason had the mask in his right hand and turning his head said, "Move up close to my side and I will pass the mask behind my back to you. When you get it put it into my pack."

Watching my footing I continued to close the distance between Jason and myself until I was within reach of the mask. He had slowly swung the mask behind his back and grasping the mask with a death grip I slipped it into his pack. The next ten minutes were occupied with pitons being driven into the wall and the ticklish handling of the masks. After securing the three masks in our packs Jason and I started to return to the landing. I had the lead with Jason bringing up the rear and retrieving the pitons as he returned.

After turning the corner and looking towards the ledge I could see Juan and Serge extending a slender pole across the room towards the mouth of the serpent. Fighting the urge to watch their efforts I continued to concentrate on placing my feet and hands in cracks that would offer a precarious hold at best.

Lowering her weapon Maria said, "It's good to have you back. A very large animal must live in the waters below and we have disturbed him. I expected he would rise up and grab you at any moment."

With a sigh of relief I said, "You're not the only one to be glad that it's over. Those rocks are slippery as could be. I expected to fall several times, especially when the water was splashing. Wait till you see the masks we got, they are absolutely beautiful."

Jason had also reached the ledge and as the others made room for us Serge said, "Juan has brought a pole to cross the room, but it will be very dangerous. We had to keep it rather small so we could hold it as we extended it across the room. The weight of the pole wanted to pull it towards the water below."

Jason looked at the pole saying, "Wow, that's going to be a trick to cross on that thing. It can't be more than 8 inches across. I see you've wedged this side of the pole, but what of the other side. It will roll when someone tries to cross on it."

Studying the pole and looking across towards the head of the serpent Serge said, "Juan has volunteered to cross. He says he is very sure-footed and can make it to the other side. He only asks that we cover him while he is on the pole, he fears that a snake lives in the water below." Looking over the side of the platform Serge says, "I agree with him. It sounds like a giant snake is moving through the watery growth below."

With a no nonsense look on his face Jason turned to me saying, "You're a good shot, take your rifle and cover him while he's on that pole. I want to see that man return with that statue and a big grin on his face."

Nodding my head in agreement and taking my rifle that was leaning against the wall I said, "If I see anything, it's dead." Turning to Serge I say, "Get a backpack for Juan. I want his hands free when he gets the statue and is crossing that pole. It's going to be rough enough crossing the pole without carrying that statue. It will probably weight quite a few pounds if it's solid gold."

Serge quickly grabbed his pack and helped Juan slip it on his back. Juan tightened the straps and shifted the weight until he was satisfied that it was securely fastened to his back. Looking at me Juan said, "Are you ready? I will be moving quickly across the pole and not looking into the pit. I will leave that to you, I will be concentrating on the pole and placing my feet where they belong." Taking a deep breath he continued saying, "Give me a minute and I will be ready."

With all the confidence I could demonstrate I said, "You take all the time in the world. I'm going to turn and concentrate on the room and not on you. Nothing will get you if I have anything to do with it."

My full concentration was focused on the pole and the area below it. I had moved to the edge of the opening to the room and within a foot of the end of the ledge. I had left sufficient room for Juan to pass me as he stepped onto the pole. Subconsciously I was aware of the total silence that had prevailed in the area for several moments, but I was unprepared for Juan to approach the pole at a fast walk. Trying to concentrate on my surroundings I could not help but be aware of the astonishing feat of balancing that was being performed before my eyes. Juan never seemed to look down, but continued a fast walk with full concentration on the statue before him. Only after reaching his goal did I realize he had removed his boots and walked barefoot across the pole.

The sound of splashing below my position quickly brought my attention back to the task I had assigned myself. I quickly turned to Serge saying, "Serge, bring some light up here, I want to look into the bottom of this room."

Waiting for the lights I chanced a quick glance across the room and saw Juan lifting the statue and placing it into his pack. He stepped away from the edge of the mouth and knelt to fasten the straps on the pack.

"Here's some light," stated Serge as he and Jason stepped to my side and began shining their lights into the bottom of the room. Stepping to the edge of the platform I caught the glimpse of a large sinuous shape disappearing below the vegetation. "I saw it, it's a large snake and I don't know what its next move will be."

"I saw it too," stated Jason as he stepped back, as if the snake had charged after him. Looking at me he said, "That thing must be as thick as my waist. Do you think he could reach us up here?"

I was still concentrating on Juan as he stood and shouldered his pack and tightened the straps. He seemed calm as he prepared himself to return to the platform. Without a signal to indicate his intention to start moving, Juan seemed to leap upon the pole and began walking towards our position. At the same time my attention was drawn to the incredible sight of a giant reptilian head rising from the swirling waters below the pole. The head was as broad as the blade of a large shovel with a body that glistened in the surreal surroundings of the ancient temple.

I snapped back into reality as I realized that the snake had seen Juan and was rising to catch him. My first shot impacted the body with little effect, other than to slow its rise to the pole. The snake had risen 15 or more feet above the surface of the water and turned towards me after the impact of the bullet. It seemed undecided whether to continue its charge at Juan or turn its attention to me. This momentary pause gave Juan the time he needed to complete his walk to the platform, and temporary safety.

Realizing that it had let its prey escape, the snake turned its full attention to me and charged. I found myself looking down the barrel into the cavernous mouth that gapped open as if to swallow me as I pulled the trigger three times and watched the head snap back several feet from the impact of the shots. The snake seemed to be stunned and swayed before me as it slowly slipped back below into its watery refuge.

I felt a hand on my shoulder and Serge speaking softly in my ear saying, "Don, it's gone. You drove it away I don't expect it will return. Let's get out of here, we need some fresh air and sunshine."

Serge's words slowly sunk into my stunned mind as the muscles in my arms and back began to relax. The strain of the attack had left me as taunt as a bow and I could hear my heart beating as if it were ready to burst from my chest. A little voice inside me seemed to be saying that I had almost paid the ultimate price for entering the temple.

I slowly stepped back from the entrance to the room and at that point I turned enough to begin walking up the stairs. Turning my back on the entrance was still not an option as I slowly sidestepped up the stairs to the platform above. Only upon reaching the platform did I find myself beginning to relax and take a deep breath.

Jason placed his hand on my shoulder saying, "Hey buddy, relax you're O.K. now. You had me worried when that snake charged and you didn't seem to be willing to give ground."

Turning to Jason I said, "Is Juan O.K.? How close did the snake get to me?"

"Would you believe 10 feet?"

Juan stepped up to me saying, "You are a brave man, that snake was ready to swallow you and you never moved. You saved my life."

Serge moved to the center of the platform and said, "I think it's time to get out of here. Jason, if you and Julio would empty some of the oil from the bowls, the wall might return to its original closed position. Hopefully that will keep the snake from coming up into the temple, if it lived through the bullets that hit it."

I decided to sit on the steps for a minute to get my bearings back and let my heartbeat return to normal. The pounding of my heart was still an audible sound in my ears and a constant thudding in my chest. I watched the wall slowly return to its original position as the oil was removed from the bowls. I think there was an inaudible sigh from the entire group as the wall finally returned to close the entrance to a room of beauty and death.

Before returning to the upper chamber Juan withdrew the statue from his pack for all to see. It was a wonder to behold. Fashioned of solid gold with the finest of engraving to present the likeness of a living serpent coiled around a branch. The eyes were fashioned of emeralds and the base of the statue was inlaid with turquoise. The statue measured 14 inches in height and weighted enough to cause considerable distortion to appear in the pack that Juan had carried.

After leaving the temple I called Serge to my side saying, "We need to record this moment on film, finding that statue is something we will always remember. After turning it over to the museum in Trujillo we may never see it again."

Serge agreed and we had Julio snap a picture of Serge, Jason and myself holding the statue near the serpent temple. We had accomplished one of our goals of the mission by finding the statue, and in the process we had also found several articles that would help finance further research trips in the future.

Esteban approached the group announcing that lunch was ready and would anyone care to have something to eat. To his surprise he was greeted by almost hysterical laughter from all six members of the group. I know for myself I felt as if we had been in the temple for more than eight hours and in reality no more than four hours had passed. As the laughter passed and everyone gained control of his or her emotions, Esteban was informed that we were more than ready to enjoy some food.

13
Protector of the City

As the last of the meal Esteban had prepared had vanished from our plates, we began discussing the morning's discoveries. The excitement of finding the statue and the three golden masks were the main topic of conversation. It was agreed that the statue would remain out of sight as it would be a great temptation for the men to try and steal it. It was decided to let the existence of the masks be known throughout the camp. Juan had pointed out that if we did not acknowledge some discoveries they would become suspicious.

"Could I see one of the masks?" asked Julio as he looked at the golden mask in Juan's hands. Juan handed the mask to Julio saying, "These were made by great craftsmen, notice the engraving on the face of the mask."

Taking the mask Julio began scrutinizing it saying, "This truly is magnificent. The eyes are inlaid with lapis lazuli and the eyes are engraved with great skill. The ears have gold and turquoise earrings that display great engraving skills." He continued turning the mask from one direction to another making sounds of wonder as he ran his hands over the artifact.

Watching Julio study the mask Maria turned to Serge saying, "We have discovered some rare artifacts today. The craftsmanship displayed in the masks and statue is of finer quality than anything I have seen in the museums. This city presents many mysterious unanswered questions concerning the inhabitants of the city. In many ways they display Inca styling in architecture and beliefs, but the building materials and finishes are of a quality far superior to what is found in the west."

Turning to Julio she says, "Do you have any ideas where these people came from and where they went?"

Setting the mask in his lap, Julio looked at Maria and said, "I've also wondered what could be the origin of these people. They display great skills in working with precious metals. The stone work is above average and some of the finishes are beyond anything I have seen in my years of research." Slowly moving his finger across the face of the mask Julio turns to Serge saying, "I hope we will be able to return these artifacts to Trujillo. The director will be speechless when he sees them, especially the serpent statue. He has suspected that it existed for many years."

With confidence written across his face Serge says, "We will make it back to Trujillo. I suspect the professor is behind us, and possibly by only a few days. If everyone is feeling well enough to continue I suggest that we follow Julio and Maria into the next pyramid. I would like to search that pyramid and use tomorrow to investigate the cylindrical tower. If the professor is behind us, he could appear within two days. If we can wrap this up before he arrives I think we will have a chance to get out of this without a confrontation."

With an expression of determination on his face Jason says, "Hey, if this guy wants trouble he's come to the right place. We found the city first and he can wait until we're finished."

I couldn't help smiling at Jason's aggressive reaction to Serge's words. Jason was right, but Serge's words of caution were good advice. Looking from Serge to Jason I said, "I like your thinking, but Serge has the right idea. It took us three weeks to get here and the trip back to civilization will be just as long. If we have a confrontation with the professor we will take casualties and if we escape from the city travel will be difficult with wounded to care for."

Jason nodded his understanding, but his resolve was evident. He was not going to roll over and let the professor take what we had struggled so hard to acquire. Without saying a word, I agreed completely with Jason. Reaching over and tapping Jason's arm I said, "Remember, we still have to travel through Indian country. This time they know where we are and they could be waiting for us to leave the city." With a grin I said, "Let's hope the professor runs into the Indians who ran us into the cave. They might help by decreasing the amount of people the professor has with him."

With a short laugh Jason says, "I like that line of thinking. If he's come this far, I doubt a few casualties will cause him to turn back. Serge are you sure this guy could be this determined?"

Nodding his head Serge reassured Jason that the professor had a reputation for tenacity. Looking from one to the other of the group Serge said, "The professor should be taken very seriously." Turning to Juan he continued saying, "Juan, please reaffirm with Esteban that the guards should remain very watchful for any strangers. I would suspect they would enter the valley from the cave. I doubt they will do this openly, but with stealth to remain undetected as long as possible."

Juan reassured Serge that he would caution Esteban concerning the possible arrival of the professor. He also informed us that Esteban had discovered a small break in the city walls behind the cylindrical tower. He felt that it would be a good means of escape if we were attacked from the front of the city.

Turning to Juan I said, "Has Esteban had a chance to determine an alternate escape route from the city if we're attacked?"

Smiling Juan said, "Esteban has discovered an animal track near the rear wall that turns towards the cliff where we entered the city. If we are attacked we could escape from the opening in the rear wall and move around the enemy. It will be a matter of timing and our ability to see the enemy before they see us. Esteban has disguised the opening so it will not be visible to anyone not looking for it."

Nodding his head in agreement with what had been said Serge rose from the ground saying, "I think Juan and Esteban have done their best to prepare for the eventual arrival of Professor Segault. Let's get moving before we have uninvited guests and see what awaits us in the next pyramid."

Julio and Maria took the lead since they were the first to investigate the structure. Approaching the pyramid I was reminded that it resembled the pyramid to mother earth in size and construction. Julio led the group up a large flight of steps to the second level and approached an opening 12 feet wide and 6 feet high. The opening quickly narrowed to a 4-foot wide opening with a 6-foot high ceiling. As I followed Serge into the confined passage I noticed a groove had been cut into the walls and floor. It was wide enough to place a finger into and several inches deep. I wondered what the designers of the temple had planned to put in the grooves. The passage was 16 feet long and emptied into a large circular chamber with a domed roof and a square structure in the middle of the room.

Looking around the room I said, "Julio, what causes the dancing lights in this room?"

Turning and smiling he said, "The sun light enters the four openings into the room and is reflected off the iridescent covered walls." Turning in a circle with his arms raised he said, "Have you ever seen anything as beautiful as this? When Maria and I first entered the room we were speechless. The walls look as if they are alive as the colors undulate around the room. You can actually see the full spectrum of colors found in a rainbow. Come look what is in the center of the room." Turning Julio led the group towards a square shaped structure about 10 feet high.

As the group walked around the center structure we found that each wall had a 6-foot diameter disk attached to the wall.

After the group had walked around the structure and gathered to speculate on the use of the room Julio said, "I have also determined that the walls are covered with the same material as the stone columns outside the city. Maria and I could find no other passages leading from this room, but I feel there has to be more to this pyramid than this room."

I was standing next to Serge and said, "I agree with Julio, there has to be more to this room than what we see. Let's spread out and spend some time searching for anything that seems out of place. I for one am going to investigate the groove I saw in the passage we entered."

With his arms crossed he turned to me saying, "I saw that groove also and thought it strange to have a groove without a door to move into it. Let's go take another look and see if there are grooves in the other passages."

The group spent the next ten minutes walking around the room and investigating the disks and any possible means of opening a concealed passage, if one existed. Serge and I confirmed that there were grooves in all of the passages. They were all placed in the same location and were the same size.

The group had slowly migrated together near the western opening and was discussing what had been found. It was agreed that the only items that were out of place were the grooves in the passageways. While trying to resolve this riddle, Julio suddenly turned and walked towards the western opening. We watched him walk through the passageway until he was standing outside the structure. He seemed to turn around looking in all directions and then stopped as if he had heard something. Suddenly he snapped his fingers and ran towards the astounded group.

"I have the answer, I should have realized where we were," Stated Julio as he raised his arms and turned in a circle looking about the room. Coming to a stop and looking at the group Julio said, "This is the temple to the sun god. The ancients considered the sun god the most important god of all their gods. Notice there are four entrances to the room and each is pointing exactly north, south, east and west. If my guess is correct, those grooves are meant for a metal disk to be placed in them when the sun is shining into that particular opening."

Juan had said very little while we were in the room, but he seemed to come alive as Julio was speaking. Turning to Julio he said, "Now I know why this room disturbed me. I have heard of a legend that spoke of a room that the sun god lived in and when he entered the room he would dwell in a chamber below the room. The sun is nearing the west, let me help you move a disk into the western passage."

The group followed Juan and Julio as they prepared to remove the disk from the wall facing the western passageway. Looking behind the disk, Julio said, "There is very little room between the wall and the disk. I cannot see any fastener that is attached to the disk. Juan get a hold of the other side and let's try to pull it from the wall."

The two men practically fell to the floor as the disk suddenly separated from the wall. Only the agility of youth kept Julio and Juan from falling to the floor with the disk, but the reaction of the group to what had been exposed on the wall caused everyone to practically ignore their near accident.

In a voice that was barely above a whisper Jason said, "Is it a diamond?"

Except for Juan and Julio, the group was staring at a large stone embedded in the wall. The stone was the size of a fist and its many facets were reflecting the dancing lights within the room.

Stepping up to the stone, Serge said, "I don't think so, it looks like a very large crystal. I wonder if it was holding the disk to the wall?"

I turned to see Julio and Juan steadying the disk and said, "Let's see what happens when you place the disk into the groove. I bet this crystal has something to do with the placement of the disk in the groove."

The group stepped away from the crystal while watching Julio and Juan take the disk into the passage. After placing the disk into the groove, the passage became bathed in a brilliant light streaming into the room. They quickly joined us and watched a stream of light being pulled into the crystal. The effect on the crystal was immediate as we watched a segment of the wall begin to recede into the structure that sat in the center of the room. Within five minutes the light from the disk had stopped and a small 4-foot wide by 5-foot high opening was revealed in the stone structure.

It took several seconds for the surprise to wear off before the group began to move. Julio stepped up to the opening and looked in saying, "I don't see anything, it's empty." Reaching for his flashlight he turned it on and moved into the opening. He had only taken a few steps when he jumped back saying, "The floor is moving." He quickly backed out of the opening and straightened his back and said, "I only entered about 5 feet and suddenly the floor began to slowly drop beneath me. This may be the way to enter into the interior of the pyramid."

Each member of the group entered the opening and tested the floor trying to come to some conclusions concerning the mysterious opening that had been revealed. It was soon agreed that Julio had found a possible opening into the interior of the pyramid. Serge was greatly concerned about how to investigate the opening without endangering the life of one of the group.

Julio motioned Serge saying, "Serge I have a suggestion. Tie ropes to Juan and I and let us enter the opening together. Have our ropes held by Don and Jason, if it is a trap and the floor drops out from under us they will be able to pull us back up. Jason knows how to secure ropes for climbing, he will make sure they are secure."

I could see Serge was very concerned as he looked at Julio saying, "Don't take any chances. Jason will fasten you and Juan securely and we will hold the ropes in case you need help. Keep your lights on and tell us what you see, don't stop talking until you come to a stop. Once you enter the opening and start down I'm going to crawl in and try to watch you from above."

Julio acknowledged Serge's advice while Jason fastened ropes to their waists. After securing the ropes Jason turned to me saying, "Let's get our gloves on and we'll use the standing hip belay method for controlling the rope descent."

With their ropes securely fastened around their waists, Julio and Juan proceeded to slowly enter the small opening. I had control of Julio's rope and had run the rope through my legs from front to rear and brought it over my left hip and across my chest over my right shoulder. My left hand stretched out from my left side securely holding the rope. This method allows the rope to run through the brake hand, which slowly applies braking action to bring the descent to a slow, smooth stop. While preparing myself for the possibility of Julio falling I continued hoping that our precautions would not be needed.

Julio announced that he and Juan were ready to move on to the slab that had previously started moving when he had stepped upon it. I noticed Jason prepared himself as I did for the rope to begin moving through our hands. As Julio had stated earlier, I began to feel a gradual moving of the rope towards the opening where Julio and Juan had disappeared. During their descent Serge crawled into the opening and disappeared from sight, but I could hear him speaking with the men as they descended.

The unexpected loss of tension on my rope caused me to quickly look at the rope in Jason's hands, it had also ceased to remain taunt. Grasping the rope and moving near the opening I asked Serge if the men were all right.

"There fine, they have come to rest on a small platform. They asked if we could tie the ropes to something and let them hang into the pit. If they have to leave in a hurry they will use the ropes," stated Serge from within the opening.

Jason quickly responded by hammering two pitons into seams of rocks within the passage. We tied the ropes to the pitons and suggested to Serge that we climb down to assist Julio and Juan.

After sliding back out of the opening Serge stood and looking at me and said, "I know you two can climb, but be careful. If you get into trouble Maria and I are the only ones up here."

Crouching low Jason entered the passage and moved to the opening that was evident as our lights shone across the floor. I could see the ropes dangling over the edge of the opening and the voices of Julio and Juan came faintly to my ears. I knelt at the opening and looked down a 20-foot drop to a small platform where the men were standing looking in opposite directions.

Without raising my voice too loud I said, "Julio what can you see?"

In a voice that echoed within the shaft walls Julio said, "This could be interesting. The floor slopes to each side of this small platform at a very steep drop. I think we can walk down the slope upright, but we will have to take our time. I can see an opening into a room to my right and the passage to my left goes off into darkness. I hope you will be coming down here, as Jason would say, it's creepy down here."

I heard Jason chuckle next to me as he heard Julio's words. Leaning over the edge Jason said, "Julio, have you seen any large spiders down there?"

Turning to Jason trying not to laugh I said, "You better be good, he already sounds like he expects those spiders to step out of the shadows and get him. Let's get moving and see what they have found."

Turning my head towards the entrance of the opening I said, "Serge, Jason and I are going to go down into the shaft and see what Julio has found below. Stay near the edge of the shaft so we can keep you aware of what's going on below."

Serge agreed that he would remain at the top of the shaft and if we needed help Maria could run and get Esteban and the men. It was evident by the hesitancy in Serge's voice that he was not very happy with splitting the group up. I tried not to let my voice betray my own concerns with dropping into a dark shaft that could end up being my tomb. If the early designers of this pyramid had wanted to catch the uninvited visitor this was the perfect place to do it.

The shaft walls were of rough cut stone that provided several crevices to place our feet as we repelled to the bottom. Julio and Juan had stepped aside as we landed on the platform providing as much room as was possible. I noticed they were careful not to step off the platform onto the sloping floors to left or right.

Releasing my hold on the rope I turned to Julio and said, "Has the platform moved in any way since you came to a stop at this level?"

With evident caution in his voice, Julio said, "No. We were concerned that if we stepped off the platform that it might begin to rise. We could be trapped here with no way to communicate with the rest of the group. We have searched for a lever or something that might be used to raise the platform, but there is nothing to be found. I fear this might be a trap prepared for trespassers."

Nodding my understanding of his concern I said, "We have to try and test the platform to see if it is made to rise after our weight has been removed." Looking up into the shaft I turn to Julio and say, "Could you and Juan climb up the ropes and hold on for several minutes? If you could do this Jason and I will climb up behind you and this will remove all weight from the platform."

Julio and Juan agreed that they could climb the ropes and hold on with Jason and myself climbing below them. I called up to Serge and informed him of what we were about to try to do. He cautioned us to climb up the ropes quickly if the platform began to rise.

With Serge's words of caution resounding in my head I turned to Juan and Julio and indicated that they should begin moving up the ropes. As they began climbing the ropes I directed my attention to the platform trying to sense if the platform had reacted to the lack of pressure exerted by the two men. I could discern no movement of the platform and said to Jason, "Well let's give this a try. I've detected no movement after Juan and Julio left the platform. If it's going to move it will be after you and I leave the platform."

Jason indicated he was ready and together we each grabbed a rope and hand over hand climbed the ropes until we were below the men tenaciously trying to hold themselves steady against the wall. Gaining a toehold on the wall I ventured a quick glance below expecting to see the platform rising to touch my feet. To my surprise the platform remained in its position and seemed to be solidly positioned where it had stopped.

Looking at Jason I said, "I think it's safe to return to the platform. Do you agree?"

He nodded his agreement and began to lower himself to the platform. Within a few moments the four of us had gathered on the platform and a discussion ensued as to which way we should move. I called Serge and informed him of our situation and that we would begin searching the passages before us.

After speaking with Serge I turned to Julio and said, "Why don't you and Juan take the right passage and Jason and I will take the left." Looking down each passage I said, "The floors of both passages are sloped to the bottom, but seem to level off. Keep your eyes open for anything that might resemble a trap. I don't trust this place, it seems to be made to catch the unwary."

It was agreed that we would split into two groups and care would be exercised in moving through the passageways. I watched Julio and Juan begin to carefully descend the sloping passageway towards a dimly revealed opening that could be seen from the platform we were standing on. When Julio had reached the bottom of the sloped section of the passage I cautioned him to return to the platform within 30 minutes. I didn't want the four of us separated for to long a period of time.

Turning to Jason I said, "Well, let's see what is down this passage."

With our lights directed towards the floor of the passage, we carefully made our way to the bottom. I could see an opening at the end of the passage and two other openings, one to either side of the passageway.

Looking back up the sloped passage I remarked, "I hope we don't have to make a quick exit from this place. It's pretty steep for running if something is after you."

Turning to me Jason said, "Thanks, I needed that. Now I'll be looking for something to jump out of one of those openings that are ahead of us."

Laughingly I said, "Sorry, I didn't mean it to sound quite so ominous. We'll probably find plenty of diamonds and fill our pockets to the point that we won't be able to climb up the passage." Holding my hands out palms up I said, "See, that's all I meant."

"Yeah right," Jason said as he shifted his weight from one foot to the other. Looking down the passageway he said, "Let's check the doorway to the right. We don't have much time and we have lots of diamonds to find." The last part of his statement was said with a chuckle as he began to move forward down the passageway.

It was evident from the thick layer of dust on the floor of the passage that many years had passed since anyone had walked in this passageway. The opening to the room on our right was several feet wide and 6 feet high. Jason had turned and entered the room swinging his light from left to right and suddenly stepped quickly to his left shinning his light at the floor.

I quickly stepped to the opening and said, "What's the matter. Why did you stop so suddenly?" The sight before me just as suddenly stopped my words and movement. Against the wall rested the skeletal remains of someone who had died many years before. It took several minutes for me to register that this might be someone who had died searching these ruins.

Jason was the first to speak saying, "Who do you think he was?"

I slowly squatted in front of the remains and said, "I don't see the remains of boots and from the size of the remains I would venture to say he was an Indian." With a touch of wonder in my voice I continued saying, "I wonder if he was with Phillip's party? Look at his feet he had opened several small clay pots and the contents are scattered on the floor."

The shock of finding the remains had begun to wear off as Jason began moving around the room. I had started to rise from my inspection of the remains as Jason said, "Look over here. They must have used this room as a storage room for pottery. I see several small pots similar to the ones he had opened." Reaching down Jason picked up one of the small pots and stated, "Huh...they are sealed. I wonder what is inside?"

Turning quickly to Jason I shouted, "Don't open that pot. I have a bad feeling that whatever is inside contributed to his death."

Jason quickly set the pot on the floor and looking at the skeletal remains against the wall visibly shivered and said, "You don't have to tell me twice. Let's see what else is in this place. I want to take something out of this place, not remain here for eternity." After a quick search of the room we decided to move across the passage to the other chamber.

We both came to a sudden stop as our lights revealed a room lined with weapons and ceremonial feathered robes. The level of preservation of the robes was incredible, I guessed partly due to the dry environment in these lower rooms. Slowly walking around the room I could see remains of embroidered garments and elaborate turbans and togas and other articles of clothing. Several highly decorated war clubs were leaning against the walls as if waiting for the owner to return at any minute.

Jason turned and said, "Let's see what's at the end of the passage. I hope it's more interesting than what we've seen so far."

I nodded and turned towards the opening we had just entered. With our lights shining down the passage I could see a large chamber being revealed as we neared the opening to the room. I also noticed our lights were being reflected back at us as we neared the opening to the room. Taking the lead I stepped into a circular chamber with a large silver disk facing the opening to the room.

Jason stopped at my side and said, "Could that disk be made of silver, and look at the stones in the disk." He continued walking towards the disk saying,

"This reminds me of Cuzco and the disk representing the moon." Standing before the disk Jason slowly ran his hands over the surface saying, "I bet these are emeralds and other precious stones. What do you think?"

When Jason failed to get a response from me he turned and said, "Where are you, why...." Jason saw me looking towards the wall adjacent to the doorway we had just entered. Approaching my side Jason said, "Oh, no. Not another one, this is not looking good."

I had entered the room before Jason but had not continued into the room as Jason had done. I had turned around and was about to survey the room when I saw the skeleton lying to the right of the doorway. I was aware of Jason speaking while I slowly surveyed the remains and the area around it. Nearing my side I turned to him saying, "I think we have found another one of Phillips Indians and at first glance I see no visible signs of what killed him. Have you touched anything?"

In a hushed voice Jason said, "Yes, the disk on the wall." He quickly turned to see if anything had resulted from his inspection of the disk. "I don't think anything reacted to my touching the disk. Do you see any of the little pots near him?"

I stepped closer to the remains and as before squatted near the feet looking closely at the area around the skeleton. I could see no pots or anything other than a bone-handled knife lying near his side. I could see no signs that he had died from a violent death. None of his bones looked broken and from the position of the skeleton he must have leaned against the wall to die.

Rising from the floor I said to Jason, "I have no idea how he died, I see no signs of violence. Let's be very careful what we touch and how we touch it. There may be traps that are operated by touch and are very subtle. A poisonous gas released by something they touched could have sprayed them."

With the realization that a silent form of death could be waiting for the unwary intruder, we decided to take our time looking around. Without a word we both turned and began surveying the room. The room was a perfect half circle with a domed roof. The incredible thing was that the cracks between the stones that comprised the walls were filled with silver. The original builders had selected a dark stone to build with and the silver shone forth as our lights reflected off the seams, which resembled flowing streams of light. The most breath-taking thing was the silver disk Jason had inspected earlier.

Walking towards the disk I said, "I think you're right. The stones in the disk look like gemstones." I also touched the disk and stones as Jason had and realized that a king's ransom was before our eyes. "Well, what do you think? Shall we take a chance and try to remove one of the gems?" I said as I withdrew my knife from my belt.

Jason had come to my side and looking over my shoulder said, "Do you see anything that might look like a trap? How are the stones set into the disk? These guys didn't die from old age so watch what you touch."

Looking closely at an emerald of considerable size I said, "If there's a trap I sure can't see it. The stone seems to be set in a small hole that had been fashioned for it. I'm going to try and remove it, just to be on the safe side move towards the doorway. If something happens get out of the room and don't hesitate."

Jason took a quick look at the stone and said, "Don't do something stupid, I don't want to be down here by myself. If you sense anything strange about the stone get away from it." With a moment's hesitation Jason slowly stepped back towards the door and continued to shine his light on the disk before me.

I had no intention of doing anything stupid, but I had to see if the gemstone was removable. A quick survey of the disk revealed that no other stones had been removed and that disturbed me. Had the last two people who had tried to remove a stone died for their trouble? I don't consider myself an exceptionally brave person, but some times you have to take a chance to grab for the brass ring. The gems in the disk sure looked to me to be brass rings that needed to be grabbed for.

Taking one last glance at Jason to reassure him and myself I turned and selected the stone I would try to remove. I estimated that the emerald was 3 karats in size with a clear deep green color. Carefully holding my knife near the edge of the stone I slowly began to wedge the point into the hole that held the stone. The stone began to move ever so slightly and than as if pushed from within almost jumped out of the disk. I quickly grabbed for the stone and caught it before it fell to the floor. Holding the stone I quickly stepped back from the disk looking for anything that might threaten me.

"Are you all right." asked Jason as I heard him step towards me. "I saw you jump back, are you O.K.?"

Turning towards Jason I raised my hand with the emerald between my forefinger and thumb saying, "So far so good. Look at this beauty, it must be 3 karats in size. It came out so quick it almost fell on the floor, I caught it just in time."

I walked towards Jason and put the emerald in his out stretched hand and said, "The stone came out with very little prying. I don't think the disk is trapped. These guys must have tripped something else that got them. Let's hurry and get some of these stones and get back with the other guys. We've been gone for quite a while."

The next few minutes were spent in silence while Jason and I pried several more emeralds, rubies and sapphires from the disk. They were beautiful stone's and would help to finance further expeditions in the future. At least these were my thoughts as I pried the gems from the disk and wondered if we would ever be able to return to civilization. I knew the professor was only days behind us and we also had three weeks of jungle travel to get through before seeing Lima.

While occupied with these thoughts I heard Jason say, "We have enough, let's get the other guys and see what they found."

Looking at the disk and the empty holes we had left I said, "You're right, we have enough. We shouldn't be greedy, let's find the others."

With one last look at the silver disk, we turned and started to retrace our steps to the elevated platform where we had entered this lower level of beauty and death. Passing the room where we had discovered the first skeleton I said, "I think I know how these men died. Neither one displayed a violent death from the position of the bones or evidence of violence to their remains."

Carefully climbing the sloped ramp Jason said, "Yeah, I noticed that they both seemed to have died leaning against a wall."

Reaching the platform I stopped and said, "I bet the small pots next to the first skeleton we found had a substance in it that when released killed anyone within a certain distance. It looked like he had opened two of the small pots and the contents were spilled on the floor next to him."

With a visible shiver Jason said, "Just think if you hadn't said something to me when I picked up one of those pots we might also be leaving our bones here." Turning and pointing down the other passageway Jason said, "It looks like the other guys are busy. I can see their lights moving around in that far room."

Before leaving the platform I informed Serge of what we had found and that we would be joining Julio and Juan in the other room. Serge was greatly concerned about the information of the skeletons and requested that the four of us quickly return to the upper level. I reassured him that we would be returning to the surface in a few minutes.

Jason and I began to descend the sloping passage towards the room where Julio and Juan were in the process of searching. Nearing the opening to the room I could hear Julio speaking with Juan and directing him to remove something from a wall. Jason and I stopped at the entrance to a room that took my breath away. The room was built in the shape of an arrowhead with an 8-foot diameter gold disk in the center of where the point of the arrowhead would be. The disk was elevated 4 feet above the floor and studded with gemstones. The walls of the room shimmered in the reflection of our lights. I could see no seams in what looked like solid gold-covered walls.

"Have you ever seen anything like this?" said Julio as he realized we had joined them. Walking towards us Julio said, "This is the private temple to the sun god. Notice the walls, they are covered with sheet gold. I have never seen such wealth displayed in one place for any deity."

Juan had just removed a gold mask from the wall to the right of the disk and brought it to Julio saying, "Julio, I have seen masks like this from Lambayeque. Is this possible that they had contact with people from Sipan?"

Juan was holding a large golden mask with large flared ears with pendant earrings attached to the ears. The earrings were inlayed with turquoise to represent the sun. They had used emeralds for the eyes and engraved around the eyes to represent the shape of an eye.

Julio reached for the mask saying, "This is amazing, they resemble masks from Sipan." In silence Julio continued studying the mask and slowly looked at me and said, "If I had not seen this with my own eyes I would not believe this. These masks should not be here, I have seen masks like these near Chiclayo on the coast."

I felt a hand on my shoulder and Jason said, "I hate to interrupt, but we better get moving. Remember this place might not be too healthy."

Nodding, I looked from the mask to Julio and said, "Jason is right. We found two skeletons in the other rooms and I suspect an airborne poison that they unwittingly released killed them. Give me a quick overview of what you and Juan have found in this room and then we better get what we can and get out of here."

Julio handed the mask to Juan with instructions to place the mask in his pack and then turning to me said, "This is a very lavish room dedicated to the sun god, it must have been used for worshipping their god. Juan and I have found precious stones embedded in the gold sun disk and we have removed several of the larger ones. There are a total of ten gold masks attached to the walls, each as beautiful as the one Juan is packing away. I have every reason to believe that the walls are covered with gold. We have truly found the grandest temple to the sun god that I have ever heard of in Peru."

Looking about the room I had to agree with Julio that this was a magnificent temple that had been made for their god. I told Jason to get one of the masks from the wall and suggested that we prepare to get back to Serge on the upper level. Juan asked if he could remove a few more stones while Jason went to get another mask.

Nodding I said, "Sure, but hurry. I feel we have to get out of here soon."

Jason returned from the wall carrying a gold mask with beautiful large emerald eyes, offering it to me he said, "Feel the weight of this, it must weigh 10 pounds. Would you put that in my pack?"

We waited for Juan to remove a few more stones and then it was decided to leave the temple before something deadly befell us. I felt we were on borrowed time and that at any minute something would happen to trap us in these under ground passages. I knew it was my imagination, but a cold chill had begun to creep up my spine while waiting for Juan and Jason to finish getting what they were after. I confided my concerns to Julio and he agreed that he also felt uncomfortable staying to long in these ruins.

After Jason and Juan had packed their treasures away we turned and quickly retraced our steps to the platform. As we assembled on the platform I informed Serge that we had found several items that we were bringing from below. I could tell from his voice that he was greatly relieved to hear we had all survived our time below and that we were ready to join him above.

Jason was the first to speak saying, "O.K., how do we get this elevator to rise? We have two openings, two passages and two blank walls. I see no levers and no visible system to raise this platform."

Jason's words brought all of us back to reality. The platform had deposited us on this lower level, but it was very evident that no visible means of raising the platform were to be found. The next few minutes were spent by the four of us in searching every square inch of the walls for anything that resembled a lever or release of the platform. Our search was fruitless and in frustration it was agreed that we would have to find another way out of these passages.

Looking at the ropes dangling from above I said, "Well, let's take turns climbing up the shaft. It's only 20 feet, we should all be able to climb that distance."

Juan stepped forward and said, "I will go first if you like. I should not have a problem getting up the rope. When I get to the top I will help pull each climber up."

I called out to Serge informing him of our predicament in finding that we could not find a means of raising the platform. I told him we would be climbing up the ropes we had left hanging from above.

Juan was as good as his word, in minutes he had climbed up the rope as if it was something that he did everyday. Turning to Julio I said, "If you're ready Jason and I will bring up the rear."

Suddenly I became aware of Julio's hesitancy to grab the rope before his face. He tilted his head back looking up the shaft and turned to me saying, "I'm sorry, but I don't think I can do this. I have never been good at climbing ropes and in addition to that I don't know how."

Jason stepped to Julio's side and said, "I will give you a lift up with my hands and you grab the rope. Hold on tight and Juan will pull you up. Before you know it you will be at the top and ready to climb out of the shaft."

Jason's words seemed to have a calming effect on Julio and stepping into Jason's cupped hands he grasped the rope with a death grip and I told Juan to begin pulling Julio up the shaft. Juan wasted no time in pulling Julio up the shaft and in moments Julio disappeared over the edge out of sight. Jason and I quickly climbed up the shaft into the welcomed daylight that was streaming in through the western opening to the upper room.

The group gathered around the opening to the lower chambers and sitting on the stone floor shared their stories of what was discovered with Serge and Maria. The masks were pulled from the packs and everyone commented on their beauty.

Reaching into my jacket pocket I looked at Serge and said, "Open your hand."

Serge looked questioningly at me and did as requested. His eyes grew to the size of quarters as he watched me pour a small stream of gems into his open hand.

Looking into his out stretched hand Serge said, "Oh, my. Oh, my. What have you found? These look like the real things."

I knew the smile crossing my face was as wide as it could be as I said, "Yes, I think they are real. We have the masks and a number of gems. When we get to camp I will fill you in on what we found below. It was truly incredible."

We sat in the round chamber discussing the success we had below and the impact that finding the skeletons had upon our decision to leave the lower level. I told Serge that I suspected that the remains could belong to men that had come to the city with Phillip. I also told him that they might have been killed by something that had been concealed in small pottery pots. Juan cautioned us that the sun was getting low and we should consider returning to the camp.

After removing the disk from the passageway, we heard the wall returning to its original position. Julio and Juan placed the disk on the crystal and by some unknown power it seemed to adhere to the crystal. Shaking my head with wonder and acknowledging that I was witnessing another unexplainable phenomena we turned and walked out of the chamber. The group gathered at the top of the stairs and began to descend to the city grounds below.

I held back a little to take in a scene that I would never behold again. The impact of my surroundings had suddenly fell upon me. I was standing 60 feet above the ground on a pyramid 500 years old. Surrounding me was a wall of green jungle that was alive with the sounds of birds and monkeys screaming out their outrage at our intrusion into their world. I watched my friends descend to the ground below and slowly tried to picture what my surroundings must have looked like five centuries ago.

I could see the stone streets below busy with the activity of the priests and craftsmen who provided for the temples. Coming through the main entrance to the city was a golden litter supported by eight warriors dressed alike. The individual sitting in the litter held a regal posture as he was carried towards the temple of the sun god. Nearing the temple I could see he wore a headdress of feathers surrounding his face resembling a sunburst. Suspended from his neck was a large golden plaque that resembled the sun. He carried a long handled golden axe, which he balanced on his left knee.

Suddenly the images before me disappeared as I heard Jason say, "Don, stop daydreaming. It's getting late and Esteban has prepared the evening meal."

I waved to Jason acknowledging his advice and began to slowly descend the steps to the ground below. I was back in the twentieth century and all about me were ruins, but I knew I had been given a glimpse of the splendor of the city as it might have looked centuries ago. I knew I would always remember the images of grandeur and beauty that I had seen that day from high on an ancient Inca pyramid in a hidden valley in Peru.

14
Unwelcome Guests

Leaning back and resting my elbows on the ground I looked towards the western sky as the last of the sun's rays caused a few small-scattered clouds to take on a brilliant vermilion hue. I realized that times like these would be engraved in my memory for the rest of my life. The jungle was still alive with the calls of a myriad of different birds and an occasional monkey would join into the evening chorus. Closing my eyes I found a certain sense of peace as I let the sounds of the jungle slowly envelop my being.

The fire had been allowed to diminish to a bed of coal with an occasional flame licking at an un-burnt fragment of wood. Silence had settled around the fire as each of us dwelled on his or her own thoughts. We had been in the city for two days and had found many artifacts of great interest and value.

Slowly rising to a sitting position and crossing my legs, I turned to Serge and said, "I was lying here thinking about the items we've found in the last two days. Especially the statue of the serpent that is truly a find of great value to us and will make the director of the museum in Trujillo very pleased."

Nodding his head with a look of concern on his face Serge said, "Yes, Dr. Seminario will be very pleased. My only worry is that Professor Segault could be very close to this valley. We have had the ability to search the city for two days, but I suspect that he may arrive at anytime." Turning towards Juan, Serge said, "What are your thoughts about the possibility of the professor finding us in this valley?"

Juan tilted the bottle of beer up for a last swallow and setting it at his side said, "If he has enough money he will find a guide to bring him to this place. There are many guides who will take you anywhere if the money is good. I know of several men that could find this place if given enough directions. If he has hired one of them they could be here within one or two days."

"I agree with Juan," stated Julio. Turning towards Serge, Julio continued saying, "Juan is correct, I have been told of many guides who are not very ethical. They would lead anyone for the right price and they would not hesitate attacking us if they could get something for their troubles."

I could see that Serge was deeply troubled hearing these dire predictions from Juan and Julio. Rubbing his chin with his right hand and looking around the fire at each of us Serge said, "I think we should consider leaving the city tomorrow. We know the professor has arrived in Peru and I would suspect he would find us shortly. We've found some wonderful things including the serpent; which was one of our major goals. I believe we should take a vote on whether we should leave tomorrow or continue searching the temples."

Stretching my legs out towards the fire and rubbing my knees I said, "I agree with Serge. Everything he has told me about the professor leads me to believe that he is determined to find this city." Slowly looking from one face to another I said, "When he gets here...notice I didn't say if he gets here. I don't expect him to share the wealth of the city with us. This man is coming here to take what he can carry out of the jungle and we had better not be in his way."

"I don't plan on sharing our discoveries with the professor," stated Jason with resolve evident in his voice. Jason crossed his arms and continued saying, "We've worked hard for what we have and I plan on taking what we have back with us. If the professor wants a fight he'll get one."

Nodding my head in agreement with Jason I said, "I agree with Jason's sentiments, but I would like to try and prevent an armed confrontation. It's very possible the professor's men will be armed with automatic weapons, as we are. A firefight could result in serious casualties on both sides. I would prefer not dying for what we have found in this city. I agree with Serge's suggestion that we leave the city tomorrow."

As silence surrounded the dying embers of our fire Serge said, "If we all agree, I suggest we move out at first light."

Raising my hand to signal Serge I said, "I would like to make one suggestion. I would like Juan to have Esteban break camp after breakfast and move the supplies to the hole in the city wall that he had located. Send one of the men to the cliff to keep watch for any intruders so we will not be surprised if the professor shows up. While Esteban takes care of the camp, I would like to take a quick look in the cylindrical pyramid. I would hate to leave here without looking inside that pyramid."

Juan reached behind his back and placed a few sticks in the fire causing it to react quickly to the added fuel. While placing the wood in the fire Juan said, "I would also like to see inside that pyramid. I will instruct Esteban to have the camp packed and all gear moved to the rear wall. I will have Efrain go to the cliff to watch for the professor. He can run very fast. If he sees anyone coming down the cliff he will alert us with enough time to escape from the city."

It was agreed that we would investigate the strange cylindrical pyramid in the early morning hours, hoping we would have enough time to evade the professor's anticipated arrival. The six of us sat around the fire and continued talking about the artifacts that had been found and the impact they would have on the scientific community. Juan added more wood as the last of the suns rays disappeared behind the cliffs surrounding the ancient valley. Conversation continued for another half-hour but as the fatigue of the day slowly took hold of those around the fire, several yawns were visible as our weary bodies demanded rest. One by one each of us excused ourselves and headed to our sleeping mats, ready to let the songs of the night insects sing us to sleep. My last thoughts before sleep closed my eyes were of the possibility of the professor surprising us while we were in the pyramid. If he captured us we might be leaving our bones in this ancient city with its many secrets.

As the first rays of sunshine touched the pyramids it also revealed a group of nine individuals busily moving around the camp site packing and arranging for a quick escape from the city. Esteban had prepared a filling meal of fish, plantains, and rice anticipating that our next meal could be many hours in the future.

After packing my gear and checking my weapons, I turned to Jason and said, "How are you doing? I think it was a good idea of Serge's to split the artifacts between each of us. The masks and fruit could get pretty heavy after walking for several hours."

After tightening the straps on his pack Jason looked up and said, "I'm doing O.K. I'm looking forward to getting inside the last pyramid." Turning to look at the cylindrical pyramid Jason said, "I don't remember ever seeing anything like that in all the research we did. Do you think we'll have the time to see what's inside before the professor arrives?"

Picking up my pack and swinging it over my shoulder I said, "If we can get things ready for Esteban to move to the city wall, we should have most of the day to search inside the pyramid." After picking up my rifle and starting to turn towards the center of the camp I said, "However, the professor could be here before we have a chance to fully investigate the pyramid. Get your gear together and let's get moving."

It had been agreed that each of the team would pack his or her belongings and stack them for Esteban and Pedro to move to the city wall behind the cylindrical pyramid. After breakfast Juan had sent Efrain to station himself near the cliffs and watch the ledge where the cave was located. Juan had given instructions that if he saw intruders he should run to give us time to prepare for evacuation of the city. It had been estimated that it had taken about an hour and a half to walk from the cliffs to the city.

Before the sun had touched the streets of the city we had cleared the camp and were prepared to search the last pyramid in the city. Esteban had indicated that he would place all the equipment near the rear wall and would return to keep watch for Efrain's return. If intruders were observed he would station Pedro and Efrain to watch for them and he would come and alert us of the impending danger.

With a few final words of encouragement to Esteban, Juan turned and quickly joined the team as we started towards the pyramid in the center of the city. Nearing Serge's side Juan said, "I told Esteban to stay alert. What you have told me of the professor warns me to expect the unexpected. He might try to find another route into the valley, such as the other passage that Don and I found in the cave. That other passage could also enter the valley and possibly closer to the city."

Overhearing Juan's conversation with Serge I said, "I had forgotten about that passage, it could be an alternate route to the valley. We could feel the moisture in the air, which would indicate that a water source was below us. It's possible that an underground stream flows from the cliffs into the valley. We never checked, but I bet the stream we got our water from could begin within the cliffs."

Nodding in agreement Serge said, "We should hurry, the professor could arrive at any time."

We soon approached the mysteriously shaped pyramid with its large octagonal base fashioned of large well-fashioned stone blocks. The pyramid had four sets of stairs rising to the main entrance level 40 feet above the ground. The exterior of the pyramid was much like the other pyramids in that it was covered with various forms of growth protruding from small cracks and crevices. A small group of very small monkeys scattered at our approach as we mounted one of the wide stairs to the level above. The small gray monkeys were only 12 to 15 inches high and had beautiful black markings around their eyes and mouths. Their high piercing screams announced their displeasure at our intrusion into their world. Watching them scamper away, I quickly resumed my climb up the stairs to rejoin the group.

It quickly became evident that the builders of this structure had used astronomical planning in their design of the pyramid. The large stairways leading to the upper level were exactly aligned with the compass points for north, south, east and west. As the group assembled on a beautifully laid base of finely dressed white stone we paused in wonder at the 100-foot diameter tower before us. The seams between the blocks that were used to form the tower were almost invisible and the finish of the stones would challenge any modern day craftsmen.

Maria slowly approached the tower wall and placed her hand on the wall in almost a reverent fashion. Turning to Julio she said, "Julio, could our ancestors make something like this? I have never seen such craftsmanship displayed at any of the sites we have visited."

Julio seemed to come out of a daze as he responded to Maria saying, "I have never seen anything like this. I have seen the round towers of the Toltecs' capital city of Tula that were introduced to the Yucatan Mayas but they are nothing to what I see before me."

Julio's words seemed to release all of us from the spectacle before us. As if on an unspoken word we all approached the wall and marveled at the construction before us. I could also see that an 8-foot wide by 6-foot high opening was directly in front of the stairs we had used to climb to this level.

Julio walked towards the opening saying, "Let's see what's inside this beautiful building."

Single file we entered the passage which led to a large circular room with a ceiling 40 feet above our heads. In the center of the room was a large white circular column that reached from floor to ceiling.

Moving about the room I could see that there were three other entrances each facing one of the exterior stairs leading to the level we stood upon. Another marvel that quickly became evident was a staircase winding up the walls of the circular room. From a distance they seemed to be suspended in air, but upon closer examination I could see that they were made of stone carefully inserted into the wall.

"Look at this column," stated Serge.

I turned to see Serge standing several feet from the white column with an expression of amazement on his face. He kept slowly moving around the column and every few feet stepping back to look up towards the ceiling.

I decided to see what he had found and nearing Serge I said, "What have you found? You sure sound excited about this column."

Pointing to the upper face of the column Serge said, "Look at the black lines on this column, they resemble constellations that are visible in this hemisphere. We need to sketch these drawings and compare them to what is visible from this area." Serge turned and looking at Julio said, "Do you have any familiarity with the constellations in this hemisphere?"

Julio was standing with his right hand rubbing his chin with a look of wonder across his face. He looked at Serge and said, "I'm familiar with some of these markings, but I don't recognize many of the others. I have walked completely around this column and only recognize some of the stars and planets that are represented on this wall. These people were very advanced in their astronomical research, I even found an elaborate solar calendar depicted on the east side of the column. Their understanding of the solar system is beyond my understanding, they have depicted the sun together with all the planets and other bodies that revolve around it."

Serge's reacting to this statement was immediate as he said, "Julio you must be mistaken. These people did not have the technology to see the planets in the solar system, much less the understanding of how they revolve around the sun."

Julio raised his hands before him saying, "Look for yourself." Saying that Julio pointed about 12 feet above the floor saying, "Is that the sun? If so, then they have accurately depicted the other planets revolving around that depiction of the sun." With evident excitement in his voice Julio moved to his right and said, "Look at this if you need further proof of their understanding of the heavens. Do you see where they indicate the earth and the small symbol next to it representing the moon? Look closely and you will see a small symbol next to the moon. Now...look over here, that symbol is repeated with a drawing of the phases of the moon with the earth in the center. What truly mystifies me are the lines that are drawn from various stars to the earth. The lines also extend from those stars to stars further away from our solar system."

Serge was standing next to Julio as he pointed to various areas on the column and in a hushed voice said, "Julio, you've made me a believer. What I see before me is truly beyond my understanding. I never would have believed that these people were so advanced in astronomical research and understanding of the heavenly bodies." Turning to me Serge said, "Please get your camera and record as much of this as possible."

It was soon decided to climb the stairs and find out what was above this room. While climbing the stairs I marveled at the engineering that was evident in the placement of the stepping stones and how they were anchored to the wall. The steps circled the room and ended at a passageway that turned to the right. There was a steady source of light from the end of the corridor so flashlights were not needed. The corridor was 6-feet wide and 20-feet long ending at a blank wall. A wide set of steps could be seen at the end of the corridor on the left-hand side. Walking up the steps I could see the daylight increased in brightness until I turned to the right and I could see a short flight of steps opening onto another outdoor level.

Stepping out into the bright early morning sunshine I found myself on a circular platform about 50 feet in diameter. In the middle of the platform stood another circular tower about 30 feet in diameter and 10 feet high.

"What do we have here?" stated Jason as he joined me. Pointing towards the wall he said, "Look at all the rectangular openings, they seem to have been placed very deliberately. That small opening could be an entrance into the tower."

Turning to Jason I said, "Let's wait for the others before entering this place. I think you're right, that opening could be a passageway into the interior."

As the group gathered on the platform it was evident that the strange structure before us had the attention of the whole group. Serge, Julio and Maria walked around the tower and returned with looks of surprise across their faces.

Stopping next to me Serge said, "Those small slots go around the whole tower and they seem to be equally spaced." Walking towards the wall he continued saying, "Have you ever seen such stone work? The seams are virtually invisible."

Unnoticed by the group Juan had entered the tower and sticking his head out of the entrance he said, "My friends, you must come and see this room." After inviting us into the tower Juan turned and disappeared from sight.

I quickly followed Juan and entered a circular room that caused me to come to a sudden stop before the entrance. Slowly moving towards Juan I let my eyes take in a sight of wondrous beauty and mystery. The floor, walls and ceiling resembled black glass with no visible joints. In the center of the room stood a 4-foot diameter column 8 feet tall covered with a white material. Brilliant sunlight was streaming in through the wall slots that were facing east giving the impression that the center column was rotating.

"Oh my," stated Serge as he joined Juan and I. In a voice hushed in surprise at such beauty he said, "This is truly marvelous, but what is its use? Look at the small pedestals circling the room they seem to be lined up with the slots in the wall."

As each of the team members entered the room exclamations of wonder could be heard as they tried to grasp the beauty and mystery of what was before them. I heard Jason state that there were lines cut into the floor from the wall connecting to the pedestals and then to the center column.

Jason was kneeling on the floor inspecting one of the slots when he looked up at me saying, "Don come here and look at these slots they seem to be filled with gold."

Kneeling next to Jason I confirmed that the slots was filled with gold and that they seemed to have been cut in straight lines from the wall slots to the inner column. Serge was the next to call our attention to the ceiling exclaiming that the ceiling looked like a night sky. He began pointing out several constellations and specific stars. Julio confirmed that several of the constellations were of the southern hemisphere.

"What is this?" stated Maria as she came from the other side of the column holding a black sphere in her hands. Lifting the sphere in both hands Maria continued saying, "I found this sitting on top of one of those slender pedestals. It is surprisingly light and feels like obsidian, but its warm to the touch."

Julio walked to her side and extended his hand to Maria saying, "Could I please see that. I have heard legends about a sphere like this, but I have never seen one until today. The legend says that the priests could speck with the gods when they had the sphere in their temple."

I watched Julio slowly rotate the black sphere in his hands as if he were looking for a hidden seam. It looked to be about 6 inches in diameter and as Maria had stated, it seemed to be very light in weight as he rolled the sphere in his hands.

We all jumped with surprise as Esteban burst into the chamber saying, "Juan, Efrain has returned and he says people are following him to the city."

Juan quickly gave Esteban orders to return to the men and have them ready to provide cover for the team as we attempted to leave the city. As Esteban turned to leave the room, Juan turned to the group saying, "Julio, place the sphere in a backpack and then we must leave this place. Esteban, Pedro and Efrain will provide a rear guard as we attempt to leave the city."

Julio placed the sphere in Serge's backpack and tightened the straps saying, "Please try not to loose that. It might be the most valuable item we have found in the city."

With a final glance around the chamber we quickly exited the small entrance opening to the room and proceeded to descend to the lower levels of the temple. In single file and in total silence we practically ran to the stone steps that led to the lower level. The stepping stones surrounding the large chamber were too dangerous to descend in a hurry. It took precious minutes to finally attain the floor of the large chamber and run towards one of the openings to the exterior of the pyramid.

Descending the pyramid I could see Esteban and his two men standing near the city wall looking towards the road leading into the city. Our group quickly gathered around the three men and Juan said, "Esteban, what has happened? Has Efrain seen people entering the valley?"

With one last glance towards the jungle he looks at Juan and said, "Efrain fell asleep on guard duty and was awakened by voices. He says he saw three white men and three Peruvians and they are armed with automatic weapons. After they passed his position he quickly ran back to the city to warn us."

Before Esteban had finished speaking Juan turned on Efrain and lashed out in Spanish with a tongue-lashing that left Efrain trembling next to the city wall. With visible control Juan turned to us and said, "Please accept my apology for this lack of responsibility that has been displayed by Efrain, I will take care of him later. If he ran most of the distance to the city we may have a half-hour before they arrive here." Turning to Serge he said, "How would you like to handle this situation? We could attempt to drive the professor away from the city or gather our things and slip out the rear of the city. It is possible we could evade the professor's group and escape up the cliff."

Serge removed his hat and rubbed his hand through his hair in thought. This was a decision that would effect all of us and he deliberately took his time before speaking. Placing his hat on his head he turned to me saying, "Well...what do you think? We have the time to set up positions to guard the entrance to the city and try to keep Segault out. It sounds like he has a group of six men including himself, we out number him by three people which places the odds in our favor. We could slip out of the city and not confront him and let him have the city to search."

Holding on to the sling of my shouldered rifle in thought I said, "I don't like the idea of being driven from our discovery, but we have a long journey back to Iquitos and it would be best not to do that with wounded. I vote that we leave immediately."

"I'm sorry, but our unwelcome visitors have arrived," said Jason as he removed his rifle from his shoulder.

Jason's words caused an immediate response from the entire group as our worst fears were realized. I looked past Serge's shoulder towards the plaza and noticed several men cautiously approaching the plaza with weapons pointed before them.

Looking at Juan I said, "This does not look good. We better set up a perimeter behind the serpent temple, this could turn into a bad situation."

Serge indicated that he would approach the professor and notify him that he was not welcome at this site. I could see his French temper was beginning to flare and I cautioned him against doing anything rash. He nodded his understanding and I proceeded to assign positions to guard Serge when he spoke with the professor.

After giving some direction to Jason and Juan I looked at Serge and said, "Take Juan with you when you speak with Segault. He will keep his eyes on the professors people while your attention is on Segault. I've asked Jason to slip into the jungle near the city wall to watch your back and Efrain will go to the other side of the city opening. I don't trust the professor not to try and flank our position."

Serge agreed to my plan of action and proceeded to speak with Juan concerning the coming confrontation with the professor. Serge indicated he would stay near the right wall of the serpent temple and speak to the professor from across the plaza. I told Maria to stay behind the city wall out of sight and to only come out if she was needed. Juan directed Pedro to cover his back and I told Julio to follow me to the left side of the serpent temple.

As I turned the corner of the serpent temple I could see several men standing on the road leading to the plaza. They seemed undecided as to their course of action when suddenly their attention swung to my right as I heard Serge call out to the professor. One of the Europeans motioned and two Peruvians slipped into the jungle on either side of the road.

"Professor, what are you doing in Peru?" asked Serge. "I hope you have not been following me, because we need no help with our research at this time."

I saw a man in his middle years of above average height with an athletic build step forward with a large smile across his face. His bearing exuded confidence as he said, "My young friend, it is so good to see you again. I must admit that the mystery of your journal has drawn me to your side." Pointing towards the city to our rear he continued saying, "I see you have found your mystery city. I hope you would be willing to give me a tour of this wonderful place." Placing his right hand on the butt of the weapon at his side he said, "I hope you would not begrudge your old professor the courtesy of a little tour of your city."

The threat was heavy in the air as the professor spoke and his gestures were indicative of his determination to visit the city. I could sense this was not a man to be trifled with and he was someone who was accustomed to getting his way with people.

"Professor, I can hear your man moving through the jungle trying to flank our position. Call him back before there is trouble. We are educated men and should be able to come to an agreeable arrangement concerning the city," stated Serge with evident concern in his voice.

I itched to join Serge, but I knew Juan would protect him if the talking came to an abrupt end. At times like this you some times feel helpless. My thoughts were interrupted as the professor responded to Serge saying, "My friend, I'm not here to take your research from you, only to satisfy my curiosity concerning the existence of the city. When you revealed the journal to me I knew that I would have to see this city for myself. I must thank you for blazing the trail for me, it was evident that you were trying to cover your movements. My guide was very good at finding small signs of your movements, but I lost him to an arrow from one of the local Indians." Rubbing his hands together with a broad smile the professor said, "Should we take a little tour?" Where upon the professor began to cross the plaza with his two assistants following him.

"Stop!" shouted Serge. "You're not welcome here. Please leave before there is trouble. We are armed and will defend what we have found."

I slowly removed my rifle from my shoulder, but kept it pointing towards the ground. At the same moment I heard movement from the jungle to my left and turning I began to motion Jason as a shot rang out and Julio gasped and staggered back towards the temple wall. Immediately Jason and Efrain responded with shots fired into the jungle as I attempted to assist Julio to the rear of the temple. I could see Julio holding his left leg as blood became visible between his fingers. As I helped Julio to get to cover I was aware of semi-automatic fire behind me and on the other side of the temple.

As I got Julio out of the line of fire behind the temple walls I called for Maria to come to our assistance. Her response was immediate, especially as she could see that Julio was injured.

With her medical bag in hand Maria said, "What has happened to Julio, was he shot?"

"Yes, I must return to the fight," I stated quickly as I turned and decided to check on Serge and Juan.

Moving away from Julio I could see that Maria was taking control of the situation in a professional manner. I found Serge and Juan standing at the right corner of the serpent temple exchanging shots with individuals in the jungle. Lying near them was Pedro who had been hit twice in the chest and was clearly dead. I could see Esteban firing from the jungle towards the plaza.

Serge turned to eject his magazine and seeing me said, "They fired from the jungle and killed Pedro. Juan fired at the professor and his men and one of them fell mortally wounded. Have we taken any other casualties?"

Nodding my head I said, "Julio has been wounded, Maria is caring for him. I'm not sure how serious the wound is. If possible it would be good to withdraw into the city so they cannot flank our position."

Placing the magazine into the rifle and chambering a round Serge said, "Check the others and see if they can start to move into the city. Juan and I will try to hold this position until your ready to move Julio."

As I was about to turn I heard Esteban fire a three round burst and shouts something in Spanish. I asked Juan what he had said and he responded without turning his head that Esteban had shot one of the men in the jungle. Nodding my approval I turned and stopped for a moment to see how Julio was doing.

Maria was concentrating on her work as I said, "How bad is the wound?"

Starting to wrap a bandage around Julio's upper leg and not looking up Maria said, "The bullet went through the leg without hitting any major arteries. He will be all right if we can get him to safety. I have given him a light sedative to help with the pain."

Confirming that Julio was in good hands I said, "We are going to try and move back into the city. Wait until I get Jason and Efrain and we will help move Julio behind the city walls."

I turned from speaking with Maria and approached the corner of the temple. Efrain was firing towards the plaza and I could see Jason firing from behind a tree within the edge of the jungle. Just as I was about to call out to Jason I saw him twist and turn to the other side of the tree and fire towards the jungle before him. At the same time I heard a scream and thrashing of someone falling in the under growth. It was evident that Jason had just shot one of the professor's men.

Standing behind Efrain I shouted to Jason saying, "Jason...try to run over here."

With a quick glance towards the plaza he turned and nodded his acknowledgement of my request. Waiting for what he felt was the right moment, he bolted from behind the tree and ran towards the temple. Several shots were fired in his direction, but they failed to find him.

With sweat running down his forehead Jason leaned against the temple wall and said, "How are we doing? I just got the guy that shot Julio. I'm not sure if he's dead or alive, but at least he's hurting."

Letting him get his breath I said, "Maria feels Julio will be fine, but he needs help to get behind the city walls. I spoke with Serge and we feel it's a good idea to pull back behind the city walls. Pedro was killed and Juan shot one of the Europeans and Esteban thinks he shot one of the Peruvians in the jungle. When you're ready get Efrain to help you move Julio behind the walls I'll cover your backs."

I informed Efrain of what we had to do and told him to help Jason move Julio. I took Efrain's place at the corner of the temple and got a quick shot at an individual that started to move around a tree, he quickly changed his mind. After a few minutes Jason announces that he and Efrain will move Julio and that I should provide covering fire during the move. I acknowledge his request with a couple of quick three round bursts into the surrounding jungle. I stepped back for a quick glance at Jason and I could see that he had everything well in hand, with Maria leading the way to the wall.

Silence suddenly settled over the jungle as shots ceased to be fired from both sides. I chanced a quick glance behind me at Serge and Juan to see if they were O.K. Serge had turned towards me with a look that asked if the fight was over. I motioned that he should continue watching for any movement from the professor's group. He acknowledged my signals by nodding his head and turning back towards the plaza.

The silence continued for the next ten minutes without a sound from our unwelcome guests. As the jungle animals began to accept the silence that had returned to their world I could hear the birds and monkeys slowly making themselves heard within the forest. It was possible that the professor had taken several casualties and wanted to slip off and lick his wounds before attempting to take the city.

With one last glance at the plaza and jungle before me I turned and quickly moved to Serge's position saying, "What do you think? It sure has gotten quiet. This might be a good chance to withdraw into the city."

Serge had turned and rested his back against the temple wall and said, "I think your right, let's get Esteban over here and move back into the city."

Serge told Juan to try and motion Esteban and get him to join us behind the temple. Juan spent several moments trying to signal Esteban, but he had moved to a position that placed him at an angle that prevented him from seeing Juan's signals. Suddenly Juan gave a call of a bird that was so real I felt the bird was next to me. The reaction from Esteban was immediate as he peered around the tree and looked towards our position. Juan motioned for

Esteban to join us behind the temple, he acknowledged with a quick raising of his hand.

Esteban seemed to erupt out of the jungle as he suddenly appeared out of the foliage and leaning forward ran as if a fire-breathing dragon were after him. Expecting to hear a shot ring out, I was relieved to have Esteban join us in total silence. Serge informed us he would cover our retreat to the city walls and taking a quick breath we bolted for the cover that the walls would provide for us.

As the group came together behind the city wall it was evident that we had not come out of the engagement unscathed. Julio had been wounded seriously and Pedro was dead. The danger that we had accepted as part of the expedition had taken a deadly turn for the worse. Without proper care we could loose Julio and we knew that medical help depended completely on Maria.

I turned to Maria and said, "Can Julio be moved? We must try to move deeper into the city."

Maria nodded and said, "I have packed the wound well and wrapped it tightly. The bleeding is under control, but he will need help. I don't want him to place too much weight on the leg."

It was agreed that Serge and Esteban would provide cover for the group as we moved deeper into the city. I had indicated that I wanted to get behind the base of the cylindrical pyramid. The pyramid would hide us from the professor as we attempted to exit the hole in the wall behind the pyramid. I knew it was time to try and escape from the city before the professor decided to move on the city.

Efrain and Juan supported Julio from their shoulders with Maria walking beside them watching their every move. Jason and I shouldered their weapons and tried to protect our retreat to the pyramid with eyes constantly searching for unexpected movement before us. We made it to the pyramid and Julio was placed as gently as possible on the ground. Maria immediately hovered over him until he motioned her to relax, indicating that he had no plans on dying any time soon. Trying to hide the concern in her eyes Maria checked the bandage and pretended not to notice the blood seeping through the bandage.

Jason and I had taken positions behind the pyramid steps and when Serge turned to look at us we motioned that they should join us. Serge waved and then he and Esteban sprang from behind the wall and ran towards our position. At the same time that I saw Esteban stumble I heard the shot ring out from the forest. He took a couple steps and fell to the ground holding his arm. Serge turned and dropped to his knee looking for a target to fire at, seeing nothing he quickly turned to Esteban.

Turning to Jason I said, "Cover me. We have to get Esteban under cover." I set my rifle down and leaped up from behind the steps and ran towards Esteban and Serge. I quickly dropped at Esteban's side and looking at Serge said, "How bad is he hit?"

With concern written across his face Serge said, "He took a round to the arm. We need to get him to Maria."

I took Esteban's weapon and slung it on my shoulder and then Serge and I helped Esteban up and moved him to our position behind the pyramid. He kept apologizing for being so much trouble and kept insisting that he could make it on his own to the pyramid. When we got him to Maria he was white as a sheet and sweat was streaming down his face. It was evident that he was in a great amount of pain even though he didn't want to show it.

With my rifle back in my hands I dropped next to Jason and said, "Have you seen any movement from the other end of the city?"

Without taking his eyes from the city entrance Jason said, "No. I didn't see who shot Esteban, but no one has tried to enter the city. They may be waiting for the cover of darkness to slip into the city."

Taking one last glance at the entrance I turned my head towards Jason and said, "I don't plan on being here when the sun goes down. As soon as Esteban has been cared for we need to get out of the city. Let's fire a couple rounds towards the entrance just to let them know that we're still here and ready for them."

I mentioned to Serge that Jason and I would be firing a few shots and he should warn the others not to panic when they heard the shots. He agreed that it was a good idea, and agreed to warn the others of the impending shooting.

Turning to Jason I said, "Let's fire two bursts of three rounds and see if they return our fire." Jason agreed and in the next few minutes we each fired six rounds towards the entrance of the city.

We waited for ten minutes for some reaction to our shots, but the sounds of the jungle returning too normal was the only reaction to our shooting. Looking up at the sun I estimated that it was near noon and if we were going to try and slip away from the city this was a good time to do it.

Moving further behind the pyramid I approached Serge and said, "After Maria has bandaged Esteban we need to leave the city. I know the professor has taken casualties, but he may be willing to disregard them and continue the attack. We've lost one man and have two wounded, I don't want to lose anyone else."

Wiping the sweat from his forehead Serge says, "I agree. The professor has come a long way to search this place and he will not let us stand in his way." Serge turns his head towards Maria saying, "Maria, is Julio and Esteban able to travel? I know it isn't the best thing for them, but if the professor attacks again we could be in bad trouble."

Maria had just finished placing a bandage around Esteban's arm and closing up her medical bag she gave Serge a stern glance saying, "I don't have much choice in the matter, do I?" She paused for a moment and said in a milder tone, "I'm sorry, you don't deserve that. This violence is so unjustified and cruel, I would strangle the professor if I could get my hands on him." With the beginnings of a smile she continued saying, "Wow...I sound pretty dangerous, the professor better watch out for me. Seriously, I think Don has the right idea about getting out of the city. Esteban can walk on his own, but we should carry Julio if at all possible."

It was agreed that we should try to get out of the city as quickly as possible and hope our leaving would go unnoticed for several hours. I asked Juan to have Efrain go into the jungle and cut two 7 foot long poles that we could use for a litter to carry Julio. Maria produced a blanket from her gear for the litter and within ten minutes a litter was ready for Julio.

During the activity Jason had remained on guard duty, but as the litter was readied for Julio he said, "Don, I see you remembered the open blanket method for making a litter. All that first aid we took sure has come in handy. Remember, it's best to have four men carrying the litter it will help keep the litter bearers from tiring too soon."

It was agreed that Serge and I with Juan and Efrain would carry the litter out of the city with Esteban leading the way. Esteban indicated that he had discovered a game trail near the city during one of the times he had been looking for food for our meals. He felt that it would lead towards the cliffs at the west end of the valley. Jason volunteered to provide rear guard for our retreat from the city. The city wall was located about 100 feet from the pyramid and using the cover of the pyramid we gathered our belongings and moved to the hole in the wall. We believe we were able to leave the city undetected, as the professor's men raised no alarm.

The next three hours were a prolonged period of torture for Julio and those carrying the litter. We tried to rotate the litter bearers, but moving through a jungle with a litter is very taxing on the patient and the bearers. It was decided to try and slowly shift our direction from the game trail to the stone road. It was recognized that it would be dangerous, but we felt we had to make the cave before dark.

The road suddenly came into view and Esteban quickly motioned for the group to stop moving. He turned and approached Juan saying, "The road is close to us, I don't see anyone. I will quietly move to the road and see if it is clear."

Juan gave his permission and Esteban turned and disappeared into the jungle. We carefully set the litter down and Maria quickly came to Julio's side enquiring about the pain. The bleeding had stopped a couple hours earlier, but I could see Julio was feeling quite a bit of pain. Juan approached Maria and said something in Spanish causing her to nod her head in agreement to what Juan had said. Juan immediately turned and stepped into the jungle and disappeared from sight.

After watching Juan disappear I turned to Maria and said, "Where is Juan going? Is everything all right?"

Looking up from Julio's side she said, "Everything is fine. Juan had seen a plant that has a medicinal use as a painkiller. He asked if I would like to use some for Julio. I asked him to get it if it's not to far from here."

Juan returned moments before Esteban appeared from the jungle around us. Juan handed Maria some dark green leaves which she immediately selected one and told Julio to chew and swallow the leaf. Esteban announced that the trail was clear and he felt we could use it to get to the cliff. It was agreed that we would take the chance and move to the road. We arrived at the trail that led to the cave above. Maria directed that Julio is turned so his head was at the head of the litter, she reminded us that it was the best way to transport a patient uphill.

Three days ago we had descended the cliff in 15 minutes with only a few areas demanding some caution. The climb this late afternoon took 45 minutes of exhaustive effort on the part of the litter bearers. Several times I doubted if we would be able to carry the litter up the cliff without making Julio get out of the litter.

Exhausted and bone tired we staggered onto the ledge that we had stood on only a few days before. The cave was in view and we carried Julio into the safety of the cave for Maria to try and make him comfortable. Jason stated he would watch the trail while we set up a cold camp for the night. Juan proceeded to open some of the canned food for a quick meal before settling in for the evening.

After checking on Julio and Esteban I found Serge sitting with his back against the cliff wall. He had drawn his knees up to his chest and had wrapped his arms around his legs. He seemed to be staring into the valley, but I felt his eyes were not focused on anything in particular. With a slight groan I lowered my aching body to the ledge and leaned against the wall.

I closed my eyes for a moment and tried to will my body to relax from the trauma that we had experienced today. Members of the group had been killed and wounded today in a fight that was generated by greed. Opening my eyes I gazed out over an ancient land filled with beauty, but disguised within the beauty, was death waiting for the unwary.

Without turning my head to Serge I said, "I hated to leave Pedro lying in the city."

"I know," said Serge in a voice that echoed sorrow and pain. Turning his head he said, "We certainly have seen death during this trip. I knew this would be dangerous, but I never quite believed that we would loose people on the trip. We have wonderful memories of this land, but pain and death over shadow them."

Slowly turning my head back to the valley I said, "You're right, but I don't regret taking the challenge to find this city. We have found incredible artifacts that will add greatly to the knowledge of this land for the Peruvian people. I have found a love for the people of this land and they're many traditions and customs."

Silence settled over us like a soft sheet as the evening shadows started to lengthen across the valley. The green carpet of the jungle started to darken as the last of the sunlight slowly lifted above the valley.

In a voice as soft as a whisper I said, "Serge, don't let the actions of today cause you to stop asking what is around the next corner. When we get back to civilization and return to our homes let's not forget what we have accomplished in the jungles of the Amazon. Within the next couple years I want to prepare for another expedition in search of the unknown. We have spent too much time and training to give up after the first research trip. There are many things that are just waiting for those who would dare to look danger in the face."

Serge turned and looking me in the eye said, "Don't worry, I'm hooked on this adventure thing. We will do this again in the near future."

Epilogue

Looking at my watch I realized the telling of the story had taken several hours and as I leaned back against the tree I sighed in memory of times past. I glanced at my son and said, "Well...as a radio personality was known to say that's the rest of the story."

My son was slowly stretching his legs out in front of him and looking at me spoke in a voice of wonderment saying, "Why in the world have you kept this knowledge to yourself? It's a fabulous story. The rest of the family should hear about this, it's incredible." Turning towards me he said, "You need to record this for the family. You're grandchildren will want to know what their grandfather did as a young man."

Nodding my head in agreement I said, "You're reaction to the story is very encouraging, I guess I never gave to much thought to keeping a journal of my adventures." With a chuckle I said, "Journal, did you get the play on words?"

With a grin on his face and shaking his head from side to side he said, "Yes, I see what you're saying. You followed a journal into Peru, now you need to write your own journal. Before you take on that task, I have a couple questions I'd like to ask about that trip."

Rubbing my stomach in exaggerated pain I said, "We haven't caught any fish to cook so we'll have to see what you're mom has fixed for supper, story telling works up an appetite." The look of disappointment that crossed his face caused me to quickly say, "Just kidding, go ahead and ask your questions. I'll try to answer them as best that I can remember."

Holding up his hands in mock defense he said, "I know you're an old man and your mind's going, but before it completely disappears fill in a few gaps for me. Did the professor ever catch up with you before you got to Lima?"

"No, we never saw him again. It took several days before we could relax and not constantly be looking over our shoulders expecting to see him ready to pounce. Serge kept insisting that we keep moving, he felt the professor would try to stop us before we got to the river. I figured that the professor had acquired what he had come for. He had run us off, so he had the time to search the city without interruption."

With a look of concern on my son's face he said, "Did Julio survive the trip to Iquitos?"

Smiling I said, "Yes. With Maria's care and his determination he was walking with a stick in a couple days."

Picking up the magazine he said, "Is this the serpent statue that you found in the city of the sun?"

Taking the magazine and looking at the picture I nodding my head saying, "Yes, that's the statue that we took from the city. We delivered it to Dr. Seminario at the museum in Trujillo and collected our reward. That gentleman was a happy camper when we walked into his office and unwrapped that serpent. He practically jumped from behind his desk when he saw the statue. I'll never forget the look on his face, it was like a dream come true."

Raising his right fore finger he said, "One last question. What was the black sphere that was found in the top of the cylindrical pyramid?"

"Ah, you remember the black sphere," I said with a mysterious tone in my voice. "That item caused many questions to be asked about whom could have made such an item. When we exposed it to day light it would turn from black to crystalline and holding it you could feel a tingling in your fingers and hands." Rising from the ground I said, "Well I'm about ready to pass out from hunger, let's see what your mom has fixed for dinner."

"Dad!" exclaimed my son. "You didn't answer my question about the black sphere. What did you find out about it?"

Looking over my shoulder and chuckling I said, "That's another story, and when you visit again I might tell you what I did in 1980. Now that was quite an adventure."

Printed in the United States
997800003B